NEIGHBORS

A TWIN ESTATES NOVEL

STYLO FANTÔME

Published by BattleAxe Productions
Copyright © 2016
Stylo Fantôme

ISBN-13: 978-1537785028
ISBN-10: 1537785028

Critique Partner: Ratula Roy

Editing Aides:
Barbara Shane Hoover
Ratula Roy

Cover Design
Najla Qamber Designs
najlaqamberdesigns.com
Copyright © 2016

Formatting: Champagne Formats

DEDICATION

To dreamers and weekend getaways and sunny shorelines and not giving a fuck.

NEIGHBORS

A TWIN ESTATES NOVEL

1

D ESCRIBE YOUR PERFECT DATE.

"I mean, c'mon," Katya grumbled, blowing a hank of hair out of her face. "What kind of question is that?"

"It's just to get an idea of the type of girl you are," her roommate, Tori, tried to explain.

"If I had an idea of what the perfect date was, I wouldn't be making a profile for an online dating site."

"Shut up and just say something generic, like long walks on the beach ... or hand jobs in the backs of theatres."

Katya burst out laughing and went with the long walks on the beach suggestion.

Online dating wasn't really her thing, but she was finally willing to admit that whatever her thing was, it wasn't working. She was twenty-three and had a good career, great friends, and a nice life. But zero love life to speak of – her boyfriend had dumped her eight months ago, and she'd barely spoken to another man since then.

She knew she was somewhat ... vanilla. She'd grown up in the suburbs, with a normal family, and a normal life. Katya didn't mind boring. Boring was ... secure.

Boring paid the rent.

Yeah, but boring doesn't get you laid.

And somewhere, deep in the darkest corners of her mind, she'd begun to admit to herself that boring simply wasn't good enough anymore. She wanted something different for herself, though she wasn't quite what she was looking for – someone who would let her escape her life a little bit. Someone who could open her eyes to new experiences. Someone who could make her feel comfortable in her own skin, and comfortable with stepping outside of it sometimes.

She might have been vanilla a good deal of the time, but there were other times when she wanted to be rainbow sherbet. With sprinkles on top, dammit.

"Okay, there, done," Katya closed her laptop. "I am officially one of the sad and lonely many on the interwebs, desperately looking for love."

"It's not so bad, Kat. Remember Jenna from high school? She met her husband online. So did Thad, the guy from downstairs – he met his boyfriend on some app. It'll be fine," Tori assured her.

"I don't even think it's necessary. I have my work, my clients – I'm satisfied," Katya tried to convince herself while she collected her belongings.

"Satisfied is lame. You want to be blown away. Knocked off your feet. *Overwhelmed,*" her roommate insisted.

"Just watch. Nothing will come of it. That profile will sit un-touched. I'll probably forget I even have it. *Byeeeee,*" Katya sang as she waltzed out the door.

Tori sat there for a couple minutes, staring at the table top. Her bestie was a great girl, she just needed to live a little. Her idea of a good time was having a second Cosmo after dessert. She'd led a somewhat sheltered life, then had kept herself sheltered ever since high school.

She needs this, I'm helping her.

With that thought, Tori opened the laptop and was pleased to see when the screen came back on, Katya was still logged into the dating website. Smiling big the whole time, Tori decided "updating" the profile wouldn't hurt anything.

Holy shit. Is that …

Liam Edenhoff stared at his phone's screen. The happy face of a woman looked back at him. She had a big smile with great teeth, surrounded by full lips. Apple cheeks perfectly showed off a pair of soft blue eyes. She had dark hair, but the photo wasn't doing it justice – it was a deep auburn, he knew, and would shine like garnet when the sun hit it just right.

My frickin' adorable neighbor is on the Eros dating site.

He lived in the building next door to her and had noticed her, of course, because she was hot. But she dressed like a librarian and acted like a Sunday school teacher, so he'd ignored her for the most part.

Looking at her profile now, on a dating site he lurked about sometimes, he was shocked to read her bio. She'd listed her job as professional baker, which didn't exactly surprise him, but under hobbies "*strip-aerobics and pole dancing classes*" did throw him for a loop. Favorite past times? "*Indulging in my kinky side*" – before that day, he would've guessed she wouldn't have even known what that word meant.

"*EDEN!*"

The voice in Liam's ear was so loud, he gave a shout and launched his phone across the room.

"*Christ,* don't ever sneak up on me like that, Ricky!" he gasped for air, pressing a hand to his chest. "I nearly had a fucking heart attack."

"Oh please. If I thought scaring you could kill you, I would've tried it a long time ago. You're fine, Eden."

"*Eden*", so nicknamed because of his last name, as well as the irony when juxtaposed with what he did for a living.

"Har dee har har," Liam grumbled as he grabbed his phone off the ground. His business partner leaned over his shoulder.

"Online dating? Sad," he made a tsk tsk sound with his tongue.

"Eh. Can't be any worse than the dates I've made in real life, I figure. Besides – see this chick? I know her. Kinda. She lives next door to me. This site cuts out the middle man," Liam explained, holding up his phone so the other man could see Katya.

"Ah. She's gorgeous. Looks like a good time," his partner's voice was low as he spoke, almost distracted sounding, but Liam didn't notice. He kept staring at his screen.

"Yeah," he agreed. "Yeah, I think she might be ..."

2

KATYA WAS GLARING DOWN AT HER CELL AS SHE WALKED ACROSS THE LOBBY of her building. Her phone was blowing up with notifications from that stupid dating site. She hadn't opened any of the messages, but there were some pretty interesting subject headings scrolling across her screen.

"Why would you do this, Tori!?" she mumbled to herself as she looked over her dating profile. Or really, her *new* dating profile – almost everything she'd typed was now gone, replaced by a bunch of sexy garbage.

She wasn't looking where she was going, so even the sound of someone shouting wasn't able to stop her in time before she practically ran a man over. Lucky for him, he was a lot bigger than her. She ricocheted off his chest and only his reflexes saved her from falling flat on her butt. His hands grabbed her upper arms, keeping her upright, while her phone and purse fell to the ground.

"Sorry!" she blurted out automatically. "So sorry, I wasn't looking."

"That's alright, cause I was looking for you."

Creepy statement to hear, that was for sure. She stared up at the man, trying to place him. Did she know him from work? The building? He seemed vaguely familiar. Oh god, had she forgotten a client's face? That wasn't good. Then again, neither was a client showing up at her place of residence. Oh god, was he a stalker!?

"I'm sorry, have we met?" she asked, glancing around, glad to see there were other people around them.

"No, not officially. I'm Liam Edenhoff, I live in the building next door," he explained, and she finally smiled. That's why he was familiar – she must have seen him around.

Katya lived in an apartment building just outside of downtown San Francisco – really it was *two* buildings, together called *Twin Estates*. Her building and the one next door were twins. Identical and managed by the same company, they shared an alleyway and dumpsters between them. She'd probably bumped into him while taking out the trash at some point.

But why was he looking for me?

"Oh, hello. I'm Katya," she introduced herself, but didn't offer her last name.

"I know."

Creepy just got bumped up to totally weird.

"Oh. Um …"

"Sorry, I'm coming off totally weird," he laughed, reading her mind. "I've seen you around the buildings, and then I was on this website, and I saw your profile."

Oh. Jesus. She was really going to murder her roommate. It was one thing to have a bit of fun and put some naughty stuff up on a website, but when it brought random strange men to where she lived, it was going too far.

"Ooohhh, yeeeaaahh. *That* website," she grumbled, finally kneeling down to pick up her bag.

"Yeah. I gotta say, I've noticed you for a while, and I always thought you were …"

"Were what?" she asked, glancing up at him. He shrugged.

"I don't know. Just … I read that profile, and I had to meet that woman."

Katya wasn't sure what to make of his statement – she was a little insulted that the woman he'd seen around the building hadn't been interesting enough to meet. But she was also a little flattered – and, admittedly, excited – that he'd sought out the woman from the profile.

"So if you hadn't seen my profile, you would never have introduced yourself?" she double checked. He chuckled and rubbed at the back of his neck, looking a little sheepish.

"Honestly? No. I mean, don't get me wrong, you seemed like a really sweet girl, and you're gorgeous, but I'm not exactly a sweet guy. I didn't want to waste your time, or freak you out," he said.

"Freak me out?"

"Yeah."

"How? What do you mean?"

"Well, like I assumed you were a Sunday school teacher or something," he explained. "I own and operate a club downtown. The two don't exactly match."

"Sunday school teacher? Why?" she was a little surprised, then was even more so when she watched his gaze blatantly travel up and down her body.

"My other guess was librarian. You just always seemed … sweet. Innocent," he said.

Sweet and innocent. Translation: **boring**. *Tori was right. I'm dull, and it took a made up online profile to get a guy to notice me.*

Katya should've been angry at him. For judging her before he'd met her, solely based on her outward appearance. For perpetuating the stereotype that a woman had to be overtly sexy in order to be interesting. For only giving her the time of day because of some ridiculous website.

But she was actually angry at *herself*. She felt like a prisoner of her own inhibitions, her own naiveté. She was angry that deep down, she *wanted* to be an overtly sexual woman, the kind that could draw men in with a single glance.

She wanted to be that woman from her profile bio.

She just didn't know how, and before her anger could boil over, all her carefully built manners and over the top etiquette cooled her off. She managed a tight lipped smile for him.

"Well, I'm sorry to disappoint you, but I didn't write that bio," she told him the truth.

"You didn't?"

"Nope. My roommate did."

"Ah. Roommate. So I take it you don't do strip-aerobics," he said with a chuckle. She shook her head.

"I didn't even know that was a real thing."

He burst out laughing.

"Gotcha. So the whole sweet and innocent thing, that *is* the real you."

She opened her mouth, then froze. Was that the real her? Or was that just who she'd convinced herself she needed to be? She was so sick and tired of everyone assuming she was this insipid goody-two-shoes. Tori telling her to get a life. This stranger assuming she was a librarian. It wasn't fair. She could be just as wild, just as fun-loving as the next person. All she needed was the chance.

Take a chance …

"Just because I don't walk around in a thong bikini doesn't mean I'm all innocence," she replied. He cocked up an eyebrow.

"I dunno. A baker, huh? You pretty much look like angel food cake to me," he teased her. She glared at him.

"Was this your big plan? Stalk me down in my building and interrogate me? Is this how you ask out all your dates?" she demanded.

"Who said I was gonna ask you out on a date?" he replied.

"Oh, please. You didn't come over here to ask me about my strip-aerobics class, and we both know it," she said, proud of herself for the quick and snappy come back.

"Touché. I was going to invite you to my club," he said. She took a deep breath and for a split second, thought about how early she had to get up for work. Thought about the design she had to work on for a client. Thought about her big plans for the evening – reinforcing all the buttons on her dress shirts.

"I'm free after eight o'clock," she blurted out. He laughed at her again, and she couldn't help but notice that he had a great laugh, and an even better smile. She'd known him for all of two seconds, but she was willing to bet "fun-loving" was his middle name. The man was made to smile.

"Whoa there, angel cake, I don't think this is such a good idea," he said, holding up a hand.

"Why not? I love to dance."

"It's not that kind of club."

"What? Is it like a book club?"

He laughed again, but she hadn't been joking. She figured he didn't need to know that and she managed to laugh as well.

"Look, you seem like a nice girl. I'm sure you get asked on lots of dates, and if I was a tax attorney, or an insurance salesman, I'd for sure want to go out with you, but I don't want to make you uncomfortable," he told her. She rolled her eyes.

"If anyone here is a 'nice girl', it's you – I've made all the moves so far. If you don't want to go out, just say so, and I can move onto the next guy, and you can go to your little club house thingy," she said.

This was so far out of her comfort zone, she wasn't sure she was still the same Katya anymore. Her Eros profile had come to life and body snatched her. The words coming out of her mouth, the tone of her voice, were completely foreign to her. Yesterday, Katya would have gotten embarrassed. Blushed at the way he talked about her, apologized for taking up his time – even though he'd been the one to stop her.

This new-Katya, though, refused to be embarrassed. He had come there for a reason, to ask *her* out, so she had nothing to be sorry about, and hell, maybe she would move onto another man.

She'd certainly gotten a lot of offers from the website. She squared her shoulders and looked him straight in the eyes, praying her bravado held out for a few more minutes.

"Club house thingy, huh," he mumbled, his eyes wandering over her form again.

"Are we done? I have some messages to catch up on," she said, then she went to step around him. He reached out and grabbed her arm.

"Alright, alright, calm down. You want to see my club?" he asked. She noticed he kept putting emphasis on that word, *club*.

"I don't know, now. You've made it weird. Am I going to show up and it's some football club? A One Direction fan club? I'm not so into those things," she said.

"How about a sex club? You into that?"

She almost swallowed her tongue. A sex club? He owned and operated a *sex club?* Did those even exist in real life? And the way he'd said it. A perfect stranger, talking about a sex club with her. In broad daylight.

Maybe I never really woke up this morning and this is all a dream.

"I'm sorry," she cleared her throat. "Are you saying you want to take me to a sex club?"

"Yes."

"Is that where you take all your first dates?" she asked, still thinking he might be joking.

"No. Usually I keep it a secret. Freaks most girls out – just like I thought it would you, until I saw that Eros profile," he explained.

"So let me see if I have this straight. Whatever you saw on my profile made you think I'd be interested in going to a sex club with you," she spelled it all out.

"Yeah. Clearly, I was mistaken. It was nice meeting you, Katya."

She was having a moment. A tidal pull on her conscience. This was a bad idea on an epic level. Going to a sex club with a man she'd just met? That's how women ended up on Dateline. Not to mention the fact that Katya simply didn't do things like that – she was more of a museum or opera house kind of girl.

But new-Katya, the woman from the profile, she bristled against old-Katya. Got mad at the way this handsome stranger was looking at her, as if she couldn't possibly be brave enough to try something new and daring. Something sexy and a little dangerous.

"Nine o'clock," she blurted out.

"Excuse me?"

"I'll need more time," she explained. "I can meet you down here at nine o'clock."

"C'mon now, this isn't like truth or dare. No points for trying, it's okay. We can just pretend this didn't happen, go back to avoiding eye contact when we pass each other on the sidewalk," he suggested.

"Awww, see? You're such a good little girl, trying to look out for me," she spoke to him in a baby-voice. His smile finally reappeared and she had to will away the blush she felt creeping up her neck.

"Alright, angel cake. Let's see how far you'll take this cute little act. Nine o'clock," he said, then he finally let her go. She nodded her head.

"I'll be down here," she assured him, then she started for the elevator.

"Oh! And a suggestion," he shouted after her. She turned as she stepped onto the lift and saw that his grin was stretching from ear to ear.

"Yes?"

"Don't change your clothing. What you're wearing is *perfect.*"

<hr>

Holy shit. Holy shit. Holy shit.

"What!?" Tori practically yelled, following Katya around the apartment as she paced.

Shit, was I saying all that out loud!?

"Quick – is what I'm wearing sexy?" she asked, holding out her arms.

"Huh?"

"Sexy! Do I look sexy!?"

"What is going on!?" Tori demanded. "Calm down and explain to me why you're acting so strange!"

"I promise, I will. Just … is this outfit sexy? Be honest, tell me the truth," Katya said.

Tori looked like she wanted to argue, but she finally huffed out a sigh and took a step back. Looked over her friend's outfit, then motioned for her to turn in a circle. When Katya faced forward again, Tori was frowning.

"Matronly," she stated.

"Pardon me?"

"Your outfit is matronly. Did you get that shirt from a maternity shop?"

"This is Donna Karan!"

"Okay. Then … comfortable. You look very comfortable," Tori amended her word choice.

Katya groaned and looked down at herself. She was wearing a loose fitting blouse, tan in color, with an oversized floppy bow that hung down at the neckline. The sleeves were wide, coming in tight at the wrists with long cuffs. Her slacks were also loose, in a shade of brown she thought had complimented the blouse, and she'd paired them with an ecru colored belt. But now looking at herself, she realized she was dressed entirely in colors belonging to the beige family.

Beige. Synonymous with **boring**.

"That stupid profile," Katya growled through clenched teeth before stomping through to their kitchen.

"Oh, yeah. I jazzed it up a bit after you left," Tori said, following along and grabbing them both wine glasses.

"I know, I frickin' read it. Hell, *everyone's* read it. My phone has been blowing up, and then …" Katya's voice trailed off as she replayed the incident in the lobby. What had come over her!?

"And then what? I honestly thought it would be funny," Tori said, pouring healthy amounts of vino tinto into both glasses before sitting down at the table. Katya sat, as well.

"This guy asked me out," she mumbled, fiddling with the stem of her glass.

"Oh. That's a good thing, right?"

"Right …"

"Uh oh."

"He lives next door," Katya spoke slowly after taking a big drink. "He saw the profile and recognized me, decided to come over and introduce himself."

"Scandalous! Who is he? Do we know him?" Tori asked.

"I didn't. I mean, I kinda recognized him just from seeing him around. Liam … something or other. Edelweiss?" Katya tried to remember his last name. "He's tall, tan, bushy brown hair. Big smile."

"Ooohhh, great smile?"

"Sure."

"Yeah, I know the guy! *He* asked you out!? You owe me one, he is *hot!*" Tori sounded excited.

"Yeah, super duper hot. Except the only reason he wanted to ask me out was because that stupid profile made me seem like some sort of kinky sex goddess. After about two seconds of talking to me, he realized that wasn't the case and he tried to back out," Katya said.

"I'm sorry, honey. I honestly didn't mean any harm, but hey, no harm, no foul. At least you didn't have to wait till after the date to find out he's a misogynistic prick," Tori said, rubbing her friend's arm. Katya polished off the rest of her wine, then poured some more.

"Oh, we're going out," she said, deciding to chug the last of the wine straight from the bottle.

"What?"

"It was like … invasion of the body snatchers. He was looking at me like I was some Girl Scout. He said I looked like a Sunday school teacher. Something came over me, I got so pissed. Like what, because I like to dress nice means I don't know how to have a good time? So I started, like, acting like that stupid profile. Saying things I figured that type of girl would say. God, Tori, I was so rude to him, and weirder, he seemed to go for it. I'm meeting him downstairs at nine," Katya said, cupping her glass between both her hands.

"That's *amazing*, Kat! I've been saying this whole time that you need to get out of your little comfort zone! Good for you! And don't worry about this guy – think of him like a spring board. Test out the new you on him, see if you like it, and if not, just never talk to him again," Tori suggested.

"Right. The new me."

"This is so fun! Is that why you were asking about the outfit? You should *definitely* change. Where is he taking you?"

Katya felt flames racing across her face. Surely, it had all been a joke. He couldn't *really* be taking her to a sex club. That he owned. And operated.

Her forehead hit the table with a thunk.

3

I T WAS NO JOKE.

Liam had been waiting in the lobby for her at nine o'clock, sharp. Liam Edenhoff – *"but everyone calls me Eden"* – he'd introduced himself again to her before guiding her out to a taxi he'd had waiting.

She felt a little nauseous. She'd chugged down the only other alcohol they'd had in the apartment – crème de menthe – before heading downstairs to meet him. She'd almost talked herself out of going, but she'd made the mistake of telling Tori about the whole "sex club" bit and her roommate had almost died. Apparently, Katya owed it to women *everywhere* (and Tori in particular) to explore this opportunity to its fullest. Her roommate had all but shoved her out the door, telling her to check in and reminding her of the rape whistle in her purse. Then the door had been shut and she'd heard the chain lock being fit into place.

"Nervous?" Liam Eden-whatever-his-name-was asked her as the cab slowed to a crawl.

"Nope," Katya's voice sounded overly loud.

"Liar. Tonight is gonna be an interesting night, angel cake."

"Stop calling me that."

"What's your last name?"

"None of your business."

"Okay then – when the gang bang starts, I'll tell them to call you Katya X."

She couldn't stop the blush from happening that time and he burst out laughing, then soothed the sting by grabbing her hand.

Even when they got out of the cab, he didn't let go of her. Normally, she would've been uncomfortable with a stranger assuming such a familiarity, but this time she was thankful for it. She held onto him tightly as they walked down a crowded street. Then they turned into an alley, and his gang bang joke didn't seem so funny. He led her to a plain door above which a simple, small neon sign spelled out "The Garden". Outside several small groups of people stood, chatting and smoking. Several folks called out greetings to him, all of them using his nickname, but a large and scary looking bouncer addressed him very properly.

"Hey, Mr. Edenhoff, wasn't expecting you in tonight. Any problems?"

"Nope, just bringing a friend to show her the place, let her see what I do for a living."

All the blood was quickly rushing from Katya's limbs, pooling somewhere in her stomach. None of this was a joke. He really did own the place, that much was obvious. She was *actually* going into a sex club, with a complete stranger.

*Oh my god, I'm actually, really, seriously doing this. Me. Katya Tocci. I'm going into a real live sex club. Holy shit, that is so **BAD. ASS.***

As Liam led her through the door, Katya felt a new surge of confidence. She was still nervous, still more than a little scared, but she was okay with it. Liam seemed like a nice guy, he wasn't going to take her into some dark room and insert foreign objects into her orifices. She could leave whenever she wanted to, whenever it got too uncomfortable. Everything was fine, and for once, she was doing something exciting. She'd *finally* have something interesting to talk about at work.

"How long have you owned this place?" Katya asked, almost stumbling as she moved behind him. They were walking down a long, narrow hallway that was dimly lit. He squeezed her hand tighter, pulling her close to keep her from falling.

"Only three years, but I've worked here for almost six. I was hired on as a general manager, the old owners had no clue what they were doing. I finally bought them out, changed a lot of stuff," he told her.

They finally came out of the hallway, and while she'd mentally prepared herself for some crazy orgy, it just looked like a normal bar. Huge padded booths curved along one wall, cocktail tables sat on the open floor, people were laughing and mingling while they drank. Jazzy music was blanketing everything, and while the vibe was definitely sexy, there was no *actual* sex taking place.

Maybe it *had* all been a weird joke. Weirder still, Katya realized she was a little disappointed. Sure, she hadn't intended on participating in anything, but still. How cool would it have been to say she went to a sex club?

"That's nice," she finally spoke again as they walked up to the bar. "I'd love to own my own bakery. I'm head baker at where I work now, and they give me a lot of freedom, but it's not the same."

"No, it's definitely not. Tim! *Timmy!*" Liam shouted, pounding on the bar top. A handsome young man finally made his way down to them.

"Hey, boss man! What can I get for you?"

"I'll take a Jack and coke, and for the lady, let me guess," Liam made a big show of looking her over. "I'm thinking … Cosmo. Definitely. You're a Cosmo girl." Katya glared at him for a second, then turned to Tim.

"Patrón, double shot."

Liam chuckled at her bravado, then full on laughed when she almost gagged on the tequila. She managed to get it down without coughing or spitting it everywhere, though it all nearly came back up when she felt his hand slide around her hip.

"This isn't a 'who's cooler' competition, you know," he whispered in her ear. "And if it was, you showed up. You came here. *You win.*" She took a deep breath.

"And *you* need to stop pretending like you know me."

"Touché. C'mon, lots more to see."

Tim had made her a Cosmo anyway, and Katya mouthed a "thank you" at him before picking up the drink. She struggled to take sips as she followed behind Liam. They walked up to a massive door that was covered in the same vinyl material as the booths. There was an antique looking doorbell on the wall and Liam pressed it, holding his thumb on the button for a while. When the door finally creaked open, he winked at her and grabbed her free hand.

They were facing a wide set of stairs that curved along a wall before disappearing around a bend. Katya shuddered at the idea of trying to navigate them while drunk. Several people were standing about on the steps, and all of them said hi to Liam as they passed. A couple women even reached out to him, running their fingers and hands along his shoulders, his arms, his back.

"Eden, it's been forever, where have you been?"

"Eden, you owe me a drink."

"Eden, you never called me back."

Katya didn't know him well enough to be jealous, but she didn't find the experience enjoyable, either. By the time they reached the bottom of the steps, she'd downed her drink and was praying there was another bar. She was excited as one came into sight, but then frowned when she realized the back-bar was entirely stocked with fancy looking brands of water. No liquor? How did people engage in public indecency without a healthy amount of alcohol in their system!?

"Why do they call you Eden?" she asked, glancing around the space. It looked like it was entirely carved out of stone. The stairs, the walls, even the bar and bar back. Sconces and recessed lighting gave the entire place a soft glow, as if they were in a cave and lit only by firelight.

"Because of my last name," he answered simply as he moved behind the bar. He had a brief exchange with the man who had been doling out the expensive looking water, then Liam dipped out of sight. When he popped back up, he had a fancy clay bottle in his hand.

"Roofies?" she asked, and he barked out a laugh.

"No, tequila. From Guadalajara."

"Why do you hide it?"

"Because, we don't serve alcohol down here," he explained.

"Why not!?"

"When sex is involved, you want people thinking with a clear conscience, and acting with good intentions. People can carry a single drink down from the bar above, but they can't go back for more, and none is kept here."

"Except that bottle."

"Except this bottle, which is my personal bottle that no one else touches. To new friends - cheers."

She grabbed a full shot glass from him and watched as he came back out from around the bar. She stared him right in the eye while she downed the fiery liquid. Before he could finish his shot, though, another woman slithered her arm around his waist.

"Eden, so good to see you. Make sure you come say hi before you leave," she breathed, then leaned up and placed a wet kiss on his cheek. His eyes never left Katya's, not even when the other woman walked off in a huff.

"I don't think they call you that because of your name," Katya said in a soft voice. He smiled and leaned down close to her, resting his hands on her waist.

"They call me that because of what I've given them," he said, his voice low. She couldn't help the shiver that ran over her body.

"And what's that?" she whispered. He chuckled, that sound she was growing to adore, and slowly forced her to turn around, to face the wall that had been at her back the whole time.

"*The garden of earthly delights.*"

She could see in most of the booths, though some had semi-sheer curtains drawn in front of them. In the open ones people were clearly visible. Some were sitting and drinking. One couple was kissing. In another booth, there was a man sitting alone. Or at least, that's what Katya thought at first. When she took a second glance, she realized there was a woman on her knees under the table.

"Oh my god."

"I warned you, angel cake. Just let me know when you're ready to go home."

She felt her back teeth grind together. Hadn't she come out with him? Hadn't she walked around his stupid club? Yet there he was, still assuming things about her. Sure, she was surprised, but she wasn't running away. What did it take to get a little credit?

"You'll know when I'm ready."

She was halfway across the room before Katya even knew she was moving. She took deep lungfuls of air in, almost hyperventilating. But she didn't stop walking. She kept going until she was in front of an emergency exit that was positioned between two of the booths. The booth to her left was empty, thankfully. The one on the right had two women and a man who were either practicing a really interesting form of yoga, or were having exhausting looking sex.

When was the last time I had exhausting sex? Never?

"Hey," she said in a loud voice. There was a young guy standing near the door, nodding his head to the beat of the music. He looked up when she spoke, then smiled as he took in her body and outfit.

"Hey, how's it going?" he asked, turning to give her his full attention.

"Okay. A little bored," she sighed, glancing around them.

"Sounds like a problem I could help you with – what's your

name?"

"Katya."

"Mike," he gestured to himself. "So what brings a good girl like you to a place like this?"

"Obviously if I found my way here, I'm not a very good girl," she pointed out.

"Baby, I've been hanging out here for a while, and you look about as good as they come," he chuckled, his eyes wandering over her clothing. She sighed and put her hands on her hips.

"You should never judge a book by its cover because under this frumpy brown exterior, I'm wearing a leather bustier and crotchless panties," she prattled off.

Did I just say crotchless panties!?

"Whoa, my mistake, baby. How about we sit down and we can talk more about bad covers on good books," Mike suggested.

"Sounds good. I …" Katya's voice trailed off as she felt warmth at her back. Almost pressing against her. Mike glanced over her shoulder, then did a double take before standing up noticeably straighter.

"Hey, Eden, nice night," he said.

"It is. *Leave.*"

Her new friend scampered off, and before he'd even passed by her, Katya felt a warm hand on her hip. Smoothing along the side of it, then gliding across her stomach. She held perfectly still. Even held her breath. Liam's large hand was warm against her body, and he splayed his fingers, his thumb brushing against the center of her bra. She finally remembered how to breathe and stepped away from him.

"I thought you said tonight would be interesting," she said as she turned to face him. "So far all that's happened is you've judged me and been unexciting."

"You still think this is a competition," he sighed. She shook her head.

"No, I'm just … tired of people acting like they know me simply because I talk or act or dress a certain way. If I were to judge you based on your clothing, I'd assume you were some out of work college drop out," she said, gesturing to his well worn polo shirt and loose jeans. He gave her a big smile.

"Fair play. Alright, no more judgement. You want to play at being bad for the night, then it's no concern of mine. I just have one thing I'd like to double check," Liam said.

"What?"

"I didn't feel any leather bustier under that pilgrim shirt you're wearing."

How far was she willing to take her little self-challenge? He was smiling, but his eyes weren't on her face. They were eating up the lines and miles of her body, almost like he could see beneath the billowy material and suss out her real figure. She *wanted* him to see her real figure.

"Maybe you should look for yourself."

While Katya was having a lot of inner turmoil about her choices and actions, her mouth was having no such issues – she was shocked at the dare she'd just issued. Liam stepped forward and while his eyes never left hers, he reached out very slowly and tapped his finger on her top button. He waited half a beat, and when she didn't move away or stop him, he pushed the button out of its hole. He continued down the line and she drew in a shaky breath when she felt the floppy bow come to rest in her cleavage.

I'm about to be topless in a night club. Who is this person, and what has she done with Katya Tocci?

"Still racier than I expected," he said in a soft voice, and she felt his finger trace along the lacy edge of her lilac bra. "But definitely not leather."

"Sorry to disappoint," Katya whispered.

Maybe it was the tequila. Maybe her sign was in retrograde, or maybe it was all the stuff Tori had been saying to her. All Katya knew was it felt like her blood was on fire and she never wanted him to stop touching her.

So when he hooked a finger around her belt, she let him. Stepped forward when he pulled her near. Didn't stop him when he leaned down so close, she could feel his hot breath against her lips.

"Katya, there is literally nothing about you that could possibly disappoint," his voice was gentle.

"Don't say that – you haven't checked for the crotchless panties yet."

He gave one last laugh, causing her heart to do a little somersault, and then his mouth was on hers. She was almost ashamed at how good it made her feel. She hadn't been kissed in a long time and she abandoned herself to the sensation. Sighed against his lips, then gasped when his tongue filled her mouth.

She returned the favor, her tongue tentatively skimming along the edges of his teeth, then when she realized he was undoing her belt, she became more aggressive. Wrapped an arm around his shoulders while she actively pressed back against his tongue with her own, waging war for space in their mouths.

"C'mon," he panted when he pulled away, and she realized he was forcing her to move backwards by shoving on her hips. "Let's go to my office. I can have some drinks brought in and we can -"

"*No.*"

Katya was just as surprised as him at the tone of her voice.

"No?" he asked.

"No. I … I want to stay out here," she told him. Since new-Katya apparently didn't care about anything of a proprietary nature, she figured being honest wouldn't be weird.

"Ah, I see. Angel cake wants to watch," he teased her, and she could feel his fingertips rubbing against the bare skin just above her belt.

"I'm curious," she corrected him.

"Then by all means, let's see if we can scratch your itch."

She had to concentrate on her feet as he moved her into the empty booth next to them. The alcohol was settling around her brain and making her body feel relaxed.

But not her mind. That felt sharper than ever. She knew *exactly* what she was doing, and was suddenly very aware of *exactly* what she wanted. It had all been a dare, to see how far she could push herself, but now, she wasn't even thinking about any of that – she was only thinking about how good looking the man next to her was, and how amazing it had been to kiss him.

They sat down side by side. Katya noticed how wide and deep the bench seats were – if she pressed herself to the back of it, she couldn't put her feet on the floor. Her knees didn't even reach the edge, though Liam's did; he was pretty tall, easily six-foot-two or so. There was no proper table, but rather a low glass coffee table with what looked like movable ottomans underneath it. Several bottles of water were gathered at one end, unopened and inviting looking.

"What made you want to do this?" Katya breathed, letting her eyes wander over the room.

"Bring you here?" he asked.

"No. Run your own sex club."

The place wasn't exactly a raging orgy, no one was having out-and-out sex in the middle of the open floor. But most of the booths held occupants, and only a handful of them were just chatting. The rest were engaging in all sorts of naughty activities, some on full display for the room, their moans and sighs audible to everyone, while others chose to be more discreet behind the sheer curtains.

"I had a background in night club management, they hired me on. I liked the place, but they were doing a shitty job. It never would've lasted without me. Then I came into an inheritance, met some … investors, kinda, and came up with the plan to buy this place," he explained.

"So it wasn't your life's ambition to run a sex club?" Katya asked. He laughed.

"No. I mean, I guess I've always been a sexual person. You know, like overtly so. I'd been to sex clubs, some swingers parties, but never thought about it as a job."

"Do you like it?"

"Yes, very much."

"So people just come here and mingle and then get it on in these booths?"

"Yeah, but not just that," he said. "See those double doors over there? They'll open up after ten o'clock. There's private rooms along the hallway – some, people pay by the hour. Some, they rent by the month. Then at the very end are two conference rooms with a removable wall between them, so they can become one huge room. Those usually get booked out for conventions, birthday parties, whatever."

Katya couldn't imagine what kind of birthday party would rent out a ballroom at a sex club. Yet for all that, the place was really … chill.

"It's different than I expected," she said, and he seemed to understand what she meant because he laughed.

"It's a Tuesday and it's kinda early. It'll pick up later," he assured her.

She turned to face him again and when his eyes dropped to her chest, she had to work hard not to blush – she'd actually forgotten that her top wasn't buttoned up.

"I've never done anything like this before," she said in a soft voice.

"I'd already guessed that."

"And not just the sex club," she continued. "Going out with a man I don't know. Kissing a man I don't know. *All* of this."

"Still not surprised."

"Can anyone come down here?"

"No. Members only, and we're *very* strict."

"How does one become a member?"

"You asking for yourself?"

She'd been looking over the room again, but cut her eyes back to him. He had a rich voice and usually sounded like he had a laugh hiding just beneath the surface of his words. But now he sounded serious. Sexy. Their kiss ran through her mind and she felt a little dizzy.

"I don't think I'd meet your qualifications," she whispered.

"We have got to cure this nasty self-deprecation habit you've developed."

"It's the truth."

Liam moved into her personal space and gently grabbed the bow on the front of her shirt. She leaned into him as he pulled her closer.

"I think you need to stop caring so much about everything, and maybe just let go for a little while."

This time when he kissed her, there was no hesitation on her part. She didn't even flinch when he untied the bow and slid the shirt away from her shoulders. She shook free of it, sat there clad in only her bra, but she didn't even think about it. Her brain was spinning from the alcohol and his words and his nearness.

"I don't think I've ever let go," she panted against his mouth.

"I'm good at it, I'll show you the ropes," he assured her, one of his hands spearing into the hair at the back of her head as he kissed along her jawline.

She felt like a teenager, making out in some dark corner. Not that she'd ever done that as one, but it was naughty. Thrilling. She tried to get closer, curling one of her legs under herself and stretching the other across his lap. His free hand immediately went to her hip, smoothed a path down to her knee, then worked its way to the inside of her thigh, his fingers digging in as they slowly traveled the length of her leg.

Katya had slept with two men in her entire life, and been "intimate" with four. Intimate meaning she gave Joey Simms a really bad blow job during her freshman year of college, and the following year, Mark Demello had received several decent hand jobs from her. All four men had also gotten their hands into her panties, but only after many, many dates, and even then – only two had been around long enough to actually see her fully naked.

She'd known Liam for all of four hours, and she was ready to strip down and sit spread eagle for him. Do anything he wanted. It was insanity. She'd been raised better than that, she'd been taught to respect herself. Been told that men only wanted one thing, and she had to protect herself from their wanton ways.

But right then, as her new found confidence washed away her inhibitions and Liam's hands burned away any concerns, she had one thought screaming through her head like a freight train.

*What if **I** want that "one thing"? What if **I** have "wanton ways"?*

There was the briefest hesitation when his fingers smoothed over the skin on her stomach, and she held her breath, praying she wouldn't have to beg him. She wasn't sure her tongue would be able to cooperate. But then he surged back into the kiss, his tongue dominating her mouth, almost distracting her from the fact that his hand was now sliding its way inside her satin underwear.

"How did I know you'd feel so perfect," he sighed, rubbing his nose along the side of her neck while his middle finger worked its way inside her body, reminding her that it had been a very long time since anyone else's fingers had been there.

"I'm not perfect," she gasped for air and clung to his neck, her fingernails biting into his skin.

"Angel cake, you are *perfection* – you just need someone to show you," he whispered, pressing the heel of his hand down against her, causing her eyes to cross a little.

"Please, *please,* show me."

"Maybe we should move this to my office."

Katya pulled back at that comment. Of course, he was probably right. She knew sex was imminent, and so did he – maybe not the classiest thing, screwing a guy only hours after meeting him, but at least in his office, they'd have some privacy. It was a sex club, maybe he had a bed in there. A nice, normal bed, where they could have nice, normal sex, because she was such a nice, normal girl.

"I don't want to move," she said, leaning in again and licking the edge of his ear. She smiled when a shiver ripped across his shoulders.

"C'mon, I told you, this isn't a competition, and if it was, you won. You are officially the coolest. Do you know how long it's been since anyone's gotten me to do stuff on the floor out here? But I don't think you're ready to have sex in the middle of a bar," he said.

He was right. Considering she'd never had sex outside of a bedroom, she probably wasn't ready for something that drastic. But she also knew she wasn't ready to stop what they were doing. She wasn't ready to go back to being the old-Katya. She'd come back soon enough, new-Katya wanted to revel in her new found freedom. Wanted to roll around in all the feelings racing across her nerve endings.

I want to be in this moment.

Katya pushed at him, forcing him to remove his hand from her pants. He sighed as she climbed to her feet. She was a little wobbly on her heels at first, then caught her balance. Liam sat upright and rubbed a hand over his face.

"Want me to call you a cab?" he asked, finally glancing up at her.

He was very good looking. She couldn't quite place his age. Twenty-seven? Eight? He looked like he spent time outdoors, his bushy brown hair had a couple natural blonde highlights running through it. His eyes were a dark brown, like chocolate, warm and sensual while they moved over her face. His skin was a deep toasty tan, more proof of his time in the sun, and she was suddenly desperate to see if he was tan *everywhere*.

She stared back at him while she kicked off her shoes. Then his eyebrows went up as she fumbled with her belt, struggled to pull it loose. Once it was free, she dropped it next to her shoes. By that point, she was breathing fast, and Liam didn't say anything, just leaned to the side and pulled a chord. The sheer curtains dropped into place, offering them a little privacy, and Katya was thankful for his intuition. Then he leaned back in his seat, and his eyes went straight to her pants.

She knew if she hesitated, old-Katya would catch up with her.

The bitch had been chasing her all night, so she needed to move fast. She undid the clasp at the top of her slacks, then slowly peeled down the zipper. The loose material clung to her hips for a second, then gravity worked its magic, pulling the soft fabric to the ground, leaving her in nothing but her matching lilac underwear set.

"See," he said, sitting forward so he was eye to eye with the bow at the top of her panties. "*Perfection.*"

Katya stepped forward then, straddling his lap. He accommodated her, grabbing her hips and holding on while he scooted back in the seat. He helped her settle in right over the bulge in his pants, and she felt breathless as she realized she had caused that reaction in him. This man, who engaged in swingers conventions and ran a sex club. *She* had turned him on, *she* had gotten him hard.

"I'm not perfection," she moaned as his mouth trailed over her breasts.

"Right now, you're pretty damn close. We're not playing around anymore, Katya. If you want this to stop, now is a good time to say so," he urged her. She combed her fingers through his hair, pulling a little.

"I never want this to stop."

One of his hands was groping her ass, and the other made its way up her back. It was only one hand, and his left one at that, but he managed to undo the clasp on her bra. It didn't feel strange at all, being almost naked in a bar, where there were other people sitting not ten feet away from her. She didn't even think about it, just let the lace and satin fall to the bench beside them.

"God, you're so smooth. You're going to feel so amazing," he groaned before cupping her left breast, raising the nipple to his mouth. He pinched his teeth around the tightened peak before sucking it into his mouth.

"I want to feel you," she gasped, suddenly realizing she was almost naked and he was still fully clothed.

She began tearing at his clothing, almost strangling him with his shirt. He'd barely pulled it free of his head before she was kissing him again, sighing at the feeling of her chest rubbing against naked skin. When he lifted his hands to cup both breasts, she leaned away, looking over his body. His tan flowed unmarred across his chest and abdomen, and as she pulled apart his belt, she saw that it definitely continued under his pants.

She was too impatient, and – to be honest – a little too nervous to deal with the intricacies that were his button fly, so she moved her trembling fingers out of the way and left him to it while she went back to kissing him. His mouth, his jaw, his neck. Her hands wandered everywhere, feeling the hard plains of his chest, the smooth muscles behind his shoulders. While she worked on giving him a hickey, he grabbed one of her hands, and before she realized what was happening, her fingers were against something very hard.

"*Now* you're feeling me," he growled as her hand wrapped around the base of his dick.

"Oh god," she moaned, pressing her forehead to his as she looked down between their bodies. His erection stood up between them, looking imposing in the dim lighting. He had to at least be seven inches, if not more, and felt hefty in her hand. Thick and hard.

"I *did not* expect tonight to go like this," he started to pant as her hand moved up and down.

"Me, neither. Am I really about to have sex in the middle of a room full of people?" she mumbled, writhing against him.

"You sure as shit are."

He jerked forward suddenly, startling her and forcing her to lean backwards. She let go of him and went to brace a hand against the table behind her, then felt something against her fingers. The water bottles. She glanced back and managed to grab one before he started pulling her upright, untwisting the cap as they moved. His hand was between them, his fingers running along the side of her panties, pushing them to the side, lightly touching against her slick skin.

Then, just as she lifted the bottle to her lips, something a lot bigger replaced his fingers. She wasn't quite prepared for the jerk he gave her hips, forcing her down a little, and she almost choked on the water. As it was, the cool liquid spilled over the side of her lips. Ran down her jaw, along her neck, then trailed to the very tip of her breast. His mouth was there to catch it, licking at the trail all the way back to her throat. By the time he'd gotten the last of it, she was sitting flat on his lap, so full with him, she couldn't remember what it felt like to be empty.

"*Fuck*," was all he managed to say. It was better than her – all Katya could manage to do was shiver and shake.

*You're having sex in a … no, wait. Fucking. You are **fucking** some guy in a sex club. Holy fucking shit, you're fucking fucking someone.* **Fuck.**

Talk about surreal. She could only moan and pant and whimper as he began pushing and pulling at her hips. Thrusting up against her. It took her a minute, but she started moving back, pumping against his thrusts, rotating her hips in time to his rhythm. He groaned again and she felt his fingers raking down her back, causing her spine to arch.

"God, yes, please, Liam. This is … everything. God, thank you," she moaned. Even at a time like that, he managed to laugh.

"God, huh? Pretty close," he whispered, biting on her bottom lip.

"Harder. Please, harder."

He moved then, startling her again. She was suddenly on her back on the bench seat, the vinyl cool against her skin, and he was on top of her. She went to touch him when he grabbed her wrists, forcing them above her head and holding them there with one hand.

Then he complied with her request, thrusting against her so hard, she was pretty sure the booth was moving. She moaned low in her throat, biting her lips between her teeth to keep from shrieking.

"Don't hold back," he breathed against her ear. "Tell me how good this feels."

"So good," she whispered back.

"You have no idea. You're so tight on my cock, *goddamn.*"

"*Holy shit.*"

Go out with a man she'd just met, check. Have sex in a club, check. Experience dirty talk, *definite check.* She finally did cry out, unable to hold it in as a tremor ripped through her body, threatening to tear her apart.

"Fuck, *yes,* just like that, baby. Let it all go, Katya. Just let it go."

She was feeling pretty brainless by then, but her body was paying rapt attention to his instructions. Her orgasm shocked her a little, with its appearance and its intensity. She trembled underneath him, letting out a long, low moan as it felt like her entire body turned into one big spasm. Just as she was coming down from it, his mouth locked onto a nipple, sucking hard and causing a fresh tremor to seize her.

"Oh my god, oh my god," she tried to catch her breath. He chuckled and laid down on her, his full weight pressing her into the booth. "*Holy shit.* We just had sex."

"You just got fucked," he corrected her, his voice muffled by her breasts.

"That … was … *amazing,*" she moaned.

"*You* were amazing. Talk about pent up. You went off like a bottle rocket," he teased.

"You have no idea."

"Thank god you insisted on going out tonight," he laughed, and she felt his breath hot against her skin.

"Samesies," she said. He shifted on top of her and she was suddenly very aware of the fact that he was still hard. And inside her. So very hard inside of her.

"If you only had any idea how good this feels," he sighed, pumping in and out, almost excruciatingly slow.

"Says the guy who owns a sex club and goes to wild parties," she laughed. "This can't be anything new to you."

He stopped moving and lifted himself up so he could look her in the eye.

"There you go again. Can't you just take a compliment?" he asked, and he sounded genuinely annoyed. The grip he had on her wrists got tighter, crushing her arms together.

"I … I just figured you've done all this before, felt all this before," she tried to explain. He dropped down again and she felt his lips against her ear.

"I have *never* felt anything like you, Katya. Can you feel how tight you are? How you milk my cock? *Fucking amazing.* Jesus, if I had known you'd feel like this, I wouldn't have waited so long to talk to you," he growled.

"That's … flattering," she managed to respond, feeling slightly breathless again.

"You fucking bet it is. The only thing I can imagine feeling better than this, would be *fucking your ass.*"

Whoa now. Having sex in a club with a virtual stranger was one thing, but *anal!?* Sure, she'd always been a little curious – who wasn't? Who didn't want to be the cool chick who took anal like a champ? But she'd never even so much as discussed it with any of her previous boyfriends. She certainly wasn't about to do it with a stranger! She'd simply tell him that would have to wait for a much, much, *much* later date.

"*Only one way to find out.*"

Hmmm, not exactly what she'd planned to say to him, but it's what fell out of her mouth. When he lifted his head, she simply stared at him. Tried to focus on his warm eyes, on the laugh lines that were at the corners. She was suddenly consumed with the thought of letting him take her. It was now or never, she truly felt. She had to do this, she had to become *that girl.*

"Careful now, angel cake. Don't write checks your body can't cash," he said, looking at her naked chest. She willed her body to stop trembling.

"There you go again, assuming things about me. Assumed I

wouldn't come here. Assumed I'd go home. Assumed I wouldn't have sex with you. I wonder what else you'll be wrong about tonight," she said, her voice dropping to a whisper.

"You've never done something like that before."

He stated, didn't question. She nodded.

"Never. I've thought about it, but was never brave enough to try."

"Then this is a bad idea."

"Hmmm, I'm sure one of the other guys here won't think so."

"Katya, I'm serious. No more competing. That's a big step, a big deal, and will more than likely be uncomfortable as fuck your first time. You should do it with someone you trust," he told her.

That moment. That's how she knew he wasn't a bad guy. She was naked under him, she'd just let him fuck her brains out on a booth in his sex club. He could've done literally just about anything he wanted to her, and she was offering it all up on a silver platter, and he was still looking out for her. Liam was a nice guy. A good guy. A *trustworthy* guy.

Also, if she stopped now, she knew it would never happen.

I'm so tired of being the good one.

"I want to do it with someone who knows what they're doing," she whispered, then she lifted her head, placing a chaste kiss on his lips. "And someone who will make me feel good. Please, Liam. *Please make me feel good.*"

He was a good guy, but Liam had his limits, and a naked woman begging him to fuck her up the ass was apparently one of them.

He was slow as he eased off of her, his hands gentle as they rolled her over. He carefully lifted her head and put a throw pillow under her cheek. His hands were heavy on her skin, almost massaging her as he ran them from her shoulders to her butt, then back up again. She was a little tipsy and it felt amazing, almost lulling her to sleep.

Then she heard a noise and when she turned her head, she saw that he was pulling one of the ottomans out from under the table. They were actually drawers, though what was in their depths, she couldn't be sure. She caught a glimpse of what looked like tubes and bottles. He rummaged around in the drawer, then pulled his hand free. He was behind her after that, out of sight, so she couldn't be sure what he'd grabbed, but when something cold hit her backside, she had a good idea.

"On a scale of sober to black-out, how drunk are you?" he asked. She opened her mouth to answer, then choked on her own words as she felt his finger between her cheeks, smoothing up and down along the line.

"Like a four? Pleasantly tipsy?" she finally managed to get out.

"I just want to make sure this isn't the alcohol talking," he said.

"It's not, I swear, I didn't even drink that much before I came. I … I feel like a different person here. I want to be a different person. I want to try -"

There was no managing words that time around. He had a finger inside her. Inside a place no one had ever been before, a place she herself tried to avoid. The lubrication he was using was cool and slippery, but gave him easy access. She was shocked that it didn't feel at all gross, or disgusting, or painful. It felt … *interesting*.

"Then you came to the right place," he chuckled, and a second finger joined the first, turning *interesting* feeling into *slightly awkward* feeling. "The alcohol will help you relax, too."

She wasn't sure how long they stayed like that – her with her face buried in the pillow, trying to hide her embarrassment and shame and *delight* at what he was doing to her. Him, kneeling behind her, holding her hips up with one hand, and using the other to work magic on her.

Just when Katya began to think that's as far as he would take it, his fingers were gone. She sighed and felt conflicted – sad that he hadn't been brave enough to take it all the way. Glad because she wasn't sure she was brave enough, either.

But then he was moving, shifting around behind her. Pulling her hips even higher. There was the crinkle of foil, followed by the sound of it ripping, then a long pause. She went to look over her shoulder, to ask if everything was okay, but then something much, much larger than a finger was against her ass, demanding entrance, and she thought her eyeballs were going to fall out of her skull.

"Oh my god," she moaned, burying her face in the pillow again.

"Relax, Katya. *Relax.*"

He could say that word all he wanted – didn't mean it was going to happen. She chewed on the pillow and chewed on her lips and so desperately wanted to be the kind of girl who could have casual no-strings-attached anal sex in a club, but she became increasingly sure it wouldn't happen. He was simply too big. It *hurt*. She blinked away tears and tried to catch her breath.

"Liam, I don't think -"

"*Relax,*" he sounded like he was clenching his teeth together. "I told you it would be uncomfortable. It's gonna hurt. But I promise you, it will feel *so good* if you see it through. Cry if you need to, scream, shout, whatever. It's okay. But just trust me."

She almost took him up on his offer to scream. He couldn't have been more than halfway inside her and the pain was causing a burning sensation up her spine. She would've screamed, but she worried that if she opened her mouth, she'd throw up. She bit down on the pillow and cried, the tears soaking the material.

"This is better than I imagined, Katya," he sighed after what felt like an eternity later, when his hips were against her ass.

"I wish … I could say … the same," she managed to pant out between gasps for air. He chuckled and she felt his hands on her back, massaging her shoulders.

"Touch yourself," he whispered.

"I can't," she whispered back. She was scared to move, scared it would hurt more.

"Just relax and let your body feel everything," he insisted, and one of his hands moved to her front, passing over her breasts and heading straight between her legs. She was still wet from the sex they'd had, so his fingers moved with ease. She took deep breaths and was shocked when she felt her body react. Felt warmth spread from his fingers to her nipples to her lips to every limb. When he started moving his hips against her, it wasn't exactly enjoyable, but it wasn't as painful as it had been, either.

"Touch yourself," he said it again, this time as a command. She did as she was told, replacing his fingers with her own. His hands gripped onto her hips, holding her still while he slowly moved in and out.

"Oh my god, Liam," she whispered.

"Told you so."

It took some time to adjust to his size, it felt like he was splitting her in half at first. Every time he plunged back in, fresh tears filled her eyes. But after a while, her fingers were moving faster than his thrusts, and her panting was staving off an orgasm, not pain. Before she fully clued into what was happening to her body, he was fully fucking her, his hips thrusting hard and fast against her ass, and even more shocking, she was pushing back into him. Wanting it harder, wanting it faster. Wanting more, period.

"Oh god, I'm gonna come," she cried out, something she'd never said during sex before, to anyone.

"*Fuck,* yes, me too. Come with me, Katya, please, baby, come again," he begged.

This time, she really didn't hold back, crying out as her orgasm rocked her world. She had three of her own fingers inside herself and she held them still when she started shaking again. Then Liam's hips locked in tight against her and as she felt his hands on her back, he let out a long growl, coming and coming till she didn't think he could possibly have anything left to give her.

"Holy shit, what did we just do," she gasped for air when she could finally talk. He laid down on top of her, forcing her flat against the bench again.

"Something amazing," he replied, kissing along her shoulder

blade. She managed to move her arm and she reached back, combing her fingers through his hair.

"Liam?"

"Yeah?"

"I'd like to reassess something."

"What?"

"I think I'm more like a six – not black-out drunk yet, but beyond tipsy."

He burst out laughing, then went back to kissing her skin.

"Don't tell me that, I want to believe it was my cunning sexual prowess that just gave you that monster orgasm," he teased.

"It totally was, and if you get me something to drink, maybe you can show me some more of your 'prowess' before we go home."

"I think I'm falling in love, angel cake. You are more fun than I ever would've thought possible."

"See? Never judge a book by its cover."

4

KATYA WOKE UP WITH A START, SITTING BOLT UPRIGHT.

Where the fuck am I?

She winced at thinking such a bad word, and at the pounding headache that was raging between her ears.

She pressed a hand against her forehead and looked around. She was in an apartment, but it wasn't hers. This one was nice, with high ceilings and ornate crown molding. A glance over her shoulder showed her big bay windows and pale yellow wallpaper.

She was stretched out on a long white leather couch. She cringed as she looked down at herself. She had her bra on and her blouse, though it wasn't buttoned. She wasn't wearing her pants, and her panties were hooked around one ankle. *Classy.* She felt around her head and could tell that half her hair was still up in a bun, though it had gotten yanked around and was hanging askew off the side of her head. The rest of her hair was in a rats nest on the opposite side.

Jesus, how drunk did I get last night!?

She swung her legs off the couch so she could sit upright, and the soreness radiating out from her backside reminded her *exactly* what she'd gotten up to last night. All the blood in her body rushed to her cheeks. She'd gone out on a date. To a sex club. Where she'd had sex. *Anal* sex. With the club's owner. Liam Edenwieselhoff-whatever.

I don't even know his last name, and I must be in his apartment. Please, dear god, let this be his apartment.

Katya refused to think about anything. If she stopped to think, she'd literally die of embarrassment, and she didn't have time to die. A glance at a huge clock on the wall showed her it was eleven in the morning. She was two hours late for work.

She got to her feet and pushed away the rush of nausea that rolled over her. She hopped around, struggling to pull on her underwear. Once the satin was in place, she searched for her pants. She managed to track down her shoes and her purse, but the pants were simply gone. Shit, she didn't even remember coming to the apartment – how could she remember where her clothing was?

Oh god, oh god, did I come back here only half-clothed!? Did we take a cab? An Uber? Oh god, oh god, oh god.

"I can practically hear your thoughts, angel cake. Keep it down, I'm hungover as fuck."

She'd been crawling around on her hands and knees, but at the sound of Liam's voice, she knelt upright. She hadn't realized it, but the whole apartment was like a giant studio, or a loft. There didn't seem to be any real walls, though there was tons of space. A huge platform bed sat on the other side of the room, and underneath a single flat sheet, Liam was completely stretched out on top of the mattress.

"I need to go," she hissed, knee-walking over to the bed.

"Shouldn't that be my line?" he chuckled, not bothering to open his eyes. She lowered herself again and looked under the bed. Still no pants.

"It would be, if we were at my place. I'm beyond late for work. Shit, did we drink more? Shit, where are my pants," she grumbled. Before she could move any farther, she felt his arm wrap around her waist from behind, yanking her till she was being dragged onto the bed.

"We drank lots more. Forget work, lets spoon," he suggested, pulling her into his chest.

"No, I have responsibilities, I *have* to go to work," she insisted, struggling with his arm.

"*Fine.* But I can't help you on the pants," he sighed, letting her go. She turned so she was facing him.

"Did I come home naked?" she was almost yelling. He smiled at her, though his eyes were *still* closed.

"I tried to talk you into it, but alas, you insisted on getting dressed. We got honey all over your pants, I think they're soaking in my bathtub," he explained.

"Honey!?"

"Yeah, don't you remember? God, you're an animal. The things you did with those cherries – I will *never* forget last night."

"*Oh god!*" she groaned, dropping her head into her hands.

"Hey, hey, hey," he said, and she felt him curl around her. "Don't start that self-hate crap. Last night was amazing. Awesome and fun and all that shit. You were beautiful."

"I was *drunk.*"

"But still beautiful. I had a great time, Katya. Thanks for going out with me."

She couldn't help it, she had to smile at him. She didn't know Liam very well – at least in the bright light of day, she didn't – but she was quickly learning that feeling bad simply wasn't an option around him. She leaned back so she was resting on his side.

"It was pretty awesome. Thank *you* for showing me a good time."

"You're very welcome. Now get out of here, I want to sleep through this hangover," he said, slapping her on the side of her thigh.

"Can I borrow some shorts or something?" she asked, sliding off his bed.

"Wardrobe. Top drawer. All yours."

Last night, she'd said his outfit made him look like a college drop out. Looking through his underwear, she lowered her estimation to frat boy. There were boxers with kiss prints, four leaf clovers, beer logos, a woman's face with her open mouth strategically placed, all sorts of goodies. She frowned and decided to move onto a different drawer. There, she found some basketball shorts. They went clear past her knees, but they would do. She knotted the draw string tight and tried not to think about how bad her walk of shame was about to look.

I've never even done a walk of shame before – but last night was totally worth it.

"Thanks, I'll make sure they get back to you," she told him as she buttoned up her shirt, heading back to the bed where she'd left her purse and shoes.

"No worries. Take it easy today, you're gonna be sore for a while," he warned her, and when she looked up, he finally had his eyes open. They were red rimmed and tired, but still so warm. Full of laughter.

"Oh. Okay."

He laughed and grabbed the bow at the front of her shirt, yanking her in close for a kiss. They both desperately needed to brush their teeth, and Katya was dying for a shower, but he still managed to take her breath away and had her contemplating how important her job really was.

"What happened to my little silver tongued vixen from last night?" he asked when he pulled away.

"She got left behind in the bottom of a tequila bottle. Thanks for a good time, Liam," she said. He skimmed his thumb over her bottom lip, pressing down lightly.

"Thanks for the *best time*, Katya."

He kissed her once more, then slapped her on the ass when she walked away.

It wasn't till she was in her apartment, showered and getting dressed for work, that she realized they hadn't even exchanged phone numbers. Hadn't set up another date. Hadn't even learned each others last names (or at least, she couldn't properly remember his, and she'd never given her own).

*Holy shit, did I just have a one night stand with my hot next door neighbor? I am, I **really am** a bad ass!*

Liam dragged himself into work not long after Katya left, but he wasn't getting much work done. He was staring at his phone once again. He'd saved the picture from her Eros profile, which was a good thing because the profile didn't exist anymore. She'd deactivated it.

Good. She's a naughty little secret that we should keep to ourselves for a little while longer.

She'd rocked his fucking world. He'd expected to call her bluff – that she'd take one look at his little club and turn tail. Her taking the shots had been surprising enough, but making out with him? Letting him take off her shirt? Jerking him off? He'd thought he was going to die.

Liam was no virginal choir boy – fucking was like an Olympic sport for him. He trained hard, and he trained often, so it wasn't like some girl wanting to have sex with him was usually so mind blowing. But that particular girl had been something else. Most of the women Liam slept with were old pros at having casual sex. Being with Katya, it was like discovering that lifestyle all over again. Her hands, trembling and full of excitement. Awkward and insistent.

It had made *him* excited and nervous. Caught between not wanting to scare her away, yet also not wanting to pressure her. Desperately wanting to touch her, but also wanting to do the right thing.

Anticipation. The best of all the feelings, in his opinion. Katya had practically had him begging her to touch him, praying that she'd go just that little bit further with her little bravery charade.

And *ooohhh boy*, did she go that little bit further. Little bit? Pfffft, try a couple extra miles. He still couldn't wrap his brain around the things she'd let him do to her. Schoolmarm to freak-in-the-sheets, in less than a day. She'd needed to cut loose, that much was clear, and why she'd chosen to do it with him, he'd probably never know, but sweet jesus, thank god she had.

Angel cake, I'd cut loose with you any time.

"*EDEN!*"

Liam groaned and rubbed his hand across his face. He tried to close the screen on his phone, but he wasn't quick enough, and his partner caught another eyeful of Katya before the screen went black.

"Hey, *Riiicckkyyy*, how's it going?" he asked, spinning around in his chair.

"You know I hate that fucking name."

"Okay, *Richard*. What's up?"

"Not a whole lot. Just checking on my investment. How're things on your end?"

"Good, good."

"How did the date with Susie Homemaker go?"

"Good."

"Just good? I already heard some interesting things from the staff. Right out there on the floor, huh. Shocking. Not like you, Eden."

"Yeah, well, this girl wasn't like anything I've ever experienced. I took my chance when I had it," Liam explained.

"Was it worth your while?"

"More than you could possibly even guess."

"Hmmm, *interesting*."

"Did you want something, *Ricky?*" he asked, glancing up at the other man.

"No, just checking in. I'll go get us some drinks, we can go over the books."

And with that, his partner walked back out of the office. Liam glared after him for a while. If random visits were going to start becoming the norm, he was going to look into working from home.

Hmmm, home. Which was roughly two hundred feet away from

Katya's home. He leaned back in his chair and linked his hands together behind his head. They hadn't made any plans to see each other again – he hadn't even gotten her phone number. But just thinking about her had given him an uncomfortable hard on.

She seemed like she lived a very structured life. Liam was a great stress reliever. Maybe they could help each other out. He chuckled and adjusted himself in his pants.

Because I could definitely use some help right now …

5

"YOU WHAT!?"

Katya yanked her cell phone away from her ear, wincing. Tori's normal speaking voice was loud, but when she got excited, she really went for being heard in the back of the room.

"Keep it down! I'm still at work," she hissed, glancing around the tiny break room.

Of course, no one had cared that she was late – Katya had never, ever been late, the entire time she'd been working there. She was also head baker, *and* highly sought after, at that. After a prominent magazine had featured her culinary skills, her appointment book had been full. Wedding cakes by Katya Tocci had to be booked a year in advance, other events at least three months. She could show up to work high on meth, and as long as she made a perfect sugar rose, she wouldn't get fired.

"I know, I know, but still, I cannot get over this! You had sex with some random dude, in some random club! This is AMAZING!" her roommate insisted.

"He wasn't random, I knew who he was. Kinda. Sorta," Katya tried to make it sound better.

"Oh, whatever, don't try to downplay it, you little slut. It's great!

I cannot wait to hear all the dirty details."

"I'm not -"

"You *are*, and you're gonna tell me everything. Length, girth, which hole, how many times."

"Oh jesus. I can't believe you weren't even worried when I didn't come home."

"I knew where you were."

"You did!?"

"Uh, yeah, you texted me about A MILLION times, don't you remember?"

"No. I told you, I don't remember anything from about midnight on."

"Yeah, you were telling me about how fucking hot he is, and how good he gave it to you, and about how it didn't hurt as much as you thought it would," Tori prattled off. Katya felt another bout of nausea sweep over her.

"Still. What if after the amazing sex, he'd taken me home to rape and murder me?" she pointed out.

"Oh, he took the phone from you after you started messaging gibberish. Sent me his address and phone number, just in case. He's one of the good ones, you can tell. When are you gonna see him again?"

A jingling noise came from the front of the store. The bell over the front door, meaning a customer had just come inside. *Saved by the bell.* Katya took a deep breath and smoothed her hand over her apron.

"I gotta go, customer is here," she whispered.

"You can't hide from me! *Everything!* I want to know everything when you get home!"

Katya didn't bother with goodbye, she just hung up the phone and took a couple deep breaths. She glanced in a small mirror and cringed again. She hadn't bothered with blowing out her hair, but had just slicked it all up into a high bun while it had still been wet.

Now that it was dry, it was starting to frizz up around the crown of her head. She was wearing the barest amount of makeup, just enough powder to kill the zombie look she was rocking.

She'd never been into wearing the whole chef's jacket and pants, usually opting for a pin striped apron and a smock. But that day, she'd barely managed the apron, and was wearing a pair of skinny jeans, ballet flats, and a loose blouse. Maybe normal clothing for other people, but unheard of for her. She could just imagine her mother's reaction at seeing her dressed that way, in public, at her job.

Her parents were very proper people.

But shitty clothing and hangover be damned – she had a job to do. She took a deep breath and pushed her way through the double doors that led to the sales floor. Normally, she almost never went on the floor, unless it was to meet a client. But the counter clerk was on her lunch break, one of the assistant bakers was on a delivery, and the other was on vacation. Katya was on counter duty till the other girls returned.

"Hello, welcome to Fondants!" she chirped pleasantly, though she could hear how scratchy her voice sounded. Whether it was from the hangover, or from Liam making her scream his name, she couldn't be sure. She took another deep breath and fanned at her face as she turned to look around the shop.

The place looked empty at first glance, but then she saw him. A man was standing in the corner with his back to her, in front of a display of cupcakes, and he was talking into a cell phone. The bell above the door jingled again and Katya turned to smile at the customer who came walking in, but she was again ignored. It was a young woman who was dressed in a smart suit and skirt, and she didn't even look at Katya, just made a beeline for the man in the corner. She stood next to him, leaning in close to say something softly, then she stood back and fiddled around on a tablet.

Wondering whether or not she'd actually be needed, Katya busied herself with checking over the racks in the display case. She didn't usually bother with the donuts and pastries and croissants, but she had to keep herself busy. If she didn't, her mind would wander back to her activities from the night before, and then she'd blush like an idiot for the rest of the day.

Bad enough that I'm having trouble walking normal, don't need to be red in the face, as well.

She was pulling one of the racks out of the case, determined to change out the croissants that she just knew were stale, when the strange couple finally turned around and came to the counter.

"*Angel food cake.*"

Katya almost dropped the entire rack. It wasn't like it was really her nickname, but still. She would never be able to hear those words again and not remember Liam whispering them while he touched her.

"I'm sorry, what did you say?" she asked through gritted teeth while she worked to get the rack back into the case.

"Cupcakes," the man said. "Do you make angel food cake cupcakes?"

"We could, sure. What were you thinking?" she finally got the display back to rights and she stood upright, brushing her hands against her apron as she turned to face the front.

"I was thinking I'd like a couple dozen."

Katya froze as she stared into a pair of very blue eyes. She flicked her eyes to the other woman, but that girl was still looking at her tablet, moving a stylus back and forth across the screen. So Katya looked back at the man.

Holy shit, how long has it been? Eight years? Nine?

"You do speak English, don't you?"

Hmmm, not long enough to forget he's a total asshole.

Katya knew him, or at least, she used to – he'd grown up in the house next door to her, their families had been loose acquaintances. He was about six years older than her, though, so they'd never been friends. Not that they would have been even if they'd shared a birthday – he'd always been a jerk. Smarter than everyone else, richer than everyone else, more talented than anyone else. A gifted swimmer, there'd been talk of him going on to Olympic trials, but he'd pursued a college career instead.

He'd never paid any attention to Katya and her friends, or any of the other kids in the neighborhood, even the ones his age. He'd always been aloof. Snobbish. When she'd been fourteen, she'd taken a job babysitting his little sister for the entire summer. She hadn't realized he'd be home for the whole time, as well. No matter how rude he was to her, no matter how selfish or thoughtless, she couldn't help the small crush she'd developed. He had just been too good looking, and her bedroom had overlooked his pool. Watching him swim everyday hadn't been a burden at all.

She wondered if he still swam.

"Yes," she finally answered. "I'm sorry, I don't normally work the counter."

"That is unfortunate. I was hoping to deal with the manager, or at the very least, someone professional," he sighed. Katya felt her feathers getting ruffled.

"I'm head baker here, sir. Anything you need, I assure you, I'm the person to help you with it," she informed him.

"So you can make my cupcakes for me?" he asked.

"Depends."

"On what?"

"On when you need them. I have a waiting list," she said.

"You have a *waiting list?*"

"Yes. If you'd like me to make them, I can have them to you in roughly three months. But if you'd prefer for one of the intern bakers to make them, I'm sure they could get something together in a couple days," she said. Normally, she never would've spoken of her coworkers that way, but he'd pissed her off.

"A wait list," he chuckled, rubbing at the side of his jaw. His very smoothly shaven jaw. Katya refused to be taken in by his good looks again and looked away from that jaw. Into his disgustingly blue eyes.

"I'm sorry, but I'm very busy today. If you'd like to look at my portfolio, I can give you our website, or I can you give you the phone numbers of some other very good bakeries," she offered, moving to grab a card from the counter top.

"No, no, three months is fine. We're having a party in about five months time, so if you think you can pencil me in, that would be great," he said.

Katya got him an order form, and while his assistant filled it out, he prattled off some details, what kind of design he wanted, other desserts he might be interested in ordering. The whole time, his eyes wandered over the display cases, or his phone, or his assistant's tablet. He hardly even looked at her, and certainly didn't recognize her. Didn't even ask for her name. By the end of the exchange, Katya was ready to shoot fire from her nostrils.

A whole summer I practically lived at his house. Fetched him food and drinks at his every command, and he doesn't even fucking remember me.

"I think that'll be it. My assistant will be in touch if we need to add anything else to the order," he said as they wrapped everything up.

"You have until four weeks before the delivery date to change your order – after that, we charge a fee. One week before, no changes allowed. We'll expect a deposit on your order in the next week. No refunds for cancellations," she said, handing her card over to the silent assistant.

"Sounds good. We'll be in touch about the deposit."

And with that, he walked out of the bakery. No goodbye, no thank you, no nothing. The assistant followed in his wake, still poking at her tablet. The door slammed shut behind them, jingling the bell.

"Prick," Katya muttered, resting her elbows on the counter and massaging her fingertips against her forehead. The bell above the door sounded again and before she could stand upright, she heard quick footsteps moving across the floor.

"Hi," Katya started. "Welcome to …"

Her voice trailed off as she watched the smartly dressed assistant hurrying towards her at a clipped pace. The other woman was tiny, even in her heels, and she had to stretch to reach her arm over the display case. She had a card pinched between her fingers and Katya tentatively took it.

"Mr. Stone said to meet him here at seven o'clock," she said in a sharp voice. Katya stared down at the card. It was simple, all white, and had a restaurant's name written on the back of it.

"I'm sorry … what?" Katya was confused as she flipped the card over, taking in the impressive name and even more impressive job title.

"Seven o'clock. Sharp – Mr. Stone does not like to be kept waiting," the assistant said, then started moving back towards the door.

"What's going on?" Katya demanded. "Is this about the order? I don't meet clients outside of work hours."

"No, Ms. Tocci," the assistant replied, shocking Katya. She'd never said her last name. "This is not about the order. Seven, sharp. Please don't be late."

Katya stared at the door, long after the assistant had disappeared through it. Long after the black town car had pulled away from the curb. *Ms. Tocci.* The assistant had known her name. Known it because someone must have told her what it was, someone who'd known Katya. Someone who'd remembered her, after all. She finally shook her head and looked back down at the card. The Stone Agency was embossed big bold letters at the top. An address was at the bottom in regular print. In between the two was a name, with the letters "CEO" after it. A name she hadn't heard in almost a decade.

Wulfric Stone.

6

KATYA LEFT WORK EARLY IN ORDER TO GO HOME AND FIGURE SOME SHIT out. She wanted nothing more than to sit in the bottom of a shower and decompress, maybe take a nap, but she was in for a surprise when she walked through the front door. Tori was sitting at their kitchen table.

"What are you doing home?" Katya asked. Her roommate shrugged while she flipped through a magazine.

"Took the day off. Had to mentally prepare for our girl's night in tonight," she teased.

"Don't get too prepared," Katya groaned as she dropped into a seat. She winced upon contact with the wood, then immediately blushed.

"Why not? You have to spill. Look at you! You look like a lobster!"

"I know, but … I think I might have a date tonight," Katya said.

"Wow! Mr. Sex Club must have really given it to you good!" Tori laughed.

"Ummm … it's not with Mr. Sex Club."

"Holy shit! Don't tell me you're a sex addict now."

"I'm not."

"Another guy from the Eros dating site?"

"No."

"Then who?"

Katya took a deep breath.

"Some guy from back home. It's not really a date, I don't think. He came into the bakery, and I thought he was just some asshole who didn't recognize me, but then snooty-pants-assistant-lady came back in, and she told me seven o'clock sharp, and -" she began to explain, talking in one big rush. Tori finally held up her hand.

"Wait, wait, wait. Let me get the wine, then we're gonna start from scratch."

Katya didn't drink anything, but she did tell Tori about the sex club. About having sex with Liam, though she left out the explicit details. Gave a run down of her morning and being at work, then told all about her meeting with the mighty and powerful Wulfric Stone. She gave a bit of the backstory on her previous relationship with Wulf – i.e., being a stupid teenager with a crush on the jerk guy from next door, and him being a jerk guy who'd never given her the time of day.

"So you see," Katya sighed, glancing at her watch. "His assistant told me to meet him at this restaurant downtown, at seven. I looked it up, it's super fancy and exclusive, I'll be shocked if we even get a table."

"Well, if he's as rich as all these websites claim, then it probably won't be a problem," Tori mumbled. She'd gotten her laptop out and had already googled Wulf's name.

The Stone Agency owned large chunks of San Francisco. He also had other companies and other realty businesses, owning property in Los Angeles and Beverly Hills and Malibu and Orange County and just about every other rich California town that came to mind. Beyond that, there were articles about investments and possible shell corporations. Wulfric Stone was a very, very wealthy man.

"Why does he want to have dinner?" Katya asked.

"Maybe he could smell the sex-kitten-vibe rolling off you," Tori suggested.

"I was only a sex kitten for about six hours last night," Katya said.

"So. Counts, and men like this, they can always smell it."

"Stop saying smell, it sounds gross."

"Who cares, Kat? You're meeting a guy you used to have a major hard on for, and you're not the little brat next door anymore. You're a successful, bright, sexy young woman who is coming into her sexual peak, apparently. Go eat dinner on his dime, see what he wants, and if he's halfway nice to you, boff his brains out," Tori said. Katya started to laugh, but then it died away.

"What about Liam what's-his-face?" she asked.

"What about him?"

"I don't know … are we dating? Was that a date last night? I mean, I can't have sex with him last night, then go on a date with a new guy tonight … can I?"

"Babe, you can do *whatever* you want. I always wondered why you had so many rules for yourself. Did Liam ask you out again?" Tori asked.

"Well … no," Katya was honest.

"Okay. Did he get your number?"

"No."

"Has he had sex with other women in that club?"

"I got the impression he had, yeah."

"So then no harm, no foul. You're not his girlfriend. Go out with this Wulf guy tonight, who knows, maybe all he wants to talk about is cake. Maybe he wants to eat you out like you're made of cake."

"I'm seriously going to be sick if you keep talking like that."

"Either way, you're not tied down or committed to anything, so why not have fun?"

Going out to meet Wulfric Stone didn't exactly sound like Katya's idea of "fun", but she found herself getting ready anyway. Her hangover was still lurking in the back of her brain, but she downed three extra strength Tylenol and pounded a beer at Tori's suggestion, then dug a decent outfit out of her closet. A skirt short enough to show off her legs, which she thought were pretty nice, but demure enough to be appropriate for a business dinner. Another flowy blouse on top, covering up her arms to balance out the amount of skin showing on her legs.

Then she got in her second shower of the day and scrubbed every inch of her skin. Shaved all the pertinent parts of her body, because obviously, one needed to be squeaky clean for a "business dinner". After she'd lotioned up, giving her olive-tinted skin a shine, she finally pulled her hair up into a loose, rounded bun, then worked on her make up. She preferred a mostly natural look, light pink gloss on her lips, long delicate lashes, shimmer on her cheeks and eyelids. *Fresh faced,* that's what she called it. But when she was done, she wondered if she looked a bit … *young.*

"What do you think?" she asked as her roommate came into her bedroom. The other girl dipped down, looking in the mirror as well.

"Cute. You're so adorable with those beautiful eyes," Tori teased, blowing kisses at their reflection.

"But I don't want to be adorable. I want to be sexy," Katya said.

"It is sexy – just in a different way. Your look, it's like … you kinda … when you look as cute and innocent as you do, it makes men want to dirty you up. Defile you," Tori said.

Hmmm, certainly did the trick last night.

So at seven o'clock on the dot, she found herself standing in the entrance to Mirage restaurant, looking around for the mysterious Mr. Stone. She paced from one wall to the other, tapped her Jimmy Choo against the marble floor, then paced again. Glanced at her phone, as if magically Liam would have somehow gotten her phone number and texted her. He hadn't, and the screen was blank. So she paced some more.

At five past, she began to wonder if it had all been a joke. The assistant chick had made such a big deal about being on time – so where was Mr. Punctual? At ten past, Katya had enough and started heading towards the exit. Just then, the maître d' glanced up from his podium.

"Excuse me, were you looking for someone?" he asked in a polite voice. She smiled at him.

"Yes, Mr. Stone, but he's late," she said.

"Oh, he's already been seated! My apologies. Please, right this way."

Katya was once again surprised. That Wulf was already there, and had been seated, not bothering to look out for her. Or obviously not bothering to tell the wait staff that he was expecting someone else. If she hadn't been sure before, then she was definitely sure now that it wasn't a date.

"Mr. Stone, you have a guest," the maître d' made a big show of pulling out her chair for her, laying her napkin across her lap.

Wulfric Stone stayed seated the whole time, barely glancing up from his menu to acknowledge her. He nodded at the other man, then went back to looking over the food. Katya stared at him for about a minute, unsure of what she should do.

"Are you hungry? The lobster here is fantastic," he said. He'd spoken to her in the bakery, but she'd been so out of sorts, she hadn't paid attention. His voice was smooth, and much deeper than she remembered it being.

"I'm sorry, are we having dinner?" she asked. He finally looked at her.

"So you have trouble with speaking English *and* don't understand the basic functions of a restaurant. You see, Katya, in a restaurant, they tend to specialize in producing food, particularly around the socially acceptable hours for lunch and dinner, and possibly breakfast, depending on the establishment."

Her blood instantly went from stagnant to full boil and she stood up, her chair scooting out behind her. She didn't owe this man anything, didn't even know him, and couldn't give two shits about his order with her bakery. She grabbed her purse and went to storm past him when he grabbed her arm.

"*Do not* touch me," she hissed, but his hand didn't move.

"I was being serious – the lobster shouldn't be missed. Sit down," he said, finally putting down his menu.

"Are you joking? I'd rather eat my own hair than have a meal with you," she said.

"Well, you can do that at this table, too. *Sit.*"

She sat down, shocking herself. He smiled at her – a closed mouth, tight lipped number, then retrieved her napkin from where it had fallen next to the table. She took it from him and smoothed it out on her lap.

"What do you want?"

"I was very surprised to see you in that bakery. I wasn't aware you were living in San Francisco," he said.

"Been here for a long time now."

"You're a baker?"

"Well, you see, Wulf, when someone makes cupcakes for order, and cakes, and cookies, and other desserts, depending on the establishment, that person is generally considered a baker," she mocked him. She expected him to get angry, but he actually smiled. She wasn't sure if she'd ever seen him smile.

"Feisty. How's your mother?" he asked, sipping at his wine.

They discussed their families for a while. Their mothers were still close, and Katya had only been two years older than one of his sisters, though she hadn't spoken much to the other girl since graduation.

After they'd ordered, Katya found herself feeling more comfortable. More confident. Why was she so intimidated by him? Because he was rich? Because she'd had a crush on him, a million years ago? Refusing to blush, she remembered the woman she'd been the night before; remembered the kind of unbridled passion she'd experienced. She'd been fucked seven different ways to Sunday, in full view of multiple people – Wulf was nothing in comparison to that kind of intimidation.

*Just another guy. You weren't scared of Liam – don't be scared of this asshole. You had **anal sex** last night, for god's sake. He wouldn't even know how to handle you.*

Though while they ate, she caught him looking at her sometimes. Looking in such a way that she had a feeling he would know *exactly* how to handle her. By the time dessert menus were brought around, she was feeling so hot and tense and *turned on*, she felt like she was about to start running circles around the room.

"The food was lovely," she said while she waited for her wine to be topped off. "And I even admit, it was fun to catch up with someone from the old neighborhood, but I have to be honest Wulf – why are we out at dinner?"

"For a bright girl, I feel like you don't catch onto things very quick," he said. His sense of humor was odd, that was for sure. So dry and sarcastic, she wasn't entirely sure when he was or wasn't joking. She decided to take a guess.

"Then enlighten me, and speak slowly, please," she joked back. She was given another tight lipped smile.

"Well, Katya, when a man asks a woman to share a meal with him late at night, that's generally considered a date."

"We're on a date?"

She'd blurted it out before she could stop herself, but she was so shocked. Her? On a date? With Wulfric Stone? The world had officially gone crazy. First she's engaging in public displays of indecency, then she's accidentally going on a date with the biggest asshole she'd ever met.

Maybe I'm in a coma or something and this is all a crazy hallucination.

"What did you think this was?" he asked, cocking his head to the side.

"I don't know, I thought maybe you wanted to talk about your order or something. I mean, you acted like you didn't even know me, then you sent your assistant in with a card, what was I supposed to think?" she asked back.

"I didn't really care, I suppose. I just saw little Katya Tocci behind a counter, all grown up, living in the same city as me. Thought it would be nice to sit down together, see what was behind that apron of yours," he said. She willed away the blush.

"Um … that's … flattering," she managed to reply, and she finally got a genuine smile out of him.

"It is, isn't it? C'mon, I have an early morning tomorrow."

He walked her out of the restaurant, his hand on the small of her back, burning a hole through her shirt. She expected him to say goodbye and sail off into the night in a fancy car, leaving her to hail a taxi. But he kept his hand on her as he spoke to the valet, and a minute later, a sleek, sporty, convertible Mercedes rolled up in front of them. He stepped forward and opened the passenger door, and Katya didn't even question him, she just slid into the leather seat.

When had she become so docile? Something about him, it was like he could snap his fingers, and she would bend over backwards. Without even a thought or a question. It was bizarre. She may have been a bit of a goody-two-shoes pushover in her day-to-day life, but she wasn't the type to just let a man strong arm her in any way, either.

"Realty is a good business," she commented when he was behind the wheel and pulling them away from the building. He glanced at her, then watched while she slid her hand along the dash.

"*Very* good. A lot better than baking," he replied, and it was her turn to laugh.

"I'm sure, though baking does alright by me."

"I bet. Three month waiting list – was that bullshit? You seemed pissed off."

"I was, but it wasn't bullshit. I'm 'in demand', as they say," she laughed, doing air quotes.

"Nice. Address, please."

She prattled it off to him, then got sucked into a conversation about school. They'd taken very different paths, with him attending a prestigious ivy league school on the east coast, and her attending a culinary school in California.

She moved in her seat to somewhat face him, her knees and head pointed in his direction while she animatedly talked about a cooking class that had gone very wrong. She hadn't noticed it happening, but sometime while telling him about the oven catching fire, his hand found its way onto her thigh. She was proud of herself that she was able to keep talking without any hint of surprise, but when he began rubbing back and forth, dipping between her legs, she stumbled over a couple words.

He illegally parked in front of her building and walked her into the lobby. He was on his phone most of the time, and only when she got onto her elevator did he stop talking long enough to notice her again.

"Thanks for being a good sport and meeting me," he said. She smiled at him, not letting on that she was just a teensy bit disappointed. She wasn't entirely sure that she liked him at all, but it would've been nice if he'd asked for her number, or another date, or anything that showed he was interested in her.

"No problem. It wasn't as horrible as I thought it would be," she teased. There was one more tight lipped smile, then he started lifting his phone back to his ear.

"Cheers, Tocci."

Then he was walking away and the elevator doors were sliding shut.

Katya dragged her feet down the hallway and clear through her front door. Tori hollered from the bathroom, and Katya dreaded telling her how the bizarre date had gone.

"Did you see his penis!?" the other girl yelled. Katya rolled her eyes and kicked off her heels.

"Jesus, I'm not some total slut, you know!" she yelled back, tossing her purse to the floor.

"Yes, you are!"

Katya went to respond, but was interrupted by a sharp knock at the door. She groaned again and turned around, wondering who it could be at that hour. It was almost ten o'clock at night. She glanced through the peep hole and was shocked to see a very familiar look-ing tie. She scrambled to pull back the chain lock and yank open the door.

"Hi," she breathed, staring up at Wulf. Without her heels and standing so close to him, she suddenly realized he was a lot taller that she'd thought. He stared down the length of his nose at her.

"I'm sorry, did you just say you weren't a slut?" he asked. She cringed.

"No. I mean, I'm not. My roommate, she said … we were just … I only mean …" Katya babbled, not sure how to dig herself out of her hole.

Turned out, she didn't need to. While she fumbled around, wav-ing her hands and searching for words, Wulf leaned down and kissed her, gently holding her chin between his thumb and forefinger.

It was simple, just his lips pressed against hers. No hint of tongue, or anything naughty, really. He kept her in place, tilted her head at the perfect angle, held her lips to his. Very chaste in comparison to what she'd experienced the night before.

And yet, her blood was on fire. She felt weak in the knees and leaned into him, gripping onto his lapels. It was driving her insane. Wulf was sex in a three piece suit, why wasn't he tearing into her? Was she ready for that? Did she even want him to tear her apart?

Oh yes, I most definitely fucking do.

"Hmmm," he hummed when he finally pulled away. "Maybe we can explore that whole 'slut' thing another time."

"Uhhh …" she responded eloquently. He smiled and she felt his hands on top of hers, gently pulling her away from his blazer.

"Good seeing you again, Tocci."

He kissed her once more, this time resting his hand against the side of her neck. She felt the heat from his fingertips long after he walked away.

"Pssst," Tori hissed from behind her, after Wulf had disappeared onto the elevator. "Was that the guy?"

"No, that was the guy from 4A downstairs," Katya said.

"Seriously?"

"No! Of course that was him! Who else would I be kissing!?" Katya snapped, finally turning away and slamming their door shut.

"I don't know, Liam?"

Liam. Two simple kisses and Katya had already forgotten the man she'd slept with just twenty-four hours ago.

"No. I think Liam was just for fun," she sighed.

"And Wulf isn't?"

"I don't know what the hell he is."

"Did you at least have a good time?"

"Yeah … yeah, I think I actually did."

"But no sexy time."

"Trust me, that kiss was *definitely* sexy time."

"Didn't look very sexy to me."

But she wasn't listening to her roommate. She had her fingertips pressed against her lips, her mind going over the kiss once again.

———◆———

Day one, Katya had made an in-the-moment decision to go out on a date with a random stranger and have sex with him in his sex club. Sex had evolved into first time anal sex, a huge step for her. It had been amazing, and eye opening, and such a change from her every day life, she couldn't believe it. She'd felt like a new woman.

Day two, Katya had gone on a kinda-sorta-date with a ghost from her past. She hadn't realized it was a date till it was almost over, and it had been a bad date, but also a good one, and a ten year old crush had gotten dusted off, and he'd kissed her, and she'd been pretty sure she'd seen the back of her own eyeballs. She'd felt like an amazing woman.

Day three, it all came crashing down. Oh god, oh god, what had she done!? Fucked a stranger, let him fuck her in the ass – which was *still* sore – and then she'd gone on a date with a man she didn't technically know, at least not anymore. A man who hadn't been nice to her ten years ago, and still wasn't very nice to her now.

She no longer felt new and amazing. She felt confused and upset. Caught between feeling bad about herself and trying to forget everything.

Katya Tocci simply didn't behave that way. Katya Tocci baked cakes and decorated desserts. Went on sensible dates, never kissing until at least the third date, and never having sex until she was at least semi-positive she actually liked the man and they had similar goals and ideals.

Katya Tocci did not take it up the back door and date assholes.

Oh god, I cannot believe I did all that.

She'd taken the morning off to collect herself. Recover some of her dignity and remember exactly who she was – not that girl from that stupid profile, which she'd already deactivated. She had goals. Plans. Her career was on a fast track to success, even possibly minor fame. Owning her own bakery wasn't too far off in the future. Acting crazy and reckless put all that in jeopardy. No matter how amazing the sex had been with Liam, and no matter how good Wulfric kissed, none of it was worth risking the future she was building for herself.

When I talk like that, I sound like my mother. I'm gonna start crying again.

After taking another skin scrubbing shower, Katya cleaned the apartment. Tori had stumbled out of her room around eleven, giving her a heart attack. Her roommate had decided to stay home after realizing Katya had stayed home, wanting to offer a comforting shoulder. Though when Katya explained why she was staying home,

Tori called her an idiot, and then asked for Liam's phone number, jokingly offering to date him in Katya's place.

After pulling on a pair of cream colored chinos and buttoning up a soft, pink, cashmere cardigan, she felt more like herself. Less like the hussy from the crazy dating profile, more like the respectable young woman her parents had raised. She worked her hair into a thick braid that coiled around the back of her head, then topped the look off with a pair of pearl earrings. As she was heading out the door, she stopped and stared at her reflection in a mirror.

What had he said? Sunday school teacher. I look like some sort of bible study tutor.

She shook the thought free from her head, refusing to dwell on it anymore. Besides, neither Liam nor Wulf had bothered to get her phone number. It wasn't like she'd be seeing either of them again anytime soon.

She decided to keep that thought in the back of her mind. Neither of these men wanted to see her again, so her worrying about her behavior was a moot point. They wouldn't be popping up to share her secrets with anyone. Perfect. Everything was *perfectly fine*.

Katya took a deep breath as soon as she got out onto the sidewalk. The weather was lovely, with a slight breeze in the air to cool down the warm summer day. She smiled to herself as she went over her plans for the afternoon. She was going to finish up the day at the bakery – she had to go over a design with a client for a graduation cake. Then she was going to stop in at a floral shop and get some bouquets. Growing up, her parents' house had always been filled with fresh flowers, and when she'd cleaned that morning, she'd realized she missed the smell of flora and fauna. Hmmm, and maybe after the flower shop, she'd stop and grab some -

"Jesus, I thought the brown outfit was sexy, but this definitely has it beat. You've graduated from Sunday school teacher to virginal valedictorian."

Katya gasped so hard, she started choking on the gum she'd been chewing. She stumbled into the wall next to her, desperately trying to catch her breath, then Liam started slapping her on the back. She finally hacked up the gum and waved him away.

"I"m fine!" she snapped, rubbing at her throat. "God, you scared the crap out of me!"

"Sorry. I've been waiting out here forever for you to turn up," he said.

"You've been stalking me!?"

"That makes it sound weird. Waiting sounds better."

"Okay. Stop. Start from the beginning. What's going on?" Katya asked, finally standing upright to face him.

It had only been two days since she'd seen him, and Katya had only known Liam for about a grand total of twelve hours, but still. His image would be burned into her brain for the rest of her life. Also, and it sounded cliché, running into him sort of felt like running into an old friend. Someone comfortable and familiar.

Ummm, there was nothing familiar about the things he did to your naked body.

He smiled when she started blushing, and she hated herself a little.

"I never got your number," he said. "I think I was still pretty drunk when you left. I was thinking we could go get some tacos, I know a great place downtown."

Katya opened her mouth, automatically ready to say yes, but then she froze. She wasn't sure why. She felt so comfortable with Liam, yes could be the only answer to anything he asked. He was also stupid hot – those chocolate eyes wandering knowingly over her body, his big, goofy smile distracting from the fact that he was a very large, very built, very sexy man.

But she'd also just had a very long conversation with herself about not being with certain men, no matter how good looking they were, or how good they were in bed. Or how their hands had touched parts of her body she still couldn't think about without turning bright red.

FOCUS.

"Liam," she sighed.

"Oh no. That tone isn't good," he said, but his voice was teasing.

"Look. You're super ... amazing. Hot and funny and all that stuff that makes girls fall at your feet. I pretty much did," she told him. "But that night, that wasn't me. I mean, you were so good looking, and I wanted to be the kind of woman you're attracted to. I wanted to be dangerous and sexy and fun, and I'm just not. I'm not that woman. I'm a schoolmarm, who wears beige and cashmere and I'm just ... *boring*. I'm boring, Liam. I'm really, really boring."

She was rushing by the end of her speech, and wasn't entirely sure what all was pouring out of her mouth. It was pure word vomit, straight from the ether to the tip of her tongue, but at least it was out. She'd said it. Liam knew the truth. She let out a deep breath and stared up at him.

"You are so ridiculous. You know that, right?" he laughed. Katya blinked her eyes.

"Did you hear anything I said?" she asked.

"Of course I did. It was all bullshit. Boring? Lady, you walked into a sex club, slammed back a double tequila, then fucked my brains out. Does that sound boring to you? You were totally all those things – fun, sexy, and yeah, even a little dangerous. You just gotta chill out and stop spending so much time in that brain of yours," Liam said, tapping a finger against her temple. She frowned at him.

"But I was just pretending," she insisted.

"Oh, okay. So you just pretended to get fucked in the ass."

Forget blushing. A five-alarm fire broke out across her face, causing Liam to laugh again.

"*We are in public!*" she hissed at him, gesturing to all the people walking around them.

"So? Who gives a shit? Do you plan on fucking any of them?" he asked.

"What!? Of course not! No! But ... they ... you can't ..." she started sputtering.

"Then who cares what they think? You're talking to me – I'm the only thing you should be worrying about right now," he said.

"No! You can't just say and do things like that, Liam! It's totally inappropriate," she said.

"You know what else is inappropriate? You wearing this sweater," he replied, then he crowded in close to her. She instinctively backed away, moving until he'd forced her against a wall. She held her breath when he reached out and plucked at the top button on her cardigan.

"There is nothing inappropriate about this sweater – it's J. Crew," she told him.

"I think it's grossly inappropriate to hide a body as amazing as yours. You've got some serious self-esteem issues, angel cake," he sighed, finally undoing the offending button. She slapped his hand away.

"I do not, I just don't want to dress like a slut. I like these clothes," she said.

"Baby, no one likes to dress like that."

"Stop arguing with me."

"I'm not arguing, I'm just stating facts."

"You're stating opinion – there's a big difference between the two."

"Careful, you're getting feisty. In danger of becoming – gasp! – not boring," he teased her. It was impossible to keep a straight face, she had to laugh.

"God, you're horrible," she chuckled, letting her head drop forward till her forehead hit his chest.

"The worst. Come have tacos with me and I'll make up for it," he whispered. She took a deep breath.

"Like go out to dinner?" she checked, then frowned when she felt him shrug.

"Lunch time is better for me. It'll be great, we can bring some home and eat them on my roof," he told her.

Hmmm. Didn't really sound like a date. Sounded like two buddies meeting up to eat tacos and hang out. Katya figured she could handle hanging out with a friend. It wasn't like she had to end the night with crazy sex. Maybe new-Katya and old-Katya could sort of meld together.

"Okay. Okay, I think I can do tacos. But not today, I have to go to work. Tomorrow?" she asked, finally lifting her head.

"Sounds good. I'll grab you from you work, noon. Oh! And phone number, please. As fun as hanging out outside this building is, texting would be easier," he said, taking out his phone. She hesitated for only a moment, then gave him her number.

"Sorry I'm so difficult," she said while he tapped away at his screen. He frowned and put his phone away.

"What is it with that? You're always apologizing for something, or thinking you're not cool enough, or good enough. Who made you feel that way?" he asked. She stared at him for a second.

"No one, I just … I'm realistic. Objective about myself. Let's not get into it now, I have to go to work and you -"

She gasped when he pressed himself to her front. While her lips were still parted, he dove in, kissing her hard. Her head hit the wall behind her, causing her braid to press painfully against her skull, but she didn't care. She couldn't even think straight. She'd already forgotten how kissing him felt – like locking lips with a runaway freight train.

"*And I* need to remind you that you are that girl who walked into my club and rocked my world. That was you naked in that booth. Screaming my name in my bed. Seems like you only remember the bad, and never the good about yourself," he growled as his fingers made fast work of opening her cardigan. She was wearing a white camisole underneath, and he yanked it free from her pants. There was a slight hesitation, as if he was giving her a split second to tell him to stop, then his hands were under her shirt, his fingers raking across her back.

"Trust me, I will *never* forget those things," she moaned, gripping onto his jacket to keep herself upright.

"Good," he said, then he kissed her again. It felt like he was going to inhale her tongue and when she started feeling dizzy, he finally pulled away. "Now remember some other things: tacos. Noon. You're a sexy beast."

Katya burst out laughing and he smiled back at her, stepping away. She adjusted her shirt, but didn't bother buttoning up the sweater again.

"I'll try to keep that all in mind," she said, running her hands over hair, trying to gauge whether or not it was still in good condition.

"And this time, *definitely change,*" he said. Katya went to argue, but then he leaned in, kissed her on the nose, and walked away abruptly, whistling a tune to himself.

Katya went to work in a daze, not entirely sure how she got there. She was of almost no use to anyone, struggling to even tie her apron. Was she going out on a date with Liam tomorrow? Had she just gone on a date with Wulf the night before? Was that okay? Shit, had she accidentally started dating two men? But wait, hadn't she decided she wouldn't be seeing Wulf again? Of course, she'd also made the same decision about Liam, but he'd changed her mind super quick. She had a feeling if Wulf was even half as insistent, she'd fold instantly.

She got herself together for her clients. Katya refused to let these stupid boys have any effect on her real life. Her libido, sure, but her career was another thing. She would no longer deny that both men had a pull on her, but she would not let them ruin what she'd built for herself.

After the design for the cake was finalized and her client had picked out what flavors she wanted, Katya was left alone again. She did a quick inventory on everything she'd need to set up the bakery for the weekend, put in an order for the supplies, then she was finally able to take off her apron again. She was almost out the front door when the phone started ringing. Before she could hit the sidewalk, her coworker was yelling her name.

"Some client," the other girl said, holding the phone out. "Said it was important."

"This is Katya Tocci," she said in her professional voice.

"I should hope so, that's who I asked for."

Again, Katya felt like she was going to fall over. Wulf. It hadn't even been twenty-four hours since she'd seen him – was he really already calling her!? He wasn't going to do the standard boy thing and wait three days before getting in touch? It was shocking. She'd already halfway convinced herself that she wouldn't see him again.

"Wulfric. Hi. What can I do for you?" she finally managed to say.

"Hmmm, now that's the million dollar question."

Seriously, if Katya kept blushing so much, she was going to permanently turn red.

"Is this about your order?" she guessed, and he chuckled. Actually made a sound of happiness and laughter – another shock. It was deep, rumbling through the phone and going straight to the pleasure center of her brain.

"No. This Saturday, six o'clock, meet me at Flannery's," he instructed her. Her head started spinning.

"You're asking me out on another date?" she asked.

"I'm *telling* you to go out with me on Saturday," he corrected her. "Why?"

"Because you have amazing legs. Six o'clock."

The phone line went dead. The disconnected tone buzzed in her ear, but Katya stood there. What in the fuck was going on? Was the universe playing a trick on her? She wakes up that morning determined to rid herself of both men, yet by the end of the day, she'd somehow managed to make dates with both of them.

You fuck a random stranger one time, and suddenly you've got more men on your hands than you know what to do with. Nice, Katya. Real nice. I am such an idiot.

On the way home, Katya stopped and got her flowers, then even grabbed pizza. She left all of them on the kitchen table, then locked herself in the bathroom before Tori could get too chatty. A hot bath and some time alone with her thoughts, that's what Katya needed.

But instead of thinking about what was going on in her personal life, her brain took a different route. She slipped beneath the bubbles and as she closed her eyes, memories from her night with Liam began floating behind her eyelids. Her kiss with Wulf got spliced in, and her brain went wild from there. Would he touch her the way Liam had? Would he be as bold? Maybe even *bolder?* She smoothed her hands over her thighs and panted in the steamy air.

Good lord, on top of being an idiot, I'm also now a sex addict.

7

"**I** NEED TO TELL YOU SOMETHING."

Liam glanced at her over the massive taco he was attempting to shove into his mouth.

"*Mo morf it,*" he mumbled around his food. Katya frowned at him.

"You're so gross."

"Not what you said the other night," he teased, then belched. She tried not to gag.

Liam was unabashedly male. His apartment was a mess, his dishes desperately needed to be done, and his laundry looked like it was trying to escape. He could probably do with a haircut, though she liked the wild and bushy look on him, and he always seemed a day or two behind the shaving train. He was crass and he swore all the time and he was blunt to the extreme.

She *loved* it.

He was so different from any other man she'd allowed herself to associate with – he actually reminded her a little of her roommate, Tori. A good friend she felt instantly comfortable with, despite the fact that they'd only met two days before, and he'd already seen her in all her glory.

After ordering enough tacos to strangle a mule, Liam had loaded her and their food onto San Francisco's "subway", the BART, and they'd rode it home together. They only stopped in his apartment long enough for her to be appalled at the state of it and to get some beers, then he led her up to the roof. Apparently, Twin Estates weren't entirely twins – they weren't allowed roof access in her building. She thought it was a little unfair, since both buildings were managed by the same company. Liam suggested writing a letter of complaint, and then told her to include a picture of her boobs for good measure.

"You gonna eat the rest of that?" he asked after he swallowed the last of his taco. Katya glared and pulled her bag of food away from him.

"*Yes,* you hoover vacuum."

"Alright, touchy. What did you need to tell me?"

Katya took a deep breath and ran her palms down the front of her pants.

"Is this a date?" she asked.

"Do you want it to be?" he asked back. She rolled her eyes.

"Don't be cute. I'm asking a serious question. I guess I'm not really sure what's going on right now, so it makes me nervous, like I'm gonna accidentally break the rules, or something," she tried to explain. He laughed.

"No rules, so nothing to get broken. I had a great time with you the other night, and you're kinda funny, when you put your mind to it. I thought tacos would be a nice segue into getting you to sleep with me again," he said. She threw her used napkin at his face.

"Whatever. I just … I think you should know something, then," she started again.

"What? Oh god, if you say you're pregnant, I'm gonna have to ask you to leave," he said. She threw the whole bag of food at him that time.

"*I'm not pregnant,* you asshat. I'm dating someone else," she snapped. She hadn't meant to just blurt it out, but Liam had a way of making her forget herself.

She wasn't sure what she'd expected. Maybe for him to get jealous, or a little upset. Or to tell her he didn't want her to see other people. She didn't know how it worked. Were they dating? Were they friends? The whole situation was driving her crazy – she needed to find her footing if she wanted to continue with either of them.

"Poor guy," Liam sighed, digging one of her tacos out of the bag.

"Why?" she asked, totally confused.

"You're dating this dude, yet gave your anal virginity to me. Must not like him too much," he said. She almost choked on air.

"You have seriously got to stop bringing that up."

"Why? It was amazing. I'm thinking of writing a song about it."

"Stop it."

"Seriously. I could have an open mic night at the club."

"I'm going to leave."

"Maybe I could do some abstract paintings, as well. Hang them about, set the mood."

Katya abruptly stood up and went to stride past him, towards the door. She'd barely made it two steps when she felt his hand on her hip. He grabbed her and yanked her off her feet. She fell into his lap and before she could get her bearings, she felt his fingers digging into her waist. She burst out laughing and immediately started squirming, trying to get away. But he was so much bigger than her, he was able to hold her in place with ease and tickle her to his heart's content.

"Stop!" she was shrieking with laughter. "Stop! Oh my god, I'm gonna pee. I'm gonna pee on you, *stooooppp*."

He finally complied, but he didn't let her go. She went lax, still laughing as she tried to catch her breath. When she looked up at him, it was to find him smiling down at her. As her breathing returned to normal, he reached out to brush some hair away from her forehead.

"See, there it is," he said softly.

"What?"

"You're beautiful when you're glaring at me or pretending to be perfect, but goddamn, Katya, you are *breathtaking* when you let go and just be yourself," he told her.

She wasn't sure what to do with that information. Bizarrely, she felt a little like crying. No one had ever particularly made her feel bad about herself, but no one had *ever* spoken to her like that before; he made her feel beautiful.

Before she could do something ridiculous, like actually cry, he suddenly yanked her upright. She was on her feet before she knew what was happening and he smacked her on the ass so hard it stung. She yelped and skipped away from him.

"So is this Casanova your boyfriend?" Liam asked, and when she turned around, he was back to his old goofy self, trying to eat two tacos at once.

"No," she said, moving back to her seat. "I don't even know if we're actually dating."

"What do you mean?"

"We went on one date on Wednesday, and we're going out again on Saturday."

"Ah, so you *just* started seeing him," Liam said, licking grease off his fingertips.

"Yeah."

"Must be a nice guy if you're giving him the time of day."

"Actually, he's kind of an asshole. I can't figure out why I keep agreeing to meet him," she said, earning a chuckle.

"It's always the assholes who get the girl, angel cake. Sleep with him yet?"

"What? No! I *just* slept with you, I'm not going to go off and sleep with some other guy!" she snapped.

"Why not?" he sounded confused as he demolished the last taco.

"Because! That would be … I mean … I can't just start having sex with every guy I meet," she said, exasperation heavy in her voice.

"Why not?"

She looked around for something else to throw at him.

"Stop being a brat."

"Okay, okay," he chuckled, rubbing a napkin between his hands. "Yeah, sleeping with every guy you bump into might be a bad idea – but where is it a law that you can't have sex with this dude, just because we just had sex? Honestly, *who cares?* I mean, I'm not telling you not to. I doubt he's gonna tell you no. So really, you're the only one with the issue. What if you want to have sex with him? Are you gonna say no, just because you had devastatingly amazing sex with me the other day?"

She chuckled at him and looked away, letting her gaze wander over the skyline. He was completely right. The only one saying she couldn't sleep with both of them was herself. Well, and society. And her parents. But ultimately – did she really care about those things? She thought she had, but since the other night …

"Lately, I don't have such a good track record of saying no," she sighed, resting her chin in her hands.

"Hey, sometimes saying yes is a good thing. Yes gets you all sorts of stuff. Tacos, movie tickets, blow jobs, cookies, all kinds of treats. You just have to open yourself up to new experiences," he told her.

"That's one way of putting it."

"And don't worry about me," he said, shoving their trash into the now empty paper bag. "We're just having fun. I mean, our friendship isn't contingent upon us having sex, but I was totally serious about fucking you. Anytime you feel like having sex, call me. I mean it, literally, *anytime.*"

"I'll keep that in mind," she laughed.

"But this dude – you should tell him about me," Liam said, his serious face making another appearance. Katya nodded.

"I will. I had already planned on it," she said.

"Good girl. And what if Mr. New Guy has a problem with you banging a hot, successful, rich, night club owner?" he asked. She snorted.

"Okay, first of all – you're just as new as him. Second of all – hot, successful, and rich are seriously pushing it. I don't know, I guess it depends on how the date goes, but if he kicked up a fit … I think I'd tell him goodbye," she said.

"Really? For me?" Liam sounded surprised. She shook her head.

"No, *for me*. I'm confused and I'm learning new things about myself and I have no clue what's going on in my head anymore, but … I think I like it. I don't think I'm ready to go back to being boring old-Katya again. I like this new-Katya. I think I want to see what she wants to do."

Liam caught her off guard by jerking forward, almost lurching across the table so he could place a sloppy kiss against her mouth. He tasted like cilantro and Corona, and she squealed and clung to him when the table rocked unsteadily under his hand, threatening to send them both to the floor.

"See?" he said when he finally pulled away.

"What?" she asked, a little bewildered.

"You're letting go again. It's gorgeous. You better get out of here, or I'm gonna fuck you on this roof top, in broad daylight," he warned her before he sucked down the rest of his beer.

"No, you're not. I'm still sore in very uncomfortable places, thank you."

"Hey, *you* begged for that, missy. But I'll keep it strictly vag, I swear."

"Right. I'm out of here. Thanks for the tacos."

Liam slapped her on the ass again when she walked past him. Before she could move through the rooftop doorway, though, he called out to her.

"Call me when you're done with your date!"

"Why?" she asked, turning to face him. He hadn't moved from the ratty loveseat he'd been occupying for the hour they'd been up there. A stylish pair of vintage Ray Bans hid his warm brown eyes, but even without being able to see them, Katya could just tell they were smiling at her.

"Because I want to hear all the dirty sex details."

She snorted at him again, then slammed the door behind her after she'd walked through it.

———————◆———————

For their second date, Wulf was the one who was late. The place he'd picked out – Flannery's – was a high end bar, and Katya was the only woman in the entire establishment. It was mostly empty, true, but the half dozen or so other guests were all men in very expensive looking suits. An older gentleman was working the bar and he kept shooting her odd looks.

He probably thinks I'm a prostitute, awesome.

Wulf strolled in twenty minutes after six. He stopped to chat with a couple people as he made his way through the bar, even ordered himself a drink, before he finally sat down next to her. Almost as if she were an afterthought.

He explained to her that the bar was a hot spot for businessmen – expensive attorneys, lawyers, accountants, and realtors frequented the exclusive, *expensive*, eatery. When she pointed out they all also seemed to be male, he'd winked at her and said how lucky it was for her, then.

He'd picked the spot to meet her because he'd known he was going to be working late. He'd walked down from his offices, and it hadn't even occurred to him that the spot might make her uncomfortable – a twenty-three year old attractive woman sitting in what was essentially a shark tank.

While they had drinks and ate, Katya tried to pin down what exactly about him made her uncomfortable. He was smart – smarter than her, she could admit. And he was ridiculously good looking, and through their chats, she found out he still did swim frequently. He even had a lap pool on the roof of his building. He was also successful, and as a result, he was very wealthy. Katya's family was upper class and she made very good money through her job, but Wulf's bank account was on another level, she was sure. All those things spelled out intimidation in big, bold letters

But that wasn't it. Katya had dated good looking, rich, successful men before, and they never made her feel tongue tied the way Wulf did. Hell, Liam was rich and successful and so good looking, it was stupid, but she felt completely at ease with him. So strange, how one man could make her feel so comfortable in his presence, and the other could make her feel so nervous.

That wasn't the only way they were completely opposite, either. Liam was all kinky silly sexy, but there was always a hint of hesitation about him. He always, in his own way, sought permission to touch her. Once she gave the okay, he was aggressive and demanding, but only when she'd made it clear she wasn't going to stop him. He was *polite*.

Wulf had no similar such compulsion. He touched her often and frequently, and without any sort of hesitation. It was like it didn't even occur to him that he should ask permission – or he just didn't care. They sat side by side at the bar and he would reach out occasionally, tucking a stray hair behind her ear, touching her thigh below the hem of her dress, running his finger down the side of her arm. It made her think of the other night, when he'd kissed her without any ceremony, any hesitation.

It made her feel stupid with anticipation, wondering how far he'd go. She liked it, that he assumed such a familiarity. Took such charge. When his hand would leave her skin, she found herself holding her breath till it came back.

If this keeps up much longer, I'm going to pass out from lack of oxygen.

"So what else do you do?" he asked as their plates were taken away.

"Just baking," she answered.

Wulf spun on his stool so he was facing her, one of his elbows propped on the bar, a glass of brandy in his hand. She had both her elbows on the bar, her hands clasped together and her cheek pressed against them so she could face him. His knee was jutting into the side of her leg and just that simple contact caused her temperature to sky rocket.

She glanced around, wondering if anyone was around to witness her spontaneous combustion. The place had cleared out. It was only them, the bartender, and a bus boy wiping down tables. The setting sun was filtering into the space, coating everything in a soft gold glow.

"That's it? Morning till night? From the moment of waking? Jesus christ, your life must be so bland," he snorted. She actually laughed – she was getting used to his odd sense of humor.

"No, smart ass. I have a roommate, I spend a lot of time with her. I like going to museums – *love* the aquarium," she told him. He nodded while she spoke, but his eyes were wandering around the bar. Like he was bored. She took a deep breath. "Though recently, I've kind of been going through a change." His eyes cut back to her.

Ha, got him.

"Really? What kind of change?" he asked.

"Like I said, it's recent. *Very* recent. I'm not sure how long it'll last," she warned him.

"I swear, if you try to convert me to Scientology, I will wring your neck."

She burst out laughing again.

"No, no cults or anything. But … I guess I should tell you, I'm kinda sorta seeing someone else," she said.

"Ah. Kinda sorta?" he asked.

"Yeah. He's a new friend, sorta."

"You sound unsure."

"We're not boyfriend and girlfriend or anything," she assured him. "But I like spending time with him, and we have slept together.

I just thought you should know."

She'd never in her life had that kind of conversation with a man. She suddenly felt very grown up. She wanted to order a gin and tonic, and start discussing the Dow Jones Industrial, or something.

"Well then. Thank you for sharing. Do you plan on sleeping with him again any time soon?" he checked.

"I don't plan on it," she was honest.

"But it's a possibility."

"I guess so."

"Are you always this unsure about people you may or may not be sleeping with?" he asked. She slapped him on the knee.

"Yes. I told you, this is new to me. Seeing you, seeing that guy. I just wanted to be honest with you, from the beginning," she said.

Wulf reached out and grabbed her knee, his fingers curling into her skin, and he gently pulled her so she spun around on her stool top and faced him. Both his hands came to rest on the tops of her thighs and she bit into her bottom lip.

"Well thank you, Katya, for your honesty," he said, sliding his hands up so his fingertips disappeared underneath her dress. "I have to say, though, I'm curious about these 'changes' you're going through. If they involve sleeping with two men at the same time, what else are you exploring?"

"Who said I was going to sleep with *you?*" she answered back quickly.

It was his turn to burst out laughing. He so rarely full on laughed, the sound of it and the site of his smile were a shock to the system. Her reaction was so visceral, it caught her off guard. She loved it when Liam laughed, wanted to laugh with him. But Wulfric's laughter … it made her feel like she could very easily lose her heart to this man. And that thought scared her.

You don't know him, so don't start thinking about something as absurd as your heart.

"Katya, please, let's be realistic – I'm betting that by this time next week, I'll know *exactly* what you sound like when you're coming."

Holy shit. *Holy shit.* She wanted to hyperventilate. Wanted to jump on him and rip his clothes off. But thankfully, she'd been holding her breath while he spoke, and it actually calmed her down. She remembered how she was with Liam, how the new-Katya wasn't intimidated or flustered by sexy banter.

"A week, huh?" she said in a low voice. "That's a long time, Wulf. Thank god I have the other guy to keep me entertained."

He didn't laugh that time, but she could see it in his eyes, in the way he watched her lips while she spoke. Could feel his delight in the way his fingers scratched at her skin, dragging their way down to her knees.

Creedance Clearwater was filtering through the speakers, singing about putting spells on people. Putting a spell on *her*. The sunset had gone from a soft glow to a full on blaze, glaring off every piece of gold and chrome, blinding her to everything but the man in front of her. It was like the room was going up in flames around them, and they didn't even care.

And on that thought, Katya excused herself. If she was going to melt into a puddle, she'd rather not do it at his feet. She had an image to uphold, apparently.

She locked herself in the bathroom and splashed cold water on her cheeks. Stared at her reflection, wondering who on earth the girl was looking back at her. Her eyes, a somewhat dull shade of blue, stared back at her, wide in their sockets. Her hair was in another boring bun, high on the back of her head. Her loose shift dress was sleeveless, with splashes of ivory and yellow on the body of it, ending in a heavy black border at the hem. Nothing exciting.

"Stop shitting on yourself."

Liam's voice rang through her head. Holy shit, he was right – she was always putting herself down. Even when she was alone. Even when she had a guy as hot as Liam chasing after her, and a man as devastatingly handsome as Wulfric right in front of her. Why did she do that? She turned around and took several deep breaths, shaking the tension out of her hands. Then she went back to the mirror, gripping the edge of the sink and leaning in close.

Her eyes were wide and expressive, the blue so soft, they were almost a lapis color. Her hair was a deep auburn, a shade she'd often been complimented on and she knew many women tried to duplicate. She almost never wore it down, but it was thick and long and healthy. And her dress may have been simple enough and not form fitting at all, but it showed more leg than she usually ever dared, and hung off her chest in a way that called attention to her pert breasts. The light fabric contrasted well with her deep tan skin, and the overall look was … sexy, she had to admit. A sort of virginal sexy, sure, but sexy nonetheless.

What in the hell are you doing, Katya? That man is out there, ready to eat you alive. What's to stop you from being the main course? Some moral compass that's done nothing for you, except keep you from having fun? Liam is right – the only one stopping you from doing what you want, is you.

She glanced at the bathroom door and started breathing fast. She wanted Wulf. Since she was fourteen, she'd fantasized about him, but he'd always been just that – a fantasy. Untouchable, unreachable, and then just *gone*. A faded memory. Someone who had never wanted her, and would never want her. Then Liam had popped up in her life, flipping her entire notion of herself on its ass, and Wulf had walked through the door, and had seen that change in her. She had already become a sex kitten once, for Liam. She had the practice time under her belt. If she could put it into use against Wulf, who knew how far she could take things.

God, I want to see how far we can go.

Katya didn't want to wait a week. She didn't want to wait another second. What if he disappeared? What if old-Katya reared her ugly head? She didn't want to take the chance. She wanted to be that girl from the made-up-profile again, so she decided to go for it. She took a deep breath, then reached under her dress. Felt around for the edges of her underwear, then dragged them past her hips. Let them fall to the floor. She stepped out of them, then balled them up in her fist.

I can do this. I can really do this. What's the worst that can happen? He laughs at me? So what, then I take the train to Liam's house and work out this sexual tension with him.

When she came out of the bathroom, the first thing she noticed was that some shading had been pulled low over the windows. They were sheer, but they dulled the glare and made it almost impossible to see outside clearly.

Then she saw that Wulf wasn't sitting at the bar anymore. He'd moved to an old piano that was tucked against a wall, taking up a lot of space in the narrow bar. He was plunking out a tune, something she didn't recognize, though she was surprised he could play. He sounded decent and she stood behind his shoulder for a moment, watching his fingers move over the keys.

"I thought you were going to be in there all night," he finally said, though he didn't bother looking back at her.

"It was two minutes, max," she replied, though she still felt a little breathless. He must have heard, because the notes on the piano died down, slowing to a stop. He climbed to his feet, throwing back the last of his brandy, then he put the glass on top of the instrument before turning to face her.

"More like five. You sound nervous, Tocci," he called her out. She nodded.

"I am."

"Why? Scared of me?"

"Not scared."

"Then what?"

She took a deep breath. A second one. Wouldn't let her eyes move away from his as she lifted her hand.

"I don't want to wait a week," she said plainly, all while she tucked her hot pink panties into his chest pocket, crushing the pocket square he had there.

Wulf glanced down at the fabric poking out. It only took him a fraction of a second to figure out what she'd just done. Then his lips twitched, quirked up into a sly little smile, and he raised his arm, snapping his fingers.

"Tom," he said, not looking away from her. The bartender cleared his throat. "Ten minutes, please. I need the room."

Nothing else was said. The bus boy stopped clearing tables and made his way to the back of the bar, disappearing through a heavy wooden door. The bartender went and locked the entrance, then quickly went through the same door as the bus boy, and Katya could hear it get locked behind him. They were completely alone.

"Do you live close by?" she asked. Wulf pulled her underwear away from his blazer.

"Not close enough."

She watched as her panties were folded up, then shoved into his pants pocket, and she halfway wondered if she'd ever see them again.

"When I said I didn't want to wait a week, I didn't mean I couldn't wait five more minutes," she tried to joke, then her breath caught in her throat when his hands smoothed over her hips.

"Pity, because I can't."

He forced her backwards, pressing his body against her. He wasn't overwhelmingly tall, maybe six foot, but his strong physique was intimidating, and his sheer presence filled the entire room. Made her feel small and helpless and overwhelmingly feminine. She braced her hands on his forearms, allowing him to move her so her back was pressed into the bar.

One of his hands ran down her leg, then gripped her thigh roughly, lifting her. Her hands flew behind her as she was sat on top of the bar. He spread her legs, moving into the space between them, and making her ridiculously aware of the fact that there was nothing between the front of his pants and her crotch.

He was slow and methodical in the way he handled her, as if they had all the time in the world for him to explore her body. As if she was a sculpture he'd bought and paid for, something that belonged to him, was his to touch as he pleased. Her teeth cut into her bottom lip while his hands moved over her dress, briefly cupping her breasts before moving back down to her thighs, spreading them wider still.

"In a million years," he sighed when he leaned in to kiss her neck. "I would never have imagined Katya Tocci giving me her panties." She laughed softly while she combed her fingers through his hair.

"Hey, I never said you could keep them."

"Katya, the moment you showed up at the restaurant the other night, *all* your panties have belonged to me. You had better get used to that idea."

Then his hands were on either side of her head, holding her in place while he kissed her, slowly and thoroughly. Stole every molecule out of her lungs. She wasn't sure what she'd expected from him – something a little wilder, a little more scary. But what he was doing was so much more. The anticipation, the expectation, he was driving her insane, building up something inside her. She didn't know how to deal with it, how to react to it. She wanted to whimper and cry, to strip herself bare and just hand herself over to him.

Too late.

When she was actually squirming and writhing against him, her fingernails leaving permanent marks on the back of his neck, he finally moved. Kissed his way to her neck while one hand returned to her breasts. His head followed suit and she soon realized he was pushing her. Forcing her flat on her back. Her head hung off the other side of the bar, so she was looking at the bottles from upside down.

Then his mouth was hot against the inside of her knee, his teeth sharp, causing her to yelp. She tried to sit up, wanted to be an active participant, but his hand came down flat between her breasts, forcing her to stay down. His tongue traced a line from her knee straight to the center of her legs and she let out a long moan.

Once again, the man blew her mind. He was such an arrogant, selfish prick. Not waiting for her at dinner, then making her wait at the bar. Not offering an apology, not offering an explanation. And yet, when she was throwing herself at him, ready to sleep with him right then and there, he was forcing her to stop and he was going down on her, giving her pleasure while taking none for himself.

Wulfric Stone – so generous. Who would've thought?

It was such an intimate act, it usually made her uncomfortable, and she'd only ever had one ex-boyfriend do it with her – she and Liam had never gotten around to it during their night, and she wasn't sure she would've allowed it to happen, anyway. It was just too intense, and she hadn't ever enjoyed it very much, so it wasn't worth it to her to explore it with other men.

All those feelings flew away under Wulf's very experienced tongue and fingers. He was making her see colors she hadn't known existed. She groaned low in her throat, whispered his name. Panted it. Used one hand to hold onto his hair, and the other to grip the side of the bar. Her shoes had long since fallen off, clattering to the floor, and she lifted her leg, balancing the ball of her foot on the heavy oak.

Jesus, she was in a bar. It was a little after eight o'clock at night. The window shading offered some privacy, but if anyone outside decided to crouch down and look underneath the screens, they'd see her spread out on the bar with a man's face between her thighs. The thought made her tremble, and remembering there was kitchen and wait staff lurking just behind the back door made it all the worse. Or better. She didn't know anymore. She cried out and then both hands were in his dark hair, holding him to her.

"Ms. Tocci," he sighed when he pulled away. She was panting and shivering, trying to catch her breath while he pushed her dress up over her stomach. "You are so sweet, in so very many ways."

He'd moved away from her and she whimpered at the loss of his weight and heat. Rubbed her legs together, trying to finish what he'd started by using friction alone. Then he grabbed her arm roughly, and before she could open her eyes, he was yanking her upright.

The kisses were still slow, but hotter than anything she'd ever experienced, burning her clear to her soul. She wrapped her tongue around his while she slid her hands under his jacket, feeling the plains and lines of his muscles. While she explored his body, he wrapped one arm around her waist and the other around her hips, lifting her off the bar. He was carrying her around, and she didn't even care where they were going. He could've taken her outside and laid her on the hood of his car, and as long as he finished what he'd started, she wouldn't care.

He sat her on the edge of a table and she had to lift her chin to keep kissing him. Had to reach to shove his jacket away from his shoulders. While he worked on getting his tie off, she nibbled on his earlobe and took apart his belt. He unzipped the back of her dress, then pushed her back, pulling the material away from her chest. When it was all pooled at her hips, showing off the matching bra to the panties he now owned, he pulled her to the very edge of the table top, kissing her hard.

It was so quiet in the bar. The music had long since stopped. Neither of them were saying anything. There was only the sound of their breathing, panting and gasping as they were. The semi-silence should've been unnerving. Liam had been a chatty cathy, and she didn't know why, but Katya had expected Wulf to be somewhat the same. But it seemed he didn't need words. The confidence in his touch, in the way he kissed her, was enough to get his message across.

She had been preoccupied with unbuttoning his shirt, so lost in the moment, that she didn't even realize what was happening till she felt his erection between her legs. Then he was kissing her at the same time as he was forcing himself inside of her. She cried out, unable to maintain the silence anymore. He was big, and much thicker than anything she'd ever experienced. Completely foreign to her body.

So fucking amazing.

She quite literally felt impaled. She needed time to adjust, and he wasn't giving it to her, and she didn't care. She dropped her fore-head to his chest, groaning in time to each thrust as he forced him-self deeper. She locked her legs around his waist, squeezing with her thighs, and he returned the favor by gripping her by the ass, forcing her harder against him.

By the time she remembered she should be a helpful partner, she was already halfway undone by him. She wanted to take off the rest of his clothes, peel off his undershirt so she could see his amaz-ing body. But that would mean pushing him away, and she couldn't stand the idea of not touching him, of not being pressed against him. She bit at his chest through the thin material of his undershirt, finally earning a sound from him. He groaned out her name, then took a deep breath.

"Look at me."

Another thing she'd never done during sex – staring into some-one's eyes. But when she looked up, it was to find that he wasn't looking back at her. He was staring between them. One of his hands moved to her jaw, his thumb wrapping around it, forcing her to keep looking at his face. Then he was kissing her again, and she could feel his restraint starting to slip. She was heady with the knowledge that she was responsible for making his cool demeanor slip and she moaned into his mouth, forcing her tongue hard against his. Began working her hips back against his, meeting him thrust for thrust.

She wasn't sure if it was because he was about to break, or if he had a master plan, but he abruptly stopped moving. She started to moan in protest, but then was stopped short when he started scoot-ing her backwards. He climbed onto the table with her, then laid her down flat, every inch of her covered by him. She coiled her arms around his shoulders, finally able to at least push his dress shirt off his body.

"God, Wulf, I -"

She was cut off by his tongue in her mouth. He wouldn't let her talk. It was like some sort of dark magic was expanding between them, and he didn't want anything to break the spell. She didn't mind at all and kissed him back, shoving her hands underneath his shirt, finally touching his skin.

His own hands weren't idle, burning up different paths on her body. Gripping her thigh, holding it high against his hip, allowing him to thrust deeper. She tossed her head back and magic or wait staff be damned, she began moaning loudly. She couldn't keep something that amazing inside. She clawed against his back with one hand, and with the other, she reached down and gripped onto his belt, yanking on it to urge him faster.

His mouth was on her breast when it started. His teeth grazed her nipple, though her bra, and the scratchy friction kicked off the first tremor. She said his name, and she could almost swear she heard him chuckle. Probably because he knew exactly what he was doing to her. His mouth went back to her nipple, soaking the material separating him from her skin, his tongue flat and hard against her. Her whole body started to shake.

"Wulf," she whispered his name, her entire body coiling around him in tension. In preparation for the explosion that was coming.

"So, so, sweet, Katya," he sighed into her skin. "So fucking good. You are so incredibly fucking good. Do you have any idea?"

Words were gone from her vocabulary. She could only moan and cry and beg. So much begging.

"From now on," he began to pant while he spoke. "*No panties* when you're with me. I will be doing this whenever, *wherever*, I want, and I don't want anything in my way. *Understood?*"

She hoped her orgasm was a good enough answer. The back of her head hit the table painfully as she shrieked, and she was pretty sure she ripped his shirt down the back. She couldn't help it. She felt like she was going to die, but in the best possible way. He was so thick inside her, that every time a fresh wave from her orgasm had her clenching down on him, it actually intensified the feeling. She was almost sobbing by the time her body started to come down from the high.

She dropped her legs flat against the table, absolutely useless to help him or give anything back to him. He'd fucked her into another state of being. Old-Katya was *officially* gone, he'd killed her with that orgasm. And if she wasn't positive about it right that moment, when he painfully squeezed her breast at the same time as coming inside her, she was *definitely* sure.

Buh-bye, old-Katya. Can't say I'll miss you. Thanks for all the beige clothing.

She was still in orbit somewhere, but Wulf was able to pull himself together and climb off the table, pulling his pants up as he moved. She still felt like a puddle of goo, but he grabbed her arm and dragged her to her feet. While she struggled to get her arms back through her dress, he pulled off his tattered and torn undershirt. Her mouth went dry at the sight of his body. She'd just been touching *that!?* Jesus, with a body like that, he could charge people to touch him, and here she'd had the chance to do it for free and she'd been too preoccupied with silly things like orgasms.

"Keep staring at me like that, Tocci, and we won't make it out of here anytime soon."

He didn't bother giving her a chance to respond, he just turned her around and zipped up her dress. Then while still buttoning his shirt, he led the way out of the bar, unlocking the door and letting her walk out ahead of him.

"Should we tell them we're leaving?" Katya asked while she hopped around, trying to put on her shoes.

"I'm sure they'll guess we've gone, once they realize you're not screaming anymore."

Flames raced across her face.

"I don't normally do things like that."

"I know. C'mon, I'll give you a ride home."

He handed her his tie while they walked, so he could put on his jacket. She slipped it over her head, smoothing her fingers over the silk. He wasn't saying anything, and she wondered if maybe sex in a restaurant wasn't anything new for him. It certainly was for her. She couldn't even believe she was walking around without any underwear on.

"You work in this place?" Katya asked after they'd walked for about three blocks and he turned towards the parking garage for a large, imposing looking office building.

"I *own* this place. Our offices are on the top floor," he told her, then he put his hand on her back and guided her through a security door into the garage.

"Must be an amazing view," she sighed.

"I'll have to show you sometime."

Wulf didn't seem to be the biggest talker. Conversation had flowed between them during both their dinners, but it was like when he was done, that was it. Time to talk was over. She was stuck feeling like maybe she should fill the silence.

"Have I mentioned how much I love your car?" she said after she was seated in the Mercedes again. He glanced at her as he pulled out of his parking spot.

"No, do you?"

"So much."

"You're not one of those girls who needs a man to have a nice car to be worthy of her, are you? I don't have patience for that," he said. She shook her head.

"No, I've never cared about what kind of car a man drives. But this isn't a car, Wulf. This is *art*. Sex on wheels," she explained. He snorted at her, but as they pulled onto the street, his hand moved onto her thigh.

"Sex on wheels, huh," he finally said after they'd driven for about five minutes in silence.

"It's just so sleek and smooth and … *sexy*," she laughed, running her hand over the curve of her door. "You *have* to take the top off for me sometime."

"I'll see what I can arrange. So tell me something," he started.

"Anything."

"This other guy you see – would you fuck him on a table in a restaurant?" he asked. She was a little shocked at his bluntness, but then realized she'd better learn to expect that, if she was gonna be the kind of chick who shoved her panties into men's pockets.

"Uh," she stuttered a little. "I don't know. It's not like I planned on doing that with you."

"Hmmm."

She chewed on her lip and it felt like his hand was going to burn a hole through her leg.

"To be honest," she couldn't stop herself. "If it wasn't for him, I probably wouldn't have done that with you."

"Really. *Interesting.*"

His tiny vocabulary was driving her insane.

"Yeah. Until this week, I was like a three-dates-minimum-before-kissing kind of girl. It was like I just couldn't be that person anymore, then I met him, and he told me I didn't have to be, so I guess I'm not," she tried to explain.

"Well, then. I guess lucky for me you met this guy."

"Yeah, lucky you," she mumbled, staring out the window.

They rode the rest of the way in silence. Katya spent most of it wondering about her choices. Sleeping with Wulf had seemed like a great idea while she'd been all hot and bothered. Now, she felt like maybe she should've made him try harder. He'd gotten what he'd wanted, so it was probably all over. Surprisingly, that's what upset her the most. The idea of not seeing him anymore.

"*Tocci.*"

The way he snapped her name, she realized he must have said it a couple times before getting her attention. She turned towards him and was surprised to realize they were in front of her building. She managed a smile and opened her door.

"Thanks for the date, Wulf. It was fun," she said, and she meant it.

"Just a minute," he stopped her.

"What?" she asked, her heart starting to beat fast.

"You're wearing my tie."

She frowned as she looked down at herself, a little disappointed if that's all he wanted to say. But then his hand reached out and he gripped the material, pulling her forward. She practically fell into his seat, and when he kissed her that time, there was nothing slow and methodical about it. She had a feeling she was kissing the *real* Wulf for the first time. Those other times had been calculated. Planned and precise, just enough to make her beg for him. This kiss, though, was all for him. Lots of tongue, his fingers in her hair, pulling. Stinging. She gasped and he took the opportunity to suck on her bottom lip, biting down hard before letting her go.

"On second thought, keep it. It looks better on you. I'll be in touch, Tocci."

She practically fell out of the car and had barely stepped clear before he was peeling out of his spot, his flashy white car disappearing into the night. It wasn't till she was inside the building that she realized he hadn't asked for her phone number, *again*. She sighed and took out her cell, wondering if she could google her way to his personal number.

She was surprised to see several missed text messages. One was from Tori, asking about the date, but the rest were from Liam. One was a close up picture of a taco, which made her laugh. The rest were generally dirty, filled with euphemisms, and teasing her about her date. When she got to her floor, she finally sent him a response.

You're awful, stop harassing me.

But it's so much fun! You took long enough to reply – how many times did you screw him?

Katya rolled her eyes as she shuffled into her apartment, fighting to kick her shoes off as she made her way back to her bedroom.

Why do you have to be so crass?

Oh, defensive. You definitely fucked him then.

I don't kiss and tell.

How about suck and tell?

You're so gross.

Just tell me one thing.

What?

When you came, did you make the same little whining sound you made for me?

THIS CONVERSATION IS OVER.

It's so hot, I swear. I can hear it my head right now. God, I'm so hard now.

Katya practically threw her phone across the room. She may have been working on expanding her boundaries and horizons, but she was not about to have phone sex with Liam, barely half an hour after she'd had actual sex with Wulf.

She took a shower, then put on comfy clothes before padding back into her room. She looked over her closet, glaring at her clothes. Normally, she liked picking out her outfits for the coming days, but now when she looked at everything, she just saw beiges and pastels.

Boring. She made a mental note to go shopping. Having decided that, she went to sit on her bed, then jumped up when something hard jabbed her in the ass cheek. She'd forgotten about her phone, and she groaned when she saw four more missed messages from Liam. She thumbed open the screen and laughed at the last one.

I scared you off, didn't I? My sexual prowess is just too intimidating.

She smiled to herself and typed out a response.

Try too annoying.

She's alive! You can't leave me hanging like that. Do you have any idea how hot and bothered I am right now?

No, and I don't want to have an idea.

Please, you have to help me. I'm dying.

No.

I'll send you a pic.

If you send me a dick pic, I will block your number from my phone.

Please, you've probably got my dick committed to memory. I have something else in mind, it'll be really hot, I promise.

No. N-O, no.

But he sent a picture anyway. Katya was too curious to look away and when she realized what she was looking at, she burst out laughing again. It was a close up picture of a thermostat, the mercury kind that hangs on a wall. The little red line was creeping up past ninety-five degrees.

Try to contain yourself.

Har dee har har.

Seriously, my air conditioning broke today and something is going on with the radiator. Let me come over to your place.

No, my roommate is here and she already wants to meet the guy who dragged me to a sex club. I'll probably look away and you two will start screwing on my kitchen table.

Ooohhh, jealousy, I like it.

Not jealous. Just protective of my table.

Then come hang out on the roof with me.

I just put on pajamas, I'm not changing to walk all the way over to your place.

Don't bother – I'll walk over to yours.

My building doesn't allow roof access.

Does now. I talked to management after you left. I'm coming over.

Katya was a little blown away. She'd mentioned wishing she had roof privileges. Just a comment in passing while he'd dished out the tacos. That he'd remembered was surprising, but that he'd actually called and done something about it?

What a sweetheart.

She grabbed a bottle of water and was pulling on a pair of sneakers when she heard someone walking in the hallway. Tori hadn't made an appearance yet, so Katya assumed she'd fallen asleep early. She didn't want to wake her up, so she cracked open the front door. When she saw that it was Liam heading towards her, she slipped into the hall.

"What, not gonna invite me in?" he asked as they headed back to the elevator.

"No, you'd probably never leave, and I can't afford to feed you tacos every day."

"I think you just want to keep me from your sexy roommate."

"Never said she was sexy."

"It's okay, angel cake. I'll always have a soft spot for you," he assured her as they rode up to the top floor. "Tell you what, we can make it a threesome. Sharing is caring."

"I swear, if you bring up having a threesome with my roommate again, I will go back downstairs," she threatened him. He leaned down close, wrapping his arm around her waist.

"Such a scaredy cat. You never know, you may like it," he whispered, causing her to shiver.

The elevator deposited them on the last floor, then they had to walk up one fight to get to the roof top door. There, Liam shocked her again by pulling a key out of his pocket and unlocking the heavy door. She walked out ahead of him and started shivering as the night air hit her still-damp hair.

"They gave you a key? Isn't that a little strange?" she asked, turning to face him.

"It's actually for you," he said, tossing the key to her. She scrambled to catch it while he pushed past her. She dropped her water bottle in the process and had to chase it around for a second.

"Me? Why me?" she turned as she spoke, watching as he unfolded some beach chairs.

"Because you're the only one allowed up here. Well, and me, of course," he said, then he sat down. She gaped until he patted the chair next to him. She finally sat down, as well.

"What did you say to them to get me exclusive access?" she asked. Liam sighed and rubbed his hands over his face. She hadn't known him long, but she already knew it was a gesture of annoyance or nervousness.

"I have to tell you something, but I don't want you to get weirded out," he said.

"Okay, then I'm definitely weirded out," she replied, taking a sip of her water.

"I sort of own these buildings."

She spit out the water.

"What!?" she exclaimed, mopping at her chin. He winced and nodded.

"Yeah. About five years ago, my aunt passed away. She didn't have any kids, so she left the property to me and my brother. A building each. I was already living in my apartment, and a management company was handling everything else, so I didn't change anything," he said.

"Why didn't you tell me?"

"I don't know, sometimes it makes it weird. I've had girls fuck me to try to get free rent, weird shit like that, and I also didn't want you thinking like 'oh no, I'm banging my landlord', or anything like that. I honestly never thought we'd hook up, so it never occurred to me to mention it," he told her.

She was still a little shocked. He was so young, yet he owned a thriving business *and* some very expensive real estate in San Francisco – her rent *was not* cheap, hence the need for a roommate.

"How old are you?" she blurted out.

"How old are *you*?" he asked back.

"Twenty-three," she said. He let his eyes fall shut.

"God bless you," he breathed.

"*Liam.*"

"Thirty-two," he answered. Her jaw dropped.

"You lie."

"Nope. Wanna see my driver's license?"

"Jesus, I was guessing twenty-eight, max," she mumbled, her eyes wandering over his face. Over his clothes.

"I'll choose to take that as a compliment."

Nine years. He was nine years older than her. He didn't look it, and he certainly didn't act like it. She couldn't believe she'd slept with someone that much older than her. Though if she was honest with herself, she found it kinda hot. Sexy older man, willing younger woman. Yeah, she'd read those books, she'd watched those movies. Besides, Wulf was twenty-nine, not exactly close to her age, either.

"Okay. I guess none of that really matters, right? I mean, unless I can fuck my way to free rent," she joked.

"You *definitely* can."

"Can we get some sofas up here, like your place?"

"Sure, I'll see what maintenance can scrounge up. But you're the only one allowed up here – no parties, no friends, no Mr. New Guy. *Nobody.*"

"Not even Tori?"

"Nope."

"Why?"

"Because," he sighed as he lounged back in the chair. "This place is special, angel cake. It's *our* place. Just for you and me. No one else. Just us."

It was so sweet, Katya couldn't argue about it, so she smiled and sat back in her chair, too. They sat in companionable silence for a while, both looking up at the sky. She wasn't sure how long they were like that before he opened his mouth.

"I've never seen your hair down before."

"Excuse me?" she asked, caught off guard.

"Your hair. In all the times I've seen you, I've never seen it down. It looks nice," he told her. She ran her fingers through the wet tresses.

"Oh. Thank you."

"So tell me about the crazy sex," he said, sitting up straight. She shook her head.

"There was nothing crazy about it. Just normal, missionary position sex, and that's all I'm sharing with you," she said.

"God, and here I thought I'd seen the last of Miss Boring Beige Pants," he grumbled. She went to snap at him, but he held up his hand. "But no worries! I had a plan in place, just for this incident. I signed you up for something."

"Oh god, what is it?" she groaned.

"Strip-aerobics," he said with a big smile.

"You did not."

"I totally did. Tomorrow, at five o'clock, have your ass downstairs waiting for me, preferably in some sexy yoga pants."

"Liam, I don't want to learn strip-aerobics. I'll probably slip and break my nose on the stupid pole," she said.

"All I'm hearing is blah blah blah. Fuck, it's kinda cold up here, isn't it? Let's head down to your place and cuddle."

"I am not cuddling with -"

"And maybe your sexy roommate can join us, too."

"Stop calling her that!"

"Alright, your sexy girlfriend can join us."

Katya rolled her eyes and complained some more. He ignored her and made jokes all the way down to her place. And while he and Tori did get along, they did not have sex on the kitchen table, much to Katya's delight. And when she went to sleep, Liam didn't hog too much of the bed.

Though his hard on digging into her hip made it very difficult to sleep.

8

WHEN KATYA WENT TO WORK THE NEXT MORNING, SHE LEFT LIAM IN HER kitchen. He was wearing only his boxers and drinking orange juice straight from the carton. Maintenance workers were already over at his place and working on the radiator, he assured her. Then he reminded her of their five o'clock date.

"*It's not a date.*"

At least, Katya was pretty sure a strip-aerobics class shouldn't count as a date. Either way, she told Liam to meet her at her work – she didn't get off till five, so if he wanted her to go, he'd have to come get her. She packed her gym bag along with her and at the end of the day, sure enough, he was waiting outside for her.

They went to an interesting sort of place. An old building, there were fliers for lots of different classes, mostly ones hosted by "community members", asking only for donations as opposed to charging a fee. The class they were at was a freebie and was hosted by a ridiculously sexy young woman, probably not any older than Katya.

"I'm trying to build a client list, start private training, that sort of thing," Candi – "*with an i*" – explained when Liam introduced them.

"Oh. That sounds nice," was all Katya could think to say.

"Have you done this before?"

"I didn't even know it was a real thing till earlier this week."

"You'll love it. You gonna join us, stud?" Candi said, poking Liam in the chest. He chuckled and rubbed at the spot.

"Eh, not this time. Maybe if the show is good, I'll sign up for the next class," he said, winking at her. She giggled and poked him again.

"You are so bad, Eden."

Then Candi-with-an-i bounced off to greet some new students. Katya turned to look at Liam, one of her eyebrows raised.

"Stud?" she asked.

"Hey, some ladies just like to call it like they see it," he joked.

"Have you slept with her?"

"I don't kiss and tell."

"Oh, please."

"You're right. I have, but not in a long time. When she moved to town, she stumbled into the club. Was a regular for a while, then discovered stripping was her passion," he explained, his eyes lingering on the stripper-turned-aerobics-instructor.

"Pity for you."

"I know. She's was … *wild.*"

"You're not actually gonna sit here the whole time, are you?" Katya asked, glancing over the rest of the class.

There were lots of women, ranging in ages from what looked like eighteen all the way up to easily seventy years old. There were even several men in the group, one of which was wearing a pair of heels higher than anything Katya had in her closet. But mostly, it was females in their late twenties to early forties, and none of them looked anything like a stripper.

"Probably not. If I wander off, I'll be back to pick you up at six-thirty," he assured her.

"I've lived in San Francisco for years, Liam. I can find my way home," she said.

"And run the risk of some other guy picking you up? No, I'll be here, don't worry," he teased.

Candi started clapping her hands, so Katya fell in rank with the other attendees. The basics of strip-aerobics were explained, and then they were led into some light stretching. While she reached down and placed her hands on the floor, Katya figured it would be an easy hour. She ran regularly, did yoga, occasionally pilates – how hard could strip-aerobics be? Especially a class that had a seventy year old in attendance? She would use the time to meditate on the ridiculous situation she'd gotten herself into, and the minutes would fly by.

But an hour later, she realized she hadn't needed to distract herself. Strip-aerobics and Candi-with-an-i *kicked her ass*. Katya had new respect for strippers. At first, it had seemed simple, with Candi showing them some basic moves. On all fours, flipping their hair, doing body rolls. Easy stuff. Katya had felt a little silly and awkward, uncomfortable doing those things with a group of strangers.

Then the moves got more difficult. She actually started to work hard, and she forgot about feeling awkward or uncomfortable. She peeled off her sweater at one point and chucked it against a wall, then went back to learning the routine Candi was teaching them. Katya didn't think she'd be getting a gig at a high end strip club any time soon, but she had a lot of fun, and it really was a serious workout. She felt great afterwards, and she had to admit it, she felt kinda sexy. Empowered.

Liam had disappeared during the stretching, and then she'd gotten so engrossed in the class, Katya hadn't paid attention to whether or not he came back. When she went to collect her gear, he wasn't anywhere around.

"Is there a changing room?" she asked, still panting. She'd planned on wearing her workout clothing home, having assumed the class would be easy and tame. Turned out, her sports bra was completely soaked in sweat. She wasn't in as good a shape as she'd thought. She couldn't wait to take a shower and put on some clean clothes.

"Oh, yeah! Two floors down, women on the right. Did you have fun?" Candi asked. She wasn't out of breath at all, and her Playboy-perfect make-up was completely in tact.

"Yeah, it was great. I'm really surprised at how hard it all is!" Katya exclaimed.

"Uh-huh, everyone always is, their first time. I hope you get to come back, I love getting new students," Candi said.

"I'd love to come back, that would be awesome."

"Yay! There's some fliers by the door, grab one. Tell Eden I said bye!"

Katya waved goodbye and made her way to the locker rooms. She wasn't the biggest fan of showering in public places, but she really was gross and sticky with sweat. She decided it was worth it and she shoved all her clothing into a locker before wrapping her gym towel around her body. Thankfully, that locker room had shower stalls, each with individual curtains. Only one other stall was in use, but otherwise, the whole room was empty. She hurried into a stall, then after she shut the curtain behind her, she hung her towel over it and turned on the water.

She stood under the spray forever, letting the hot water soak into muscles that she just knew were going to hurt in the morning. Then when she remembered Liam was probably waiting for her outside, she finally turned the water off. The locker room was eerily quiet, the other user must have left. She wrung out her hair as best she could, then wrapped her towel back around her body. Once she had it secured, she yanked back the curtain and stepped out of the shower.

"Took you long enough."

Katya shrieked, leaping back into the stall. She almost went down, slipping on the wet tiles, and she gripped onto the curtain with one hand while holding up her towel with the other. Liam was directly across from her stall, leaning back against a sink.

"What do you think you're doing!?" she demanded, finally pulling herself upright.

"Waiting for you, like I said I would," he said.

"Yeah, but you can't wait in here! This is the *women's locker room*," she hissed.

"Oh my god, it is!? I can't believe it!"

"Get out. Get out right now, before we get in trouble."

"Angel cake," he chuckled, pushing away from the sink. "We're all alone in here. Who's going to tattletale on me? You?"

"Someone could come in!" Katya insisted.

"Hmmm, good point. Maybe we should hide."

He was crowding in close, forcing her even farther back into the stall. The faucet knobs hit her in the spine and she gasped when he pulled the curtain shut behind them.

"Stop it, I'm not hiding in a shower with you. Just get out, then I can change, and then we can go," she said, pressing a hand against his chest when he took another step forward.

"You were amazing," he said, covering her hand with his own. She blinked up at him.

"Huh?"

"Up there. I came back, and you were so into it. I never imagined you'd be so good at it," he explained, his eyes raking over her semi-naked form.

"Oh. Um. Thank you?" she offered.

"I mean, I've seen you do some pretty hot moves," he said, and she could feel herself blushing yet again. "But now I'm curious as to how hot you can *really* get."

"It was just exercising, Liam. You thought I wouldn't do it, I did, it's done with. Over."

"Oh no. No, I don't think so."

Katya honestly had no intention of ever sleeping with Liam again. It had been a one time adventure. Like strip-aerobics – something new and fun and different, but probably best not to repeat, or something bad might happen. Someone might get injured.

Liam had no such fears, however, and he continued crowding her till her back was pressed up against the tiles. She held still when he bent his head down to kiss her, bit back a moan when his tongue was swirling through her mouth. She felt bad – but only because what they were doing *didn't feel bad at all*. Shouldn't it? She'd been taught all her life that good girls didn't behave like that – but Katya was an exceptionally good girl, and she didn't feel bad at all.

Yet part of her still clung to those societal standards and those gender roles that had been driven into her head. Liam's fingers were at the top of her towel, and as he always did, he hesitated. Waited for some signal of permission. For the first time, she was reluctant to give it to him.

"I feel like ... like this is wrong," she whispered.

"Oh, no," he moaned. "Baby, what about right now could possibly feel wrong?"

He had an excellent point.

"You don't think I'm acting like a slut?"

"Katya, of the two of us, *I'm* the slut. Do you have a problem with me being that way?"

"No."

"Then why the fuck do you have a problem with *you* being that way? You're giving me more respect than you're giving yourself, it's insane. *No,* you're not a slut. You wouldn't know how to be one if you tried. You're just a woman enjoying her body with a man who would also like to enjoy it – and there is *nothing* wrong with that, whatsoever."

Impossible logic to argue with – in fact, she'd been won over by the end of the first sentence. He'd barely finished speaking when she pushed away from the wall, forcing herself into his space. She yanked his head down so they could kiss again and he took that as all the permission he needed.

The towel was jerked away so fast, it left a friction burn in its wake. She hissed into his mouth and began pulling apart his belt. Liam didn't waste a second, he was pulling off his shirt and stepping out of his shoes at the same time. She figured he must've been feeling what she felt – if they didn't hurry, old-Katya would keep opening her mouth, trying to stop them. So when she had his pants pulled away and was working on getting them past his hips, he stopped playing around and picked her up.

"God, we should not be doing this here," she groaned, letting her head fall back as he shoved her into the wall. All his weight came down on her, pinning her into place.

"Please – it's tile, there's running water, we can shower afterwards. Name a better place," he challenged. She started laughing, but then two very long fingers were thrusting in and out of her body, robbing her of words and breath.

"Yes, please, thank you," she murmured into his hair. He had his head bowed forward, his teeth nibbling at the edge of her collar bone.

"So polite. So sweet and innocent and wholesome and so very, very wet, Katya," he whispered. "Slick and smooth and tight. I have been dreaming about this moment, so thank *you*."

Shyness was gone. She was panting and moaning loudly, begging him to fuck her. A gentleman at his core, of course he complied, but when he moved his hand to push his pants further down, he lost his balance. He now had a human weight at his front, and Katya shrieked as they slid to the right. They crashed into the pipes and he grabbed a faucet to keep them from falling. It spun under his hand and water shot out from above them. She couldn't help it, she started laughing.

"What was that you said about being very wet?"

"Just stop - it's only cute when I'm punny."

"Ha ha."

"Time to be quiet now. I'm trying to fuck you and your giggle fits are ruining the mood."

She laughed harder.

He eventually moved them out of the spray, back to their original spot, and was able to plant his feet while she worked her hand between their bodies. They both grabbed his dick at the same and both groaned out loud, their hands slippery and moving over each other while stroking him. She loved the feeling of power that came with holding his length in her hand, but they didn't have that kind of time. He moved in even closer, his chest flush to hers, and she bit into his shoulder as she slid onto his length.

"You're so …" she gasped, holding onto him tightly while he adjusted his stance.

"Amazing? Handsome? Huge? Good at this?"

"All of the above."

She'd always figured sex while standing up would be awkward. Having to find the right angle, the guy having to hold all the weight, yet also thrust, gravity working against them, so many things. She'd never even wanted to try it, it had seemed like a waste of time.

She was glad she'd waited till Liam, because it was perfect for the two of them. She was on the tall side at five-foot-six, but she was very slender. Liam was lanky, as well as built – he was able to hold up her tiny frame, no problem. Strong enough that he could pin her in place, tall enough that he could thrust upwards at a perfect angle, and his dick big enough that he could hit all the right spots.

And even better, in her mind, was the fact that she couldn't really do anything in return. She could only receive. She was being held in place, and she was being *fucked*. It was glorious. The steam was rising around them, sweat was mingling with water, and she wasn't taking in oxygen anymore. Only him.

"*Fuck*," she finally managed words. "Too soon. It's too good."

"No such thing," he was breathing hard as his hips slammed against her, over and over again.

"But I'm gonna come," she warned him. Words that had embarrassed her once upon time, now falling so easily from her lips.

A good against-the-wall fucking will do that to me, I guess.

"*Yes*, please, baby, come again. I want to feel this pussy come again, *need* to feel that on my cock," he begged.

"Oh god. Oh my god. Holy shit. Oh my god."

"Just let go," he whispered. "Just fucking come for me. Come so fucking hard for me."

She hadn't really needed to be told twice, but his dirty talk turned her on so much, she still appreciated it. She also did as instructed, coming so hard she elicited a shout from him. All her muscles clamped down and she shrieked. He yelled again and she vaguely realized she'd startled his own orgasm out of him. She could feel all his muscles tensing up with the effort to hold her in place. She should've been concerned about him dropping her, or them both falling, but she didn't care. She even went limp in his arms, basking in the aftershocks of a humongous orgasm.

She wasn't sure how long they stayed like that, both of them desperately trying to breathe in the steamy air. Eventually, he couldn't take it anymore, and Liam sat in the bottom of the shower, Katya still wrapped round him. After a couple minutes, though, the hot water became too much for her. She kissed her way across his chest as she backed off him.

"That," she sighed, dragging her teeth over his nipple. "Was *amazing.*"

"No," he argued, cupping one of her breasts. "*You're* amazing. Now help me up."

They adjusted the temperature of the water and rinsed off together. Katya started laughing when she realized all of Liam's clothes were in the shower with them – he even still had his pants around his ankles. She continued laughing when he put all the wet clothing back on and walked out of the stall.

They trekked onto the BART together, joking around and teasing each other. They were both standing up near a door, clinging to hanging straps, and when he kissed her, she didn't care that they were in a very public setting. That he was soaking wet and they were making other passengers uncomfortable. She kissed him back just as hard, and they made out the rest of the way home.

111

Only a big shindig at the club had Liam pulling away at her front door. He hugged her goodbye, which oddly felt more intimate than anything they'd shared just an hour before – sex was just sex. A hug, that was kinship. *Friendship*. She squeezed him hard, but wondered what exactly it all meant.

*Wait. I'm dating Wulf. And am apparently friends-with-benefits with Liam. How is **any of this** a good idea!?*

———◆———

"I think something's wrong with me," Katya whispered.

"Huh? Did you say something?" Tori asked, turning away from the pot of boiling water.

Monday was Katya's day off. It wasn't usually Tori's, but when Katya had crawled out of bed around noon, still sore from her strip-aerobics work out – and the workout she got in the shower – the other girl had been puttering around the apartment. She'd come home early to check on her friend, she'd said, but then after seeing her, Tori had decided to stay home.

"This isn't normal," Katya cleared her throat and spoke up.

"What isn't normal?" Tori asked, adding pasta to the water before heading back to the kitchen table.

"This. What I'm doing."

"Which is …"

"Dating one guy while sleeping with another."

"Oh, you're still on about that."

"Because it's not normal!" Katya yelled. "I thought I didn't want to sleep with Liam again, but it just … happened. How is that possible!? Like, it's not like '*oops, I ate this whole bag of chips on my own*' or '*oops, I went the wrong way down a one-way street*', or something. '*Oops, I fell on this dudes dick, over and over, for thirty minutes straight*' – even I know it doesn't work like that!"

"I'm sorry, I honestly don't see what the problem is," Tori said.

"You're complaining about two good looking, nice guys wanting to bang you. *Actually* banging you. Talk about a problem I'd like to have."

"But it's weird for me. It's like when I'm with Wulf, he is literally all I can think about. All I can focus on. Seriously, everything just stops existing – my career, my goals, Liam, everything. But then when I'm with Liam, he's just so fun and nice and sexy. It's like I can't help myself," Katya tried to explain.

"So why bother? I'm being serious. You said you've told both guys about each other, and neither of them flipped out. If anything, Liam encourages your relationship with Wulf. If they're both okay with it, why shouldn't you be? Have fun, be young and reckless. When you get tired of one, drop him and focus on the other," Tori said.

"I guess it just feels wrong. And I had this thought …"

"Oh god. When you think, I get scared."

"I'm worried I'm a bad person, because while I like being with Liam, and sex with him is sort of bizarre and new and different and all that jazz, I worry that I'm using him," Katya said.

"How do you mean?"

"Well … okay, for instance. That date I just had with Wulf? I was nervous and freaked out. But then I was like wait a minute, I did the whole sex-kitten routine on Liam, and it worked, so why not try it on Wulf? And after our hot shower sex escapade, after I got home, I kept thinking … wow, I have to try some of those strip-aerobics moves on Wulf. I have to have sex in the shower *with Wulf*. It's like Liam is my practice dummy – Wulf is the real deal. That's so fucked up!" Katya finished explaining.

"Okay, so normally, I'd agree with you, except one little thing – Liam knows all this. You guys talked about it the other night when he was here, about him being like your Jedi master and how the other guy should be thanking him for making you so freaky now. You're not dating Liam – you're dating Wulf. Liam is well aware of all of this," Tori said.

Katya glared at the table while she picked at the label on her beer bottle. It was all true, but that didn't mean Katya felt good about it. She was still hung up on the fact that sleeping with two men at once was … *wrong*. She felt like she was doing something bad. Wrong. Like she was a *slut*.

And why does thinking all those things get me so hot!? I'm broken. Liam cracked me, and Wulf broke me, right down the middle.

"Maybe I'll just go over it with him again, just to be sure," Katya mumbled. Tori groaned.

"Why!? You're just gonna scare him away, Katya. You push people away! Just let him be your friend. Let him sexify you and turn you out, and then use those tricks to catch you a wolf, okay?"

"But I still feel like being with two men at the same time is -"

"Just stop it right now," Tori's voice suddenly got serious, and she was pointing her finger in Katya's face. "When George Clooney or James Franco or whatever famous slutty dude wants to bang however many chicks, no one cares. But you sleep with two guys, who both say it's okay and give you approval to do so, and you still feel guilty. *That's* what's fucked with society. There is nothing wrong with what you're doing. You're not hurting anyone. You're actually making people feel good. Jesus, *you're* finally feeling good. If you honestly feel like it's wrong, then fine, stop. But if you like what's going on, you like sleeping with both of them, then fuck it. Ride this train for as long as you can, cause the only one who is going to stop it, *is you*."

Katya stared at her friend for a couple moments. Tori was rarely ever serious. If anything, Katya was the level-headed "adult" between the two of them. Tori dated lots of men and slept around. Katya had never thought less of her because of it, but for whatever reason, she held herself to a different standard. Why? She shook her head and managed a laugh.

"I don't give you enough credit, I swear. You're beautiful and smart. I should listen to you more often," she sighed.

"Duh. Oh, pasta!" Tori leapt out of her chair and hurried to the stove, stirring at the pot that was threatening to boil over.

"What about the garlic bread?" Katya asked, glancing at the loaf that was sitting on the counter.

"Oh, this fucking oven is broken again!" Tori growled, kicking at the front of the stove.

"Again?"

"Yeah! And I'm positive it's dead – you can't fix it this time."

"I could try -"

"No," Tori interrupted. "It's not your job to fix it. It's the management companies job to fix it, and have they ever? No. It's ridiculous. You're a fucking baker, and you can't bake in your own home."

"I'll talk to Liam."

"Good. Tell him how shitty they are about fixing stuff."

They were silent for a while. Tori puttered around, straining the noodles and leaving the colander in the sink before moving onto the sauce. Katya stared at the broken stove for a while, mourning the scones she'd been planning to make. Then her mind went back to what they'd been talking about and she heaved a big sigh.

"Soooo … if you were me, you'd keep seeing them both?"

"Honey, if I were you, I wouldn't be sitting here right now. I'd be in the middle of a sexy-man-sandwich," Tori snorted.

"Okay, that's definitely not happening for me."

"Hey, don't knock it till you've tried it."

"I like penis, but not that much."

"I think this is good for you. I really, honestly do. I've never seen you so confident, so vibrant, so … happy. These men are good for you, so that tells me that whatever you're doing, it can't be bad."

Tori's voice was soft, but there was weight behind it. She really meant what she was saying, and she wanted her friend to hear it. Katya smiled and got up, walking around the table so she could hug her friend from behind.

"You really are the best," she sighed.

"I know. Now go set the table. After I dish us up, you are going to finally give me all the explicit details on naughty Mr. Sex Club Owner."

9

"... WHAT DO YOU THINK?"

Wulfric Stone cocked his head to the side, eyeing a large piece of artwork. It was by some local artist. Up and coming, supposedly. The simple frame worked well with the minimalist style of the living room, but the artwork itself looked out of place. Heavy slashes of black across stark white. Nothing soft or gentle about it.

Since when do I like soft and gentle? Hmmm ...

"Get rid of it. Something with blues. Blues and yellows. We're showing this house in two days, and I want it to be perfect."

Normally Wulf didn't bother with the staging of homes, he left that to the designers and decorators. This particular house was worth a lot of money, though, and had been on the market for a long time – the owners had only recently switched to Wulf's agency. He wanted the home sold, and he wanted it sold *yesterday*.

Wulf's businesses, combined with the multiple properties he owned throughout California, made more than enough money that if he never wanted to work again, he didn't have to – he'd thought of retiring early plenty of times. But Wulf was a mover by nature. He hated being still. He always had to be in motion. Doing something, going somewhere. Making a deal, swimming a mile, solving a problem.

Swimming had been his passion in school, but then his parents had gotten divorced. It had gotten nasty, and though his mother had managed to hold onto the house, it hadn't necessarily been a good thing. It meant a lot of changes. She'd had to work for the first time in her life – and so had Wulf.

That's why he'd never pursued swimming as a career. Watching his mother struggle had killed something inside him. Had placed a solid, unbreachable wall between him and his father. He'd promised himself he'd never be stupid enough to jeopardize his own well-being, or his financial stability, for another human being. If his mother had been less concerned with "being in love" and more concerned with being able to take care of her family, she wouldn't have found herself in such a mess. What if it hadn't been divorce? What if his father had just died? His mother had never worked before the divorce. Had never even thought to save money for herself, to have an education so she could work, if ever there was a need.

Stupid. So stupid.

That would never happen to him. He'd concentrated on his grades in high school, and swimming had been his escape. His stress reliever. He got a full ride to Princeton because of his abilities in the pool. Graduated with honors because of his abilities in the classroom. As a present, his father had given him his first building – an expensive, historic, apartment building in downtown San Francisco, a property his dad had inherited and cherished.

Wulf immediately sold it. Fuck his father's legacy, he didn't want any ties to the man that weren't necessary. Wulf turned around and invested that money in more buildings, then even more. Thus The Stone Agency was born.

He had a knack for business. Marketing came easy to him, and when he put his mind to it, he could be very charming. He was good at making sales and he fostered great relationships within the realty community. His agency grew, and his reputation even more so.

He was a train of success that couldn't be slowed down. Couldn't be stopped. Couldn't be derailed.

Though if he was completely honest with himself, an intriguing little baker was coming the closest, of anyone or anything, to doing all those things.

He was playing with fire where she was concerned, he knew. Wulf rarely dated, and when he did, it was for one purpose only. Women were just another business deal to him. Sex was a transaction, and sometimes that took work. Katya was just another transaction. Sweet, innocent, former girl-next-door, Katya Tocci.

Only, she'd surprised him. No, not with her boldness – he'd been expecting that, he paid attention. It was the woman herself. She wasn't scared of him. Nervous, maybe, but not intimidated like some women were. She also didn't give two fucks about his money or his reputation. She was more interested in talking about their families, asking after his sisters, curious about his time in school.

It was kind of a novel experience. She was genuinely interested in him. She was nice to him. And sometimes she looked at him with so much fascination and adoration, it stole his breath away. Like he was a present for her.

He'd never felt that way before – like he was a gift to someone. Like a money train, yes. Like he owed something, like he could do something, like he was a trophy, or a prize, sure. He'd grown up with his father treating him like he was an afterthought – then when he'd become a successful adult, as a business partner. His mother loved him, but she was always so concerned with his sisters, so worried about if he was eating right, if he was going to settle down, if she needed to be doing something, saving someone, mothering everybody. His partners, the women he slept with, most of his friends, they were all more interested in what he could for for them. How he could help them.

But to Katya, he was just Wulf. Just a pleasant surprise, in her somewhat dull life.

She had no clue that she was turning out to be exactly the same for him.

Not good. *Not good at all.* He didn't want to look at her with fascination and adoration. He didn't want to think of her as a gift. She was a sexy mystery that he was helping to unravel. Seeing how far she was willing to bend for him, before she broke and realized what an asshole he really was – then life could return to normal.

A sexy mystery, Tocci. That's all you can be to me.

10

KATYA SPENT HER FIRST DAY OFF WITH TORI, AVOIDING BOTH THE NEW MEN in her life. Not that she got a chance to ignore Wulf – he didn't call or text. After she remembered that he didn't have her number, she checked at the bakery to see if he'd called there, and she told them to let him have her number if he asked.

He never did.

Liam texted often. Her lack of responses didn't seem to deter him whatsoever. She got pictures of food, dogs he met on the street, and even a naughty one of a couple at his club. Tori tried to steal the phone so she could send a response, but Katya managed to wrestle it away from her. She needed some downtime. One day without men and without sex wouldn't kill her. She'd gone eight months without it, she could certainly go twenty-four hours.

The next day, she had the apartment to herself. She called her mother and checked in with the family. She was an only child, and though she was now realizing that her parents were prim-and-proper to the extreme. She and her mother were particularly close. After an hour long talk, they made loose plans for her to visit them. Her baking schedule didn't usually allow for a lot of traveling, but she'd purposefully scheduled some vacation time for herself.

She also went back to the strip-aerobics class. She went to an earlier one, it started around eleven o'clock. She had to admit it, she liked Candi-with-an-i. They got along surprisingly well. Not a lot of people showed up, so the two of them chatted for a while, before and after the class. By the time Katya left, she'd made a date with the other woman to go shopping. She felt like Candi would know a thing or two about spicing up a wardrobe.

Katya was feeling so good about herself that when she got a text from Liam during her bus ride home, she decided to get off at the next stop and she caught a bus to his work. He'd sent some rambling message about needing tacos to survive, so she stopped in at the first Mexican restaurant she came across and ordered several different kinds. She was still carrying her gym bag and she lumbered along with that and the tacos for the next several blocks, trying to remember exactly where his club was; her memory of that night was blurry at best. She finally found her way into the alley and the same big bouncer was in front of the same door with the same neon sign. The Garden.

"Hey! Good to see you again!" the bouncer called out jovially. She was surprised at the reaction, since they'd been face to face for maybe five whole seconds.

"Hi, uuhhh …" she struggled to remember his name.

"Jan," he said, and she barely stopped herself from laughing. A mountain of a man, and his name was Jan. "You don't remember, do you?"

Oh god.

"Um, no, I'm sorry. Remember what?" she asked.

"You were pretty lit, little girl. Your taxi took a while to show up that night – you helped me check IDs, showed me what I'm doing wrong with my lemon meringue pies. We danced right over there, you're good at two-stepping," he said, gesturing down the alley. Katya couldn't help it, she had to laugh at herself.

"Well, at least I'm a fun drunk."

"You sure are. And you made boss man smile – a *real* smile – which don't happen too often. You're always welcome here, as far as I'm concerned."

"Thanks, Jan."

"You're welcome."

He held the door open for her, and she surprised him and herself by standing on her toes and kissing his cheek. Then she wondered how she'd find Liam's office – her hands were full and her cellphone was now buried in her gym bag. But the bartender recognized her right away, even gave her a hug, thanking her for the big tip she'd left him.

Please, please, let him be talking about money.

Tim led her downstairs, chattering the whole way down. The upstairs bar opened at noon, but downstairs was still closed. There were people moving around, cleaning and setting up for the coming evening. Tim showed her down the long hallway with all the doors, then gestured to an offshoot, telling her it was the last door.

As Katya walked down the hallway, she became aware of voices and she stopped moving. Liam's, loud and laughing, as usual. Then another voice – someone was in his office with him. A man, by the sounds of it, but speaking so low she couldn't make out the words. Hmmm, she didn't want to interrupt him if he was busy, but she did have her hands full of tacos. Liam lived and breathed for tacos. Figuring he couldn't get mad at free food, she started for the door again, deciding to just drop off the goods and offer to meet up with him later. She knocked on the slightly ajar door.

"Yeah?" Liam called out.

"Hiya, it's me – I brought you lunch, just wanted to drop it off," she called back. There was an odd pause. No one was talking, but it sounded like Liam was trying very hard not to laugh.

"Through there, yeah. It's fine," his voice was low, obviously talking to his guest. Then he cleared his throat. "What are you doing? If you've got food, woman, then by all means, get in here!"

Katya toed open the door and glanced around. Liam was sitting behind a big desk, smiling up at her, his hands linked together behind his head. There were some liquor boxes stacked against one wall, and a life-sized cardboard cut out of a beer wench, but no other human beings.

"Sorry," she mumbled, looking around again. "I thought you had someone in here with you."

"Oh yeah, my business partner."

"I don't want to interrupt anything."

"Trust me, you're not. He's supposed to be a *silent* partner, but he's been busting my balls lately," Liam explained. There was a loud coughing noise from behind a door in the far corner, then a toilet flushed.

"I didn't know you had a partner," she said, finally dropping the bags of food onto his desk top.

"Yeah. When I wanted to buy the club, I didn't really know what I was doing. Never owned a business before, any of that stuff. Didn't know how to get the capital for it. Needed some investors. He backed me on the whole thing, so he gets his name on the license, on the lease," Liam said, leaning forward to grab a card out of a holder. He held it out to her and she turned it over in her hands after she took it.

"Richard Mason?" she said his name out loud.

"Yeah. *Riiiicky*, as he hates to be called," Liam stretched out the name. "He's a good guy, means well. Just gets under my skin."

"Well, I'll leave you two alone so you can commence with the skin irritation," she said, re-shouldering her gym bag and backing up towards the door.

"Wanna meet him? I'm sure he'll be done in a second," Liam offered.

"Like this? No, thank you," she laughed, gesturing to her crazy hair and her gym clothes. "Tell him I said sorry, though, and that I hope he likes tacos."

"I think you look great," Liam said.

"You would, you have horrible taste."

"Roof top tonight?"

"We'll see."

"Okay, meet you there at two."

"I am not going to the roof at two in the morning."

"Good point, it'll probably be closer to three when I get out of here."

"I'm not meeting you up there."

Katya left his bar with every intention of going home and taking shower and going over her budget, then catching a movie with Tori and going to bed early.

She managed everything but the bed part. Of course she found herself on the roof at two-thirty, throwing back beers and laughing at Liam's stupid jokes. He'd made good on his word and a well-worn loveseat had been brought up for them, as well as an old corduroy couch. Katya fell asleep on the couch, and woke up in the middle of Liam attempting to carry her downstairs and almost dropping her as he got off the elevator.

Good times.

The rest of the week was a blur. She made good on her promise to herself to hold off on sex – it was one thing to get adventurous and a little loose with her morals. It was quite another to become a raging sex fiend. She wouldn't allow Liam to come to any more of the strip-aerobics classes, even though he begged.

"What did you do before you met me? Did you have a life?"

"Angel cake, I still have a life. I just worry that you might sponta-neously combust if I told you about it."

Wulf even made an appearance, on Thursday. Right after she'd gotten home from work, she'd been setting up her nail kit in her room when there'd been a knock at her front door. Assuming it was the Chinese food she'd ordered, she'd opened the door with money in her hand. Then she'd gaped as Wulf had stared down at her.

He'd gotten off work a little early, and had decided he wanted to see what she was up to – he hadn't expected her to be in pajamas at only five-thirty at night. She'd pointed out that normal human beings called before just showing up at other peoples' houses. Would he like it if she showed up at his apartment?

"If you took off the pajamas first, yes."

He stuck around, ate Chinese food with her. Scared Tori a little, with his quiet demeanor and very direct stare. Then he'd followed Katya into her room and after watching her do her nails for a while, he'd taken off his jacket and rolled up his sleeves, then told her it had been ages since he'd had a manicure.

It was silly, but while it was happening, Katya could feel something. It was a moment. A memory in the making. Something she would hold onto long after Wulf was gone. Them together in her room, surrounded by her feminine décor, sitting on her bed, both fully clothed. Him watching her carefully while she looked at his hands intently.

*I can **feel** his stare. Like hands on my body. He's touching me.*

While she pushed back cuticles and filed nails, they talked. He asked a lot of questions about her time in school, about learning to bake. He seemed particularly curious as to how she'd known it was her passion. How could she be so sure baking was what she wanted to do for the rest of her life? Didn't she worry the bottom might fall out of the market?

She'd just laughed at him and told him what she'd always told herself – if it's her dream, who cares what else happens? As long as she's healthy, happy, and not hurting anyone, then she would continue to pursue her dream, regardless of whether or not it brought her fame or fortune.

"The bottom can't fall out of a dream, Wulf. There's no market for them. Sorry, but it's one thing even you can't buy and sell – my dream is all my own, purchased, paid for, no returns, exchanges, or refunds."

He never said it, but she got the very distinct feeling that real estate wasn't exactly his dream. She wanted to ask him about his dreams. About swimming. But she didn't want to ruin the evening. He was being so soft and open – she was seeing a side of him that she was positive not many people got to see. She wanted to cherish the moment, show him thanks for it. Show him that he could trust her with moments like that; that he could always feel safe to build memories with her.

That's it – his tough as stone act. It's because he doesn't feel safe letting go, doesn't feel safe just being himself. He's just like me.

The thought made her feel closer to him. Almost uncomfortably so. He clearly enjoyed her company, and was obviously attracted to her – it hadn't been said, but she knew sex was an option any time she felt like throwing her nail stuff out of the way. But he'd never once said anything in regards to how he felt about her as a person. Far as she could tell, he was having fun. She got the impression it was almost like a game to him, the ever popular "*How Uncomfortable Can I Make Katya*" game. It wasn't right, she didn't want to feel close to him if his feelings were that she was only good for a laugh. Good for a lay.

Once again, she fell asleep early. Ridiculous. It was only nine o'clock, and the sexiest man alive was in her bed. But she was Katya Tocci, she specialized in ridiculous. She was vaguely aware of being moved around on her bed, of a sheet being pulled over her body. When he got off the mattress, she woke up all the way, but didn't open her eyes. He hadn't moved away. She could tell he was standing beside her, not moving. Watching her. She held her breath, wondering what he was going to do. What he was thinking.

In the end, he simply grabbed his jacket and left her room, shutting the door sharply behind him.

What's wrong with me? Liam is so sweet to me. Sweet, and caring, and nice. He tried to carry me to bed. He makes me feel good about myself. Yet I'd rather wish for making memories with a man who never smiles and rarely talks, and quite possibly thinks of me as little more than a vacation.

She went to sleep thinking about dreams – lost ones and new ones.

11

B Y THE TIME THE WEEKEND ROLLED AROUND, KATYA WAS MORE CONFUSED than ever. She'd gone back to Liam's club one night – there was a BDSM convention in town, and a group had rented one of the big rooms. He walked her through the set up, even strapped her onto what he called a St. Andrew's Cross. There had been a moment, when he'd reached to loosen her wrist bindings. He'd stared at her for a long time, his fingers hot on her skin. She'd stared right back, wondering what new trick she was going to learn that night. But then he'd let her down, only spanking her playfully on the ass. They spent the rest of the night in his office, laughing at cat videos and eating Chinese food with their fingers.

Later on, she'd had a lunch date with Wulf – her bakery wasn't too far from his office building, and he'd informed her that she'd be meeting him at a food cart between them. It had been windy out and he'd lost his burrito. She'd laughed as it rolled away, but then yelled at him when he simply ate hers. Before she could complain too much, though, he was kissing her. A *real* kiss, so hot, she'd forgotten they were sitting outside. He'd worked one hand into her hair and yanked, holding her head at an angle. He liked to pin her into place, she realized. Position her how he wanted, then would *do* whatever he wanted. *She loved it.* It was him who stopped them, finally dragging his lips from hers when she tried to undo his tie. He'd laughed at her, kissed her once more, then pulled the tie over his head before slipping it around hers. His next kiss was slower, sweeter, and before she could even open her eyes, he was walking away without a second glance.

The rest of the day, she felt like she was glowing. Her co-workers noticed it. Tori noticed it. Hell, she was pretty sure strangers on the street could notice it. And even better, she didn't care. She wasn't embarrassed. If anything, she was wondering why she'd been such a prude for so long. Is this what dating two men at once felt like!? God, why hadn't she been doing it all along? Why wasn't everyone doing it?

And what's going to happen when it ends and you have to make a choice?

A sobering thought, had just before she turned in for the night. Liam had texted her, offering to meet her on the roof. Wulf had messaged her, something vaguely inviting and definitely sexual. She ignored them both and stared at her ceiling, consumed with her new thought.

How is this going to end?

"What's going on with you, angel cake?"

Katya frowned and concentrated harder, sticking the tip of her tongue between her teeth and biting down. She didn't know why that helped, but it did.

"Nothing, I'm getting the hang of it."

"I'm not talking about the game."

They were playing Need for Speed. She liked it well enough, but she preferred playing Call of Duty with him. She was in the mood to shoot things.

"What do you mean?" she asked, focusing on taking a turn and not wiping out.

"You're all quiet. Introverted."

"Uh, that's kind of how I am," she laughed, then let out a shout as she almost lost control of her car.

"No. Not with me, you're not," he pointed out. She finally glanced at him, and it cost her. Her car slammed into a wall, rolled back, then surged forward again when she fumbled with the control.

Game over. Would you like to play again?

"Just been thinking about a lot of stuff lately," she said. It was his turn to laugh.

"Oh sweet jesus, that can't be good. Your brain has a way of ruining every good thing that happens to you," he teased.

"That's not true."

"It's truer than you like to admit. So what have you been thinking about?"

"Ummm …"

Katya chewed on her lip. She'd never felt comfortable with this part of her little situation. Wulf never ever asked about the other man in her life, and Katya never talked about him, but Liam was a curious little bunny. He wanted to know all sorts of things – what she and her "New Guy" talked about, what kind of sex they had, why had they only had it once!? Was New Guy frigid? Bad in bed? Tiny penis?

"Are you thinking about New Guy's tiny penis?"

She picked up a pillow and threw it at him.

"He does not have a tiny penis!" she shouted.

"Whoa, defensive! That small, huh? We talking micro? It's okay, you can tell me," he said. She picked up his dirty laundry from off his floor and began launching things at him.

"If you must know," she was laughing as well, ducking when he started throwing clothing back. "It's amazing. The perfect size, thick in all the right ways, and makes me see god. Happy!?"

"Wow, that is amazing. God, huh? What did you see when I

fucked you?"

"I didn't see anything – I blacked out. What does that say about *you?*"

He tackled her then, diving with all his weight. She grunted as she was crushed into his white leather couch – the same one she'd woken up on after their first night together.

"Alright, that's it! The infidel must be punished," he growled as he began tickling her.

"ACK! Stop! *STOP!* I'm sorry, *I'm sorry,*" she gasped for air, kicking and pushing at him.

He kept it up for another minute, but then they were both laughing too hard to keep fighting. He pressed his face into her chest and she could feel his laugh against her skin. She panted underneath him.

"You have to admit that I made you see *something,*" he finally mumbled. She chuckled.

"What is this, jealousy? C'mon, you're the one always telling me, '*it's not a competition*', remember?" she pointed out.

"Yeah, I know. I'm just curious, I guess. You're so … different. From any other woman I've been with – it's like you unfold for me. I just wonder if he brings that out of you, too," he finally explained.

"Wow, Liam. That's actually kinda sweet."

"Shhhh, don't say it too loud, people might hear you."

They both laughed again, then he propped himself up so he could look down at her. He was still smiling, but his eyes were serious as he looked over her face. She swallowed thickly and stared back at him. Took in his boyish good looks and messy hair.

You should really, really fall for this man.

"Liam," she whispered. He lifted his hand and played with a strand of her hair.

"Hmmm?"

"You created this monster. Before you, I never knew I could even be this girl. Never knew it was something I wanted. And that's amazing, and I'll never be able to thank you for it."

"But …"

Katya shook her head.

"No buts. The things he brings out in me are different. It's like … you make me expand. You open my eyes and widen my boundaries. He makes me contract. My eyes only see him and he's my only boundary. You're both just so … different. Completely different, in what you do for me, and how you make me feel," she tried her best to explain.

"*Hmmm.*"

He wasn't looking her in the eyes. Was just staring down at her shoulder, where he was playing with the hair. She'd worn her hair down – for him, because he'd said he liked it down. She suddenly got very scared that a shift had happened, that she'd said too much. She didn't want to lose him.

"Liam, maybe we shouldn't -" she started to say, but then he dropped down on top of her. So abruptly, she actually shrieked. His mouth hovered barely a millimeter above her own.

"You know what I've been thinking about?" he whispered, so close she could feel the brush of his lips.

"What?" she whispered back, then gasped when he moved again. His nose was against her neck, his lips against her pulse.

"That aerobics class. How good you were. How much better you probably are now," he hissed, then she felt his teeth clamp down on her skin. She arched against him.

"I'm not stripping for you," she said.

"Sounds good. Want me to put on some music?"

"Liam, I just said I wouldn't."

"I heard '*yes, my sweet and gentle lover, I will slowly strip for you and then allow you to fuck any orifice you please*', isn't that weird?"

"There is nothing sweet and gentle about you, and I will not let you fuck any orifice you please."

"But you've already given me access to two very important ones."

Katya took a deep breath.

"I'm not stripping," she said again.

"Ah, you've already weakened on one stance. Let's just cut out the begging and get to the stripping."

He kept kissing her shoulder. Eventually, his lips moved to her chest, which meant her sweater would have to go. But as his fingers curled around the hem, he hesitated. He always hesitated, and in that moment, she thought to herself "*Wulf never hesitates – he sees what he wants and he goes for it. He wants me.*" – fucked up, man. She knew Liam wanted her, she could feel his erection. Knew he cared about her, they were very good friends. But his lips were on her skin and his weight was on her body, and all she could think about was another man.

This isn't right. For the first time ever, this really isn't right.

"I'm sorry," she whispered as his hands moved away from her sweater.

"Never apologize, angel cake. Rain check?" he asked, his breath hot on her shoulder. She struggled to breathe.

"Yeah. Thank you, Liam," she sighed, wrapping her arms around his neck.

"Thank *you.*"

His arms wiggled their way around her waist and finally, he was hugging her back.

"If I ever become a successful stripper," Katya started, desperate to lighten the mood. "I will be sure to let everyone know they have you to thank."

"Damn straight you will. And don't be expecting any tips from me. I only make it rain for strippers I don't know."

"How chivalrous of you."

"I know, right?"

―――――◆―――――

Beyond not feeling right about having sex with him, Katya hadn't wanted to strip for Liam because the thought had made her feel nervous and a little embarrassed. What if she messed up? What if she wasn't as good as he'd remembered?

But the woman he'd described had been sexy and uninhibited, and not scared of anything. Katya *wanted* to be that woman. Liam made her feel like she *could* be that woman. Wulf was going to *experience* that woman.

"I've never been to your apartment."

Wulf didn't believe in setting up dates, that much she'd figured out. He'd called her just as she was getting off work and told her to come to his office. He wanted to take her to dinner, he explained, but a meeting was running late. She could wait for him, he'd probably be done once she got there.

Only, he wasn't – his meeting ran *very* late. After thirty minutes had gone by, he'd texted her. Gave her directions to his private office, where she could wait more comfortably.

It didn't seem to occur to him that maybe she'd rather just go home.

But of course, Katya didn't suggest it, either. He still had that strange hold on her. If Wulf said it, then so shall it be. She walked down several hallways, passed a bunch of cubicles, and was met by the same assistant who'd come into the bakery on that fateful day, already so long ago.

Wherever Wulf was, his assistant was sure to be close behind – Ayumi Nakada moved around him like a shadow, and was barely more visible than one. She was tiny, a hair's width over five foot, and usually very quiet. When she did speak, though, it was in the same tone of voice Wulf used. Brisk, no nonsense, authoritative. She'd always come off a little bitchy to Katya. Cold. Like she thought she was above other people.

Probably comes from years of working with someone like Wulf.

Ayumi showed Katya to a set of huge double doors, opening one for her and gesturing for her to enter. The door was closed behind her, and then she was alone. In Wulf's private domain.

There wasn't anything personal about the office. He had a huge oak desk that sat in front of floor to ceiling windows. A wall to her right held a floating shelf, which was covered in awards and trophies and certificates. His desk top was perfectly clean, everything in order, even the pens and pencils lined up, and for the first time, she wondered if he had a light case of OCD.

When she sat in his chair, she actually shivered. He was such a powerful man, sometimes it was easy to forget it wasn't just for her benefit. He controlled a lot of peoples' lives, in a way. Their fortunes, their futures. All from that chair. She took a deep breath through her nose, could smell his cologne. She rubbed her legs together and sighed, wondering if there was at least a lonely little magazine she could use to distract herself.

While searching his desk, it hit her. The lack of personalization. No photos of his family, which really wasn't too much of a shock. But no photos of him with impressive clients, or business partners. No art work. Everything was very standard, clearly picked based on appearance and not personal preference.

Jesus, what does his home look like?

He'd been to her building three times, and to her apartment twice already. He'd commented on her room, on how *adorable* it was, on how it suited her, which it did. Katya knew she had a very girly style, and she indulged in it often, decorating to suit her own tastes. She had a small office at the bakery, and it reflected her personal style, as well.

He must be such a lonely person.

So when, *two hours later*, she was told she was wanted in his conference room, the first thing she asked him was about his home.

"Of course you've never been to my apartment," he answered her, not looking up as he shoved some papers into a file. "It would be awfully strange if you had – you've never been invited."

Katya snorted and refused to be offended.

"You've never been invited to *my* place, yet you keep turning up there."

"Please. I'm invited anywhere you are."

"Cocky."

"Yes, as well as *not wrong.*"

She looked away from him, glancing around the room, not wanting to admit he was right. There was a massive table, surrounded by twenty-six chairs – she counted them all. Wulf was at the head of the table, his back to more big windows. Katya had sat closer to the door, with about ten seats between them.

"I didn't have to wait two hours, y'know."

"And yet you did."

"I could still leave."

"And yet you won't."

"I want to go to your apartment," she finally stated. He glanced up at her.

"Why is this so important to you all of a sudden?"

Because I want to do a strip tease for you, and I want to sleep with you, and I want it to mean something. I want to be as important to you as you are quickly becoming to me. Because I want to know you. The **real** *you, not the man you give to everyone else. I want to make you feel special.*

"I don't know," she lied instead. "We always meet somewhere, always your choosing, usually close to your work. Maybe I'd like a choice."

He laughed then.

"That you think you get a choice is funny."

"It won't be so funny when I make a choice you don't like," she warned him.

"Oh my. Tocci has grown some balls since I last saw her," he teased.

"You have to give me something, Wulf. I haven't asked for anything. If anything, I've been very compliant. I want to see where you live," she said. He stared at her for a long time, then sat back in his chair.

"And if I say no?"

She shrugged, feigning nonchalance.

"Then maybe I'll start saying no more often, too."

He quirked up an eyebrow at her bravery, but then let out a deep sigh.

"I'm a very busy man, Tocci. I'm not keeping you from my place, or anything. It's just all the way across town – I don't have time to pick you up, drive there, fuck you, take you back home, and come back to work all on my lunch break."

She had to laugh, and was glad when he smiled again.

"Okay, I get that, but someday. *Soon.* I want to see this mysterious lair of yours."

"Alright. Someday, in the near future, I will take you to my apartment."

Something else occurred to her.

"What about your days off?"

"Excuse me?"

"We could go on your days off," she suggested.

"I don't have '*days off*' – I'm either here, or I'm at a viewing, or I'm making a deal, or I'm dealing with a problem," he said.

"Jesus, your life sucks," she blurted out.

"Yes, my life sucks – I live in a multi-million dollar penthouse, own more real estate than you can imagine, and I have a very sexy woman as my own personal fuck toy. Life is awful."

"That poor, poor woman."

"I'm talking about *you*."

"What about after work? You usually leave around six, right? We could go there, I could cook you dinner – I can do more than just bake," she offered.

"I'm sure you can, but once I'm there, I don't want to make the trip all the way back down town to take you home," he explained.

"Wulf, if I come to your house for dinner, it's almost a sure bet you're going to get lucky. You could take me in the morning on your way to work," she told him.

"I know I'd get lucky, but *you* won't be staying the night."

"I won't?"

"No. I don't let women spend the night with me."

"Ever?"

"Not in my own place."

"I thought I had a lot of rules for myself," she mumbled. They were so much alike sometimes, it was almost unnerving.

I should introduce him to Liam. Would that be weird? I think Liam would be good for him.

"How many women have you taken to your apartment?" she asked.

"This specific apartment?"

"Jesus, you real estate moguls and your multiple properties. In all your sexually active years, how many women have you actually slept next to? Like all night?" she was curious.

"I don't know, a handful, maybe – if you hadn't fallen asleep the other night, I would've woken up with you the next morning."

She was suddenly cursing herself for not forcing a pot of coffee down her throat when he'd shown up.

"You're very annoying," she groaned, rubbing at her forehead. "In all your sexually active years, how many women have you invited to your residences, and then allowed them to spend the night?"

He stared at her for a long, long time.

"One."

Katya was a little shocked. She'd spent many a night at her ex-boyfriend's place, as well as the boyfriend before him. Hell, she'd spent the night twice at Liam's already. What had happened to Wulf in his life that he didn't want to let anyone inside? And more importantly for her, was he a lost cause? If he was always going to keep her at arm's length, she'd rather know now, so she could protect her heart from him. Or protect what little he hadn't already stolen.

Just one. I wonder who she was – must have been someone pretty important to him.

"One," she sighed. "You underestimate the power of a good cuddle session."

"I'm sure, but I've survived pretty well so far without them."

"Okay, okay. We don't have to go to your apartment, on one condition."

"What?"

"You can't come to mine anymore."

"Good luck with that."

"I'm serious. You don't get to see mine until you show me yours," she told him.

"I've already seen all you've got to show."

She sucked air through her teeth, but refused to be rattled.

"Wulf, you haven't even begun to see all I have to show."

Such complete and utter bullshit, but she held his stare and refused to back down. He was very good at making correct assumptions about her, but just maybe she could bluff her way through some things.

"Holding out on me, Tocci," he finally said in a low voice. "Very naughty. I think a punishment is in order."

"I'm trembling in fear."

"You will be. Get on the table."

"Why do you -"

"*I didn't ask a question.*"

Just like every time he said a command, her body automatically heeded it. No conversation with her brain or heart whatsoever. It was like she was standing outside herself, watching as the cute auburn haired girl stood up and moved to kneel on the edge of the table.

"Good enough?" she breathed.

"Stand up."

She did so.

"Anything else?"

"I was hoping for a show, since you were bragging about having so much to see."

Katya wondered what the hell she was doing. What the hell he was thinking. If the fucking door was locked. She wasn't sure what it was he was asking for. A show? Did she know any magic tricks? Was she supposed to get naked and just lay down?

Get naked …

Liam's words from the other day started whispering around in her brain. About how sexy and confident she'd been at her aerobics class. He'd gotten hard just describing it to her. What would happen to Wulf if he saw it in action?

*You can **do** this. You've **done** this. Be **that** woman.*

There was no music, but Katya started rolling her shoulders to an imaginary beat. Moving her hips from side to side. Wulf looked a little intrigued, but not half as much as when she kicked off her shoes. He stared at her fingers as she slowly pulled her dangly necklace off from around her neck.

She sank to her knees at the same time as she peeled her shirt off. She dropped it off the edge of the table while she crawled forward. Then she rolled onto her back, looking at him from upside down while she arched her back. She was wearing all black that day, even down to her underwear, and his eyes lingered on the cups of her bra.

After fanning her legs in the air, she spun back around, always moving slightly closer to him. She moved her hands over her body as she walked down the table. When she was only about five feet away, she finally stopped and did a straight-legged bend, forcing her ass up and high, all while she slid her leggings off. With a flick of her foot, she kicked them into his face.

By the time he'd thrown the fabric into a corner, she was on all fours, crawling towards him again. He'd looked aloof for the most part of her dance, but now that she was closer to him, she could see the hunger in his eyes. Like he wanted to take a bite out of her. She stretched out flat on the table, kicking her feet up behind her and making sure her butt was popped up. Then while still staring at him, she reached out and grabbed his tie, gently yanking on it. He rolled forward in his chair till he was against the edge of the table.

"Not what I was expecting, Tocci. I'm impressed," he said to her, his voice low. She smoothed her hand down his tie. Over his chest. Across his stomach. Clear to the bulge in his pants, which she cupped in her hand before stroking up and down.

"I'm flattered. I get the feeling there isn't much you've seen that impresses you," she said. His hand went down over hers, pressing down harder, showing her how fast to stroke.

"Katya," he whispered, and she shivered. He so rarely said her first name. "I've never seen *anything* like you."

Words like that, and Wulf didn't need to make any deals. She never had to see his apartment. He'd barely finished talking, and she was all over him. His assistant was somewhere in the building, Katya was positive the conference room door wasn't locked, and she didn't care at all. Not even one little bit.

She dropped into his lap with such force that his chair rolled backwards, almost threatening to tip over. She was able to kiss him once, but then his hands were in her hair, yanking her away.

"Ah, but this is supposed to be a punishment, remember? Who said you could kiss me?" he said, and she felt him nipping at the side of her neck.

"Wulf, please, I don't want to – *AH!*" she ended in a shriek when he bit so hard, she wondered if he broke skin.

"Dissension. Tsk tsk, Ms. Tocci. You're on a roll tonight. *Get off me.*"

She wasn't given a chance to comply. He pulled harder on her hair, and she was forced to follow his hand. She slid off his lap and managed to get her feet under her, still following him as he stood up.

Katya was dragged across the room and pressed up against the window. She gulped at the feeling of cold glass on her hot skin, then moaned when she felt his lips on the back of her neck. She wasn't sure what had gotten into him – their last time together, he hadn't been so aggressive. Maybe she was seeing a new side to him. Or the real him.

Very pleased to meet you, Mr. Stone.

"Please," she said again, pushing her hips away from the window and rubbing her ass against his crotch. "Please, I need you."

"Hmmm, that's nice, but I don't think that's what you mean," he whispered. As he kissed his way down her spine, his hand slowly slid out of her hair and crept over the back of her neck.

"Please, Wulf."

"*'Please, Wulf'*. She begs so sweetly, yet still can't get what she wants."

His free hand was at her hip, yanking and pulling at her underwear. Shoving them down, letting them fall to her ankles. Leaving her in only her bra.

"*Please.*"

She could feel his suit against her bare skin as he stood upright, and his hand slid around her neck, gently wrapping around her throat. She gasped as she was pulled back, her spine forced to arch as her head was drawn into his shoulder. She planted her palms against the window and started panting when his free hand moved across her stomach.

"Please *what?*"

"Wulf, I want ..."

The hand on her throat squeezed tighter, the hand on her stomach moved lower, but neither pushed her over the edge she was so desperately seeking. She stood on the balls of her feet, almost crying from the tension running through her body.

"If you can't even say what you fucking want," he growled, his breath hot against her face. "I don't know why I should bother giving it to you."

"Please, I want you to fuck me," she whispered. The chuckle she heard sounded more like a growl, and she moaned when she felt his tongue against her ear.

"What was that? I couldn't quite hear you," he hissed.

"Just fuck me," she hissed right back.

"*Just* fuck you? That's it? My, your demands are so very simple."

Alright, Wulfric. You win.

"Please, Wulf," she purred, placing one of her hands over his own and moving it down between her legs. "Fuck me right now. Right here. Against this window. Fuck me so hard, people down on the street will hear me screaming your name."

She'd never spoken like that before, to anyone. She briefly wondered if it was too much. If she sounded ridiculous. But then he was slamming his dick into her, and she realized it wasn't too much at all.

Jesus, I should've been talking like this years ago.

"I thought that was going to take you all fucking night," he groaned as he bucked his hips against her. Slow and gentle certainly wasn't on the menu that night – he just instantly started fucking her like it was his job. She couldn't even respond. Could barely breathe. He was pounding the air from her lungs, and the hand on her throat was ensuring she couldn't suck any of it back in.

"See what happens when you do as I ask? You get rewarded," he panted, finally moving his hands. She sucked in air greedily and managed to nod.

"Yes. Yes, thank you. God, thank you so much," she moaned. He gripped her hips and yanked them further away from the glass, forcing her to bend at almost a right angle. The new position enabled him to fuck her even harder, something she hadn't thought was possible. She shrieked with every thrust, her hands beating against the window.

"So polite. So sweet. Katya Tocci, best fucking dessert I've ever had."

She shrieked again as she was whirled around. She thought she was going to fall over, the position she was in wasn't favorable when competing against gravity, but she didn't have to worry. Wulf always had a plan. She was slammed down against the conference table top. She pressed her cheek to the hard wood and let out a long groan when his hips started slamming against her again.

"The best. God, you're the best," she was whispering. Babbling, unsure even of what exactly she was saying. She had her arms stretched out to the sides, gripping the edges of the table, but he roughly grabbed her right arm and yanked it back.

"Touch yourself," he commanded, lifting her hips enough so she could work her hand between them and the table.

"*Oh my god.*"

One press of her fingertips, and she shot off like a starter pistol. Screamed as an orgasm rocked every single nerve ending. She went to pull her hand away so she could bathe in the sensations, but Wulf's hand flattened over her own, his fingers working above hers. She whimpered and cried out as wave after wave of pleasure coursed through her. Became too much for her. Overwhelmed her. Yet still, he forced more, his fingers pressing even harder. It wasn't until she was lifting her feet off the ground, her free hand pounding on the table top, begging him for mercy, begging him to stop, that he let her go.

And immediately, she missed his touch.

Before she could plead with him to start all over again, though, he had his own orgasm. He came with a shout, dragging his nails down her back before grabbing onto her hips. Digging his fingers into her flesh. While he throbbed inside of her, bruises throbbed on the outside of her, and every nerve ending throbbed within her.

"Holy shit, Tocci," he panted, and she felt him lean forward. Felt his forehead against her back.

"You … you were … that was incredible," she whispered, still finding it hard to breathe.

"I know."

"Jesus, it was like you were angry at me."

"I was. You should've given me that show a week ago, how dare you keep something so wonderfully inappropriate from me."

She managed a laugh.

"Duly noted. Next time I learn a new trick, I'll share it with you immediately."

"You had better," he growled, and she yelped when she felt his teeth against her skin.

"You're going to leave marks," she commented, raising a hand to rub at the bite on her neck.

"Good. Every time you see one, you'll think of where it came from. Who gave it to you."

Before she could respond to such a bold statement, he moved away from her and yanked her upright. She stumbled a little and he laughed, then helped her wiggle her panties back into place. He put his own pants back to rights while she struggled with her leggings, but before she could put on her shirt, he was kissing her again. She coiled her arms around his neck and sighed.

"I thought we were having dinner," she snickered as they stumbled around the room.

"We were, but then someone decided to do a strip tease on my conference table. Do you know how hard it's going to be to have meetings in here now?"

"Good, you deserve it. Jesus, that was amazing," she moaned, rolling her head on her shoulders. "What got into you? You were so wild."

"*You,*" he whispered, bending his head down to kiss the hollow of her throat. "You sit there, so pretty. So perfect. So completely unaware of how fucking sexy you are. Sometimes … I can't help myself when I'm around you. I have to *make* you aware."

She made him lose control. Never in a million years would she have thought she could have that effect on a man, let alone one as amazing as Wulfric Stone. Katya groaned and lifted her leg to his hip, trying to get closer to him. Wanting to feel all of him, all over again.

"You can do that *any time*," she whispered.

"I know – I wasn't asking permission," he whispered back, and then his hands went down the back of her leggings.

Who needs to eat when I can just feed off his passion? Food is overrated, anyway.

12

LIAM WAS IN TROUBLE.

Smiling and selling himself came second nature to him, it's part of what made him such an effective business owner. He could smile in someone's face and make them laugh, even as he fired them. He could sell a woman in white gloves a ketchup popsicle. He could certainly sell himself to Katya as a charming, happy-go-lucky, only interested in sex kinda dude.

Because that's what he was, usually. He'd seen her profile, learned about her, and wanted to push her buttons. Tease his prim-and-proper next door neighbor. He'd never expected her to explode out of her shell the way she had – he was still blown away by their first night together.

But he hadn't expected her to be so endearing. Sassy. She was funny, and watching her discover herself, seeing her test her own boundaries, was special to him. She was a very willing student, and Liam was an excellent tutor, so they fit well together in bed. They fit even better outside of bed.

That was the problem, right there. Every time she smiled at him, teased him, complained about him, he liked her even more. Less and less of his time was being spent thinking about what new and nasty thing he could get her to do, and more was being put towards figuring out how to just spend time with her. How to get her to look at him the way he looked at her.

Stupid fucking *New Guy. Fuck him.* And fuck Liam for taking it so far. It was all his fault, he was very aware of that – everything. He should've fucked her, then just let it go. Goal attained, mission accomplished. It had all been for a laugh.

Now, he was in too deep to pull away from her. He spent almost more time at her building than he did his own. He was addicted to pushing her buttons, to seeing her reactions, to hearing her laughter. They hadn't slept together in a while, she'd backed away from that aspect of their relationship, and he didn't even care.

"I am so fucked," he whispered, dropping his head to his desk.

*This is gonna be bad. This is gonna be so bad. How do I tell her everything? It won't end well. Correction, it **will** end. Completely. She'll never speak to me again. And I don't know if I can handle that.*

Katya spent most of her time in a lust induced haze, anymore. She managed to turn everything off for work, that was the only time she could concentrate. She would *not* put her job in jeopardy for those boys. But from the moment she woke up till she got in the door of the bakery, and the second she left the bakery till she went to bed, she was thinking about them. Answering texts from Liam, making plans to meet on the roof and have pizza. Talking to Wulf, meeting him for stolen kisses in alleyways between their work places.

It was overwhelming in the best way possible, but still – despite all that and her case load from work, she was finally able to pull her head out of her ass long enough to realize something.

"Holy shit, you lost your job, didn't you?"

She and her roommate stared at each other. Katya had gone home for lunch, something she rarely did. Tori had left the house at the same time as her, around eight in the morning, yet there the other woman was, sitting at the kitchen table, wearing shorts and a hoodie. It was like tumblers fell into a lock in her brain, opening Katya's eyes. Tori had been home a lot, always showing up at lunch time, staying home when Katya stayed home. *Always around.*

"I'm … I'm sorry," Tori whispered, then burst out crying.

I'm an awful friend.

Katya dropped the bags she'd been carrying and she hurried to her friend. Tori had been there long before boys had ever been a thing to Katya – they'd met their sophomore year in high school, had been inseparable ever since, much to Katya's mother's chagrin. Tori was a "bad influence". Oh, if Mrs. Tocci only knew how much.

They sniffled and cried, then Katya bundled Tori up in a blanket. While her friend tried to get control of herself, Katya made soup and got down the special reserves. *Vodka.*

"Why didn't you say anything?" Katya asked. She'd called in at work, letting them know she wouldn't be back, then she'd changed into her yoga pants and a hoodie of her own. She sat next to Tori, her legs propped up on a chair across the way. Tori's feet were in her lap and Katya was absentmindedly massaging them.

"I didn't want you to be mad," Tori sighed, slurping at her soup. "It happened a couple days before we made that dating profile for you. I was freaking out, I didn't want you to think I couldn't pay rent."

"How could you think I'd be mad? I mean, yeah, if you can't pay rent, we'll need to figure something out, but that's it. I'm not gonna kick you out," Katya told her.

"I know, I know. I'm awful. I just felt so … stupid. Here you are, with this amazing career that just sky rocketed. And I'm some paper jockey in a stupid marketing agency. Then you met those guys, and you were so happy. Like for the first time ever, for reals happy with yourself, and I didn't want to ruin it, or distract you. I figured for once, we could overlook my issues and concentrate on yours."

It was a sweet sentiment. Tori had always been a wild child, they'd spent many a night cursing her ex-boyfriends, of which there were many. Katya'd had to bail her out of jail once, when she'd keyed one of the unfortunate dudes' car. She'd bounced from job to job, but she'd been at the ad agency for over six months. Katya had thought something had finally stuck.

"Hey, you know what would make me feel better?" Tori sniffled.

"What?"

"One of your coffee cakes."

"Can't," Katya sighed. "Oven is still broken."

"Still!? Did you send an e-mail?"

"Several."

"And Liam?"

"He said he'd talk to the management company, but he's busy with his club, I don't want to bug him."

"This is stupid. No job, no boyfriend, and now no cake. My life sucks," Tori grumbled, burying her face in her arms. Katya heaved a sigh.

"How about we make a pact now, that no matter what is going on in whose life, we always take time to help each other?" she suggested.

"Sounds good."

"And my career isn't that amazing. I'm lucky, and I work really, really hard. Sometimes … sometimes I honestly wonder if it's worth the stress I put myself under. Sometimes, Tori, I wish I was more like you," Katya was completely honest. Her roommate looked shocked.

"Seriously!?"

"Yeah. You never care what people think, you do whatever you want. I've never gotten to be that free."

"Maybe I need to be less free …"

"Maybe I need to be less closed off …"

They were both silent for a while, deep in their own thoughts. Then Tori took a deep breath and pulled the vodka bottle closer.

"Alright then. Let's get royally fucked up – it's the only thing that can save today."

A couple hours and most of the bottle later, Tori made good on her word. Both of them were proper drunk. They'd moved to sit on the floor in the living room, sharing a bag of popcorn. Tori had just gotten done telling a story about the time she'd tried to date a guy who was heavily into the world of BDSM. She hadn't been able to get into it, the whole sexual lifestyle thing, though she'd appreciated his very thorough approach to sex.

"Liam put me on one of those cross thingies," Katya said, then hiccuped.

"*No fucking way!* You had sex on a St. Andrew's Cross!?" Tori gasped.

"No. I'm like you, I'm not really into all that, I think. But at his club," *hiccup*, "there was some sort of convention. He showed me some stuff, some things. Strapped me in," *hiccup*, "and I almost thought it was going to happen, but then we had Chinese food instead." *Hiccup.*

"That man is a waste on you, I swear. When you're done playing with him, send him my way," Tori groaned. Katya frowned and poured herself another shot.

"Wouldn't that be kind of weird? Hey, my roommate's dating this dude I used to fuck," she pointed out. *Fuck.* A word that used to make her feel guilty. Now it spilled out of her mind and out of her mouth with ease.

Times, they are a changin'.

"Who said I wanted to date him?"

"I just assumed …"

"*You're* not dating him, yet you two fuck."

Katya waited for the blush to take over her face, but it never came. She smiled. She was finally becoming desensitized.

"Very true. Still. Kinda weird."

"Whatever. Describe his dick to me, so I have something to look forward to."

Okay, not that desensitized. She coughed on her shot of vodka, dribbling it everywhere.

"I'm not describing his dick to you, sorry. If he wants to show it to you, trust me, he will," Katya assured her.

"You're so lame. Then what about the other dude? You've told me everything about sex club man, but you never talk about the lone wolf man," Tori said. Katya frowned deeper and poured yet another shot, cleaning out the last of the vodka.

"It's ... different," was all she managed to say.

"How so?"

It's special.

She felt awful thinking it – her time with Liam was special, too. Liam was *very* special. But her moments with Wulf were something else. If Liam was discovering a new side to Katya, then she was getting to discover the new pieces of Wulf. The ones he normally kept hidden away from the world. It was beyond special to her. She didn't want to share it with anyone. She wanted those moments, those memories, to only belong to the two of them.

I want to be special to him, too.

"It just is, I don't really want to talk about it," she finally answered.

"Oh my god, Katya, you *loooooove* him," Tori sang at her.

"I do not. I've only been seeing him for a few weeks."

"So? Your vagina is certainly in love with him."

"My vagina and my heart are two very different things. One is a lot smarter than the other."

"Hmmm, I'm still putting my money on your vagina."

Katya took the last shot, then stood up while Tori searched for her phone. The other girl was demanding pizza, struggling to call Dominos. While she did that, Katya stumbled back to her bedroom, looking for her own phone. When she picked it up, she glared down at the screen. A wedding cake she'd done for the mayor's daughter stared back at her. Katya had been proud of the cake – was still proud of it. And yet ... was that really her biggest joy in her life? Her job?

She looked around her room. It was simple enough. Big by San Francisco standards, but much smaller than the one she'd had while growing up. It was a narrow room, so she'd had a lot of space at the foot of the bed, and she'd put in a nice drafting table. She used it to sketch ideas for future desserts, things she wanted to try, stuff she wanted to show to clients. Underneath it were random cooking accessories, promotional items from the bakery, stuff she kept meaning to try and use. A dresser sat on the opposite wall, and on top of it were rows and stacks of cook books.

Is my whole life about my work? When did that happen?

Before she knew what she was doing, Katya thumbed open her phone and pressed a button. It rang and rang, then went to voicemail. She frowned and called again. Kept calling, back to back, for two minutes straight.

"Goddamn, Tocci, you better be fucking dying," Wulf's voice growled down the line. "I was in a meeting."

"I'm very drunk," she slurred, kneeling on her mattress.

"What?"

"Tori lost her job, we got drunk," she explained.

"You're drunk."

"Sooooo drunk."

"And you called me."

"Sooooo called you."

She expected him to get mad. To snap at her. Call her silly or stupid, then hang up on her. But he didn't. He was silent for a moment, then his warm chuckle filled her ear, and all was right in her world. She slowly laid down, stretching out below the pillows.

"This is very cute, and I'll admit, I'm curious to see just how wild you're willing to get while in this condition, but I'm a very busy man."

Yet he wasn't hanging up on her, so she took that as encouragement.

"You're always busy. I'm always busy. Let's be busy *together*," she suggested.

"Hmmm, what did you have in mind?"

"Come over and I'll show you."

"Tempting, Tocci, but I'm trying to close on a fifteen million dollar property."

"Is fifteen million dollars worth more to you than pussy?"

She slapped a hand over her own mouth. Had she really just said that!? She'd never in her life said anything like that to a man. To *anyone*. She'd completely shocked herself and she glanced out her open bedroom door, wondering if Tori had heard her.

"My, my, you do get wild. You've managed to impress me once again, Katya."

There it was, her name. Her first name. She stretched her body again, moaning into the phone. His voice was wrapping around her like a blanket, making her hot and uncomfortable. She pulled at her shirt, yanking it so it was bunched up underneath her breasts.

"Come over," she whispered.

"I would love to, and I'm sure I will later, but I can't."

"I'm gonna be gone soon," she blurted out.

"What?"

"Gone. I'm going," she tried again, her tongue thick in her mouth.

"Where the fuck do you think you're going?"

She had to laugh at the anger in his voice. Her interrupting his mutli-million dollar meeting was fine. Her leaving town without telling him first? Bad news bears, young lady. No one leaves without the wolf's express permission.

"I'm going home," she sighed, smoothing her free hand down her leg. "For a week."

"Like you're going to be sleeping there, spending every night there?"

"Yes, Wulf. What do you think I mean when I say I'm going home?"

"Jesus, it's only two hours away. You could come back, you know."

"Says the man who won't drive across traffic to let me see his apartment."

She wanted to sound angry and vengeful, but she was pretty sure the slurring and hiccuping ruined it.

"That's completely different – that doesn't get in the way of me fucking you."

"Sorry. I want to see my mommy," she spoke in a sing song voice. "Want to see my home. My dad is out of town, she's lonely. We're gonna bake cookies."

"Cookies, huh," he grunted out.

"It's just a week, Wulf."

"A week, huh."

She finally laughed at him.

"I leave on Sunday. That gives you tonight and tomorrow to fuck me," she assured him.

"Hmmm. I'll be in touch, Tocci."

Then the line went dead, and she was laughing again. Her head was spinning and her heart was pounding. She stayed that way till she fell asleep, chuckling to herself while she was stretched out on the mattress. When she woke up sometime later in the middle of the night, she immediately remembered the phone call and started smiling again. She picked up her phone and turned it on.

Several missed messages from Liam.

Only one from Wulf.

Liam's never got opened, but she stared at the one line text from the other man.

Behave yourself tonight – I'll see you soon.

"You're ignoring me."

She could hear the smile in Liam's voice, so she didn't worry too much that he was really offended. She squished her phone between her ear and her shoulder while she tore around her apartment.

"I'm not, I swear," she lied, jamming clothing into her bag.

She'd spent most of Sunday hungover on the couch with Tori, caught between being embarrassed at her sassy phone call to Wulf, all but begging him to come fuck her, and angry that he hadn't taken her up on it. Not only hadn't taken her up on it, but hadn't even bothered to call her the day after. She'd stewed about it so much, she'd thrown herself into a design for a client, trying to forget. She'd fallen asleep at her table. She woke up at seven in the morning with an awful crick in her neck, and the realization that she hadn't packed for her trip. Hadn't reserved a car, hadn't done anything.

Nope, just pined away over a stupid, arrogant, antagonistic, son of -

"You're literally ignoring me right now," Liam brought her back to reality.

"I'm sorry, I'm just kinda running late. I was supposed to leave for my mom's at eight, but I woke up late, and just got out of the shower, so I'm running around, trying to grab everything," she explained. Not a total lie.

"Oh, I forgot about that trip. A week, right?"

"Just five days, then you can start raiding my fridge again."

"Who said I'm going to stop? Tori's gonna be home, right?"

"Actually, I was meaning to ask you about that," Katya started speaking in a hushed tone. She stepped into the bathroom, then leaned out and peeked down the hall, making sure her roommate wasn't close by.

"Ooohhh, we're whispering now, must be something good. Yes, I will fuck your roomie, thank you for the invitation."

"No. She needs a job."

"And what do you want me to do about that?"

"Well, she has a background in food service. I figure you know people in the bar industry. You know her, too. Maybe you could put in a good word with some bars and restaurant people you know?" Katya asked, chewing at her bottom lip.

"Hmmm, I could do that ..."

She groaned. She hated when his voice trailed off. It usually didn't bode well for her.

"Oh god, you're not gonna turn this into extortion, are you? I'm not fucking you just to get her a job," Katya stated.

She hadn't slept with Liam since that time at the gym. It didn't feel right, not after the moments she'd had with Wulf. She didn't know what was going on, really, she was just going with the flow. Her heart was pointing at one man. Quite possibly the wrong man, but that's just the way her particular cookie crumbled. She didn't want to lead Liam on, and something in his smile, in the way he looked at her, made her think maybe she was, just a little.

"Please, I could get sex either way, I don't have to extort anyone. What I meant was, I could talk to some other bars, *or* she could work here," he offered.

"There? At your sex club?"

"Well, upstairs – people have to work their way up to coming downstairs. But I need a bar back and a waitress. If she can do both those things, she's hired."

"She can. I'll tell her to stop down there?"

"Yeah, I'll be there today, after two. Tell her to ask for me."

"You're the best, Liam Edenhasslehoff."

"*Edenhoff*. Jesus, how can you not have it down yet? We've seen each other almost every day for the past three weeks."

"Has it really been three weeks!?"

"Glad to know it's been magical and special for you, too. You're awful, you know that?"

Katya rolled her eyes and finally opened the medicine cabinet. She put her bag on the sink and began shoveling supplies into it, watching as toothpaste, lotion, birth control, Tylenol, and Q-tips fell into her luggage. She closed the cabinet and shoved her toothbrush in her mouth.

"Yes, and it's about time you caught onto it, too. I have to go, Liam. I'm already almost an hour late, she probably thinks I'm dead," she mumbled around the brush between her teeth. She stepped into her ballet flats, wiggling her feet around while she combed her fingers through her wet hair.

"A bad friend *and* a bad daughter. You are racking up some seriously bad karma."

"Tell me about it. Tacos when I get back?" she asked, scrubbing the dry toothbrush around her teeth, hoping to get off at least some of the hangover film.

"You know it. Five days, right?"

"Correct," she said, hoisting her bag up with one hand and opening the door with the other.

"A whole five days. How are you going to survive without me for that long of a time?"

"I'm sure I'll find a way -"

Katya stopped talking when she went to step through the door and found herself blocked in. Her jaw fell open, dropping her toothbrush to the floor. Not exactly classy, but she couldn't help it. She was shocked.

Wulf was standing outside her door.

"What? You cut out, are you still there?" Liam's voice sounded tinny and far away. She couldn't answer, could only stare up at the man in front of her.

"Time to get off the phone, Tocci," he said in a simple voice.

"I have to go now," she mumbled into the phone, reaching up to grab it.

"Okay, text me when you get there, alright?"

"Sure."

She hung up, then went back to staring at Wulf. What in the hell was he doing there?

"You look surprised."

159

She finally got control of her faculties and managed to nod.

"I am. What are you doing here?" she asked.

"More importantly, what are you wearing?" he asked his own question, his eyes traveling over her body.

She'd gone on her shopping adventure with Candi-with-an-i – it had been an interesting experience. Katya had refused to buy anything leather, despite the other girl's insistence. Debates were had, but in the end, she'd come home with a wardrobe dramatically less … pastel, than her normal one. Small for a normal girl, but a big deal for Katya.

She was wearing a pair of very short jean cut offs – she'd remembered Wulf's comment about her having great legs, and Liam usually paid special attention to them, so she had decided it was time to start showing them off more. Her tank top was loose and flowy, cut low on the neckline, but if she raised her arms, she'd also be showing off a large slice of her stomach. If she turned around, Wulf would see that the shirt didn't really have a back, but was just straps of fabric criss-crossing.

Typical for probably any other twenty-three year old, but very different from anything Wulf had seen her wear. She usually dressed on par with him, professional at all times. That morning was no different for him – he wasn't wearing a suit, but he was in a dress shirt, a casual blazer, and jeans. All of it well tailored and expensive looking.

"What are we doing right now?" she suddenly blurted out, as if she was just coming to. They'd been standing in her doorway just staring at each other. "I have to go."

"I know."

"Then what are you doing here?" she asked, bending down to grab her toothbrush off the floor. She tossed it over her shoulder and finally moved into the hallway, pushing past him and closing her door.

"I came to see you," he said. She snorted and turned to lock up.

"I told you I was leaving. You missed your chance. I'm running late, I have to call my mom, go get a car, so many things," she said, then she shivered as she felt his fingers on her spine, tracing down her back. She was only wearing a bandeau bra under her tank. There was very little fabric between her and him.

"No, you don't."

When she went to turn around, he took her bag from her shoulder. Slung it over his own. She was a little surprised at his chivalry, but then he turned his back on her and walked away without saying anything. She had to jog to make it onto the elevator with him.

"What is going on?" she asked when he'd hit the button for the lobby.

"I called my mother yesterday."

"Huh?"

She knew Wulf kept in touch with his mother. They weren't particularly close, but he checked on her, asked about his sisters. Still. What kind of phone call had it been, if it had him showing up at her place at nine in the morning?

"My mother. I realized it's been quite some time since I went home. She's visiting her sister, but she'll be home on Tuesday. Seemed like fate. I told her to tell your mother I'd give you a ride."

Katya was so stunned, she forgot to move when the elevator stopped. He was halfway out the front doors before she remembered herself. She chased after him.

"You cannot be serious," she gasped as they went outside. "I mean … what if I'd already left?"

"I called earlier, your roommate answered your phone, said you were in the shower. She's very interesting."

She certainly is. Thanks for the heads up, Tori.

"Wulf, stop," she insisted, grabbing her bag. He stopped so abruptly, she stepped into his back.

"I'm parked in the street, make this quick."

She moved to stand in front of him, shielding her eyes from the sun's glare.

"What is going on? What are you telling me?"

"I'm going home for the week, too. I'll drive you down."

"Why?"

They stared at each other for a while and she realized she was holding her breath once again. On the verge of passing out.

"Because," he said in a low voice. "A week is a long time, Katya."

It was happening. One of those moments. He could've told her to walk into traffic and she would've done it. As it was, he grabbed her hand and pulled her out into the street, and she went without hesitation. Sat in the passenger seat of his car without even being aware of him opening the door for her.

"Oh my god," she breathed, looking up while he threw her bag into the trunk. "You took it off!"

"Yes. You said you wanted to ride with the top down. It's nice weather all the way to Carmel. I figured why not."

He'd done something nice. Just for her. Several nice things. She couldn't bare it. Even though they were driving down a crowded, busy, two lane street, she squealed and grabbed his head, yanking him in for a kiss. He hissed a couple curse words, fighting to keep the car under control, but he managed to kiss her back.

13

NORMALLY IT ONLY TOOK ABOUT TWO HOURS, MAYBE LESS, TO GET FROM SAN Francisco to Carmel. But Wulf once again surprised her by heading out to Highway 1, the Pacific Coast Highway that traveled all along the shoreline. It was twisty and turny, hugging the ocean clear down to Santa Monica.

It was fun. She felt her age, probably for the first time ever. She pulled her hair up into a sloppy ponytail and wore Wulf's shiny aviator sunglasses. Took off her shoes and propped her feet on his side view. Laughed at him while he tried to eat a hot dog and navigate the winding road. She offered to drive, but he laughed at her and gripped the steering wheel tighter.

He tried to shrug out of his blazer at one point and she climbed onto her knees in her seat, reaching over to help him strip it off. Her hands had a mind of their own, though, pulling at his shirt. Unbuttoning it and scratching across his chest. She had her tongue in his ear, one arm around his shoulder, and the other hand was making a quick trip down to his crotch. His free arm was wrapped around her, his hand squeezing her butt, fingers worming their way under the bottom of her shorts. Only a passing truck blowing its horn brought her back to reality. She looked up in time to see a grizzled looking man give her a thumb's up. Wulf just laughed, smacked her on the ass, then pushed her back into her seat.

A little over two and a half hours later, they were rolling through the old neighborhood. It was surreal, returning with Wulfric Stone. She'd grown up on the street and had never once so much as stepped foot on a sidewalk alongside him.

"So, um …" she suddenly felt shy as they pulled into his driveway.

"What?" he asked, shutting off the engine and climbing out of the car. She followed suit.

"What did you tell your mom?" Katya asked.

"I told her I was coming down for a couple days."

"Oh. Okay. Did you mention me?"

"Yes. I said I would be giving you a ride."

"Ah."

She wanted to know how to handle her own mother. Mrs. Tocci was ridiculously obsessed with her daughter's love life. In her mind, a proper young lady was settled down and married by no later than twenty-five. Preferably earlier. She was going to lose her shit when she found out Wulf gave Katya a ride down.

Just get it over with. Crush her dreams. Maybe it'll help to remind you that this isn't a real relationship – no one has made any sort of declarative statements, least of all Wulf.

Katya smiled at him and pulled her bag from the trunk. While he went about getting his own belongings, she headed for her house, cutting across the grass divider between them. She didn't bother saying goodbye – Wulf never did, and he was right next door, after all. She pushed her way inside her parents' home, hollering as she did so.

"Mom! I'm here!" she called out.

"*Eeeekk!* My baby girl!"

Mrs. Elena Tocci came trotting out of the kitchen and hurried down the hallway. Katya took after her mother – they had the same slim build, blue eyes, and deep auburn hair. If Katya aged half as well as her mother, she figured she'd do alright in her old age.

"Oh my, what on earth are you wearing?" her mother asked after they'd hugged for a moment.

"Oh, I wanted something casual for the drive down. Don't worry, I have something nice for dinner tonight," she assured her.

"Phew! I was afraid you were turning into a ragamuffin! We raised you better than that," Mrs. Tocci shook her finger in her daughter's face. "Now, speaking of the drive down -"

"Mom," Katya held up her hand. "Just stop. Wulf is a new friend, we found out we work close to each other. That's it. He offered to give me a ride because he's visiting his mother, too."

"Dear, his mother isn't even here."

"Stop it. Stop planning out your future grandchildren – I can see it all over your face."

"But they would have such beautiful eyes!"

"*Mother*. I'm serious. No matchmaking. Don't embarrass yourself in front of him. Just a friend, just giving me a ride," Katya insisted. Her mom rolled her eyes.

"Alright, alright, I'll contain myself. You can't blame me for hoping. Is there anyone else? Tony?" she asked, her voice full of hope as she referred to Katya's ex, a pro-golfer.

"No," Katya was honest, even though Liam's image flitted across her mind. "No Tony, I haven't spoken to him in almost a year. Nobody. Just me and Tori and my job."

"Oh, honey. Maybe you should try to have something with Wulf! He's such a respectable boy."

Katya remembered the way he'd fucked her in his conference room. "Respectable" wasn't exactly a word she'd use to describe Wulf.

"Don't get your hopes up, Mother."

"Hopes up for what?"

Katya whirled around, shocked to see the object of their discussion shoving his way through the open door. She'd assumed he'd just go to his own place, settle in or whatever. But there he was, holding a small roller bag in his hand as he strolled down the hallway.

"Wulfric! So good to see you again, dear, it's been ages," her mother gushed, leaning in to air kiss Wulf's cheek. "I keep telling your mother we need to plan some sort of get together. I'd love to see Genevieve and Brighton."

Wulf's younger sisters, *Vieve* and *Brie*, Katya knew he hadn't seen either of them in a long time.

"You'll have to discuss that with her, I don't speak to my sisters very often," he answered honestly while he pushed his sunglasses onto the top of his head. Katya didn't miss the way her mother's eyes bounced between them. She wanted to melt though the floorboards.

"Oh, that's a shame. Are you kids hungry? I was just making something for a light lunch."

"Starving. Thank you, Elena. Katya, show me to the bathroom."

Wulf had never been in her family's house before, though she'd been in his plenty of times. Genevieve was only two years younger than her, Brie around four years younger. Vieve had been away at soccer camp that fateful summer, when Katya had been talked into babysitting the youngest Stone child. The same time she'd first noticed the cranky, rude, boy next door was the sexiest thing her tiny fourteen year old brain had ever comprehended.

When Wulf passed the elder Tocci woman, she gave the thumbs up to her daughter. Katya swallowed a groan and put her hand on his back, pushing him towards a door. She should've warned him about her mother. She hoped he wouldn't do anything else to encourage her mom, but just before he disappeared into the bathroom, he stepped out and wrapped his arm around her waist. Leaned down close to whisper in her ear.

"You had better warn your mother that I never plan on giving anyone grandchildren."

Katya wanted to die, but he gave a small chuckle and squeezed her once before letting go. The door had barely clicked shut behind him before her mother started squealing.

"Oh, honey," she breathed, fanning herself. "I think he likes you.

I think he *really* likes you."

"It's not like that, Mom, I promise. Just go get lunch," she urged, ushering her mom into the kitchen.

"The way he touched you! Katya, if he doesn't like you, then I don't know what's what anymore," her mom said, hurrying to the fridge and pulling out a tray of tiny finger sandwiches.

"*It's not like that,*" Katya spoke through clenched teeth as she took the tray and carried it out to the sun porch.

"Oh really," he mom huffed, joining her with a pitcher of lemonade. "Then enlighten me, what is it like?"

She stared while the other woman went about arranging the food on a decorative serving platter. Katya had been expanding her boundaries over the past few weeks. She wanted to become her own kind of adult, independent of the way she'd been raised, and more in line with what she actually wanted. Now was the moment to prove that she wasn't all talk. She took a deep breath and squared her shoulders.

"It's casual," she said, as close to the truth as she was brave enough to get.

"Excuse me?"

"Our relationship. Mine and Wulf's. We bumped into each other, and yeah, sparks kinda flew. But neither of us is interested in a relationship right now. He really came down here to see his mom. He knew I was coming down here to see you. He offered to drive me. *That is it.* I don't want to explain this again," she stated.

Her mother stood upright, looking shocked at the words she was hearing.

"A casual relationship? Oh honey, I don't really think that's good for you," she tsked tsked. Katya took another deep breath.

"I'm sorry, Mom, but *I* know what's good for me, now. And whatever it is, it's none of your business."

She waited for arguing. Some cajoling. The common sense talk. But none of it happened. Her mom stared at her for a long second,

167

making worry lines across her brow. Then she smiled. Reached a hand out and smoothed her fingers down Katya's cheek before cupping it.

"Of course you know what's best for you, dear. As long as you're happy, that's all I worry about."

Katya fell into her seat while her mom wandered back into the kitchen, looking for the fruit bowl. That was it? It was a big moment in her life, standing up to her mother's antiquated views of how a woman should behave and handle herself. For god's sake, it was noon on a Sunday, and the woman was wearing full makeup, heels, and a dress just to make snacks in her own home. Katya had assumed her admission would've caused a minor breakdown.

Of course, she realized it wasn't a fair assumption. She'd never ever once stood up to her parents before – how could she have known how they'd react? It was unfair of her, really. Her parents had always encouraged her talents and done their best to steer her in the right direction. They'd never really punished her for anything. How could she have thought they'd think less of her for wanting to live life her own way?

I had no idea my narrow-mindedness expanded to so many different parts of my life. I really need to thank Liam when I get home.

They ate lunch on the sun porch. She got to watch Wulf turn on the charm – he'd never done it for her. He smiled and teased her mother, flattering her. Distracting her from the fact that his hand spent a majority of the time on Katya's thigh. After they finished eating, he excused himself to go back to his own home, so he could unpack and take a shower, but he asked about their dinner plans.

Mrs. Tocci had made reservations at a very good restaurant downtown, but Wulf said that wouldn't do. After a few phone calls, he got them reservations at the very *best* restaurant. When six o'clock rolled around, he took the keys from Katya's mom, then drove both women downtown. Ordered fancy wine and fancier champagne, really showing off.

"I know it's casual, dear," her mother had whispered while they'd waited for valet to bring the car around. "But you could consider making it serious. Any man who knows wine that well is a keeper."

Katya actually laughed.

Wulf left them at their doorstep, kissing them both on the cheek before saying goodnight. Then Katya got to spend some real one-on-one time with her mom. They put on their pajamas and finally made those cookies. She'd always wondered where her baking talents came from – her mother was awful at anything involving an oven. How she managed casserole was a mystery. Half the batch turned out runny, the other lumpy. Katya's turned out perfect. They took all of them into the sitting room and sat on the couch together, watching an old movie.

"I'm very proud of you, honey."

Her mother said it randomly, without ceremony, at the end of the film.

"What?"

"It occurred to me that we don't say that to you enough. Your father and I are both so proud. I worried a lot while you were growing up that we weren't giving you enough," her mom said.

"Why on earth would you think that? I went to a private school, I grew up in this amazing home," Katya was stunned.

"Well, I always thought you deserved brothers and sisters, but it just didn't happen. I never wanted you to be lonely, so I tried my hardest to help you become the type of girl that would have lots of friends. Be well liked. Get a good job. But I don't want you to think that's all that mattered to me. Lord, no."

"Jesus, where is this all coming from!?"

"Your thing with Wulfric. It was hard for you to tell me that, which made me feel bad. I don't care who you're dating, honey. I don't care if you never get married. I mean, I'm your mother, of course I would like grandchildren, and I hate the thought of you being lonely up there in that big city. But your happiness is all I care about – not Wulfric, not your fancy job, not the way you dress. None of it. Your well being is my only concern. I never want you to feel like you can't tell me something. Just because we may view things differently, doesn't mean we can't talk about them. I always want to know everything that's going on with you," her mom assured her.

She couldn't help it, Katya started crying. Of course, it set her mother off, and soon enough they were a Hallmark cliché. Mother and daughter, hugging each other and crying, though neither was really sure why they were crying. It devolved into laughter, and then into wine and more cookies. And eventually, into talking. Katya told her mom about her relationship with Wulf. And about her relationship with Liam. She left out all the naughty bits, but gave enough that her mother knew she was sleeping with both of them.

It was very late by the time she was done talking and answering questions. When she finally closed her mouth, her mother sat still for a while, munching away at a cookie.

"Alright. I think I understand. Liam is your friend, whom you have a casual, sort of open, relationship with."

"Yes."

"And Wulfric you go on dates with, you see each other, and you feel something for him."

"Yes."

"But he doesn't for you."

"I don't know. I don't think so, most of the time. But sometimes …"

"And what about Liam? Does he like you?"

"I think he genuinely does. More than what's going on between us."

"Do you feel anything for him?"

"I feel like I should, because wow, Mom, the way that guy treats me. He's crazy and he's sloppy, but I really think you'd like him. He's so nice and caring and thoughtful."

"So what's not to like?"

"Literally nothing. He's amazing. But whenever I think maybe I should try to have a real relationship with him … all I can think about is Wulf."

"Whom you think doesn't like you."

"Yup."

It was all making Katya depressed. She shoved an entire cookie into her mouth, then washed it down with a healthy chug of red wine.

"I know I'm just your clueless mother and you think I'm oblivious to everything, but I am speaking to you as a fellow woman right now – I think Wulf cares about you. He had no plans to see his mother, until he found out about *your* plans. Ms. Stone told me this herself, she said it was very strange, the way he was acting. We both agreed that something was going on, and now that I've witnessed it, I believe it more than ever. The way he looks at you when he thinks no one is watching, the way he finds reasons to always be touching you. Give him a chance, Katya. It may take him a while to get there – Wulf's had a rough life. But I think he'll find his way to you."

The tears threatened to make a reappearance and Katya was pretty sure she'd never loved her mother more than she did right in that moment. But she took a deep, fortifying breath and locked onto one part of the speech.

"Rough life? Mom, he practically owns San Francisco and he was a nationally ranked swimmer when he was growing up. Their house is even bigger than ours, and he drove a Corvette in high school. In what way was that rough?" she asked with a laugh.

"Oh, honey, you didn't know? I assumed Genevieve had told you – when the Stones got divorced, it got *really* nasty, his father took *everything*. Imelda didn't even get alimony or child support. That's why Wulf never pursued swimming as a career. He worked all throughout school and college to help his mother pay for the house. That's why he works so hard now, to take care of the family. He's putting his sisters through college. He owns that home over there, bought it outright from the bank. Imelda doesn't pay a dime now. I think it was rough on him, all that pressure growing up. Having to give up his childhood dream so he could support his family. That's why your father spent so much time over there, he wanted Wulf to have some kind of positive male figure in his life," her mom explained.

Jesus. So much about Wulf had just been explained. Their conversations about dreams, him asking how she could have such faith in hers – he'd never been allowed to have faith in his own. Of course he couldn't understand hers.

She felt kind of like an asshole, and realized for the first time that she had a serious problem with making assumptions about people. She had basically thought Wulf was just some spoiled rich guy, who'd gotten that way because he'd been a spoiled rich kid. She'd also assumed that while he'd obviously worked hard to achieve the kind of success he had, he'd done it just for himself. He didn't talk about his family, he didn't have any real relationships, who else could it be for?

*This whole time, **I've** been the real asshole.*

"I never knew any of that," Katya mumbled.

"Well, maybe you should spend less time being 'casual', and more time trying to get to actually know him."

Sage words.

It was well past Mrs. Tocci's bedtime, so mother and daughter said good night before heading to their separate rooms. Katya took off all her clothing, rolling her head around on her neck before pulling on some shorts and a loose tank top, not bothering with underwear. Carmel was having a heat wave and she was covered in a fine sheen of sweat. It took some fiddling with the old panel, but she finally got the AC blasting in her room.

She was contemplating stripping the comforter off her bed when she heard a noise. Like a splashing sound. Her room was in the back left corner of the house, with windows marching all around the walls. She peeked through the blinds and felt like she was stepping back through time. Wulf was in his pool, swimming laps back and forth, and she was spying on him from her room. Just like high school.

Only not at all. Now I know exactly what's under his swimsuit.

Debating with herself for only a second, Katya hurried from her room. Tip toed down the stairs, then turned off the house alarm before slipping out the back door. She sprinted across the lawn, then crept around a hedge, wanting to surprise him. She didn't need to worry about it, though. He was completely absorbed with what he was doing. Their properties were divided by a wooden fence that had a gate, and she was able to stroll right up to the pool without him knowing she was even there.

It had been a long time since she'd watched Wulf swim. It was kind of beautiful. All those muscles, working together and doing what they were built for – all of them toned and tight as they pulled him through the water. She briefly wondered if she should leave him alone. He worked so hard, maybe he needed this time for himself. But then she decided screw it. She worked hard, too.

The Stones had an Olympic sized pool – built especially for Wulf when he'd been in middle school. He was half the distance to her, doing a slow crawl stroke, moving in a perfect line. She sat down on the tiled ledge and lowered her legs into the water. She shivered once, then put her hands behind her on the grass, resting back on the them. Waiting for him.

His finger tips brushed against her first. If he was startled, he didn't show it. He pulled up short of the wall, though his momentum carried him into her legs, her knees pressing into his chest. He slicked his hand over his hair, pushing it all back as he looked up at her.

"Hey," he said, wiping the water clear of his eyes.

"Hi."

"Did you need something?"

"No. I like watching you swim."

"Have you ever even seen me swim before?"

She took a deep breath.

"I used to watch you. You swam every night for a whole summer."

Wulf finally smiled and his hands went to her thighs, spreading them wide so he could move to rest between them.

"You used to watch me? Naughty girl, Ms. Tocci. I was a lot older than you."

"I know. You still are."

"Yeah, but it's sexy now."

"It was sexy then, you were just too self-absorbed to notice me."

"It would have been illegal if I had."

His hands were hooked onto her hips, and when she didn't say anything else, they moved, sliding down to the top curve of her ass. He urged her forward, and she didn't resist as he pulled her into the pool. She wrapped her legs around his waist, hooking her ankles together behind him. He walked them away from the ledge, carrying her easily around the shallow end.

"I'm not very good at swimming," she warned as she leaned back, bending and stretching away from him so she was floating on top of the water, but still anchored to him.

"I'll teach you."

It was said simply, more in passing than anything else, but it made her smile. She waved her arms around in the water, like she was making snow-angels. Then he moved one of his arms away from her, and she felt his hand against her stomach, pushing her shirt up.

"Wulf," she breathed his name as she sat up. He'd walked them so they were deeper, the water halfway up his chest. If she stood on her own, it would be up to her chin. He didn't let go though, and pinned her against the wall of the pool.

"No one can see us," he whispered back as he tugged and pulled at her wet shirt, working it over her head. She almost snorted at him. Please. Like she was going to put up a fight. He hadn't caught on to the little fact that all he had to do was say jump, and she would say how high. How many feet. Would he like a sandwich while she was at it?

He tossed her shirt onto the lawn and all she thought about was how good they felt when they were skin to skin. How right. Her arms went back around his neck.

"Why did you come here with me?" she asked, letting her hands glide around his shoulder blades.

"I told you, I called my mother. I thought it would be a good idea to come down and see her."

"She's not here till Tuesday, you could've waited till then."

"It made more sense to give you a ride."

"*Wulf.*"

"Katya."

She sighed and looked down between them, letting her eyes wander over his chest before she opened her mouth and repeated herself, "Why did you come here with me?"

He was silent for so long, she began to think he wouldn't respond. The only noises were some crickets in the distance, and the water around them lapping at the edges of the pool. He lowered his head to trail his lips across her shoulder, making her heart beat pick up speed. She was about to return the favor when he leaned away, staring down at her.

"I came because I like the way you look at me," he said in an easy voice, almost bored sounding. As if he hadn't just said the most amazing thing she'd ever had anyone say to her.

"What?"

"You look at me like you really see me. Like … I'm Christmas morning. And when you said you were going away, I hated the thought of not getting to see that look for five whole days."

She couldn't speak. Couldn't even think. It was such a sweet thing to say. Wulf was never sweet. Maybe cute, at best, but that was pushing it. It was silly, but she felt a little like crying. Had no one ever looked at him like that before? Like he was their favorite present?

Has anyone ever looked at me like that before?

It was grossly inappropriate, being naked in the pool behind his mother's house. Engaging in lewd acts in full view of her parents' house. Katya had trouble saying no to him, even at her strongest moments.

And this certainly wasn't one of those moments.

14

WULF HAD NEVER TREATED KATYA LIKE A TYPICAL GIRLFRIEND, SO SHE'D assumed they weren't girlfriend and boyfriend. After all, when she'd first started seeing Wulf, she'd been sleeping with another man – nothing typical about that, at least not for her. However, she was discovering that some of her assumptions had been so far off base, it was probably a good idea to question her others.

After their fun in the pool, she'd gone back to her own room, laughing at herself as she made the walk of shame through Wulf's backyard. The next day, she got up early and made breakfast with her mom, who seemed none the wiser to her daughter's illicit night time activities.

Mrs. Tocci did ask about Wulf, hoping he would spend the day with them again. But he hadn't mentioned anything to Katya, and she explained to her mom that he wasn't really a "make plans" kind of guy, preferring to just show up whenever he felt like it. Her mother didn't like that one bit, but she didn't say anything. Just pursed her lips together and fussed about in the kitchen.

The ladies went shopping for a while, walking around the mall more than anything else. Katya dragged her mother into some stores that she wasn't used to, even convinced her to buy a funky hoodie.

She was still laughing about it when she carried her own bags up to her room. When she opened her door, though, she found she was in for a surprise.

"Goddamn, Tocci, I thought you were gonna be gone -"

She screamed before she could stop herself. The sound caused her mother to scream, even though the other woman was all the way downstairs, on the other side of the house. Wulf stopped talking and stared at her like she was crazy. Katya let out another yell and threw one her shopping bags at him.

"*What the fuck is wrong with you!?*" she shrieked.

"ARE YOU ALRIGHT!?" her mother hollered from the bottom of the stairs.

"Yeah," Katya took a deep breath, running her fingers through her hair. "Yeah, everything is fine. I just got startled."

"Well, thank goodness! And watch your language, Katya Tocci! You were raised to speak English better than that!"

She rolled her eyes, then turned to glare at Wulf. He'd regained his composure and was rummaging through the bag she'd chucked at him.

"What are you doing here?" she demanded, putting her hands on her hips.

"My conference call got canceled – I was going to see if you wanted to go have lunch, but no one was here. You should tell your mother to always double check that her front door is locked."

"I will. So ... what, you found the house empty, and decided to walk around it anyway?"

"Pretty much. I wanted to see your room – it's like a time capsule of a stereotypical American suburban teenage girl. And I gotta say, hell of a view you got there, Tocci."

"Thanks, I know."

"It's too late for lunch now – I looked in the fridge, ate some of those little sandwiches," he sighed. "I have to go and see if I can re-schedule ... hello, what is this?"

He pulled his hand out of the bag and a neon orange bikini top was dangling from his fingers. She stepped forward and yanked it out of his hand.

"That was supposed to be a surprise," she growled, grabbing the bag from him, as well.

"A surprise? That involves you in a bikini? You know me very well."

"It comes with a price."

"Maybe you don't know me."

"The bottoms are even skimpier than the top," she informed him. "And you can see the whole package when you invite me to the pool on the rooftop of your apartment building."

She expected arguing, or even outright denial. Instead, he started laughing.

"It's adorable that you think you'll be wearing clothing while in my pool. Dinner at eight?" he asked, pushing past her to move into the hallway.

"Wait!" she snapped, grabbing his bicep. "You can't just walk down there, my mom will wonder what you were doing up here!"

"Oh no, we'd hate for her to think her adult daughter is sexually active."

"Yeah, I actually would hate for my mom to think her adult daughter is sexually active, *literally*, while she's only fifty feet away from *her mother*."

"Katya. You've been up here a grand total of three minutes – as good as I am, even I can't fuck you that fast."

"You don't know my mom, Wulf. She finds out you were up here waiting for me, she'll read into it, and next thing you know, she's printing wedding invitations or something."

"You're ridiculous. What do you propose I do, shimmy down the trellis under your window?" he snorted. She smiled at him.

"It would be kinda romantic. Complete that whole teenage fantasy thing."

"Forgive me for being rude, but you can fuck right off with that idea. I'm not climbing down shit. Be ready at eight."

He didn't wait for a response, like usual, and she stood at the top of the stairs as he headed down. He was able to walk out the door completely unnoticed, which made Katya glad. One last thing she had to explain away.

She spent the rest of the day putting away her new things, did some laundry, then went about getting ready. Her mother sat in her room with her, helping her pick out clothing and fussing over her. The little things that Katya loved when she visited home, and missed when she was away.

When she was ready to go, though, she realized it was only six o'clock. She was two hours early. She thought about just sitting down with her mom and having some wine, then she decided screw it. Wulf needed a dose of his own medicine. So in her dress and heels and pearls, she stomped through their backyards, then walked through his patio door like she'd done it a million times.

It was like a portal in time. Ms. Stone hadn't changed a thing about her house, not in almost ten years. Katya stood in the den, remembering all the nights she'd spent there, coloring with little Brighton Stone. Sitting awkwardly while a nineteen-going-on-twenty year old Wulf moved about the room. Of course, she hadn't known it at the time, but the first summer she'd ever noticed Wulf as a very attractive male neighbor, was the last summer he ever came back home.

She wandered around till she found him in an old office on the second floor. He didn't seem shocked or surprised when she strode into the room. He glanced at her, then went back to whatever he was writing.

"I was bored," she explained, even though he hadn't asked.

"I feel like that happens a lot to you. Sit, I just need to make some calls."

"Oh, I can leave."

"Sit down."

She sat on the edge of the monster desk he was sitting at – the thing took up most of the wall. She remembered that his father had been a famous architect, then later a contractor. It must have been the elder Mr. Stone's desk, once upon a time. She moved so she was sitting at the corner and her legs were spread out along the length of the desk, crossed at the ankles. She shook up a snow globe while Wulf made a phone call.

"Do you collect these?" she asked, glancing around the room and seeing a bookshelf full of them.

"My mother," he replied. She shook the globe again.

"She got all those herself? Wow."

"No. I send her one every time I go somewhere."

"Jesus, Wulf, if you get any sweeter on this trip, I'm gonna re-name you Romeo."

He dug his pen into her side, painfully. She squeaked and pushed at him, but then he held up a hand and started speaking into the phone.

She barely understood half of anything he said, though she did figure out that he was talking to his assistant. He prattled off dates and case numbers and addresses. While he spoke, he dragged the capped pen up and down Katya's leg. From the hem of her dress to just under her knee, then back up again. Slowly, over and over.

Feeling like she was going to go crazy, Katya pulled out her own cell phone, then winced when she saw the screen. Several missed calls, then multiple missed messages. A few from Tori, just checking on her and asking after her mother. Most were from Liam. She'd forgotten to check in with him.

Hey, so sorry! Things were kind of a whirlwind yesterday and I totally forgot.

Thank god. I was half ready to come down there. Don't scare

me.

Sorry. But you don't need to worry about me so much, I'm tougher than I look. Besides, turned out, I didn't come alone.

There was a long pause before he sent a response.

New Guy?

Yeah. He showed up and offered a ride.

What a sweetheart.

She could feel the sarcasm rolling off the screen.

Hey, it was nice. I didn't have to rent a car.

Yay for you. I could've come with you. Your mom would love me.

I bet she would. I doubt there's many women who don't like you.

Damn straight. How many more days?

Just three more, not counting today.

Too long, angel cake.

You survived thirty-two years without me – you can survive a couple days.

I'm not so sure anymore.

Katya didn't know how to respond to that. She frowned and stared at her screen, her teeth digging into her bottom lip.

"Hey," Wulf's voice broke through her thoughts.

"Huh?"

"I'm done. Who are you messaging?"

"Oh," she mumbled, fumbling while she tried to lock her screen. "Just a friend."

"A friend, huh. Is this the friend you occasionally sleep with?"

Since their date in the fancy bar, Wulf had never asked about the other man in her life. She had figured he just didn't care. The tone of his voice right then, though, made her think that he actually cared very much.

"Yes. Sort of."

"Again with this 'sort of'. He must have an awfully small dick for you to be so easily confused as to whether or not you're fucking him."

"Shut up," she laughed. "It's been a while."

"Slacking off, huh?"

"More like stopped entirely. It just isn't … as fun as it used to be."

"Hmmm, and I wonder why that is."

They stared at each other for a long moment, and she willed him to say whatever it was that was bouncing around his head. She could see it behind his eyes. He was such a caged beast. Once again, she thought about how good Liam would probably be for him, and wondered if she should introduce them some day.

Then Wulf broke the spell by slapping her sharply on the thigh, hard enough to sting. She cried out, but then the sting was soothed when he leaned forward and kissed the same spot.

Dinner was nice, though she was still a little distracted, thinking about Liam. Hoping he was okay. She really did care about him, and she knew he cared about her. She didn't want to hurt him, and she worried that's where they were headed.

She wasn't the only one with problems, either. During dessert, she noticed Wulf glancing at his phone, then glaring at it like it had personally offended him.

"Bad news?" she asked. He shook his head and tucked the device into an inside pocket of his blazer.

"An investment that's gone bad. Nothing for you to worry about."

But she did worry. He'd gone back to being silent-Wulf. They finished eating without another word, drove home in silence, and she was left to walk herself to her door. She couldn't help thinking that Liam would never treat her like that, not even when he was upset. Wulf was aggravating. So petulant, like a child. So infuriating, like an asshole.

Yet an hour later, when she heard the splash, Katya was at her window. Watching him swim all those laps. Wondering when, or if, he'd ever let out his demons.

Can't swim away forever, Wulf.

Katya went to sleep worrying that Wulf would still be grumpy the next day. But when she wandered downstairs in the morning, still in her pajamas, she was pleasantly surprised to find him in the kitchen.

"Katya, just in time. My mother is finally home."

Wulf looked nothing like his mom. One wouldn't even think they were related. He was so tall and big and broad. Beautiful, with his dark brown hair and his striking blue eyes. Ms. Imelda Stone had fair hair, now liberally streaked with gray, that went well with her warm brown eyes. She was short, at least four inches shorter than Katya, which made her almost a foot shorter than her son, whom she quite literally seemed to look up to – there was so much love and awe in her gaze, it almost made Katya uncomfortable. It was as if the woman couldn't comprehend that she'd created such an amazing man.

He took care of her. He supported her. Still does – he owns the house she lives in, he pays for her daughters to go to college. He amazes me, even.

"Katya, it's been ages," Ms. Stone sighed, leaning in to give her a hug.

"A very long time, ma'am. Please excuse the way I'm dressed, I didn't know we had company," Katya prattled off automatically.

"Oh, don't worry about it at all. It's an ungodly hour to be visiting, but Wulfy insisted."

Wulfy!?

Katya raised her eyebrows at the pet name, and there was no mistaking the look Wulf gave her from over his mother's head.

Don't you fucking dare.

"It's not too early at all."

"So tell me, has my son been nice to you? I know he can be a little … *abrupt.* Heaven knows where he gets it from, his father and I, and even *your* father, certainly tried to teach him better," Ms. Stone chuckled.

"Nice isn't exactly the word I'd use," Katya replied, unable to contain her smile as Wulf's glare grew even worse.

"Oh, dear! Tell me everything."

"Well, first he put in a huge order at my bakery, all while pretending not to know me, just to make me nervous. And then he took me to a fancy restaurant, the awful man. And you'll never believe this, but he even showed up at my apartment once, on my day off, and *forced me* to give him a manicure. Can you believe it?" Katya teased. She was pretty sure Wulf's glare had reached *burn-to-a-crisp* levels, but she just ignored him.

"Sounds *terrible,*" Ms. Stone laughed. "Just awful. Best to get rid of him while you can."

"If only," Wulf finally cut into the conversation, making all the women laugh.

Katya dashed upstairs to shower and change, and by the time she felt presentable, the Stones had already gone back to their own home. She discovered that the mothers had made plans for a barbecue. It was short notice, they weren't sure a lot of the neighbors would show up, but both had already started making some phone calls. Mrs. Tocci had their housekeeper dust off the grill and move it into the backyard, near a picnic table, and a grocery store delivered a ridiculous amount of food.

"Mom! Did you invite the neighborhood, or all of Carmel!?"

"Hush, it's not often my beautiful daughter comes to visit."

"Oh, stop."

"And even rarer that she brings home a man I actually approve of!"

*"Hey! I **did not** 'bring home' Wulf, it is **not** like that. And I thought you loved Tony!"*

*"Because I thought **you** loved him. I always thought he was boring. I was dreading going to those PGA tournaments."*

The Toccis had always been popular in their neighborhood, and of course, Wulf was somewhat of a legend, so a lot of people turned out. The gate was opened between the Stone and Tocci properties, and people milled about, chatting while eating gourmet hot dogs.

Katya was sidelined by a neighbor's son. She felt awful, she couldn't remember his name, even though they'd gone to high school together. He was living in Carmel and his parents had invited him to the barbecue.

"Real estate, huh? I hear that's good business," Katya mumbled, only half listening to him while her eyes scanned the yards, wondering where Wulf was – she hadn't spoken to him since that morning.

"Yeah, it is. Carmel has some great property values. I'm still kinda new, but I think I'll go far," what's-his-name babbled.

"I'm sure you will."

"I heard Wulfric Stone is here – isn't he into real estate?"

"Yeah, he owns his own agency in San Francisco."

"Tough market. I should meet him, he could probably give me some good advice."

"Don't hold you breath," she muttered.

"What was that?"

"I said don't you like this bread?"

She took a huge bite of her hot dog and he went back to going on and on about his fascinating job. She was just about ready to excuse herself when her eyes finally locked onto Wulf, and for the first time ever in her life, Katya saw pure green.

Jealousy.

He was in a group, but standing next to a woman. She didn't know who it was, just that she was tall and blonde. Not crimes in themselves, but the fact that his arm was draped casually around the woman's waist made Katya want to commit murder in the first. When he leaned in close to speak directly to the girl, jealousy turned to nausea. She was going to be sick all over her mother's lawn.

"Excuse me, I don't feel so well."

She made her way inside and went straight into the pantry, where she knew no one would be, and shut herself in. She leaned over a utility sink and turned on the cold water.

She was being ridiculous. Wulf wasn't technically her boyfriend, she'd been over and over this in her mind. She was the one actively seeing another person, so it was wrong *and* unfair for her to get upset at seeing Wulf with another woman.

*Doesn't change the fact that I'm **really** upset.*

Making her feel doubly stupid was the fact that she didn't even know what was going on. For all she knew, that girl was a cousin of Wulf's. An old school friend. An old girlfriend. A current girlfriend. *His mom's girlfriend.* Who knew? Certainly not Katya, because she hadn't asked. No, she'd taken the very adult approach of freaking out and locking herself in a pantry.

Right there, surrounded by canned goods and cleaning supplies and jars of pickles – when had her mother gotten into pickling!? – she had an epiphany. It wasn't about expanding boundaries anymore. She'd been trying to keep her feelings for Wulf at bay for a while, but really, she'd only been ignoring what had been happening all along.

Ignoring the insane death fall she was taking into caring for a very, very cold man. Right then, she was suddenly very aware of the steps she'd taken, and it was too late. She'd gone over the edge. She was falling, falling, falling, gone.

I have to tell him. I have to tell Liam. I have to end everything. God, I can't talk to him, not like this. I'll burst out crying and he'll laugh at me and then I'll puke on him. Would serve him right. He's such a dick. Jesus, I'm falling in love with a total dick. **I cannot tell him that**.

Though she still kind of wanted to throw up, and very much wanted to cry, Katya pulled it together enough to go back out to the party. She would make one more round through the yard, saying thanks to everyone for coming, then she would lock herself in her room and try to figure some shit out.

When she stepped out onto the back deck, her eyes immediately zeroed in on Wulf and the blonde. They were laughing together, standing even closer than before, his arm still wrapped around her. Jealousy and self-pity took up root in Katya's chest, making her heart hurt. She took a deep breath and strolled onto the grass.

She said thanks to their pastor. Kissed Mr. and Mrs. Patel's baby on the forehead and commented on how much he'd grown. Oohed and aahed over old Mrs. Hoover's new needlepoint. Made light conversation as she moved through the crowd, weaving in and out of different groups. She'd almost made it back to the deck when a shadow fell over her from behind.

"If I didn't know any better, I'd say you were avoiding me, Tocci."

Wulf's voice was low in her ear, and though they weren't touching, he was standing far too close to be considered appropriate. Katya took a deep breath and held herself as still as possible.

"Not avoiding you. Just mingling."

"Bullshit."

"You were busy."

"I know, so were you. How's Kenny Bartlett doing, anyway?"

Aha! While I was eyeballing him, he was eyeballing me. Works both ways, wolfman!

"Great. He's in real estate, you'd probably have a lot in common."

"I bet we would – we certainly have similar taste in women."

"I don't know, seems like you prefer blondes."

He chuckled in her ear, but it sounded more like a growl. Then his arm was slipping around her, his hand pressing flat on her stomach and pulling her back into him.

"Jealousy looks good on you, Tocci. *I like it.*"

"Not jealous," she sighed. "Just tired. And have a headache. I think I'm going to go lay down."

She went to step away, but he refused to let her go.

"Hmmm, I'm calling bullshit again. I have to share you with another man, yet I can't even talk with an old friend from school?"

"Never said that, not even a little bit. You're allowed to talk to, see, do whatever you want, with anyone you want."

"That's really impressive, you know."

"What?"

"Getting those words out around all the *bullshit* in your mouth."

Katya stepped forward with enough force that he had to let her go, unless he wanted to actually struggle with her. She glanced back over her shoulder once, when she went to step through the sliding glass door. Wulf had already moved on and was laughing with a group of guys. She shook her head and continued inside, making a beeline for the stairs.

Stupid, stupid, Katya. At least you didn't start crying in front of him. Then you'd really belong to him.

———◆———

She hadn't been lying, she really had a headache. Probably brought on by a sudden case of massive heartache, with a little guilt and self-pity sprinkled on top. She paced around her room for a while, resisting the urge to spy on the party. Her mother checked on her once, bringing her some water. Then at eight, Katya gave in to the pounding between her ears and she swallowed a couple Tylenol PMs before burrowing under her covers. She was out within twenty minutes and had strange dreams about being in the woods. Going over rivers. Heading to her grandmother's house.

Sometime later she was startled out of her sleep. She sat up, struggling with her blanket as she tried to figure out what had woken her up. Her alarm clock said it was just after eleven-thirty. The only lighting in the room came from the glow off Wulf's pool, making everything look eerie and ethereal.

Then Katya heard it again – a thumping noise, outside on the roof below her. Was this a home invasion!? She clutched the blanket to her chest and reached for her lamp, but only succeeded in knocking it off the end table. She cursed at herself, then gasped as her window started to slide open.

"I thought this would be appropriate."

Holy. Shit. Was this really happening? Was Wulfric fucking Stone really crawling through her bedroom window? It was literally her biggest high school fantasy, but come to life. She tried to keep from panting as she scrambled out of bed.

"What are you doing?" she whispered, picking up the lamp before hurrying over to him. He finally stood upright, dusting himself off.

"You said you used to dream about me, when you were in high school."

"I never said that."

"Please, it was written all over your face."

"What are you doing?" she said it again.

"Fulfilling a fantasy."

She hadn't realized it, but he was looming over her, crowding in so close she was forced to walk backwards. She sucked in a sharp breath of air when his hand moved onto her hip. The air conditioning had turned off sometime while she'd been out, making the air heavy and warm. She'd kicked off her yoga pants in her sleep, leaving her in only a small t-shirt and her panties.

"I never fantasized about having sex in my parents' house while my mom was sleeping downstairs," she hissed. The back of her legs hit her bed and Wulf's chest was pressed against her front.

"Wait – you've never had sex in here?"

"No! What kind of girl did you think I was back then!?"

"You were a sexy seventeen year old girl at one point in time, so I assumed you'd had sex in here."

"Well, you assumed *wrong*. I was a good girl, I couldn't do something like that in my parents' house," she informed him. His head dropped down and she gasped when he sucked at the sensitive skin where her neck met her shoulder.

"Hmmm, then I must've been a bad boy, because I never once thought it was wrong when I did it at my house."

"Not shocked."

"What if I had snuck in back then?"

"Huh?"

"If I had crawled through your window when you were seventeen, would you have been a bad girl for me?"

"I would've been creeped the fuck out – you would've been twenty-three."

"*Smart ass.* You know what I mean."

She did, but she didn't want to give him that sort of power over her. He already had so much. But as his teeth clamped down on the side of her neck, and his hand fisted in the material of her t-shirt, she couldn't resist him.

Like always.

"Yes," she whispered.

"Yes *what?*"

"I would have been a very, *very,* bad girl for you."

He shoved her abruptly, forcing her to fall onto her mattress. He

was on top of her in an instant, and the usual Wulf – the slow, tor-
turous, methodical lover – was nowhere in sight. His knee drove up
between her legs, forcing them wide apart as he settled in between
them, and he let his hands wander anywhere they damn pleased.

"Prove it."

She gasped into his mouth, moaning softly as his hands pressed
down hard over her breasts. She knew she had to keep in mind that
they weren't alone in the house – she would not embarrass her mother, not even for Wulf. But she also couldn't possibly stop what was
happening, not anymore. She sucked her lips between her teeth and
bit down.

"Ooohhh, silly girl, think you can keep quiet with me?" Wulf
chuckled, as if she had challenged him.

"Wulf," she whispered. "You don't understand, I can't -"

Another moan cut her off, and her eyes rolled back in her head
as his hand dove into her panties. She felt his tongue, flat and warm
on her collarbone, and he licked a path clear to the back of her ear.

"Did you fantasize about this?" he breathed, then bit down on
her ear lobe.

"God, yes."

"Me tasting you, touching you?"

"Kissing me. All the time."

His tongue was in her mouth, smooth and warm. She could taste
brandy on him, and something smoky. Dark. She mewled against his
lips and dragged her nails down his chest.

"What else?" he asked at the same as he slipped two fingers inside her.

"God, I don't know, I don't know," she cried out, scratching at his
arm. Holding onto his wrist.

"Tell me, so I can make this as authentic as possible."

Something about that line struck her as odd. Was it not authentic already? He was taking her teenage sex fantasy very literally, it
seemed. Then he started sucking on her nipple through her shirt and

she forgot her own name.

"Wulf," she was able to remember his name and she said it on an exhale as she tried to catch her breath.

"Tell me what you want, Katya," he growled, his fingers moving double time.

"I want … I want …" she didn't know how to articulate her thoughts around him. Didn't know how to express exactly what she wanted. Words came easily for Liam, but Wulf always managed to chase them away.

"*Say it.*"

"*I can't.*"

He pulled away abruptly, and she cried out at the loss. Then he was grabbing her t-shirt again and he yanked hard, jerking her up off the bed. She stayed limp, her weight being held up by his grip on the fabric. He was staring down at her, almost looking a little angry. It was hard to tell in the ethereal glow from the pool. She stared right back, refusing to be scared of him.

Yeah, right, good luck with that.

"Tell me what you want from me."

The moment had gone from intense to surreal. Everything was quiet again, just like their first time together in the bar. Only instead of everything catching fire and turning gold, the entire room was coated in silver and blue, washing over them both. She took a deep breath.

"*I want you to let go,*" she breathed. "I want you to feel free when we're together."

Something broke. Electricity crackled in the air, but before she could contemplate where it was coming from, he dropped her. Before she'd even settled on the mattress he was gripping her shirt again, but this time at the neck line, and with both hands. She let out a shout as the material pulled tight, then ripped in half. He tore it right down the middle.

When Wulf let go, apparently, he *really fucking let go.* There was clawing and tearing. Movement that would leave marks. It was *amazing.* While she pushed and pulled to get his shirt off, her panties disappeared in a similar manner to her shirt. She had just gotten his belt undone when he grabbed her by the wrists. She cried out again as her arms were pinned above her head.

"Turn around."

Before he'd even finished speaking, she'd rolled onto her stomach. Her body always heeded Wulf's commands. Remembering her lessons from the strip-aerobics class, she drove her knees into the mattress, forcing her ass high in the air while leaving her upper half flat on the mattress. She stretched her arms out and pushed against her headboard.

When she felt the first slap, she was a little shocked. The second one was harder, earning a moan from her. She braced herself for a third, but it never came. Instead, his hand fluttered up between her thighs, his thumb was swimming in the wetness he'd created.

"Are you so eager when you're with the other guy?"

He could've spanked her, whipped her, put a ball-gag on her, and she would've been less shocked. He was asking about Liam, *again.* Something he *never* did, and now he'd done it twice in as many days. God, was he jealous? *Threatened?* When they were having sex, Katya could barely even remember her own identity, let alone anyone else's. Wulf had absolutely zero to worry about.

"Jealous?"

"Curious. Do you get this wet for him?"

His thumb was replaced with his dick and she gave a full body shudder. She tried to push back against his intrusion, tried to take him deeper, but he gripped her hips and held her in place. It took her a moment to realize he was waiting for an answer.

"Only for you," she whispered.

He slammed into her with such force, she couldn't help it, she shrieked. She bit down on her sheet after that, moaning into the Egyptian cotton while he pounded her from behind.

"Jesus, Katya, if you were fantasizing about this when you were seventeen, I definitely should've taken notice," he groaned. She managed to nod.

"Oh god, I wish you had."

His hand was suddenly in her hair, pulling so hard and sharp, he earned another shriek. She was jerked away from the mattress, her back arching as he continued yanking. While he pressed his forehead to the side of hers, she reached out and gripped the top of her headboard, trying to maintain her balance.

"Does he fuck you as good as this?" he hissed, and she felt his teeth against the apple of her cheek.

"Oh my god, I can't ..."

The conversation should've made her uncomfortable, but it didn't. Her body temperature was sky rocketing, and her stinging scalp was sending a pulse of pressure straight to where he was fucking her oh so good.

"Tell me, Tocci. Who's got the better dick? Who makes you come faster? Better? Harder?" he grunted out his words as his thrusts almost became brutal.

Katya went back to biting her lips between her teeth. No, he wouldn't force that out of her. Even drunk on his passion, intoxicated by his touch, she wouldn't betray herself. Betray Liam. Turn herself over to him completely.

Or at least, I pray I won't ...

"You feel so good," she finally moaned. He stopped moving and she actually let out a sob. He let go of her hair and she fell forward. His fingers trailed through the sheen of sweat on her back, twining around her vertebrae. Then he backed away completely and she couldn't feel him at all.

"That wasn't what I asked."

She was panting, half suffocating on the blanket that was in her face. Then she felt his hand around her ankle, and she squealed as she was jerked down the length of her mattress. He flipped her over

195

and his hands were on her thighs, his grip painful. Being quiet was already out the window and she cried out when he started thrusting into her again, over and over.

"Did you ever fantasize about this? Me fucking you in your bed?" he was speaking loudly, sounding out of breath while he fucked her like he was angry at the whole goddamn world.

"Yes, yes, god, so many time, yes," she cried, her hands squeezing her breasts.

"Did you fuck yourself while thinking about me?"

"*Yes.*"

"Do you still?"

"All the time."

"Do you picture me when you're fucking him?"

Her whole body started to shake, and she could feel the orgasm blossoming in her chest, causing her breasts to tighten up. It moved lower, finally meeting that point where his dick was burrowing its way to a new home inside of her. There her orgasm took root, coiling around her lower stomach, growing larger and hungrier.

"Tell me," Wulf whispered, leaning down close, crushing her hands and breasts under his chest. "Tell me who's the best for you. Tell me who makes you feel things you've never felt. Tell me who fucks you better. *Tell me, Katya.*"

All his commands and demands hadn't worked on her. She had thought she could stand strong in his presence. She was wrong, though, and her own name was her undoing. She let out another sob as her entire body erupted in orgasm, clamping down on him so tight he actually hissed. She thought she was babbling incoherently, almost on the verge of tears as the orgasm consumed her, body and soul. It was causing every nerve ending to fire off and shut down. But as her body unclenched and he started moving again, so gentle as he pumped in and out, she could finally hear herself.

"You. It's you, Wulf. Only you. Always you. *Just you.*"

15

KATYA WOKE UP WITH A START THE NEXT MORNING. SHE WAS COMPLETELY under her sheet, her head covered and all. She struggled with it before finally pulling it away her face.

The morning sun was coming through her windows. That perfect kind of light, where everything glows white, but isn't hot to the touch. She glanced at her end table, but her lamp and alarm clock were on the ground. When she looked up, the picture that usually hung over her bed was gone. It had fallen behind her headboard.

Hmmm, might've gotten a little crazy last night …

She glanced to her right and instantly, warmth spread across her chest. Wulf was asleep next to her. Hadn't he said he didn't like to spend the night with women? Maybe he'd meant only in his apartment. Either way, she didn't care. He'd never spent a full night with her before, and that's all that mattered.

She sat up and took her time looking him over. God, what a body. He had such fair skin, especially contrasted with her own naturally tan skin, and almost no body fat. Just sleek muscles, long and lean, built from a lifetime lived in a pool. A pillow was covering his face, hiding a strong jaw and a sharp nose – even in repose, he had a tendency to look like he was glaring. Like he was ready to fire somebody. His face was just structured that way, but he was still gorgeous, with his thick brown hair softening the overall look. His blue eyes were charming almost to a fault, and when he smiled, he could stop her dead in her tracks.

She dropped her eyes lower, but a sheet was loosely draped low across his hips. Hair trailed low on his stomach, becoming thick before the fabric cut off her view. She glanced down at herself. She was still completely naked. Wulf was obviously naked – if the low sheet hadn't given it away, the massive morning erection he was sporting would've. She chewed on her bottom lip for a moment, then turned and leaned over her bed. Grabbed at the alarm clock and picked it up.

Almost six in the morning. She laid back down and stared at the ceiling for a second. Let memories from the night before wash over her. What a bad man, making her admit such horrible things. She felt like such a disloyal friend, and Liam had been so good to her. But the truth was the truth, and Wulf had dragged it from her screaming, traitorous, orgasmic body. And if she was still willing to be truthful, *it had been hot.* He'd been so demanding of her. So forceful. So out of control. Her ass was sore, her thighs were weak, and her scalp was still tingling. She *loved* it.

Her teeth pressed down into her lip as she looked over his sleeping form. He rarely ever spent the whole night with women, he'd said. No one had ever looked at him like a Christmas present, he'd implied. She wanted to reinforce both of those things for him. Unwrap him, and show him how good the morning after could be.

Katya slid across the mattress, turning as she met his side. He mumbled in his sleep, twitched once, but didn't wake up. She smiled and smoothed her hand across his chest. Paused over his heart for a moment. Then worked her way south, wrapping her fingers around the base of his cock.

He let out a deep sigh as she began pumping her hand up and down, oh so slowly. She smiled to herself and moved lower down on the bed, kissing along the side of his abs as she went. As she was trailing her tongue over the side of his hip bone, he finally moaned. Then she felt him, his hand was on the back of her head. Combing through her ratty hair.

"Wow, Tocci, if I'd known you liked to wake up guests this way, I would've spent the night a lot sooner."

"Just being a good hostess."

She didn't give him time to make another smart ass comment – she wrapped her lips around his head and sucked hard, all while sweeping her tongue in a circle. He hissed and his fingers clenched tight for a second, then let go.

"*Goddamn.* You've been holding out on me," he panted. She let him go and chuckled, smoothing her hand over the sensitive head.

"Don't get your hopes up, I'm not very good at this. I was hoping you'd sleep through most of it."

He laughed, then groaned again when she lowered her mouth back to his dick.

She hadn't been lying – Katya had only given blow jobs a handful of times. As little as possible with her previous boyfriends. Hazy memories of her first night with Liam had come back to her over the last couple weeks, and she could remember him helping her go down on him; holding her head at the right angle, telling her what he liked, what he wanted. It wasn't much, but she was glad to try out her new techniques on Wulf.

"Not great," he grumbled through clenched teeth. "But pretty damn good, Tocci. Definitely something we can work with."

He let out a shout when she unsheathed her teeth, and he pulled at her hair again. But then they both moaned when she deep throated him. A talent she'd never known she'd possessed until recently, she was more than happy to share it with him – turned out Katya had a practically non-existent gag reflex. Lucky for Wulf.

It wasn't long before her jaw was aching and her arms were tired. When his hand clenched in her hair once more, she moaned, encouraging him. That was all he needed – he took over after that, showing her the quickest way to make him come. He set the rhythm and the pace, forcing her down as low as she was able to go. Eventually, both his hands were in her hair and he was cursing her name, his hips pumping up to meet her mouth.

"Fuck, Katya, you're gonna make me come."

Thank god. Sure, it made her feel all womanly and powerful, bringing him to his knees, reducing him to a puddle of orgasmic goo, all that good stuff. But she was also ready to take a break, and maybe a few full sized breaths. She purred around his dick, causing it to jump and twitch in her mouth. One hand was against his thigh, helping to keep her upright, and her other hand was wrapped around his length, moving in sync with her mouth, moving to play with his sac. She was prepared to swallow – it wasn't as awesome as porn stars made it out to be, but she would finish him like a champ.

Turned out, though, Wulf had other plans.

Just as she hollowed her cheeks, ready to push him over the edge, he suddenly yanked painfully on her hair. She let out a cry, which was thankfully muffled, but had to move with his grip. He pulled her up his length and while she was still gasping for air, he kissed her hard, filling the void with his tongue.

Her hand was still on his dick, and his fingers wrapped around hers, both of them stroking him. He forced her to squeeze hard and when he bit down on her bottom lip, he finally came. She jumped a little as she was hit in the chest, but then his tongue was back in her mouth, his hand pumping up and down again, milking himself to the very last drop.

"So much …" he was panting. "So much for keeping things strictly PG in your parents' house."

Katya laughed, panting as well. His hand was still in her hair, keeping her forehead pressed to his own. She was kneeling between his legs, her hands on his thighs, and she let her eyes fall shut.

"So, still think spending the night with a woman is such a bad thing?"

"I never said it was."

"Do you ever admit when you're wrong?"

"Has yet to happen. But I promise, I would if I ever was."

"Smart ass."

She wanted to kiss him again, but when she leaned forward, she went to brace her hand against his chest. Her palm landed in something sticky and she opened her eyes, looking down between them.

"Messy, Wulf. I'm surprised," she laughed at him. He chuckled and pulled her closer, kissing along the side of her neck.

"I like seeing you covered in me," he whispered in her ear. "Like a brand. *Showing who you belong to.*"

Her body lit on fire at his words and she instantly regretted the blow job, wanting to fuck him right then and there.

Luckily, Wulf was very good at knowing her wants and needs. Before she could even beg for it, he had her flat on her back, his tongue making her even wetter than she already was.

A very impressive feat.

<hr />

She woke up again later in the day, but that time, Katya didn't care what time it was. Every muscle in her body was completely relaxed, something she hadn't felt in … *ever*. She knew it was a lot later in the day, because the light streaming through her windows was distinctly more gold and the room was already heating up again. She really had to talk to her mom about fixing the air conditioning.

She stretched her arms out to her sides and when she didn't encounter anything, she glanced to her left. Wulf wasn't there. She sighed and closed her eyes, raising her arms above her head. He'd stayed the night. They'd fallen asleep once wrapped around each other, and a second time with sheets clinging to sticky skin. She really could not have asked for a better night with him. She wondered if he'd gone back out the window, or if he'd braved going down the stairs. Wondered if she should call him, or wait for him to call her.

She finally retrieved her phone from off the floor and scrolled through her messages. A couple were from her boss, with some questions from clients. Despite having a no-changing-your-mind-after-a-certain-point policy, people always wanted to push it. She sent the best answers she could give, and was on the verge of calling, but then remembered – she was on vacation. She'd scheduled this time for herself months in advance; she deserved it, and she'd earned it. She finally texted that she was busy, then moved onto her other messages.

There was one from her new friend Candi-with-an-i, asking how she was liking the new wardrobe, and more importantly, how Liam liked it. Which led Katya to look at his messages. They were mostly all asking how her sex life was doing without him, and if she missed him yet. She smiled and felt bad that she hadn't called him. Then she remembered the stuff she'd said the night before, and her smile fell away. She frowned and started dialing his number, suddenly desperate to talk to him, to explain how she felt. Before she could push the last button, though, her bedroom door burst open.

"Mom!" she snapped, dropping the phone and scrambling to cover herself with some blankets. "You could knock!"

"Why would I knock? I've seen it all before, Tocci," Wulf chuckled as he kicked her door shut behind him. He walked over to the bed and held out a coffee mug. She didn't take it. Just gaped up at him.

"What are you doing here?" she asked. He pulled the cup away and started drinking out of it.

"I've finally fucked you stupid, I see. It's a problem I have, I should've warned you. We had sex last night, which happened in this bed – for the first time ever, apparently – and then we fell asleep, and then you woke me up with an inexperienced yet still incredible blow job, after which -" he prattled off their adventures from earlier that morning. Katya growled and smacked him in the chest.

"Shut up, you know what I mean! I thought you'd left, gone home!"

"Clearly, I didn't."

"Wait a minute," she gasped, her eyes bouncing between his face and the coffee mug in his hand. "*Wait a minute.* Where were you, just now?"

"The kitchen. If you tell me there's a coffee maker in here, I'll be pissed."

"No. No, no, no. What time is it?"

"Almost noon."

Katya dropped her face into her hands, then peeked at him through her fingers. He was wearing his pants, thank god, but nothing else. No socks, no shoes, no shirt. His hair looked wild and crazy, as if someone had been pulling it all night.

Probably because someone had.

"Jesus. Tell me you didn't -"

"Your mother says hi. She's going to some charity meeting. She left some lunch in the fridge for us."

"Oh god. My mother. My mom saw you like that," Katya clarified, finally dropping her hands and staring up at him again.

"We had a nice chat. She makes a good cup of coffee."

"I'm so glad for you."

"Hey, I offered you some."

"Wulf."

"Yes?"

"You're half naked."

"Hardly."

"Did she say anything? About all … that?" Katya asked, waving her hand in a circle, gesturing to his bare chest.

"No, we talked about landscaping. Did you want your mom to hit on me?" he asked. She resisted the urge to gag.

"*No.* I just … I don't know. I didn't want to her to know what we'd done last night," she struggled to explain. Wulf chuckled and moved to kneel at the foot of the bed.

"Cat's out of the bag, Tocci, cause I'm pretty sure she had a good idea of what her daughter had been up to," he warned. He started crawling up the mattress and she felt her mouth go dry. She finally looked away and stared out the window.

"I didn't want that," she sighed. She felt his arm wrap around her waist, over the sheet, and then he was dragging her into him. Pulling her down so they were laying side by side. She still refused to look at him.

"You're an adult. *We're* adults," he informed her, tapping a finger against her chin before pushing, forcing her to look at him. "We did nothing wrong."

"You don't understand, Wulf. She … she's one of *those* moms, she's always trying to set me up. Always asking me when I'm going to settle down, get married, have babies. She sees you, and she sees hope. She sees the good looking, successful, rich, boy next door, and then she sees us together, and then she's going to start thinking about all that other stuff. Thinking you're perfect. Perfect for me," she told him in a soft voice. He chuckled and leaned close, kissing her softly on the lips. It didn't make her feel better, though. It made her heart pound and constrict, warning her that what she was about to do was irrevocable.

"I am pretty perfect, Tocci."

"Please stop."

"*You* stop," he sighed, rubbing his nose against the side of her jaw. Kissing along the side of her shoulder. "We just had an amazing time together, didn't we? Yet here you are, trying to tell me I'm not perfect."

"I'm not saying that," she said, finding it hard to breathe. Everything was already too difficult – she wanted him to stop touching her.

Don't want him to ever stop touching me.

"Then what are you saying?"

"I *do* think you're perfect for me, and that scares me."

"Why?"

"Because I've never felt this way about somebody," she whispered, placing her hand over his. "I don't want you to break me."

He had no sharp comeback for that, no smart ass response. The kisses stopped, but he didn't move away. His forehead was pressed against her jawline, his breath hot against her neck. His hand stretched and flattened against her skin, then slowly slid out from underneath her own hand. She closed her eyes, preparing for him to leave her.

But he didn't. His hand moved over the top of hers, his fingers splaying wide apart. He took a deep breath, then fit his fingers into the spaces between hers. He squeezed tight and balled his hand into a fist. Linking their hands together. She gripped as tight as she could, wanting to hold onto the moment forever.

They always go away too soon. Give me this one, for just a little longer.

"You're right, Tocci. That is very, very scary," he breathed.

She was pretty sure he'd never spoken truer words to her.

They laid like that for a long time, neither moving as the room grew hotter and hotter in the noon sun. She tried to move away at one point, so full of nerves and tension, she was afraid she'd burst out crying if she didn't get away from him. But Wulf wouldn't allow it, wouldn't let go of her. As she rolled away, he held her in place with their hands against her chest, then scooted up close behind her. Spooning her. He was on top of the sheet and she was under it, but still. It was the closest she'd ever felt to him. When he sighed and kissed the shell of her ear, it finally happened. A tear escaped, running down the length of her nose. It balanced on the bow of her lips for a moment, then dropped sideways to the bed.

What happens now?

16

THE SUN HAD BECOME TOO MUCH, THE HEAT OPPRESSIVE. DESPITE HER BEST efforts, Katya fell back asleep, warm and comfortable with Wulf pressed against her from behind.

When she woke up an hour or two later, it was to find herself alone in the bed. She sat up, holding the sheet to her chest. Wulf was sitting on a chair near her bed, bent over with his elbows on his knees, his hands steepled together. He was completely dressed, even looked showered. She wondered how long he'd been sitting there, watching her. She glanced around the room.

"Your mom is still gone," he offered.

"Oh. Thank you."

"Are you alright?"

"Yeah. Hungry, but alright."

"Katya ..."

She stared at him with wide eyes, her hands clutching the sheet in a death grip. Usually when Wulf said her first name, it made her heart dizzy and her pulse pound with happiness. Now, though, it made her worry. Something in his tone.

"Yes?"

"I have to go back home."

"Oh. Okay."

Okay. Super duper okay. So okay. Never mind my heart puking into my stomach, that's totally normal. Totally okay. Super fucking goddamn extremely fucking o-fucking-kay.

"A Malibu property requires my personal attention," he stated as he stood up and began to pace her room. His voice was serious, his cadence clipped. She knew this Wulf, the all-business-all-the-time Wulf. The man she'd been getting to know was miles away. If she wanted to have any hope of ever seeing the other Wulf again, she had to let him go. She had to give him space.

"I understand," she assured him in what she hoped was a calm voice. "Work is work. Go."

His eyes cut to her.

"Most women like to say something is okay, when in reality, it's the least okay thing they can think of."

"Lucky for you, I'm telling the truth. I'll see you when I get home," she said it flippantly, as if she took it for granted they'd keep seeing each other. Maybe if she acted like it was no big deal, the moment they'd shared, then he would, too.

"Yeah," he said, his voice soft.

"Are you leaving right now? Do you have time to eat?"

"I'm leaving now. I'll order a car for you for Friday."

"Oh no," she waved him away. "That's ridiculous."

"I drove you down here. I'm leaving you stranded. I'll send a car."

"Seriously, Wulf, it's fine. I'm a big girl, I can rent a car, or my mom can drive me, or I -"

"I'll send a fucking car, and when it shows up, you had better be here."

Whoa. She wasn't sure that she'd ever heard Wulf angry before. For whatever reason, her getting home was a big deal to him. She nodded and took another deep breath.

"Okay, Wulf. Okay. Friday, whenever is fine."

"Good."

"Thank you."

He'd been looking out a window. As she watched, he did an about face and strode towards her bedroom door. He was going to leave. That was it. No goodbye, no acknowledging what had happened between them. It was another moment, she could feel it, but not a good one. She stared at him as he moved, committing him to memory. Wulf always looked good, but his body was made to be in motion. When he got to the door, he yanked it open, then held still. Katya bit down on her lips.

"I'll be in touch, Tocci."

Then he was through the door, slamming it shut behind him. She bent in half, pressing her forehead to her knees.

See? Ruined it. I completely, totally ruined it. Should've kept my mouth shut.

But she couldn't have, she knew. Even right then, when she was feeling hurt and sick and confused, her feelings for him were bursting out of her. Ripping her at the seams and tearing her apart.

Wulf had said he was good at deals, but apparently he'd never acquired a heart before. It was safe to assume that he didn't even know what to do with one. She would be his learning curve, and she had a feeling that it would be a very steep, very sharp one.

This is going to hurt like a bitch.

17

WULFRIC STONE WAS NOT A STUPID MAN. HE'D GONE TO GOOD SCHOOLS, gotten excellent grades, excelled at everything he'd put his mind to – his bank account and his business accolades were proof.

But he could admit when he was acting stupid, and when it came to Katya Tocci, he'd been *beyond* stupid. Idiotic. Dense. *Imbecilic.* See? All those synonyms, and he'd thought of them on his own – a very smart man.

Yet rendered completely stupid by the mere presence of a former neighbor.

The first time he'd seen Katya, he'd thought to himself "wow, the girl next door really grew up", and then he'd wondered exactly how much she'd grown. He hadn't paid any attention to her at all when she'd been a neighbor in Carmel. Now as a neighbor of sorts in San Francisco, she captured *all* his attention.

He'd been curious – Wulf was curious by nature. Always poking, always prodding. Always testing boundaries. How far would little Miss Tocci bend? Would she break? What all would she do for him? And for how long?

He'd expected her intoxicating mixture of naiveté and bold

sexuality. Been ready for the way she'd responded so eagerly to him. Was happy at how easily she took commands and heeded demands.

What he hadn't been ready for, in any way, was her blinding honesty. Katya hadn't needed to confess how she was feeling – it shined out of her. She looked at him with such adoration. Such happiness, at simply being near him. Not his money. Not his power. Not his intelligence or connections or family name. Just him. Just Wulf.

But when the words weren't spoken, it was easier to ignore. To pretend he didn't notice any of it. How could he acknowledge any of it? It would have meant the end, and he wasn't finished yet. No, not by a long shot – not when there was so much more of her to be had.

Why the fuck had he gone home with her? Wulf never went home. He hadn't been home in years, not since Vieve had graduated – he'd made excuses for Brie's graduation, missing it entirely. Yet Katya Tocci drunkenly mentions that she's going home, and he cancels a weeks worth of meetings and takes the top off his car.

She's not the only one who had some words that needed to be said.

He couldn't say them, though. Was scared – yes, *scared* – to even whisper them to himself. To admit, out loud, that he cared about her. Very much. That way she looked at him … it meant everything. Somewhere along the line, he'd grown to depend on it. *Need* it.

Horrible. Needing something meant depending on it, and *that* he could not abide. That's all he'd thought about when he'd been curled around her, while she'd cried and slept. If he needed her, and she left him, he would be broken. He couldn't afford that, not the way he lived his life, not when there were people who depended on him to be whole and strong.

His mother had loved his father, very much. Wulf was pretty sure she *still* loved the man, and they hadn't spoken in years. The elder Mr. Stone had cheated on his wife, multiple times, before finally leaving her for a much younger woman. Wulf hadn't begrudged his father his happiness – if he needed to leave, then he had to go. Wulf would've been okay if it had been as simple as that, a man following his heart.

But it wasn't that simple, and what Wulf couldn't understand was why his father had to make it hurt so much. Why he'd rubbed the new relationship in his ex-wife's face. Why he'd tried to leave her destitute and penniless with two young girls, and a son who had a very expensive hobby.

It had broken his mother. He could remember thinking that very clearly, finding his mom hiding behind the couch, curled up in a ball and sobbing. She'd never returned to her old self. It had been Wulf who'd looked after his sisters for the first year, taking them to their soccer practices and ballet recitals. Eventually, his mother had bounced back, but still. It wasn't the same. Her smile never reached her eyes. She never so much as looked at another man. And she never, ever stopped working. Almost like she was afraid to stop.

That *could not* happen to Wulf. So he cut out the middle man. Remove the potential for heartache from his life, skip straight to working all the time, and never be afraid.

Cut to fourteen years later, and you're terrified of a baker with big blue eyes.

Because Katya would break him. If he let her in, he'd have to be honest with her. Let her inside his heart and his brain and his secrets. She'd have to know everything about him. And then she'd leave, it couldn't end any other way. He couldn't let that happen. He didn't want to be broken.

So he broke her, instead.

18

AFTER WULF HAD LEFT, KATYA HAD MANAGED TO DRAG HERSELF INTO THE shower. Scrubbed his scent and his fluids and his touch off her body. When she was scraped raw and shiny pink all over, she'd finally gotten out.

Her mother didn't say anything, much to Katya's shock. The older woman did send her some knowing looks, though, and she smiled to herself, *a lot*.

They spent the day together, taking the barbecue leftovers to a homeless shelter. Walked around a park for a while, talking about Katya's job and her mother's charities. Laughed about her silly father, who was a well respected former professor, and now did historical consultations for books and movies. He was in New York, helping with a play, and was sad to have missed his only child's visit home.

The next day, Katya kept herself busy with cleaning her room from top to bottom. Her mother had an amazing housekeeper, a woman who felt more like family than an employee, so Katya hated leaving behind any sort of mess.

She also had to keep busy because if she didn't, she would go insane. She kept checking her phone, desperate for a message from Wulf. She'd sent him one, saying she'd hoped the trip home hadn't been too bad. He never responded. Never called. Nothing.

He said he'd be in touch. He had to go home. Stop freaking out. It doesn't mean anything.

When she finally went to bed, though, she wasn't quite as strong. In her head, she whispered that it meant everything. They'd shared a very powerful, important moment, and then he'd ran away. She'd pushed him too far, asked for too much.

You didn't ask for anything.

You asked for everything.

The next morning, she woke up even more of a wreck. Still no texts from him. It had been almost forty-eight hours. She was counting them – since reconnecting, they hadn't gone more than a couple days without speaking, at least via text. If he didn't text the next day, she was going to lose it.

She'd gotten so worked up, she'd convinced herself that he'd already completely forgotten her, which meant she needed a way to get home. Blinking away tears, she sat on the sofa in the living room, her laptop open in front of her and a car rental site already pulled up. Then someone knocked on the door and her mom called out for her.

"Katya, dear! Your ride is here!"

A man in a simple black suit stood on the porch, smiling politely. At the curb was a huge, black Lincoln Navigator, with super tinted windows and shiny rims. Wulf hadn't been joking around – she would be riding home in style.

The driver loaded her one bag into the back of the car, then opened a door for her while she hugged her mother goodbye. It was silly, but she actually got a little teary eyed. Katya visited home fairly regularly and had never gotten choked up before, but it had been a different kind of trip. Special in its own way. She'd grown even closer to her mom, learned more about her.

Oh, those boundaries. Ever expanding.

During the ride she chatted with the driver for a while, but then fell silent and stared out the window. Tried not to think about a very cold, serious man that had left her naked and all alone.

As soon as she walked in her front door, she got attacked by Tori. Her roommate outweighed her by quite a bit – Tori was all tits and ass, while Katya was all knees and elbows. The flying hug sent Katya crashing into the wall, then they both fell to the ground.

"Good lord, I was only gone for five days," Katya gasped for air, shoving the other girl off her.

"I know, I know, but what a five days!" Tori exclaimed, finally backing away and helping her friend up.

"Why? What happened?"

Katya chucked her bag into her bedroom, then followed Tori to the kitchen. They had a decent sized living room – well, by San Francisco standards – but always wound up in the kitchen. She never knew whether it was because she just felt most comfortable in a kitchen, or it was because that's where the alcohol was located. She sat down while her roommate poured them some pre-mixed margaritas.

"I started at The Garden," Tori all but squealed as she dropped into her seat.

"Liam's club? And it's going good?"

"Oh mah gurd, it's *amazing!* I can't believe I never went to a sex club before!"

"He told me you'd be working upstairs."

"Pffft, for like five whole seconds. My superior waitressing abilities and fantastic cleavage streamlined the process. Once I proved that I could carry a tray without dropping it, and that I could count down a till, I was pretty much in. I mean, it helps that my roommate is banging my boss," Tori snickered.

"Don't say that," Katya almost snapped. The mood in the room instantly sobered.

"Whoa. Sorry. Didn't realize it was a … sensitive subject …" Tori mumbled. Katya groaned and rubbed her hands across her face.

"It's not, I'm sorry. Just had kind of a weird weekend with Wulf, and I haven't slept with Liam in a while. I think I need to be done with boys for a bit," she sighed.

"No way. Working around that man every day has me wondering how you ever keep your hands off him. Goddamn, that body? That smile? So sweet. So funny. You should see the way women fall all over him."

"Do they?"

"Yeah. But don't worry, he doesn't pay any attention to them."

Katya frowned and slurped at her margarita. She'd prefer it if he did – she wanted some of the attention off herself.

They talked about Tori's job for a while, until it was time for her to actually put in an appearance at the place. She changed into a sexy outfit, then blew a kiss as she breezed out of the apartment. She was gone for all of two minutes when there was a knock at the door.

"Did you forget your keys?" Katya groaned, stomping down the hallway. "I always tell you, check your pockets before -"

When she swung open the door, it was to find Liam standing there. Not Tori. They blinked at each other for a moment, then Katya finally smiled. She had missed him. Maybe not as a lover or as a romantic interest, but as a very good friend. His warmth and caring always surrounded her, making her feel comfortable in her skin. A feeling she wasn't entirely used to.

Especially after spending a few days with Wulf.

"I actually do have the keys to the building, but I thought it might be creepy if I used them to let myself in whenever," Liam teased. She leaned through the doorway and wrapped her arms around his middle, surprising him a little. It was a moment before his own arms were settling over her shoulders, holding her head tight to his chest.

"It would be very creepy," she sighed, breathing in his warm, familiar scent.

"You okay?"

"Now I am," she said, pulling back a little so she could look up at him. He was still smiling.

"I have a surprise for you. Come with me."

They went back up to the roof. Katya wasn't sure what she'd expected, but it certainly wasn't what was waiting for her. She burst out laughing as she took in the small, blue, plastic kiddie pool that was now sitting in front of the old loveseat.

"You dragged this up here?" she snickered, walking around it. It was filled with water, which she discovered was ice cold when she leaned down to drag her fingers through the liquid.

"Yeah. There's a hook up over there, I stole a hose from maintenance."

"Naughty. I won't tell if you don't."

"It's okay, I'm pretty tight with the owner."

She laughed again, glancing back at him. He wasn't looking at the pool. He was only looking at her. She cleared her throat and reached up to pull her hair into a ponytail.

"Let's take this baby for a spin."

She'd carried her margarita up with her and they shared it while they sat on the loveseat. They'd both rolled up their pant legs and were soaking their feet in the subzero kiddie pool. It was funny, she'd spent a lot of time trying to talk Wulf into taking her to the pool he said he had on his own building – and here Liam had brought one to her. It was kind of a beautiful moment.

So many moments. Moments with Wulf. Moments with Liam. So different.

"So, how was your vacation? How is Mom?" he asked, leaning back into the sofa.

"Mom is good. Really good. I, uh, I told her about you."

"Really? That's nice."

"And the other guy."

"Wow, angel cake! You're getting braver every day!" he laughed. She threw him a glare over her shoulder.

"Hey, it was hard for me. My mom and I don't talk about stuff like that," she told him.

"I know, I'm teasing you. I'm impressed. It couldn't have been easy. Good for you," he said, and she felt his fingertips near her temple, gently pushing a stray hair behind her ear.

"She was totally cool about everything, I was kind of shocked. You'd really like her."

"I'm sure I would."

"Yeah."

"And what about the new guy?"

"What about him?"

"Did Mom like him?"

Katya cleared her throat again, turning to stare out over the neighborhood.

"Yes. My mom likes him very much."

"Lucky for him."

"Yeah."

"Katya," Liam sighed, and she felt him lean forward. "Is everything okay?"

She bit into her bottom lip. This was not something she could cry about to Liam. What could she say? "*Hey, thanks for all the great sex and opening my mind to new possibilities and ways of life and fucking me six different ways to Sunday, but I think I'm falling in love with this totally closed off douchebag asshole, and I don't know how to stop it from happening, and I don't know how to make him love me back*" just didn't sound like something she should blurt out to him.

Why couldn't you just fall for Liam!? He's so perfect! He owns his own property, runs a successful night club, is so hot he burns just to look at him, and is the best thing to happen to the female sex since vibrators.

But she hadn't fallen for him, and that's why she couldn't talk to him. It was between her and Wulf. Their moments were their own, she wanted them kept private. Things they'd only ever share with each other.

"Yeah. Just a long week. New guy can be kind of temperamental, and my mom threw a huge neighborhood barbecue right before I left. Just drained. Ready for a couple more margaritas and a nap," she said, finally managing a smile for him.

"Margaritas I can help with. But a nap? Are you five? I can think of some other activities that might help relax you."

She felt his hands on top of her shoulders, squeezing and massaging. She closed her eyes. It felt natural when Liam touched her, but she knew it was wrong. She was just helping him dig himself into a hole with her. The same kind of hole she was standing in with Wulf. She wouldn't do that to another person.

Katya moved so her back was against the arm rest, then she put her feet in his lap. Let him massage those. They laughed about life in suburbia and he talked about his childhood and his family. His parents were divorced, but it had been amicable, and they were still really close friends, which was encouraging to hear, she felt.

She also learned about his brother, the other sibling who had inherited one of the Twin Estates buildings. For some reason, she had always assumed it was a younger brother. Maybe because of his age, she didn't know, but then Liam casually made a comment about his brother being his twin, and Katya almost fell off the couch.

One Edenhooferhoffen was almost too much for the world – there were two of him!? Another carbon copy of Liam running around somewhere? She wept for the women of the world and prayed that his brother was at least the settling down type. Those were some genes that needed to be propagated.

"Edenhoff. Say it with me, angel cake. Edenhoff."

The second Edenhoff brother – *"technically he's older, by about four minutes"* – was in Guatemala. He was a former ER doctor and he traveled around with different aide groups, providing medical services in third world countries.

Talk about night and day. One twin runs a sex club at night, the other saves starving children in Latin America. She almost wondered if Liam was making it all up.

The sun set and the stars came out and it got too cold for the kiddie pool. Cold enough that he wrapped his massive hoodie around her. She'd figured he would go back to his club, but when she asked him, he told her he was where he was needed most. Then they finally went back to her apartment, where they drank margaritas till Tori came home. Katya left them together, laughing around the kitchen table, while she quietly slipped into bed.

I do need Liam. I would've stayed home all day pining for Wulf if it wasn't for him. But I don't want to use him. I just want ... this all to not be so complicated anymore.

Katya had the rest of the weekend off, and she refused to spend it whining and crying over Wulfric Stone. He had a life. He had a business. He had property in Malibu he was trying to sell, apparently. His life didn't revolve around her, and that was okay. So he hadn't gotten in touch yet, so what? She was a modern woman, having a very modern relationship. She would not freak out. He'd get in touch when he had the time.

She kept herself busy, going back to her strip-aerobics class. They'd served their purpose, but she really did enjoy it. Candi was glad to have her back – the classes were always fluctuating, so it was nice to have a regular.

Sunday was spent with Tori, who'd been given the day off. They went out shopping with her tip money – The Garden was proving to be lucrative. Membership there was not cheap, which meant neither were the clientele. Tori made *excellent* tips, on top of the very impressive wages Liam gave her.

After buying some sexy dresses for Katya, and even sexier outfits for Tori's new job, the girls went into a dive bar on a whim and proceeded to get *hammered*. Completely wasted. Tori was celebrating finally having a job she actually liked. Katya was burying her self-pity under a fifth of tequila. They made a bunch of new friends and were the belles of the bar, till a very nice and polite bouncer kindly asked them to leave.

On the car ride home, Katya called Liam. Tried to tell him how much she appreciated him, all while Tori blew raspberries into the phone. He sounded concerned, but she couldn't really understand what he was saying, so she shrugged and hung up on him. Then she closed one eye to help with her aim and stabbed her finger at a different contact.

He didn't answer. *Of course* he didn't answer. Why would he? Not like she mattered. Not like she was anything important. Not like they hadn't just shared the most intimate moment she'd ever had with anyone *ever*, so *OF COURSE HE DIDN'T FUCKING ANSWER*. After she yelled the last part, Tori took her phone away. Clearly, one of them was slightly drunker than the other.

When they pulled up to their building, Liam was stepping out of a taxi at the same time. Tori had one arm slung around Katya's waist, trying to hold her upright, but she was laughing more than she was helping. Liam simply strode over and scooped Katya up, cradling her in his arms as he carried her through the building.

"You're very strong," she mumbled, completely limp in his arms, her head hanging upside down. Tori was holding onto her ponytail, as if that helped somehow.

"Not that strong. It's like carrying a dead body. Did you gain weight down in Carmel?"

Both girls burst out laughing, and even through her drunk haze she was able to hear him chuckle. He was fine, she was sure. He was so tall, so strong. Easily as strong as Wulf, and Wulf would never drop her.

Except he did. Like a bad habit, angel cake.

The tears started after they got into the apartment, thank god. Tori fell face first onto the couch and Liam carted Katya into her bedroom. While she hiccuped and sobbed, he peeled her jacket off her. Took off her shoes and socks and skinny jeans. While she laid there, desperately trying to catch her breath, he crawled into bed next to her.

"What's wrong?" he whispered, smoothing his hand down the side of her face. "Do you need to be sick?"

"No," she wailed.

"Tell me. This is killing me. Let me help you."

Katya rolled onto her side and pressed her face into his chest.

"I did something awful."

"What?"

"Awful, awful, awful."

"Jesus, Katya, did you kill someone? Run over a small child? What?" he demanded.

"I said too much," she whispered.

"You … what?" he sounded confused.

"I … I … I think I …"

"For the love of all that is holy, *what!?*"

"I think I do need to be sick."

She was carried into the bathroom. She tried to push him out the door, but that only made the nausea worse. Besides, he wouldn't allow it. Liam was okay with every single part of her, she knew. The workaholic Katya, the stick-up-her-ass Katya, the sex kitten Katya, the crying Katya, and yes, even the drunk and puking everywhere Katya. As he held her hair away from her face and he rubbed her back and he got her glasses of water, her mind spiraled around one single thought.

You're so stupid for not loving this man.

19

"H*ERE.*"

Liam raised his eyebrows. Katya had just burst into his office. She looked very much the worse for wear. Her hair was all scraped up into a messy bun on top of her head. She had dark circles around her eyes, and her normally olive tinted skin was an ashy gray color. Her full lips were thin and pinched, and he really hoped she wasn't going to throw up in his office.

"What are you doing here?" he asked, jumping up and hurrying around the desk. "You should be in bed, I'm surprised you're even up at this hour."

"It's three in the afternoon, Liam," she said as he urged her into a seat.

"Yeah, but in hangover time, that's like six in the morning."

"I wanted to say thank you, for taking care of me," she started, then made a gagging sound in the back of her throat. She pressed a hand over her mouth and held up a paper bag.

"What is this?" he asked, gingerly taking it from her.

"Tacos. God, the smell. I think I'm actually dying."

Liam laughed and threw the tacos behind his desk before calling upstairs. He had a large ginger ale and a really cold beer brought back for her. He'd been working in the bar industry for a long time, and it was his opinion that hair-of-the-dog was the best hangover cure. Apparently Katya felt the same way, because she immediately grabbed the beer and chugged it down.

"Better?" he asked with a laugh. She burped in response, then slapped both hands over her mouth. He laughed even harder.

She spent the afternoon in his office, talking and laughing with him. She certainly wasn't her usual perky, sassy self, but at least she didn't look like she was gonna throw up, anymore. He offered her a taco, but she waved him away, sticking with her ginger ale and some goldfish crackers he'd managed to scrounge up.

After a while, she became absorbed with something on her phone, so Liam went about his work. Most of the bar's accounting and payroll needed to get done. He would glance up at her every now and then, smiling to himself. He liked having her there, was comforted by her presence.

He frowned at his last thought and stared at her. He had to tell her how he felt. If she hadn't figured it out already – he wasn't exactly being subtle, but fuck it. When he fell, he fell hard. He'd never been afraid to love.

His only fear was that she'd never love him back.

"Katya, I ..."

———◆———

Katya glanced up at the sound of her name, but before Liam could finish the sentence, his office phone rang. He glared down at it for a moment, then looked back up at her.

"Just a sec," he sighed.

"Want me to wait outside?"

"No. No, not at all. It's just my partner."

She nodded and was about to go back to the book she was reading, but when he swiveled in his chair, she got a little curious. His back was to her and he was speaking in a low voice. Normally, Katya wasn't much of a snoop, but she couldn't help but lean forward in her seat, trying to hear him better.

"No ... no, don't come down here ... I know ... I'm aware ... you think so? ... oh, you *know* so, excuse me ... fine ... fine ... why don't you call and check for yourself?"

Katya was surprised to hear that Liam sounded kind of pissed off. Not fully angry, but there was a tightness to his voice, and his tone was snide. She wondered why he hadn't just bought his partner out. The club was thriving, and he had his property. Surely he didn't need Richard Mason's help anymore.

"That's good ... real good ... how about you handle your business the way you want to, and I'll handle my business the way I want to ... sure, sure ... I'm hanging up now ... goodbye ... goodbye ... hanging up ... wow, I've never heard you this angry before, it's kind of amazing, I'm actually – hello? Hello? *Motherfucker*," Liam growled, and he slammed the phone down with so much force, he startled her.

"Bad news?" she asked. He glared at her for a moment, then took a deep breath.

"Yeah. Yeah, he's a dick. We have this sort of side investment, and we can't agree on anything."

"Why would you start a new project with him, when you hate him?"

"What makes you think I hate him?"

Katya shrugged.

"You never have anything nice to say about him. Your whole demeanor changes when you talk about him, or when he's around," she said, remembering the time she'd interrupted their meeting.

"It does?" Liam sounded surprised.

"Yeah. I always assumed you didn't like him," she explained.

He was suddenly out of his chair and stalking towards her. She sunk down in her seat, swallowing thickly as he bent over her. She sucked in a breath of air when he reached out his hand. Again, that brief moment of hesitation. His eyes flicking to hers, seeking permission. She didn't know what was going on, so she didn't say anything, didn't move. He went ahead and touched the top of her head, pulling the pins out of her bun. She could only stare up at him as her thick hair fell in waves around her shoulders.

"You should wear it down," he said in a husky voice.

"You think so?"

"Looks sexier."

When he kissed her, it was a little bit of a shock. They hadn't kissed in a while. Also, just a couple hours ago, she'd been puking her brains out. She'd brushed her teeth – several times – and had swallowed half a bottle of Listerine, but still. Between the hangover and her conflicting emotions, his tongue was making her want to gag. Not the reaction she usually had to him. She grumbled and pushed at his chest till he backed away.

"What is going on?" she panted for air.

"Nothing. I just haven't kissed you in a long time. Wanted to give you a little reminder," was all he said. She stared at him like he was crazy.

"Okay, well, maybe while I'm hungover, we should *not* do that," she said, trying to laugh a little to break the mood. He had one hand in her hair, holding it away from the side of her face, and he stared down into her eyes.

"I think I have something that could make you feel better," he whispered, leaning close enough that his lips brushed against hers.

Katya was a red blooded heterosexual female – of course she was turned on, a sexy man was trying to kiss her. One whom she knew for a fact could make her hear colors and taste sound. It was very tempting. But as good as all those things were, they wouldn't banish a different man from her mind, and Liam deserved better than that.

"I can't," she whispered back, pressing her hand to his chest.

He stared at her for a long time and Katya felt like she was falling into a black hole. She'd already been knocked down by Wulf. If Liam turned his back on her, she wasn't sure what she'd do. Two support systems, gone in two days. She felt sick again.

"Maybe when you're feeling better," he suddenly said, then he kissed her on the nose before walking away. She suddenly became aware that she was holding her breath, and with a gasp of air she sat upright.

"Liam, maybe we should -" she started to confront the situation, but he held up his hand as he sat down.

"I have to call him back," he interrupted. "Do you mind if it's in private this time? Sorry, I have a full schedule today."

"Oh. I'm really sorry, I had no idea. Yeah, totally, I'll get out of here," she said quickly, standing up and gathering her things.

"No, don't be sorry. I'll see you later, okay?"

"Yeah. Yeah, sure. Okay."

"Angel cake."

She finally looked at him, just as she was about to leave.

"Yeah, Liam?"

"Thanks for the tacos."

Then he winked at her, and she felt a little better about the situation. She closed the door behind her as he picked up the phone and started dialing.

Katya went home and spent the rest of the day feeling weird. Confused. Her phone was glued to her hand. She could remember calling Wulf during her drunk fest, and her phone's log said the call had been several minutes long, but she couldn't quite remember *what* she'd said. While Tori moaned and hobbled around the kitchen, Katya bit the bullet and called Wulf.

"You've reached Stone."

She almost burst out laughing at his voice mail message. How appropriate, *"you've reached stone"* – because that's literally what a person was doing when they called Wulfric Stone. Reaching a man made out of cold hard rock. Carved out of marble. She didn't leave a message and let her phone fall beneath the couch.

The girls huddled together on the sofa and shared a pizza. Tori finally got the whole story out of Katya – everything that had happened in Carmel. Around two in the morning, someone knocked softly on the front door. It could only be Liam, but neither of them said anything. Just waited in silence till he went away.

"What are you going to do?" Tori whispered, after they'd moved into Katya's room and stretched out on her bed.

"I don't know."

"You can't just keep … existing like this."

"That's a little dramatic, it's only been a couple days since we've talked."

"Show up at his work."

"I am *not* doing that."

"You have to do *something*, Katya. What happened to the girl from the profile, who walked into a sex club and took it up the back door?"

"Jesus. If I'd known everyone would be so obsessed with my anal sex shenanigans, I wouldn't have done it at all."

"See! That's the kind of spunk I love seeing – this new, aggressive you! You like this guy. Really like him. So *fight for him*. Sounds like no one else in his life ever has, which really sucks. Maybe that's all he needs, to know that someone else will step up to bat for him," Tori offered.

Katya frowned. It was kind of true, Wulf had only ever had himself to depend on, and it was a very sweet sentiment. Which killed the whole idea before it could even get off the ground. Sweet and Wulf didn't mix. Orange juice and toothpaste were a better combination.

"I don't really know how to be this way. I mean, it was always an act," Katya tried to explain.

"Bullshit. An act doesn't get two gorgeous guys falling all over themselves for you."

"Ummm, there's a lot of gold diggers out there who would beg the differ."

"That's my point – these guys don't want gold diggers, they would spot a faker a mile away. They reacted to *you*, *this* is the real you. *The Evolution of Katya Tocci*. Enjoy it. Embrace it. And then go get this guy, before you lose him for good."

Sage words from a hungover bartender. Tori fell asleep soon after her grand speech, but Katya stayed awake for a while. Staring at the ceiling and still trying to figure out what the fuck she was going to do. She had one day before she had to go back to work, and she had a big week – she had to be on her A-game. She may have been taking steps towards realizing her entire life didn't need to revolve around her career, but she was also proud of what she did and she wanted to put out good work. People had booked her in good faith, she would not let them down.

I will not let these boys ruin me.

20

TUESDAY WENT BY WITH MORE CRIPPLING AGONY AND SELF-DOUBT. SHE couldn't bring herself to take Tori's advice and confront Wulf, so she contented herself with staring at her phone and praying for him to call. Liam finally went the creepy route and let himself into her apartment with his master key set, but she didn't mind too much. He was back to his normal self, teasing her and laughing with her. They spent most of the day together at his apartment – her oven was *STILL* broken, she reminded him – trying to teach him how to make macarons.

"Why do you want to learn how to make a French dessert?"

"Because you like making desserts."

"So?"

"And I like doing things you like."

She hadn't known how to respond to that, so she'd busied herself with the prep work. The macarons didn't turn out horrible – maybe not perfectly round, but they tasted delicious, and she assured Liam that in the end, that's all that really mattered in baking. She went home with a plateful, barely dodging a kiss before slipping through his door.

Nighttime was rough. She couldn't quite keep her thoughts at bay. It hurt that she could so easily be disposed of. It had been a week. She'd actually gotten out a physical calendar and counted the days – Wednesday would mark one week since she'd last seen or spoken to Wulf. He wasn't returning her phone calls or texts. It was like he'd disappeared.

Or like I died.

It *hurt*. And not just to know that he didn't care for her the same way she cared for him, but also because it showed that he'd *never* cared about her. Not even as a friend. There were moments when he'd seemed so bright and perfect to her, she'd almost been blinded by him.

She missed his voice. Missed him teasing her. Missed his tongue, the way it could burn a path across her body. His hands, squeezing and pinning and pulling. Missed seeing those all-too-rare smiles, and missed being happy when she put one on his face.

Apparently, looking at him like he was a present wasn't enough. If I'd known he was gonna cut me out of his life completely, I never would've gone to that stupid restaurant.

She took her time waking up on Wednesday morning. She wouldn't be in the bakery much that day – she had to go on-site to work with a client in their reception hall. She was glad because that meant work would be a bigger distraction than normal.

She slid into a dark pair of skinny jeans, then pulled on a tight, long sleeved shirt. Red, with thin navy stripes. Not exactly punk rock, but a definite departure from pink cashmere and pearls. She left her hair down on a whim, pinning one side back away from her face, but that was it. She just coaxed a couple soft waves out of the tresses, then called it good. She grabbed her binder and her sketch pad, then took off.

"Wow, Lauren," she sighed when she walked into the building. "This place is gorgeous."

Lauren, the bride-to-be, hurried forward to take Katya's hands in her own.

"Isn't it!? I can't believe I'm having my reception here. I never, in a million years, would've imagined myself here."

Lauren was a very special person. She was in her mid-forties with four children of varying ages. She'd lost her first husband to cancer when the youngest kid had been a newborn, but nothing kept Lauren down. She'd rallied, gotten a second job, then took night classes so she could become a vet tech. She was fun loving and had a big laugh, forcing everyone around her to be in a good mood.

Including, it turned out, the vet at the first clinic she interned for – "*San Francisco's best vet*", as he was hailed by multiple news sources who cared about that kind of thing. The man had more money than he knew what to do with, so he'd decided to share it all with Lauren and her kids, whom he'd taken into his home like they were his own.

So if anyone deserved a huge wedding and a reception hall that probably cost more to rent than one of Katya's paychecks, it was most definitely Lauren. They'd clicked instantly, from the first time she'd come into the bakery, a year and a half before – she'd seen a magazine featuring one of Katya's designs. One picture, and she'd just known that's who needed to make the cake on her special day.

"It's beautiful, Lauren, I'm so happy for you. And I'm super excited about this cake!"

Katya had brought a rolling trolley with her. It was filled with samples. Lauren was working in a medical clinic and getting away was hard, so they'd agreed to do the tasting and designing at the reception hall, a halfway point between their two jobs.

"And I'm super hungry. I'll eat, you look around, and then we can talk about my design."

Katya set up the samples on a high table, then left her client to eat while she walked around the building. She made notes as she went, poking around the kitchen area. Lauren wanted a massive cake – the main one would have six layers, and then there would be two satellite cakes, each with four layers. The layers were all four inches thick. It was a monster and Katya wanted to make sure it could be safely delivered to the hall, or else she'd have to assemble and decorate it there in the morning, which she *really* didn't want to do.

Luckily, there were huge loading doors that opened directly into the kitchen, and then double doors could be propped open leading into the hall. She could bring the cakes all in one piece, load them onto carts, then wheel them onto the floor. Easy peezy.

"Looks good, Lauren. This is a great space," Katya said, jotting down notes as she hurried across the huge ballroom.

"I told you! Did you see the chandelier? And those stairs in the lobby?" the other woman squealed. Katya nodded, trying to remember the measurements for the cake. While she flipped through her notes, she heard the doors at the front of the room open. She glanced up, then returned to her notepad as a group of men and two women walked into the room. Another party wanting to look over their rental space.

"Yeah, it's amazing. I'm excited – I've never seen a wedding here," she said, sliding onto a stool and putting down her pad.

"Oh, well, you'll see mine here," Lauren said around a mouthful of red velvet. "You'll love it. Champagne fountain, sprays of lilies and hyacinth *everywhere*. And white. Head to toe white. I'll be in white, my bridesmaids will be in white, *you'll* be in white – I cannot wait."

"Okay then, so buy a white dress," Katya laughed, jotting that down in her notes.

"Definitely. A little white dress. What flavor is this one, the pink? I love it!"

"Strawberry lemonade, I thought it might be fun. For the satellites, you can choose a filling to match whatever flavor you pick, but for the main, I wouldn't …"

Katya's voice died off. Lauren glanced at her, then did a double take and put down her fork. Patted her friend on the arm and said her name a couple times.

"I'm sorry," Katya breathed. "Would you excuse me for a moment? I just need to say hello to an old friend."

She stepped down from the stool, then took a couple steps onto the dance floor. Was impressed with how calm and composed she was – she wasn't shaking. She wasn't trembling. Sure, when she'd first heard that laugh, a laugh she'd never heard often enough, it had rocked her a little. Shocked her into movement. But she was calm. And she was composed.

"*Wulfric.*"

The party that had entered the room had moved to within a couple yards of her tasting. What they were doing there, she didn't know. Was Wulf throwing a party? Were those his business associates? She flicked her eyes down to where his hand was resting on the one woman's hip.

"Hello," he said, his smile still in place. It made her feel sick. "What a small world. Gentlemen, Natasha – this is Katya Tocci. We used to be neighbors."

That was his introduction. She'd slept next to him and seen him naked and he'd been inside her, and that's what she got? They were neighbors?

"Do you work here at the reception hall?" one of the men asked in a polite voice. Her eyes didn't move away from Wulf's.

"No, I'm here with a client, going over some wedding details," she answered.

"Ah, yes. Ms. Tocci here is a baker!" Wulf explained.

His voice was heavy with condescension – he was saying it to be rude. Putting down her profession. He'd never cared about what she did, before – he'd once told her he wouldn't give a shit if she pumped gas for a living, that's not what their relationship was about. Yet here he was, using it as a weapon to undermine her. To put her down.

"I am. I design and make wedding cakes," she said proudly.

"That's cute," the other woman said. "My son is having his eighth grade graduation in a week, maybe you could make him a little something!"

"Can I speak to you?" Katya blurted out, her voice loud in the room. She swore she could hear it echo. The painted on smile never left Wulf's face as he removed his hand from the other woman and placed it on the small of Katya's back, guiding her away from the group.

"*Do not* create a scene," he whispered when they were out of hearing range from his friends.

"*Are you shitting me!?*" she hissed, slapping his hand away as she turned to face him. "What the fuck is going on, Wulf?"

"I didn't know you'd be here," he assured her. "I wouldn't have come if I'd known. This building is for sale, those people are looking to buy. That's it."

"That's it? *That's it!?* I haven't spoken to you in a week, you won't return my calls, my messages, my voicemails, *nothing*, and that's it?" she demanded, folding her arms across her chest.

"I am *at work*, Tocci. You're *at work*. We have clients here. Act like a professional," he warned her.

Act like a professional? Oh, Wulfric. Katya had moved way beyond acting like anything. She gave literally zero fucks. Her anger had reached its boiling point.

"Don't you ever fucking tell me what to do!" she snapped at him, and was pleased when he looked shocked. "And act like a professional!? HA! I'll do that when you learn how to act like a *human being*."

"Watch your fucking mouth," he growled.

"Fuck you."

"We've done that dance."

How did we get to this point? From laughing and playing in my bedroom, to hurling swear words at each other in front of strangers? Who is this person in front of me?

"What did I do to you?" she suddenly whispered, catching him off guard. She cleared her throat and spoke again. "I was nice to you. I was kind to you. I never asked for more than you were willing to give. I'm sorry I told you how I felt, I'm sorry if I made things awkward. I would have apologized to you a week ago, but you wouldn't let me. You wouldn't even do me the courtesy of just ending it. No, you were too busy being a mean, nasty, hurtful, *asshole. What did I ever do to you to deserve that!?"*

By the end, she was yelling. Before, their voices had been at a level where it was obvious the conversation was intense, but still within the realm of polite. Now, the cat was out of the bag. She was shouting and breathing hard and probably red in the face.

And she wasn't the only one.

"Asshole? I'm an *asshole?* I have bent over backwards for you," he yelled back. "I was nice to you. I went to your home. I met your god-damn mother. *I let you fuck some other guy,* almost the entire time we were together, and I never said shit! Didn't fucking complain once. And *I'm* the bad guy? Sorry, Tocci. You've got it backwards. *You're* the asshole."

"Me!?" she shrieked. "*You* should've said something! Wulfric fucking Stone, so high and mighty, looks down on everyone else, treats us all like we're peasants, and you couldn't even fucking open your mouth and just tell me what you were feeling!"

"I didn't have to tell you shit."

"Maybe if you had, you could've learned that I stopped sleeping with him – *weeks ago!"*

"I don't owe you anything."

She shoved him in the chest.

"No, you don't *feel* anything, that's the problem."

"Fuck off."

"*We've done that dance,*" she mocked him.

"Yeah, you have done that dance with me – and who knows who else."

She slapped him across the face, then stepped up close to him.

"You're a pussy," she growled. "Mad at me for seeing someone else. Scared of what I was feeling for you. Scared you might be feeling something for me. So you ran away. *Pussy.*"

She didn't wait for his response. The moment was too much. She was most definitely *not* this girl, no matter what Tori, or Liam, or some made up profile, said about her. She stepped around him and strode back to her table.

"Tough talk, Tocci," he called her out, matching her step for step. "Is that the first time you've ever said that word?"

"Just go away," she grumbled, grabbing at her notepad and pens and sketchbook, trying to ignore the fact that everyone else in the room was staring at them with rapt attention.

"No. You started this, so I'll fucking finish it. You want to know what the real problem is?"

"*No.*"

"You're a scared little girl, who decided she needed to get fucked. So you went out and found a man. Found *two* men. So much attention for little Katya Tocci! The dull girl from next door scores with the hot older neighbor. But the moment I take some space for myself, you freak the fuck out. Did you think we were special? That you were my girlfriend?" he started laughing at her. "You knew what we were from the beginning. You're the one who slipped those panties into my pocket. You knew *exactly* what you were getting into. Stupid fucking girl. Gets fucked right and thinks she's in love. *Pathetic.* I hope you -"

She couldn't take it anymore. She was going to have a mental breakdown. He was beating her with his words, she could feel it in her muscles. Feel it all the way to her bones. *To her heart.* But he *would not* break her. She wouldn't give him that satisfaction. So in the middle of his rant, she let out a shriek and grabbed the closest thing to her – the half-eaten strawberry lemonade cake – and threw it at him.

"*Shut the fuck up!*" she shrieked, following up with a piece of chocolate ganache.

There was complete silence in the room. A pin drop could've been heard. They stared at each other, both breathing hard. She'd definitely crossed the line, throwing food at his suit that was worth thousands of dollars – but he'd fucking burned rubber as he'd gone over the line. Had left it in the dust and never looked back. So she figured cake throwing was warranted.

"Are you serious?" he breathed, running his hand down his tie, flinging frosting to the floor. Katya didn't say a word, just stared at him, one of her eyebrows boldly raised. Then, from behind them, came a snort. Then a snicker. A laugh being suppressed.

"I'm sorry, sir, but you kind of deserved it," Lauren interjected.

Shit hit the fan. Or more correctly, *cake* hit the fan. Wulf lunged at the table top, shocking Katya and causing her to shriek. While her mouth was still open, she got a face-full of vanilla dessert. She coughed on it and blindly reached out, squeezing whatever was closest to her and rubbing it all over Wulf's suit. That earned her another piece of cake, this time splattered all over the left side of her head.

"*You fuck!*" she was shrieking, almost incoherent as she kept adding more dessert to his chest. "I hope it fucking stains! I hope it never fucking comes out! I fucking hate you! *You stupid fuck!*"

She wasn't sure how long their food fight lasted – it could only have been a couple seconds, but it felt like forever. Everyone was shouting, not just them, and then Lauren was in the middle of it, getting cake all over her scrubs.

"Hey, hey, hey! Knock it off, you two! *Hey!* I know you're pissed off, buddy, but that is a woman you're currently whitewashing with chocolate cake! *Calm down!*" she demanded.

"Mr. Stone! Ms. Tocci! Please! Show some decency!" that was Wulf's assistant, the tiny woman who rarely said much, screaming at both of them.

They were yanked apart. Some strange man had his arms around Katya's waist, holding her away from the table. Lauren was in front of Wulf, both her hands on his chest, and the assistant was standing in the middle of it all, slipping and sliding in the mess on the floor.

When Katya cleared the frosting out of her eyes, she gasped. From his collarbone to his belt, Wulf was covered in cake. There was a little smeared down his cheek, and a chunk in the side of his hair. She was almost proud of herself – she'd certainly gotten him at least as good as he'd gotten her.

"What is the meaning of this, Mr. Stone!?" the man holding her demanded.

"Get your hands off me!" she shouted, pulling herself free. She quickly moved around, putting the table between her and Wulf. He also stepped away, creating more distance between them.

"It didn't have to be like this," he said in a scratchy voice.

"No, it didn't, Wulf. I hope you're happy with yourself," she replied, not backing down one inch.

"Always am, Tocci. Ayumi, we're leaving," he turned to his assistant. The woman took a deep breath and held her ground.

"No, sir."

"Excuse me?"

"I said no. I'd like to stay and help clean up *your mess.*"

There was a tense moment, with Wulf's glare bouncing between Katya and Ayumi. Then he gave her a curt nod, and with that, he walked out of the room.

Out of her life.

His clients lingered for a moment, still obviously in shock over what had happened. Lauren finally chased them away while Katya dropped to her knees, attempting to scoop up the cake from off the floor. After hesitating only a moment, Wulf's assistant moved to help her.

"What are you two doing!? Stop that, it's filthy! I'll get someone from the building to clean it," Lauren said, grabbing Katya by the arm and pulling her to her feet.

"No, no, I'll take care of it," Ayumi spoke in her normal terse voice, but she looked at Katya like she was hurting for her. "It's the least I can do. I'll go find someone. I'm … I'm so sorry."

The petite lady scampered from the room, leaving a shocked Katya in her wake. They'd never really spoken, except for Ayumi to pass along messages from Wulf. That she'd stayed behind and was helping Katya, it was a little mind blowing.

Or it would be, if I had any brains left in my head. You just had a screaming match and a food fight in front of your client, you idiot.

"I am so, so sorry, Lauren. So sorry. I don't know what came over me. I … I completely understand if you don't want me to do your cake anymore. I'll find you a new baker – the best baker in San Francisco. I'll pay for it," she gushed, raising shaky hands to her head, shoving her doughy fingers into her hair.

"Are you kidding? Honey, after that show, I cannot wait to have you at my party! Shit, if I didn't have to go back to work, I would be taking you out for drinks and demanding the backstory to that little scrap!"

"Little scrap!? Lauren, I called him a pussy, he called me a slut, and then we threw cake at each other. Nothing about that was little!"

"You're right. It was *epic*. Look, go clean yourself up. Don't worry about a thing, we can go over the design some other time."

"This isn't right. I was beyond unprofessional."

"What would be right? Firing a girl who just got very publicly dumped by a guy who looks like he might be the world's biggest asshole? No, sweetie, you've had a rough enough day. Who you sleep with or fight with has no impact on how my cake tastes, and frankly, that's all I care about."

Katya started laughing, and didn't stop till the laughs turned into tears. Lauren had an arm wrapped around her when Ayumi came back into the room.

"They're sending a janitor," she said. "Please, don't worry – I'll make sure any cleaning fees are billed to The Stone Agency."

"No offense," Katya managed a watery laugh. "But I think you chose your side when you stayed with me. Why did you do that?"

"Mr. Stone is ultimately just a paycheck – I still have ethics, and I still know when wrong has been done. Even if he's not ready to apologize yet, I wanted to stay behind and at least apologize on his behalf.

My job can wait for an hour or two while I help clean up."

"Honestly, I'll be surprised if you still have a job."

"Please. That agency couldn't run without me. I *will* be going back to my job, and he *will* be getting a piece of my mind. Besides, Mr. Stone would never let me go, I'm invaluable to him," Ayumi stated.

"Huh. Must be nice. I wouldn't know how that feels," Katya whispered.

And with that, the tears started all over again.

21

JESUS, I KNEW IT WAS GONNA BE BAD, BUT GODDAMN, I TOOK IT TO A TEN.
Wulfric couldn't remember ever losing so much control before – Katya had that effect on him. He lost his mind when he was around her. Usually it worked to both their benefits. That day, it had worked against them.

He had thought he could keep her separate. In a special place in his mind, well away from his heart. Similar to where he kept everyone else, only a little darker. Only a little farther back. Turned out, he'd pushed her so far back in his mind, she'd fallen straight past his defenses and taken up root in his chest, blossomed inside his heart. Made a garden there. A bright and sunny spot, right in the middle of his life.

There was no other ending for them, *but* an ending. He knew that, had known it since the beginning. He'd wanted to spare her the pain, so he'd walked away. Built up walls around her in his chest, tried to protect her from his negativity by removing himself.

Then she'd been in front of him. Nowhere to hide from her big blue eyes. So sad as she looked up at him. So soft and gentle and beautiful. *So hurt.* He couldn't handle that kind of pain.

So he'd ripped out that garden, right out of his chest. Thrown it in her face. He knew what was best for her, even if she didn't, and he would make her see the light. He would make her hate him.

Problem was, when something took up root, those roots stayed behind. Each step he'd taken away from her, those roots had pulled tighter and tighter. Stretched to their limit. By the time he'd left the building, each one had snapped clean in half. The dying rootstock festered in his chest, poisoning him. Making him want to throw up.

I make myself sick.

He only had himself to blame. She'd been a plaything – he'd even told her "*... my own personal fuck toy ...*" and he'd meant it. Pity he hadn't listened to himself. While he'd been playing his game, he'd been sharing so many moments with her. Growing something wonderful with her. He remembered having lunches with her, sitting by street carts and laughing with each other. Sitting on her bed, getting a manicure and discussing dreams. Sitting in his conference room, telling her he never took anyone to his home – though all the while, he'd been planning on taking her there.

He dropped his head and stared at his floor. He'd given her more than enough reasons to hate him. To never want to see him again. Their little food fight had worked much better than his silent treatment ever could have – had gone better than anything he could've planned.

Good for Katya, that she would be able to let him go. He could do that much for her.

Wulf, however, was going to bear the pain of losing her for a very long time.

This is for the best. This is for her. After all the things you've done to her, you certainly don't deserve to keep her. You're Wulfric Stone, and stones don't love.

22

KATYA STOOD IN HER APARTMENT FOR ALL OF TWO SECONDS WHILE SHE mulled over her options. She could call Tori, beg her to come home. Call her mother, beg her to come get her. Call Liam and just sob incoherently. Or just take a shower and forget Wulfric Stone ever existed.

She went with option five – she grabbed the vodka out of the freezer and went straight up to the roof. She sat down and put her feet in the kiddie pool, chugging the alcohol straight from the bottle. She raked her hands through her hair, not caring that she was spreading more of the cake into the strands, and yanked everything up into a ponytail. Then she scooted off the sofa and sat directly in the pool. While completely dressed. She propped up her knees and wrapped her arms loosely around them, staring off into the distance while sipping at her booze.

She wasn't sure how much time passed before she heard the lock jiggling in the door. Enough that she'd polished off maybe a quarter of the bottle or so. Not enough to dull the pain. She sighed as Liam strolled across the roof top, but she didn't look at him.

"You alright, angel cake?" he sighed, coming to a stop at the edge of the pool.

"Peachy keen. How'd you find me?"

"I knew you'd be here. This is our special spot."

The sentiment just depressed her more and she took another swig of alcohol.

"Did Tori send you?" she asked. He squatted down low, rubbing his hand up and down her thigh, getting cake on his fingers.

"Your boss called her," he said by way of an answer.

"Oh great. I'm sure they're just thrilled with me."

"She said they sounded concerned."

"And you? Are you concerned?"

"Always."

He stood up and shrugged out of his jacket, toed off his shoes, then climbed into the pool with her. They moved around – he was so lanky, his legs took up a lot of room. Finally, she was back in her position with her legs bent, sitting with his knees on the outside of hers.

"Thanks," she sighed, offering him her bottle. He took it, watching her as he threw his head back and took a healthy shot.

"Wanna have angry sex? Might make you feel better."

"No thanks."

"Sorry, bad joke."

"No," she groaned, letting her head fall forward. "It was a good joke. You're so … so good to me, Liam."

She couldn't help it. She sniffled and watched as a tear fell onto her pant leg.

"I told you, say that shit softly, it'll ruin my reputation if it gets out," he teased her.

"He was so awful," she suddenly whispered.

"He was?"

"God, the things he said. He was … hurtful. He said things *just to hurt*. Why? I don't get it. I didn't do anything to him. I was standing there, and he just kept lashing me. He wouldn't stop. Why? What did I do to deserve that?" she cried, pressing her face into her jeans. She felt Liam's hand on the back of her head, smoothing over her ponytail.

"Nothing. *Nothing,* Katya. He's an asshole. He's such a dick, and he doesn't deserve to even breathe the same air as you. *Do not* take any of this on yourself," he urged.

Easy for Liam to say. The things Wulf had said, the things he'd implied. Did he really think those things about her? Did he really feel that way? He'd laughed at her. *Laughed,* because she was stupid enough to think they were something special. To think *she* was something to special.

Nothing is special to a man carved out of stone.

"This is dumb," she finally laughed, lifting her head and wiping at her face. "I'm crying over a man who is quite possibly evil incarnate, and who also doesn't like me one little bit. What a waste of time."

"That's the spirit."

Katya snatched the vodka back and took a long pull.

"Yeah. Yeah, fuck him. I'm not wasting another minute on Wulfric Stone."

As soon as she said it, Katya regretted it. She never, ever said their names to each other. She kept them very separate, didn't want Liam cyber-stalking Wulf or something. Hadn't wanted Wulf to have a name in his head.

Not that he would've cared, anyway.

"Wulfric. That's … an *interesting* name," Liam's voice was soft as he played with the end of her ponytail. She sighed. Cat was out of the bag, couldn't hurt if she explained a little.

"They've all got weird names like that."

"They?"

"He has two younger sisters, Genevieve and Brighton. I think his mom was obsessed with Old English history," Katya chuckled, rubbing at her eyes. "Good lord, look at me. I need to take a shower."

She couldn't help but laugh as she looked over herself. Cake all over her shirt. Smeared down the sides of her pants. She'd wiped most of it off her face, but could feel it drying and getting crusty in her hair.

"You look perfect," Liam said.

He was just sitting there. Smiling at her. She stared at him for a moment. This amazing man. So good looking, it raised her blood pressure. So sweet, it swelled her heart. It was overcast, the warm spell they'd been having seemed to be over, yet he was sitting in a freezing cold kiddie pool with her, getting completely soaked.

"Why do you put up with me?" she sighed, finally climbing to her feet. He stood up as well, taking the vodka bottle from her.

"Because you are so sweet," he told her, collecting his belongings as he followed her to the door.

"I don't know. I wasn't very sweet in that reception hall. The things I said to him …"

"I would've paid to have been there."

"You would've laughed."

"I would've ripped his fucking head off."

Katya was shocked at the tone of voice Liam was using. They were waiting for the elevator and she turned to face him. She'd never heard him angry before – not *really* angry. And he sounded beyond that, even. He sounded *pissed the fuck off*.

"It's done," she said, stepping into the lift as soon as the doors opened. "Nothing you need to get upset about – it's over. So over, it's hard to believe it ever even began."

"Katya … you're a good person. There is literally nothing you could've done to deserve that kind of treatment," he said.

"Yeah, well, try explaining that to him."

"*Maybe I should.*"

They stopped on her floor, and as soon as the doors opened, she went to step out into the hallway. Liam grabbed her arm, though, halting her mid-way. She put out her hand, stopping the doors from closing her.

"Coming?" she asked, nodding towards her apartment door.

"I have to go back to work," he said, though something in his voice made her doubt him. He sounded off, like his brain was a million miles away.

"Oh. Okay. Well, thank you for checking on me, I really appreciate it."

"Come out with me," he said in an abrupt voice.

"What, to the club?"

"No, this weekend."

"I don't really feel like tacos," she laughed.

"I'm not talking about tacos."

Again, that very serious tone of voice. Angry. She stopped laughing and stared up at him.

"Then what are you talking about?"

"I'm talking about a date," he said, not looking away from her eyes. "Go out with me this weekend, on a date. Let me take you somewhere and help you forget him. Let me show you how special you really are."

She almost laughed again. Liam? Asking her on a date? Liam didn't date. Liam ate tacos, played video games, and liked to have sex. Lots and lots of kinky, loud, hilarious sex. They'd known each other for a month now, and he'd never once asked her out on a date. Why now?

*Because he knew how you felt about Wulf. He knew, and respected that choice, and didn't make you choose between them. Because he's a good guy. He's an amazing guy. **He's the best guy**.*

"I don't know ..." she let her voice trail off as she worried at her bottom lip.

"Please, Katya. I think I could be really good for you, and you already know that we're great together. It didn't work with that guy – give this one a chance," he said, pressing his hand to his chest.

God, had anything simpler and sweeter ever been said? Certainly not to her. She had to work to not start crying again. Here Liam was, knowing she was heartbroken over another man, knowing she probably still had feelings for Wulf, yet still – he was putting himself out there. He was putting his heart in her hands and saying *"here, this is for you"* – what was she supposed to say to that?

Yes. You say yes, and you try very hard to fall in love with this amazing man.

"Yes," she breathed. His eyebrows shot up and he seemed genuinely shocked at her response.

"Yes, you'll got out with me?"

"Yes, but Liam, I can't promise that I'll be a very good date. I'm … I'm a little broken right now," she tried to explain, trying to protect herself. Protect him.

"Then let me try to fix you," he whispered, leaning in close and giving her a soft kiss.

She really was going to cry again, so she stepped back. Gave him a watery smile as the elevator doors finally slid shut. Then she turned around and went home, crying in earnest while she tried to unlock her door.

If Liam is so right for me, then why does this feel like it's so wrong?

Things were not good. The universe gave her the rest of Wednesday to deal with her inner demons. She locked herself in her room, climbed in between her sheets – still wearing her clothing and cake mess – and stayed that way for a solid eighteen hours. She ignored all the phone calls and messages and even Tori, when the other girl finally came home. She just needed some time. Time to catch her breath. His words had carved her open, she was barely holding everything inside.

Thursday was a new day, though, and no rest for the wicked. It rained on and off, adding to her mood. She finally showered and realized sleeping in cake mess was definitely a mistake. When she got out, Tori was standing in the hallway, her hands on her hips.

"Glad to see you're alive," she said. Katya grunted.

"That's a matter of opinion."

"Look," her roommate sighed. "I'm not going to press you for the whole story, *yet*. I got a murky version from your boss, who you really need to call. Just know that whatever happened, I know it's not your fault, and I wouldn't even care if it was, and if we need to go out and bury a body, then just give me a heads up. That's all I wanted you to know."

Katya finally laughed. For the first time in an eternity, she genuinely laughed.

"You're too good to me, Tori Bellows."

"Don't I know it."

Katya crawled into the middle of her bed and called the bakery. It wasn't a comfortable conversation, but it wasn't awful, either. She'd apprenticed at the bakery at the age of eighteen, and had worked there ever since. The little shop was owned by a young husband and wife team, and Katya had stuck with them through lean times, through her rise to popularity, through sharks trying to steal her away – she had a good relationship with the owners.

But she also knew she'd crossed some definite lines. *Huge* lines. The staff at the reception hall had been the ones to call the bakery. Lauren had kept her lips shut, and when Katya's bosses had finally called her to check out the story, Lauren had defended Katya staunchly, threatening to pull her business from the bakery if they so much as looked at Katya wrong.

Of course they wouldn't look at her poorly. They also weren't going to let her go, and not just because of the business she brought in, but because they cared about her. She was like family to them, they assured her. They didn't want something like that to ever happen again, of course, but they were worried about her. Concerned. Was everything alright? What, exactly, had happened?

She couldn't tell them the full story, so she boiled it down to basics and said it had been a nasty break up with her estranged boyfriend. Since Katya's personal life had never ever interfered with her job before, they figured it must have been a *really* nasty break up to have exploded that way.

They brought up the idea of a sabbatical. She'd been working very hard. Maybe too hard, it was suggested. She'd gone straight from school to work, immersing herself in the industry. Maybe it was time she take a moment for herself. She would still get paid, and she could come in and work on wedding cakes for clients if she wanted to, but everything else would be handled by the bakery – they could call the other clients and redistribute the work or cancel the orders.

Katya had no choice but to agree. She was beyond humiliated, having a conversation like that with her employers. To be told, however politely, that she needed to take a leave of absence. She silently cried as they wrapped up the conversation.

I promised myself I wouldn't let those boys interfere with my work. What the fuck happened!?

After the tears stopped, she dragged herself into the kitchen. It was late afternoon, but Tori was wearing boy shorts and a tight t-shirt – sleep wear. Working at the club had her sleeping in till crazy hours. She was yawning while she flipped through a magazine, though she perked up when her friend entered the room.

"How did it go?" she asked. Katya dropped into a chair at the table.

"I'm on sabbatical," she sighed. "They think I'm just burnt out. I'll still get paid, and I can still fulfill wedding cake orders, collect commission on those, if I want to. It just …"

"Sucks?" Tori offered.

"Big time."

"I'm sorry, honey. Maybe it is for the best – you work harder than anyone I know, and you're only twenty-three. Time to relax. Maybe go to Mexico for a weekend, get wasted and flash your boobs to frat boys."

"*Pass.*"

"Well hey, wanna go catch a movie this weekend?" Tori suggested. Katya groaned and dropped her head down.

"I have a date this weekend," she mumbled.

"Excuse me!?"

"I'm going on a date."

"Whoa, whoa, whoa. The guy you were crushing on just shit all over your heart, and you already have a date lined up?"

"When you say it like that, it sounds -"

"*Fucking epic!* Legendary! I'm so proud of you! Fuck that wolf guy and whatever high horse he rode in on, you don't need him. Onto the next man," Tori proclaimed loudly.

"It's Liam."

"It's Liam what?"

"The date. Liam asked me on a date. I'm going on a date with Liam."

There was silence for a long, way too tense, moment. Tori froze in the act of pouring some creamer into her coffee. Katya stared at it, worried the cup would overflow. At the last possible second, the carton tipped upright.

"I thought you and Liam were casual. That you weren't even having scx anymore," Tori said, not looking up while she slurped at the coffee.

"We aren't – we haven't in a while. He came to check on me yesterday, and when he dropped me down here, he asked me out. He was just … he was so good to me. I felt like I needed to say yes," Katya tried to explain.

"Oh."

She was shocked. Tori was never silent. Never short on words. The woman even talked in her sleep. She was always interested in everything around her, and particularly in anything to do with Katya's love life. Her lack of interest was a little stunning, and once again, Katya felt the tumblers falling into place.

"Holy shit, you like Liam."

251

"What!?"

"You do. You like him."

"No, I don't."

"You do."

"I don't."

"It's okay, Tori. God, I'll call and cancel."

Katya had barely stood up when Tori reached out and grabbed her arm. Halted her movements.

"No! No, don't do that. And don't say anything to him," she insisted.

"But you do like him," Katya checked.

"No. Fuck, I don't know. Maybe? Not really? Like," Tori struggled with words. "You know how he is with women. It's like he can't *not* flirt, so am I just reacting to that? Or am I reacting to him? He's always smiling and flirting with me, but he's like so nice and funny and understanding. It just sort of ... happened. *If* it even really happened. Fuck, I have no clue."

"I really think I should cancel this date, then," Katya said.

"No. Because even if I do really like him – which I'm not even sure I do! – it doesn't matter, because he doesn't like me. That boy is crazy in love with you," Tori said.

"No he's not!"

"He is. You should hear him, Kat. He talks about you all the time."

"Only because I'm your mutual friend."

"*To everybody*. To the bouncer, the bartenders, the clients, everybody."

"Well ... I know some of them ... too ..."

"He's got a picture of you two as his wallpaper on his phone. He looks at you with those eyes ... God, Katya, I hope someone looks at me someday, the way Liam Edenhoff looks at you. So you see – I could be head over heels in love with him, and it wouldn't matter, because he's head over feet for *you*."

"I still don't think that's true, but even if it is, it's not worth it to me. Not if it's going to hurt you," Katya insisted.

"It won't hurt me, I promise. It's a crush, at the very most. That's all. Just a crush."

Yeah, just a crush, won't hurt a bit. That's what I thought before I met the man made of stone.

"Tori, I still think -"

"If you miss out on this amazing man who has the potential to love you better and harder than you've ever been loved, I will move out, right this instant."

They stared at each other for a long second, then both burst out laughing.

"You could never move out," Katya snickered. "Who'd cook for you? Clean up after you?"

"And who'd get you to leave your room? Show you new music videos?"

They laughed for a long time, both feeling better about their shitty situations. Tori was able to convince Katya to go out with Liam. At least one date. If it worked out, then Katya could find the new great love of her life. If it didn't, then Tori could pick up his broken pieces.

Feeling a little wrong for plotting out Liam's love life, Katya decided to call it a night. Right after she laid down, her phone pinged. For just a second, a stupid, foolish, embarrassing second, she hoped it was Wulf. What he could ever possibly say to rectify the situation, she didn't know. Didn't think it was possible. But she still hoped.

It was from Liam, and was only three lines.

Sunday. Wear something nice. Can't wait to see you.

She cried herself to sleep all over again.

———◇———

Katya spent most of Friday and Saturday alternating between pre-tending to be happy, and trying not to cry so much. Her eyes would be puffy for the rest of her life if she didn't get a grip.

Her parents called Saturday afternoon. That was a joy. They didn't know about her little incident, and she didn't want them to know. Her parents babbled away on different lines in the house, both talking over each other. Her father was sad to have missed her, and she said she missed him, too. She wished he had been there, it had been an eye opening experience, being so open and honest with her mother. She was curious what it would be like with her dad.

They wanted her to visit. Her mother wanted her to bring Wulf. Her dad thought that was a great idea. Katya took deep breaths through her nose and tried to remain calm. She laughed it off and talked her way around it, not really answering them. *"He never really liked me and possibly hates me"* wouldn't go over so well, and she didn't want to make things awkward between her mother and Ms. Stone. She agreed to visit as soon as she could – probably sooner than they expected. They all got off the phone making kissy noises at each other.

Then she went back to her room and spent the next couple hours deciding on an outfit for her date. She almost cried again when she pulled out the dress she'd worn to her date with Wulf, when they'd slept together for the first time. She chucked it to the floor and kicked it to the corner of the closet.

She settled on a soft, salmon pink dress. It was short and flowy, very typical for her style. It was made out of a sheer chiffon-like ma-terial and harmonized perfectly with her skin tone. She remembered how Tori had described her – sweet and innocent, but in a way that made men want to defile her and make her dirty. Yup, the dress fit that description to a T.

She went to bed feeling a little better about the date.

And a lot worse about Wulf.

She was keeping him at the edges of her mind, but just like in real life, he was threatening to crash through anyway. She remembered their times together at her parents' house. Thought about his smile and his laugh. The way he'd looked at her sometimes.

Was it all a lie?

Then she thought about his words. The things he'd said to her. The way he'd talked to her. How angry he'd looked, his eyes like ice and fire. Like he hadn't cared that she was broken and bleeding out – he'd just wanted to keep hitting. Wanted to keep hurting.

Was it all a lie?

Katya fell asleep with tears in her eyes, and only sure of one thing.

Not for me, it wasn't. Not one little bit.

23

KATYA WAS NERVOUS.

She hadn't spoken to Liam since he'd texted her what day to be ready.

Hadn't spoken to Wulf since she'd ruined his suit.

At four o'clock on Sunday, Liam finally texted her. Just one short sentence.

Be ready at seven.

It reminded her of Wulf, the way he'd never planned anything, had always just called her. And of course, when Wulfric Stone called, Katya Tocci always came.

She shook off those feelings and got ready. Teased her hair out big, then scraped it all back into a massive round bun. She felt like a ballerina, in her gauzy pink dress and high top hair-do. She put on a pair of strappy stilettos, then went downstairs. She was striding across the lobby when Liam walked through the front door.

"Ah, man, I was gonna come to your door, do this shit right and …"

His voice dropped off and he even stopped walking. Katya came to a stop in front of him, searching his face. He kept staring down at her.

"What?" she asked.

"You look fucking incredible."

She blushed and looked down at herself.

"Do I? I know it's not over the top sexy, or anything, but I always liked this dress," she said, smoothing her hand over the skirt.

"No self-deprecation tonight, angel cake. You are too pretty and too perfect for that," he said, his hand coming to rest on the side of her arm. She finally smiled.

"Alright, deal. I look fucking incredible," she even managed a laugh.

They walked out of the building, Liam's arm around her waist. She felt it like it was a weight. Like it was dragging her down. Like it was *wrong*. She told herself it was because she still felt so upset about the fight with Wulf, so she banished him from her mind and concentrated on the man in front of her.

They took a taxi to a far away restaurant. It was very posh, and as they sat down, she noticed for the first time how nice he looked. Liam always looked good, even in his worn t-shirts and ratty plaid flannels. But in a dress shirt and blazer, both pressed and tailored, he was drop dead gorgeous.

We make a good couple.

She'd never really thought about it before, looking good with someone. Matching someone. She wondered how she and Wulf had looked together. She was so feminine and soft, he was so hard and aggressively male. They'd probably looked ridiculous. Like a wolf taking his pet bunny out for a walk.

Liam was charming, but of course she knew that about him. He was funny and he was smart, and he'd turned all those things up to ten for their date. He smiled and smirked at her, teasing her and making her laugh. Touched her knee under the table, ran his hand up to her thigh.

By the end of dessert, Katya felt like she was going to strangle herself with her napkin. She wanted to be in love with Liam, so badly. She *did* love him, in a way. And she'd grown to care about him, *so much*.

But if his hand moved one inch higher, she was going to throw up all over her leftovers.

The whole ride back home was even worse. He was talking into her neck while he nuzzled her, telling her how much he cared about her. How much he'd grown to appreciate her. How special and wonderful and beautiful she was to him.

Hear him, Katya Tocci. He's actually saying these words to you – wearing his heart on his sleeve. He would never call you names. Never make you feel bad about yourself. Never mistreat you or use you.

It was no good, though. She could tell he wanted to come up to her apartment, but she managed to laugh it off and keep him at bay. She couldn't, however, stop the good night kiss. The date was over, the gentleman expected a kiss. He wrapped her up in his arms, crushing her to him and lifting her onto her toes. She'd always liked the way Liam kissed, so out of control and full of passion. Nothing chaste about those kisses – his tongue was always part of the action. Normally, it made her want nothing more than to have his tongue in other places.

Not that night, though. She kissed him once, twice. A third time, very slowly as she stepped away. They made promises to speak in the coming days, discuss their "feelings". When he turned to walk away, she actually held her hand over mouth, trying to keep her "feelings" inside – as well as her dinner.

She could not go home. She couldn't face Tori – the other girl would take one look at her, and know. Paradoxically, she wanted to talk to Liam. In the short time they'd known each other, she'd grown to depend on him as someone she could tell anything to; someone who could help sort out her problems. This was one problem she had to deal with on her own, though.

A man who could really love you, but you can't love him back. A man who never even liked you, and you might already be in love with him.

She burst out of her building and ran down the street. She looked ridiculous, she knew, sprinting in her high heels and short dress. She went for a couple blocks before finding a BART station. She took the stairs two at a time, almost biting it once. She managed to cling to the railing and got down without injury, then raced for the train. She slipped onto a train just as the doors were closing and she bent over, putting her hands on her knees and trying to catch her breath.

"Running late?"

Katya lifted her head to find a little old lady smiling at her. She stood upright and tucked her clutch purse under her arm.

"No, just running," she chuckled, smoothing her hands over her hair, hoping it hadn't fallen loose.

She didn't even know what direction she was headed in, where all the train went. She stared up at a map, listened to the stops as they were called out. She rode for a while, letting the rolling motion calm her down. She leaned against a pole and even closed her eyes for a bit, just trying not to feel.

She finally got off in a neighborhood she'd never been to – she'd started to feel motion sick and had to get fresh air.

It was almost ten o'clock at night. She couldn't believe it, she'd been riding the train for almost an hour. There weren't any people around, which made her happy. It looked like it might even start raining again, which made her even happier. Something to drown her sorrows.

The next time she looked at her phone, it was after ten-thirty. She was pretty sure she was lost and she wondered if she should order an Uber. The neighborhood she'd wound up in was upscale, nice. While she was thumbing through her phone, debating whether or not she should order a ride, she wound up in a park of sorts. A long, oblong grassy space, with Roman-esque columns at one end, and a huge fountain at the other. Across the fountain was a concert hall of sorts, and music was floating out of it. Some sort of orchestral music. She smiled and made her way down to the water.

She took off her shoes, leaving them and her purse on the ground as she stepped over the cement lip of the ornate fountain. The water was cool, almost reaching her knees. She held onto her skirt and stared at the sprays of water, desperately trying to clear her head.

What had happened? Just over a month ago, her life had been so predictable. She got up, she got dressed in her plain but nice clothing, she went to work. She made cakes for people. Then she went home. Made dinner for her and Tori. Worked on designs. Then cleaned up and went to bed.

Sure it was boring, but was that so bad? One moment. One conversation with Tori, and it was suddenly like boring was the worst thing ever. Join the Eros dating site! Make a profile! It'll be great!

She'd gotten so wrapped up in pretending to be some fake profile, she'd forgotten that's not who she was – Katya *was* a little boring. Sweet and nice and a cake baker. And there was nothing wrong with that. She didn't need men to validate her existence. Not Wulf, and though she appreciated him, not Liam either.

She'd had her little adventure. Gone from sexual novice to sleeping with two men at once. From missionary position to anal sex. She was proud of herself, proud of the leaps and bounds she'd made. But maybe it was time to say goodbye to new-Katya, finally. She'd only brought heartache. At least old-Katya had never gotten as hurt. Of course not – old-Katya played by the rules, how could she have possibly ever gotten hurt?

Sure, you got hurt, but there were some pretty pleasurable moments, too. And some downright beautiful moments. Words said and hearts touched. It wasn't all bad.

Nope. Most of it had been great, really. It had just ended badly. She sniffled and held back tears as she waded to the edge of the fountain. Ended *so badly*. She climbed onto the ledge, then turned back to face the fountain one more time. There was applause coming from the hall across the street, the show was ending. The night was over.

Take a bow, call it good, and gain some control over your life.

She took a deep breath, finally ready to do just that. She was on her toes, gingerly turning around, when a voice came out of the darkness behind her.

"What in the fuck are you doing down here?"

She actually shrieked, she was so startled. She also jerked her head up, which caused her to lose her balance. She windmilled her arms, attempted to tap dance her way back to standing upright, but in the end, gravity won. She screamed again as she fell backwards, landing hard on her ass inside the fountain. Freezing cold water was surrounding her, her dress becoming a second skin as it was instantly soaked. She gagged and choked on water, coughing while she cleared her eyes.

"You're joking," she gasped when she could finally see again.

Wulf was standing at the edge of the fountain. A street lamp was directly behind him, outlining him in shiny white light. He looked like a dream.

More like a night terror.

"Did you come looking for me?" he asked.

Katya was immediately enraged and she climbed to her feet, smacking away the helping hand he offered.

"How the fuck would I know you'd be here!?" she growled at him, wading towards the edge. He offered a hand once more, and again, she slapped it away. She tried to march to the right, to get away from him, but he just followed.

"Because I live down here," he finally answered her. She stopped moving for a moment and gaped at him.

"You do not," she breathed.

"I so do. My apartment is about a mile from this park, I walk down here almost every night."

"Well, I ..." she stuttered for a second, then started stomping in the opposite direction. "I didn't know that, did I? I never went to your apartment."

"Awfully coincidental, Tocci," he teased her, matching her step for step.

"*Do not* talk to me in that tone of voice," she hissed, her teeth starting to chatter.

"What tone? You're going to get frost bite, let me help you," he insisted, grabbing her by the elbow.

"*Don't you fucking touch me!*"

She had shrieked at him, but still he pulled. It was almost a wrestling match, getting her out of the fountain. The moment her feet touched the ground, she yanked away from him, almost stumbling in her haste to get away.

"If you touch me again, so help me god, I will start screaming so loud, and I won't stop until you're arrested," she threatened him.

"Kinky."

"*And don't fucking flirt with me!*" she yelled, shoving him in the chest.

"Oh, I can't touch you, but you can touch me?"

"Fuck off."

"It's okay, I don't mind. You can -"

"No," Katya suddenly held up her hand, stopping him. "I'm not doing this. *Goodbye*, Wulfric."

She stepped around him and hurried to her belongings, collecting them in her arms. She barely made it two steps before he was next to her again.

"Katya, wait. I was caught off guard by seeing you. I'm sorry."

She was completely shocked.

Wulf. Apologizing.

"I'm surprised you even know that word," she sneered. He pulled her to a stop.

"It's a surprise to me, too. Look, can we cut the theatrics? I was going to call you, but jesus, fuck, what could I say? After all the shit that went down," he told her. "I needed some time. I said that even, I needed space. If you had respected me at all, you would've given it to me."

She narrowed her eyes.

"Respect you? Is this a joke? And if you wanted space, you should've asked for it. I'm a pretty generous person, I would've given it to you. But I wasn't asked. I wasn't consulted. There was no discussion. You disregarded me, you ignored me, and then you *hurt me.* Where the fuck was my respect?" she demanded.

"It was bad. I admit it."

"Was the way you treated me respectful? Were the things *you said* respectful? No, they weren't. You purposefully tried to *dis*respect me. You tried to make me look low, you tried to embarrass me, and then you tried to hurt me. On purpose. Maliciously. *You hurt me.*"

He winced at that comment, and for a moment – just a moment – Katya wondered if she could get blood from a stone. Then he opened his mouth and she remembered who she was dealing with.

"I wasn't the only one trying to be hurtful – you were in that room, too. You fucked up, too."

"*Are you fucking joking!?* You want to keep a score card on who was a bigger fuck up that day? Let me clue you into something, Wulf – I could've pissed on that floor, and I still wouldn't have fucked up as bad as you," she called him out.

"I'm not keeping score. I was just angry. I'm *still* angry. This is ridiculous, we're shouting in the street. Let's go back to my place, and we can -"

"You're a *riot* tonight!" she burst out laughing. "Go back to your place? To YOUR place? It's funny, you know, because for weeks I wanted to see your place. See where Wulfric Stone laid his head at night. Now I couldn't give a fuck. *Get out of my way.*"

She again went to storm past him, but Wulf was having none of it. He stepped directly in her path, forcing her to walk into his chest. When she glared up at him, it was to see that he was every bit as angry as her.

"I'm fucking talking, so that means you fucking listen," he informed her. She barked out a laugh.

"See! There's that humor I -"

She ended on a squeak when he grabbed her upper arm. His grip was painful as he started dragging her down a cement walkway. She was forced to walk on her tiptoes, still in her bare feet.

"You know what your problem is, Tocci?" he said as they walked. "You don't pay attention. I'm fucking trying to say something – hell, the *universe* is trying to say something by bringing us both here tonight – and you're not fucking paying attention."

"I don't remember signing up for a lecture tonight. Take your hand off me, you have no right to touch me."

"Your body belongs to me more than it ever did to you."

Enough is enough.

Katya ripped free of his grasp, stumbling away as she did so. She clutched her purse and shoes to her chest, using them as a shield to protect herself from him. To protect her heart.

"Don't say things you don't know to be fact," she hissed.

"Oh, I *know* it's fact – I don't care what some other guy says to you, or whatever special kind of date he took you on tonight, or if he fucks you eighty different kinds of ways. Doesn't change who you belong to."

"It's very cute that you think you have some ownership of me," she sighed, bending down to put on her shoes.

"I don't think it, *I know it.*"

On the other side of the park, there was a commotion. She lifted her head and watched as the doors to the music hall opened up. The concert was over, the attendees were leaving. People spilled out onto the sidewalks, going to their cars, walking down the road. Heading into the park. She and Wulf were about to have a decent little audience for their tête-à-tête.

"We're done here. We were done over a week ago. Goodbye,

Wulf," she said, standing up straight and trying not to shiver in her soaking wet dress.

"You are not going home like that – you look like your naked," he growled, then shocked her when he began unbuttoning his shirt. She glanced down at herself. The sheer material of the dress only had a muslin backing. He wasn't lying, the wet color and sheerness of the fabric did have her looking pretty scandalous.

"I'm hardly naked," she said, watching as he shrugged out of his expensive dress shirt and held it out to her.

"Close enough. Put this on."

"Are you kidding?"

It was another wrestling match, him fighting to get her arms into the sleeves, her pushing and pulling at him. When he succeeded in getting the right sleeve on, she finally gave up. She gave him a hard shove in the chest and slipped into the left sleeve.

"You're being ridiculous."

"And you're being an idiot, trying to walk around like that."

"Well, that's my problem, not yours."

"I have a big fucking problem with people seeing you like this."

"Oh, do you? Do you, really? Well, I would hate to be a problem for you, Wulf! I would hate to be a burden on your conscience in any way!" she said in mock shock, then she whirled around and began striding towards a group of people that were heading their way. She barely made it ten feet before his hands were on her hips, twisting her to face him.

"Burden is an appropriate word for you," he said through gritted teeth as they struggled with each other. "Just come back to my place, I can call you a fucking taxi from there."

"Oh, good. I should be getting home anyway – I apparently need to get fucked eighty different ways," she snapped, slapping at his hands.

"That is *not* going to happen, so you can fuck right off with that plan."

"Why not? I mean, you said it, right? '*Little Katya Tocci needs to get fucked*' – right? Your words. *Right?* So that's what I'm going to do, I'm gonna go *get fucked*, so you can just *fuck right off*, and get the fuck out of my life, you stupid massive *fucking fuck!* I fucking -"

Katya was very aware that she was losing her marbles. They were possibly already gone. Wulf was probably using them to play his mind games on her. She was screaming and shouting, hitting him in the arms with her clutch. She could hear his mean, nasty words in her head, hear the hurtful tone in his voice. She wanted to cause him pain, wanted him to feel a tenth of what she was feeling.

Before she could inflict any real damage, though, Wulf declared full on war. He bent over and before she knew what was happening, his arms were around her waist and she was being picked up. She let out a shot as she came down hard on his shoulder, then he stood upright. He hoisted her into place, then locked an arm around her hips before he strode off down the walkway.

"Fuck, burden isn't a big enough word for you. You're a god-damn pain in my ass, Tocci," he bit out through gritted teeth.

She was completely shocked. He'd picked her up. He was … he was carrying her away. He was *stealing* her, right in the middle of their fight. She propped herself up as much as she could and started hitting him in the back with her purse.

"What do you think you're doing!? Put me down, Wulf. Put me down, *right now*," she demanded.

"No."

"I wasn't asking, Wulfric."

"*No.*"

"I swear to god, I really will start screaming."

"Go ahead. I'm not putting you down until we get to my apartment."

"I don't want to go to your apartment."

"Tough. You're running around practically naked."

"*I don't care.*"

"*I do*. I'm done sharing this body with anyone else. No one gets to see you like this *but me*."

Katya was stunned into silence. It was gruff and it was rude – he was being a complete barbarian. But in his own awful Wulfric way, he'd just made a huge admission. He was done sharing her? No one else could see her like that? A hell of a statement, coming from him.

"Wulf, put me down," she said in a low voice.

"Katya, I'm fucking tired, I'm letting you ruin my fucking five hundred dollar shirt, and on top of all that, I have a huge fucking meeting at eight in the morning, but this is *not* over. So shut the fuck up, or so help me god, *I will shut you up*."

Good god, he sounded pissed. It sent a shiver down her spine and for a couple minutes, she held still. Allowed herself to be carried around like a rag doll.

"I can walk, Wulf. People are going to think you're kidnapping me."

"That's what I'm going to do, if it means you'll shut up for five fucking seconds and let me talk."

"I'll let you talk. I'll do whatever you want, just let me walk on my own."

He put her down so abruptly, she yelped and started to fall over. Before she could completely tumble, though, he was grabbing her wrist and continuing on his war path. She was dragged along in his wake, almost jogging in order to keep up with him.

She couldn't be sure how far Wulf's home really was from the fountain – he'd carried her quite a ways and she hadn't been paying attention. Their almost-jog went on for a while, easily five minutes in silence. Half a mile? More? It seemed like an eternity. A shivering, wet, cold, awkward eternity.

They rounded a corner and she was met with an impressive, modern looking apartment building. It was a high rise, all gleaming windows and sharp corners. Intimidating – not at all like the simple, inviting building she lived in, with its seven stories and classic San

Francisco facade.

Wulf had to use a key card to get in the building, then again to access the elevator. By the time they were rising up the length of the building, Katya was shivering, her arms wrapped around herself. She would never admit it to him, but she really did need to get out of her dress. Riding home in her state would have been awful.

Of course he lived in the penthouse, she wasn't surprised one bit when he hit that button. She was surprised, however, when there was a ding and the elevator came to a stop a good ten floors below the one he lived on. Katya clutched her bag to her chest, then folded her arms, hoping she didn't look too frightening to whoever was about to join them.

She didn't have to worry, though. As the doors slid open, Wulf calmly turned and stood directly in front of her. So close, she almost went cross eyed staring at the neckline of his undershirt. She took a deep breath and felt her shivering crank up a notch. His arm came around her, and it felt like the bottom fell out from under her feet. It took her a second to realize it was the lift moving again.

They stopped two floors shy of their destination, and their guest got off. Then they rode the rest of the way up, still pressed against each other. It was surreal. She was scared to even breathe, lest it would wake her up from whatever dream she was having. When they came to their final stop, Wulf pulled away and walked off without her. She took the opportunity to remember how to breathe, then she followed after him.

The entire floor was his – all one big apartment. Absolutely spectacular views, all the way around the penthouse. Floor to ceiling windows surrounded them, showing everything San Francisco had to offer. It was awe-inspiring.

The rest of the apartment was amazing, as well. Black marble floors, brand new appliances, polished concrete counter tops. Lots of shiny dark surfaces, lots of brushed steel. Beautiful, really. A marvel of modern architecture.

She noticed something else, though, right away. It had the exact same feeling as his office. There wasn't one single personal touch anywhere. Not a picture of his family or friends, no knick knacks, no plants even. She was willing to bet a designer had picked out every single thing in his apartment, from his hampers to the art on the walls to his flatware. Nothing of himself was in that place, there was nothing to indicate a human being lived full time in the apartment.

Like it's not his home. It's just a place he stays.

"How long have you lived here?" she found herself asking as she tip toed around. She felt like she was in a museum. Out of habit, she spoke in a soft voice.

"About five years."

"Jesus," she whispered, peeking around the living room. Not a pillow out of place, not even a remote left out on a table.

"You don't approve, Tocci?"

She finally turned to face him. The living room and dining room both abutted the front windows, and he was between them. He was standing up very straight – a defensive pose for him, she knew – and he had his hands shoved into his pockets. He should've looked odd, wearing expensive slacks and shiny black shoes along with only a sleeveless white undershirt on top. His hair was mussed up from their struggles, and she hadn't noticed in Carmel, but it had gotten long since their first date. It looked good. Wulf needed a little ruffling.

"It's beautiful here," she was honest.

"Thank you. I paid a lot of money to make sure it was beautiful."

"Money doesn't buy everything, Wulf."

"I am very aware of that, Katya."

It was such a charged moment. They were both saying very little, but it all meant so much more. Again, she found herself wishing he would just let go. Just say whatever it was he had to say. Get it all out, scream, yell, break something, *anything,* so she could have some closure, at least. She held her breath and waited, but his stubbornness won out over her body. A cold shiver raced down her spine, causing everything to shake for a moment.

"You should go get changed," he sighed, moving from his spot. Those weren't the words she wanted to hear. Something in her brain snapped. What was she doing there? What was she *really* doing in his place? He clearly didn't have the balls to say what he wanted.

Well, good thing she did.

"What do you want from me?" she asked in a loud voice. He stopped mid-walk, one foot in front of the other, barely three feet away from her.

"Excuse me?"

"I never understood," she said, holding out her hands. Her purse fell to the floor. "Why did you ask me out? You asked me out on a date. Why?"

"I told you why."

"Then why'd you keep seeing me? You pursued this, Wulf. You showed up at my work, you showed up at my house. If all you wanted was sex, you had it. Why the long talks? Why the meals? *What do you want from me?*" she demanded.

He was silent for so long, she almost gave up on him. She'd already wasted so much time on the man – maybe he was just a lost cause. But as she took a deep breath, preparing herself for the final goodbye, he opened his mouth.

"Everything," he said softly, staring straight at her. "I want everything."

It almost killed her, but she refused to be taken in by beautiful words.

"That's not good enough," she said, shaking her head. "You could've had everything. *You* walked away. And now you've brought me here. *What do you want.*"

"I ..."

"Jesus, Wulf. *Just say it.* Have you *ever* said it? About anything? What do you want for Christmas? For your birthday? Just for you. Only you. *What do you want.*"

"I just want you."

"Really? Could've fooled me – you basically called me a naive slut, and then said I was stupid for thinking there was anything special between us."

"I know I did. I was so angry at myself, and I took it out on you. I'm sorry."

"Don't tell me you're 'sorry.'"

"Then what do you want me to tell you?"

"*What you really want from me.*"

Katya could just tell – he was still holding back. It was almost fascinating to her. A rich man, a powerful man, a successful man, yet he was completely unable to articulate his feelings. His basic wants and needs.

He sighed and rubbed a hand across this jaw, then took a couple steps towards her. He stopped in front of her. Not quite touching, but she could feel his body heat. Could see the confusion in his eyes while he seemed to search the floor for his answers. Eventually, he took another sigh and finally looked at her.

"I want you to look at me in that way you do – like I'm everything," he said in a simple voice. "I want to see that look every single day. When I wake up, when I go to sleep, all the time. I want to be the only man that gets to touch you, hold you, kiss you. I want you to know … know that I look at you the same way. Like you're everything. You're everything to me."

So many words strung together. Wulf rarely said a lot, but damn, when he did, he didn't mess around. She was blinking away tears by the time he was finished speaking. She looked away from him, trying to break the moment.

If she didn't, *she'd* end up broken.

"That's nice to hear," she whispered, and out of her peripheral, she watched him hold his breath. "But if you felt that way, how could you say those things to me? I felt like I was going to die. Like you were hitting me. I don't understand how you could treat someone you care about that way. I just … I can't. I can't understand it, at all."

Suddenly, he was in her personal space. Chest pressing against her shoulder, head bent to stare straight down at her. She refused to return the look and kept her eyes trained on the view. On the twinkling lights of the city.

"I wanted you to hurt. I was trying to put an end to your feelings," he whispered back. "I thought … *I knew* if I didn't end it, you'd eventually leave me. And I couldn't handle that kind of pain."

She finally looked up at him. It was heartbreaking. He looked like he was in pain right then. She was certainly in pain. So much hurting between two people who only wanted to love each other.

This is a very broken man.

"Why would you think I'd leave you?" she asked.

"Because, Katya. I'm a very bad man, who does very bad things, and you're a very good girl. It can't end any other way."

She sucked in air quickly, dropping her gaze. It hurt, hearing him talk about himself that way. She remembered how Liam would get so angry at her whenever she said anything negative about herself. Now she understood. Hearing Wulf say that, it felt like hearing someone else say it. She wanted to get mad. She wanted to defend him, against himself. She wanted to hold up a mirror so he could see what she saw in him.

If she spoke, though, the tears would come. She didn't know how to help him. She'd already given huge pieces of herself, she wasn't sure she had anything else to give. Would he have to consume her, in order to feel whole? Would she have to break, in order for him to bend?

He seemed to understand that it was too much for her. He stepped away, cleared his throat, then walked back down the hall towards the entrance. She heard a door open, then a light was switched on. She took a couple fortifying breaths as he walked back into the living room.

"Go get changed," he said. "Vieve stayed here last year, left some clothes. I put them in the bathroom for you."

He followed close behind her as she walked down the hall, but he didn't touch her. She stepped into a guest bathroom and he yanked a towel off a rack, handing it to her. Then he left, shutting the door behind him.

Katya immediately sat down on the closed toilet. What. In the actual. *Fuck.* How ... how had this all happened? She'd been on a date with Liam. Now she was on the other side of town, with Wulf. And what the hell was that about – she hadn't known where he lived, she'd gotten on a random train at a random stop and gotten off at a random time, then walked. She'd walked forever. San Francisco wasn't exactly huge, but it wasn't tiny either.

Talk about a cruel twist of fate.

She finally stood up, shivering as she did so. He kept the apartment ridiculously cold, she could feel the air conditioning washing over her. She took her shoes off and shimmied out of her dress.

When she looked up, she saw her body from her thighs up in his huge mirror. She was wearing her special black matching bra and panties – only brought out for good dates. Her eye makeup was a little smudged, giving her a slightly haunted look, and her hair was a frizzy ball on her head. She chuckled as she took out all the pins and bands, allowing the heavy tresses to fall around her shoulders.

Good lord, he'd said those beautiful words to a train wreck.

She shook her head. Such negative thoughts about herself. Who gave a fuck what she looked like when they were both on the verge of nervous breakdowns?

We need to stop this. He beats himself up, I beat myself up, and pretty soon, we're beating on each other.

She glanced at the door and started breathing fast. Whenever Katya was hurting, she wanted comfort. She wanted her mother, or Tori, or Liam, to wrap their arms around her and hold her. Tell her everything would be alright. That she was loved and trusted and that they would never, ever hurt her.

Wulf was hurting, and his first reaction had been to lash out. To hurt someone else. Because he hadn't known any better.

She didn't bother with the clothes he'd left her – she slipped back into his shirt and hastily fastened a few buttons before leaving her tiny sanctuary.

He was back in the same spot, between the living room and kitchen. His back was to her and he was staring out over the city. One hand was in a pocket, the other was hanging at his side, holding an old fashioned glass. There was a sliver of amber liquid in the bottom, though she knew him well enough to know that it had probably been three fingers high when he'd poured it.

I know you, Wulf. I know you.

Suddenly feeling nervous and shy, she gathered her hair over one shoulder, then made the slow march towards him. In her bare feet, she was barely a whisper as she moved through the apartment. It wasn't till she was almost right behind him that he heard her. He glanced over his shoulder, then turned around. He quirked up an eyebrow at her appearance but didn't say anything. Just drank the last of his cognac.

"I need to tell you something," she said, staring up at him, refusing to be afraid.

"Okay," he said, leaning over and setting the glass on his table.

She didn't speak, though. She kept staring. He held so much weight on his shoulders. His businesses, his family. He was so strong, it was unbelievable. Maybe, though, just maybe it was time for someone to be strong for him, for once. She stepped even closer, her breasts brushing against him.

"You need to hear this," she whispered, reaching up and pressing her hand over his heart. "You're not a bad man."

"Katya, you don't -"

She moved her hand from his heart and covered his mouth.

"*You're not.* I know you're a good person, because I care about you, and *I'm* a good person. It's okay to not be perfect. It's okay to feel things, sometimes. Even scary things. Because I'm here, Wulf. After everything. You're not alone, I'm not leaving. I *wouldn't* leave you. I care about you. I trust you. And I would never, ever, hurt you," she promised him. His eyes fell shut and he leaned forward to press his forehead to hers.

"Don't say these things. You can't take them back," he said. She now had her hands on either side of his face.

"*I don't want to take them back.* You can't take back the truth. It's already there – we just need to be brave enough to say it out loud."

"I'm bad for you," he whispered, his voice low and scratchy. He tried to step back, to break their connection and get away from her – get away from the truth, but Katya stepped even closer, bringing herself flush with him. Refusing to give up on him.

"*You're everything to me,*" she whispered back.

"I'm going to hell for what I've done to you."

"And I'll bring you back," she insisted, already over the fight they'd had. Over the walls they had between them. His hands slid onto her hips, and she thought maybe he was over them, too.

"There's no going back from this," he warned her.

"It's way too late for that," she agreed.

"Say it again," he breathed.

"You're not alone. I'm here."

For the first time ever, when Wulf kissed her, she could feel his nerves. Feel how unsure he was. Like he was afraid of her. What a shocking revelation. She'd brought such an amazing man to his knees, had him quaking in fear. Her, *little Katya Tocci.*

She wouldn't allow it. He tried to pull away, and she got closer still. He tried to stop the kiss, she pressed her lips harder. Stood on her toes and combed her fingers through his hair, smoothed her tongue over his bottom lip.

Even Wulf had his breaking point, and he finally reached it. His hands balled into fists, pulling the shirt tight across her back. His tongue slid between her lips and he leaned into the kiss so much, she was forced backwards. He followed and they sidestepped into the living room.

"You don't understand," he breathed into her.

"I don't need to," she cut him off.

He gripped the front of the shirt and yanked. Buttons went flying, then his hands were on her skin, skimming across her hips. Caressing her back lightly before squeezing her sides. Gripping her tightly around her ribs.

She wasn't surprised that he could pick her up – all those years in a pool had ensured Wulf could pretty much do any physical activity he wanted. She braced her hands on top of his shoulders while she was lifted high enough that she had to look down at him. She wrapped her legs around his waist, then coiled her arms around his neck as she settled into place.

"No going back," he repeated his earlier statement, kissing and licking along her neck. She let her head drop back.

"I know."

He carried her into the living room, then he sat down on a plush sofa. She stayed wrapped around him, wanting to envelop him in her love. She'd been given so much, all her life. By so many people. It felt right to pass some of it on to Wulf. He needed it more than her.

His dress shirt was shoved away from her shoulders, fluttering to the ground without another thought. Between kisses, she tugged and pulled at his undershirt. He lifted his arms and she was finally able to yank it free from his body.

While they were still locked at the mouth, he wrapped an arm around her waist and twisted to the side, forcing her to lay down. He hovered, keeping his weight off her while his tongue dove into her mouth, over and over again.

When he pulled away, she tried to follow him, but he pressed a hand to her sternum while he licked a path down her cleavage. Kissed his way across her stomach, nibbled on her hip bone. Her legs were already parted for him and when he reached their center, he paid no attention to her panties. She gasped as she felt his tongue through the fabric, moaned at the friction meeting wetness.

She could never imagine doing something so intimate with anyone else, ever again. He was the only one she trusted to take care of her needs, to do it oh so perfectly, without her having to say a word. She moaned and arched her back, thrusting a hand into his thick hair.

She was panting and desperate when he pulled away to suck at the inside of her thigh. She groaned and reached for him, but he was gone. She writhed around on the couch, trying to find him, needing his touch.

He didn't deny her for long. She felt his hands gripping her knees, and she was startled as she was dragged down the length of the sofa. He was back between her legs and without question, she locked them around him. His hands had a desperation to them she'd never felt before, as they prodded and pawed at her. Yanked her up into a sitting position, then hoisted her into his arms.

He carried her into his bedroom, kicking the door open with enough force it bounced off the wall behind it, leaving a crater in the sheet rock. He didn't seem to care – he was too busy pulling her bra apart and flinging it across the room.

She was laid out after that, her underwear stripped away. Before she'd even sat up, he was stepping out of his pants and covering her with his body.

They rolled around for a bit, making the room almost humid with how hot they were getting, with how heavy they were breathing. Everything became damp, her fingers skating around on his sweat soaked skin, her tongue sliding along his slick lips.

"On top," he panted when she wrapped her fingers around the base of his dick. He didn't wait for an answer, he rolled them again so she was astride him, straddling his hips. He put his arms behind him, propping himself upright. "I want to see you. I want you to look at me."

"You see me," she whispered back, working her hand up and down his shaft a couple times before shifting over him.

She stared him straight in the eye the whole time she was sliding down his length. Kept staring as she let her mouth drop open so she could moan at the intrusion. At the effort it took for her not to shake. Not to cry.

She sat for a long moment, adjusting to his size. He had his forehead to her clavicle and was breathing heavy. Then she worked her hips back and forth once, and they both moaned. He fell back onto the mattress as she set up a rhythm, one of his hands cupping her breast while the other squeezed her thigh, urging her faster.

She didn't want to even be that far away from him. She fell forward, her auburn locks becoming a curtain around them as she kissed him. Both his hands speared into her hair, holding her in place while his own hips started moving. Pumping back against her. She rotated her hips, he thrust forward. Rotate, thrust. She felt like she was going to take off, shoot forward, blast off. Like they were going to break the sound barrier.

She didn't want to ever stop kissing him – it was always a unique experience with Wulf, but when he was wild and unhinged, it was something else entirely. But if she didn't get some oxygen, she was going to pass out, and she couldn't allow herself to miss a single moment of that night. She sat upright, tossing her hair over her shoulder. He followed suit, propping an arm behind himself. He leaned into her chest, laving his tongue across a nipple.

"Wulf, I can't ..." she couldn't even think, not one little bit. "I can't ... please ..."

He didn't say a word, just grabbed her hips and pushed her onto her back. He was so fast, he followed in time, not breaking their connection. He kissed her once, then jerked her roughly across the mattress. She was still shoving the comforter away from her face when he thrust his whole length into her again. She shrieked, then raked her nails down his chest.

"No one has ever been as good as this," he started panting over her. "Only you. So goddamn good to me."

"You deserve it," she moaned. He chuckled and bent forward, clamping his teeth around a nipple. She let out another cry.

"You don't know what you're doing, Katya. You don't even know who you're dealing with," he said when he backed away.

"I know *exactly* who I'm dealing with."

He wasn't paying attention to her words, though. He grabbed her left leg and shoved it higher, letting it fall over his arm. The back of her thigh rested against his bicep, the two slipping and sliding against each other. His hand briefly smoothed over her ass, then moved onto her breasts, squeezing and pinching. Her breath started to hitch.

"I want to see this every single night," he said in a low voice, looking between their bodies so he could watch himself thrust in and out of her.

"Yes, please, every night. Please," she agreed, clinging to his shoulders as her whole body started to tremble.

"I want to make you wet and make you come and know I'm the only one who is allowed to do that to you," he continued.

"Only you, I promise," she assured him, her hips starting to move erratically against him. Something big was building in her core. Something explosive and dangerous. She would be obliterated by their time together, she was sure.

"I want you to live with me," he kept going. "I fucking hate it here. I want your presence everywhere, I want you to make it feel like home. I want you to be my home."

"Anything. I'll do *anything you want.*"

His thrusts were brutal at that point, and she couldn't tell if she was feeling blinding pleasure, or stinging pain. Whatever it was, she wanted to feel it *all the time.* He was pushing with enough force that he was driving her across the mattress. Her head finally fell over the side.

"I want you to love me," he whispered.

Too late.

She couldn't say anything in response. She could only shriek as an orgasm ripped her straight down the middle, making her tremble and sob. She couldn't catch her breath, he wouldn't let her. He just pushed harder, and when she felt his hand moving between them, felt his fingers pinching sensitive wet flesh, she honestly thought she might die. The orgasm swelled again, becoming a tsunami. A force of destruction, threatening to wreck them both.

It was Wulf's turn to be strong, to stand against the wave. He laid down flat, crushing her as he forced his tongue into her mouth. The action distracted her from impending death, and while she tried to remember what planet she was on, he thrust so hard, he broke every last boundary she could've possibly had – cleared a path straight to her soul. While he came inside her, his teeth bit into her bottom lip, most definitely leaving a mark.

It took a while for both of them to calm down. Multiple orgasms were not only real, she'd just discovered, but they were at once the most awesome and most terrifying thing she'd ever experienced. She pressed a hand over her eyes, trying to stop the room from spinning.

Wulf laid still, but continued to twitch inside of her for a while. Even as his body relaxed, his hips continued to very slightly pump against her, slowly and languorously.

She wasn't sure how long they laid like that together, and even less sure of when she'd started crying. She could feel the tears under her fingertips and she tried to keep her breathing even, not wanting to scare him away from such a big moment.

"Hey," he said, finally lifting himself up. "Hey, stop it."

"No, it's not bad," she assured him, her voice watery. "I'm not upset."

"No, I meant stop hiding from me."

He pulled her hand away from her face and stared down at her. She blinked up at him, her vision blurry.

"I'm not hiding, I'm just …" she started. He gave her a sad smile and traced a thumb under her eye, wiping away the tears that had collected there.

"It's okay. I know."

"*I'm happy.*"

24

KATYA HAD LIED. ONLY A LITTLE, BUT STILL.

She'd said she trusted Wulf, but she didn't fully – only about ninety-nine percent. The other one percent had her afraid to go to sleep. Afraid that when she woke up in the morning, the magic would be gone and the old-Wulf and the old-Katya would be back. Those two people wouldn't get along. They wouldn't be able to laugh and love each other and have mad passionate sex. She would hate for that to happen.

I'm afraid none of it was real, that he didn't mean any of it.

When she opened her eyes, it was to bright morning sunlight outside the windows. She blinked a couple times, half asleep yet still in awe of the view. Then she took a deep breath and glanced over her shoulder.

The bed was empty.

A huge digital clock on the wall read nine o'clock. Hadn't he mentioned having an early morning meeting? She curled up into a tighter ball, trying to hold herself together. He hadn't even woken her up to say goodbye. Maybe it hadn't been real, after all.

Before she could work herself up into a proper fit, though, the bedroom door creaked open from behind her. She squeezed her eyes shut tight, trying to feign sleep and hoping the maid or whoever would just go away.

When the mattress dipped down, though, Katya couldn't stay still. She sat up, clutching the sheet to her chest, wondering what the hell kind of cleaning lady tried to make a bed with a person in it. It wasn't a maid, it turned out. Wulfric was crawling up the mattress.

"I made coffee," he said in a low voice before rolling onto his back. He was wearing a loose pair of black pajama bottoms and nothing else. His hair was total bed-head, and he hadn't shaved. He clearly hadn't left the apartment at all.

"I thought … you said you had a meeting. I thought you had to leave," she said, tucking her hair behind her ears. She was still sitting up, so all she could see of him was from the waist down. But she felt him move and his hand came to rest on her bare back.

"I don't have to go anywhere."

"But you said -"

"This is more important, Tocci."

Katya laid back down, as well. She stared at the ceiling while Wulf folded his arms across his face, covering his eyes. They stayed silent for a really long time. Long enough that she felt like she might scream, just to fill the void.

"Why do you call me that?" she burst out.

"Call you what?"

"Tocci. You mostly call me by my last name. I always wondered why."

There was a long pause, and when she glanced at him, she could see a sly little smile playing across his lips.

"I came home during spring break," he started, clearing his throat. "I was twenty-two? Twenty-three? I was in graduate school. My mom asked me to pick up Vieve at her soccer camp. You were there, and I'd never paid much attention to you, but I was waiting by the fence, and I kept hearing this guy screaming at you. '*Raise those knees, Tocci!*', '*pass the ball, Tocci!*', '*get your head out of your ass, Tocci!*, over and over. And there you were, all gangly and awkward, running around in a jersey with TOCCI in big letters across the back. Then when I saw you again, in that bakery, *'go out with me, Tocci'* was the first thing that came to my mind."

Katya started laughing.

"That's actually kinda amazing."

"Yup. My neighbor, the shitty soccer player, Katya Tocci."

"I wasn't shitty – I was actually pretty good. I was probably just having a bad day."

"If you say so."

"Wulfric," she sighed his name. His arms moved, and when he went to rest them at his sides, he covered her hand with his own. Squeezed her fingers.

"My mother named me after a romance novel," he said in a quiet voice. Katya glanced over at him, but he was staring up at the ceiling. "If you knew her, it would make sense. I think she was kinda … swept away by my dad. She thought she was *in* a romance story. Genevieve and Brighton, well, I think she was just trying to stick with the theme. It wasn't easy growing up. Do you have any idea what it's like having a name that sounds like wolf?"

"I think it suits you."

"You would."

"I like it. I always liked it."

"Hmmm."

"My mom told me that your parents' divorce, it wasn't a good one," she said, still staring at him. He smirked at the ceiling.

"Is any divorce a good one?"

"Some people can end amicably. Not all of us want to end up screaming in a reception hall, flinging cake and insults."

"I never thought of it that way," Wulf whispered. She squeezed his fingers harder.

"Sorry. I was trying to be funny."

"Try being the operative word. The things my dad did to my

mom. The way he would talk to her. Did your mother tell you how it ended?"

"No, not exactly. Just that it was messy."

"We came home one day, and he was just gone. *Gone*. Like he'd never been there. I mean, we'd never been close, he was always working, so I wasn't too bothered by it. But Vieve was only seven, and Brighton was five. They couldn't understand why Daddy left them, and I sure as shit didn't know, and my mom wasn't saying anything, because she was having a goddamn mental breakdown.

"Then the phone calls started, her begging him to come back. It was pathetic – he'd left her for his personal trainer. Like fuck him, if he didn't want us, then we shouldn't have wanted him. But my mom wouldn't stop. She would show up at his work, at his new apartment, call him in the middle of the night. I listened in on one phone call. It was horrible. He called her stupid and fat, said she was worthless. Boring. So many things. I couldn't understand why she wanted him back. Why she just broke down and even shut out her kids, for this man who was fucking awful."

Wulf was almost growling by the end of his story, his hand crushing her fingers. She didn't try to break free, though. She wanted him to give some of his pain to her.

He's probably never told any of this to anyone. God, how long has it been rotting inside him?

"Sometimes it's hard to shut off love. Even when someone is awful and you should know better," she offered.

"Yeah, well, love shouldn't be exclusionary, either. What, he couldn't love us because he loved someone new? She couldn't love us unless my dad loved her? What a fucking fuck show. She'd never held a real job, she had no savings, he took it all – suddenly she's got three fucking kids, a huge goddamn house, and no way to pay for any of it, and what's she doing? Crying in a corner for a man who'd broken her. I will *never* understand that thought process, and I would *never* let that happen to me," he stated.

"Talk is easy. Sometimes you shock yourself with the things you allow people to do to you, if you convince yourself that you love them enough."

"What about when you allow it to affect other people in your life? I'm almost sixteen years old, and one day my biggest concern is rotating the tires on my 'vette, and the next, I'm fucking scouring the want ads, looking for anywhere that would hire a teenager at a decent wage. I eventually sold my car, sold her car, sold practically everything in that house. I knew I wouldn't be going to the Olympics. I only kept swimming because I knew a scholarship was the only way I'd get into college, so I swam my ass off. I dug in and I sacrificed and *I worked,* all so she could spend two years begging some asshole to come back to her."

He sounded so bitter. So angry. She remembered her thoughts from the night before, about realizing that even Wulfric Stone needed someone strong to lean on.

"That's awful, and I'm sorry. I didn't know any of that growing up, Vieve never told me."

"She didn't know, I kept a lot of it from the girls. *The girls.* Y'know, they almost feel more like my daughters than my sisters. How fucked up is that?"

Katya took a deep breath and rolled onto her side. She wrapped her arms around one of his, holding it tight to her chest. He finally looked down at her.

"I'm going to say something, and I want you to listen. Don't react right away, just listen."

"Oh god."

"I'm just repeating what you've told me, okay? This is what I've heard," she started. "Your dad was a workaholic, always too busy for his wife, never spent time with his kids. Then he just left one day, without a word. Without an explanation. And when your mother confronted him, he was mean to her. Said horrible, awful things to her. Tried to make it so she wouldn't want him anymore," Katya's

286

voice dwindled to a whisper as she spoke.

"Oh my god."

"I don't think you're -" she tried to preemptively stop what she knew he was going to say, but he barreled right through her.

"I'm just like him. I hate that motherfucker, I haven't talked to him in almost four years, and I'm *just fucking like him.* Do you know, I can't remember the last time I spoke to Brie? I didn't even go to Brie's graduation. I just said they felt more like daughters to me than sisters, and I fucking treat them the same way he did. I'm no better than he is," Wulf was speaking faster and faster.

"Stop it."

"And jesus, the things I've done to you, Katya. Fucking awful. I'm a horrible goddamn human being. Why are you here?" he asked, turning to look at her again.

"Because I care about you," she said. "Because I would never leave without a word, and I would never try to hurt you. Maybe you don't know how to fight for what you want, but I do. I would fight for you, Wulf. You're worth it."

He abruptly rolled onto his side as well, crashing into her. She didn't have time to process what was happening, just gasp into his mouth as he kissed her. One of his hands was on the back of her head, holding her close.

No one had ever said that to him, she suddenly realized. That he was worth it. Worth more than a blank check. Worth more than strong shoulders. His father didn't care about him, his mother had emotionally abandoned him, and his sisters had been too young to understand the sacrifices he'd made for them. But Katya saw all those things about him, knew that it proved he wasn't a lost a cause. That he was most definitely worth fighting for.

Definitely worth falling for …

"I don't deserve you," he whispered against her lips, shifting her onto her back.

"Probably not," she teased.

"I don't, Katya. I really, really don't."

"Stop it."

"I want … I *need* this," his voice stayed soft as he kissed along her jawline, behind her ear, then down her neck. "I don't want to be like him. I don't want to be that person. I want you. I want you to stay with me. I want you to fight for me. I *need* that, Katya. I really, really need that."

"I'm not going anywhere, so you don't have to worry."

"*You make me want to be a better man,*" his voice was barely a breath as he kissed between her breasts. Katya wrapped her arms around his head, hugging him to her.

"Good," she answered, her throat thick with unshed tears. "Because I want to be a better woman, too."

"You're already the best, Katya."

"Really?"

"Better than anything I've ever experienced."

The tears couldn't be stopped, and she didn't want them to stop. She wanted to keep touching him and kissing him and falling further and further in love with him. She kissed his fingertips and his pulse points and his cupid's bow. Wanted to imprint herself on his skin. On his soul.

You already are a better man, Wulfric Stone.

They stayed in bed for a long time. Wulf didn't so much as look at his cell phone, which made her feel giddy. When they'd dated, he'd been attached to the thing half the time. Now, it wasn't even in the room with them. She was his priority – he was making that very clear.

Finally, when the sun was setting and their backs were starting to ache, they got out of bed. Katya took a shower, and Wulf joined her halfway through. After they got out, he gave her one of his old college sweaters – she didn't have any real clothing, and her dress was a wadded up mess in the bathroom. The sweater only hung to the tops of her thighs, but they didn't have any plans to leave, so she didn't care.

She finally texted Tori, who was near frantic with worry in her messages. Katya asked her roommate not to say anything to Liam – that conversation needed to be had in person, in private. It wouldn't be pretty, and she could only pray that he understood. Just thinking about it caused her stomach to knot up, but then she looked up and watched Wulf as he pulled a shirt on, and just like that, she didn't feel bad anymore.

They snuggled on the couch and watched old movies. Ordered Chinese food and ate it in his living room – something he'd never done before, she found out. He always ate in his kitchen. She fed him pieces of barbecue pork with chopsticks, then wiped up the mess on his chin with a napkin.

They whispered to each other, about things they'd always want-ed, but had never said to other people. Katya wanted to own a bak-ery, knew she had the talent and client list to make it a success, but she knew nothing about running a business. Handling that much money, having employees to worry about, it all terrified her. So she stayed where she was, getting a paycheck that she knew she was worth more than.

Wulf confessed to having a massive fear of rejection. "*Duh*," she'd replied, earning a tug on her hair. It extended to all parts of his life, and was something he played very close to the vest, he ex-plained. Considering the business world he moved in, it was imper-ative that his competition never find out, obviously. He didn't keep close friends, didn't have long term relationships, couldn't even hold a conversation with his own sisters, because he was afraid they'd see what an asshole he was capable of being, and they'd turn their backs on him.

"*So I turn mine first.*"

Katya liked the asshole-Wulf, she admitted to him. She liked that he was brash and blunt and even sometimes rude. He wasn't afraid to do whatever it took to get a job done, to make sure he ultimately got whatever he wanted. He just needed to learn how to turn it on and off.

"So what you're saying," he chuckled as he stretched out behind her on the sofa. "Is I need to learn to be a little less of an asshole, and you need to learn to be a little more of one."

"I guess, yeah."

"Well, you came to the right teacher."

They laughed more than they ever had in all the time they'd spent together. She learned his laugh lines, knew how to find them around his eyes. Traced her fingers along them. He looked so good when he smiled, he needed to do it more often. She would help him.

And they talked. For hours. About everything. Her family, his family, school, jobs, past relationships, life, love, the universe. They teased and told jokes and he chased her around the apartment, making her laugh endlessly. He pushed her up against one of the windows and peeled off the sweater, kissing his way down her spine while she looked out over a sleeping city.

"*We were made for each other*," he whispered late in the night, his lips wandering over trembling skin.

"Yes," she agreed.

"Who would've thought, all those years ago. My next door neighbor, little Katya Tocci. I never even noticed you."

"Not so little anymore."

"No. Thank god we were able to keep the house."

"Yeah, cause good neighbors are hard to find."

25

KATYA WOKE UP TO THE SOUND OF AN ALARM BUZZING. SHE JERKED ONCE, still half asleep, then moaned and stretched out. Slowly lifted her head up to look around. Her hair was everywhere, falling all over her face. She blew on it till she'd cleared away a strand that allowed her to see. Wulf was laying on his back next to her and was rubbing his hands over his face.

"What time is it?" she asked, her voice creaky from all the talking they'd done.

"God, it's late," he groaned, lifting his watch off his night stand. "It's almost noon."

"You're lucky I've been banned from work, Mr. Stone, or you'd be in big trouble," she said, stretching again before rolling onto her back.

"Paid leave is hardly the same as getting banned, Tocci. Fuck, it's so late," he repeated himself as he sat up. He scratched his fingers through his crazy hair, obviously trying to wake up.

"Sorry," she laughed, pressing her palm against his back. "You're the one who wanted to stay up so late."

He glanced at her, one eyebrow quirked up in irritation, then he fell backwards. Rolled so he was on top of her.

"I think you're partly to blame for that," he reminded her, biting into her lip. It was swollen from the night before, and she moaned as her pulse throbbed in response.

"Guilty."

They kissed for a while longer. It was different, now. Kissing Wulf had always been a treat for the senses, but now, there was nothing methodical about it. He wasn't planning an attack on her body. He was enjoying it. Reveling in it. She never wanted to let him go.

"I want to stay with you," she whispered into his hair as his tongue traced along her clavicle.

"Good, I want you to be here."

"But I have to go home. I need clothes, a toothbrush, and I have to … I have to talk to some people," she said. He stopped moving, which made her freeze up. That damn one percent lack of trust – he'd given her emotional PTSD. She was scared of his reactions.

"Some people, huh. Would this have anything to do with the date you were all dressed up for?" he asked.

"Possibly. And my roommate is pissed that I didn't call her that first night, she almost called the police. She thought you found me and killed me."

"I did kidnap you."

"Hardly – I was awfully willing."

"You beat me with your fucking purse."

"Don't be such a baby, you can barely see the bruises."

He dug his fingers into her side, causing her to shriek and laugh.

"Okay," he said, silencing her with a kiss. "Okay, let me go into work real quick. I have to clear something up with a shitty investment. I'll come back and I'll drive you to your apartment."

"Wow, you're going to drive me all the way across town? This must be love."

"I might even take the top down for you."

"Stop, I might swoon."

He kissed her on the nose and jumped out of bed. She watched him while he got dressed. He didn't pull on one of his suits, his normal attire for work. He went casual, just grabbing jeans and a polo shirt. She hoped that meant he wouldn't be gone all day. She didn't want to lose the momentum they'd built up.

As he slipped on a blazer, he came back over to the bed. Crawled over it and kissed her soundly, forcing his tongue down her throat. She was almost panting when he finally pulled away.

"Please be here when I come back," he whispered, tracing his finger down the side of her cheek.

"I will. Don't be gone too long," she replied. He shook his head and stood upright.

"Two hours, possibly three. Not a minute longer, I promise."

"See you in three hours."

He kissed her one more time, just as soundly, then he was striding out of the room. She heard the front door click shut, then she was left in silence.

She wandered out to his kitchen and decided to poke around. She was a chef, through and through, so she loved to be in a kitchen. Wulf's was sad, really. He had a great stove top, and a double oven built into the cabinets. Neither looked as if they'd been used. He had cast iron skillets and copper cookware, all shiny and new, except for one small frying pan that had seen a lot of action.

His refrigerator was in a similar state. He had a carton with seven eggs in it, a carton of non fat milk, a half a loaf of bread, and a jar of pickles. That was it. His freezer held a ridiculous amount of ice cubes, one lonely tub of mint chocolate chip ice cream, and some frozen chicken breasts. His cupboards weren't any better, with a couple boxes of pasta and cans of soup. She finally hit gold when she found an almost empty box of Cheerios. She pulled it down, then went in search of bowls.

She sat on the edge of his table and ate her cereal while she looked out over the view. She tried to pick out where, exactly, they were in relation to her apartment. Tried to pinpoint landmarks to help her along. But they were too far away, or the buildings were too small. She needed Liam to get her a flagpole for her roof, so she could raise up something bright and eye catching.

Liam.

The milk soured in her stomach. He'd been so good to her, and it really had been a great date. Any other time, any other girl, and it would've been a magical night. And what had she done to say thanks? She'd ran away, gone home with Wulf, and had sex all night with him.

Katya lurched away from the table, her guilt suddenly overwhelming. She grabbed at her phone and scrolled through his messages. They were all about how awesome the date had been, how much he cared about her. One asked her to bring him tacos, because he had to go into work early every day as they attempted to catch up on inventory.

Feed me, she-devil. I'm starved for you.

She couldn't bear it. She couldn't stand there in Wulf's apartment, relaxed with afterglow and half naked in his sweaters, while Liam was sitting somewhere, falling in love with her. She felt like the devil. She had to talk to him.

Okay. Two, maybe three hours, Wulf said. That's plenty of time to go downtown and speak to Liam. To at least stop any crazy thoughts he might have pinging around in his head.

She remembered Wulf offering her some of his sister's clothing, leaving them in the hall bathroom for her. She raced into the room and started yanking on clothing. Genevieve Stone was a little bit curvier than Katya, the soft knit sweater was roomy in the chest, the expensive slacks wider in the hips, but she made it work, then turned to look at her reflection. The sweater was a pearl gray color, the pants a charcoal gray. She almost burst out laughing.

Old-Katya and her all-brown-outfit would've gotten along well with Vieve, I think.

Her hair looked psychotic, but she didn't have time to make it presentable. She yanked everything up into a high ponytail and just hoped for the best. All she had were her strappy stilettos, so she put them on, grabbed her purse, then rushed out the door, looking like she was applying for a secretary job somewhere very unexciting.

While she waited downstairs for a taxi, Katya messaged Tori, asking her if she was at work. She wasn't, but yes, she did know that Liam had planned to be in office around ten that morning.

"*Why?*"

"*No reason. I'm gonna stop by the apartment in a bit, okay?*"

"*Okay, see you then.*"

The rain had made an epic return, beating down on top of the cab as they rushed through traffic. When they got to the club, she held her clutch over her head while she made a mad dash down the alleyway, trying to avoid puddles.

"Hey, long time no see, Ms. Tocci!" Jan, the bouncer, lifted a hand to her. He had an umbrella, and as soon as she got close enough, he held it over her.

"Yeah, I've been busy!" she had to yell to be heard over the rain. "Is Liam here?"

"Yeah, downstairs already!"

"Thanks!"

Katya stood in the hallway for a moment, shaking the rain water away and trying to decide what she was going to say. What could she say? "*Hey, thanks for the date, but remember how I said that guy was an asshole? Well, he's not, and I spent the last thirty-six hours with him, and I think he's the best thing that's ever happened to me*" just didn't sound very good.

Just be honest with him. Liam's always been upfront and honest with you. He's a big boy. He can take it.

With that thought, she squared her shoulders and strode the rest of the way into the bar.

"Hey, it's angel cake!" Timmy the bartender hollered. She rolled her eyes.

"Yup, it's me. How are you?"

"Can't complain. Hey, thanks for sending us Tori, she's a doll. Love working with her."

"She's really the best."

"She is. Still raining outside?"

"Pouring. Is Liam here?"

"Yeah, Eden's downstairs in his office. Here."

Normally, she could push a button on the big vinyl door, and it would ring a doorbell in a security room. Cameras would show her face to a whole team of security workers, they would establish that she was a member, and she would be let in. But the buzzer was broken, it turned out.

Timmy had a key and he let her down into the lower level. He offered to send down drinks, and though she thought some liquid courage might help, she turned him down. As nervous as she was, she might just spew it all up.

She slowed her steps as she entered the lower bar, and eventually came to a stop. She looked around the space. That part of the club wasn't open yet, people were just moving and cleaning. Some decorations had been hung, and she wondered what was being celebrated.

It was so strange – six weeks ago, she'd thought sex clubs were an urban myth. Now she was calmly standing in the middle of one and wondering about the décor. Could look across the room and see the booth she'd had sex in; the memories still made her blush. But she refused to feel even a tiny bit embarrassed.

I'm proud. Proud that I can be this open minded, this accepting, this uninhibited. So thanks Liam, and thanks The Garden, and thanks Eros dating site, and thanks Wulf. Thank you all, for making me a better person.

Feeling good about herself, Katya made her way into the hall with all the doors. Most of the apartments were open, with people setting up the private rooms for the coming night. The locked doors belonged to members who rented the rooms by the month, she knew. The big conference room doors were open, and when she peeked her head in, the space was filled with seats. She wondered what was going on this time, was glad there was no St. Andrew's Cross to really bring out her blush.

Liam's office was down a small offshoot from the main hall, just off the conference room. There were no other doors, just his, and as she approached it, she saw that it was ajar. She raised her hand to knock, but then his raised voice floated out to her, causing her to stop.

"I don't give a shit," he was snarling. "Say whatever you fucking want – keep saying it, doesn't matter. I don't fucking believe you. Get the fuck out of my office."

Whoa, talk about an intense moment. Katya felt guilty for eavesdropping on what sounded like a *very* private meeting, and she started backing away. Someone else in the room said something, the voice so low she couldn't really hear it, but then Liam got even louder, stopping her in her tracks.

"*Yours!?* Are you fucking shitting me? You've never given a good goddamn about this business, just the money. I don't care what the deed says, this place is mine. Stop with the bullshit – you can't bully me into leaving her alone."

That sentence right there brought Katya back to the door. She all but pressed her ear to the heavy wood, desperate to know what was going on and who was on the other side of the argument. She held her breath, not wanting to get caught, and listened carefully.

"I'm not bullying. And I'm not asking. I'm *telling* you – this little game is *over.*"

Katya stumbled away from the door, falling into a wall. She pressed a hand over her heart, to feel if she was still breathing. She wasn't taking in any oxygen. Nothing was working. Not her lungs, her brain, her heart. Everything had just spun to a complete standstill.

What. THE FUCK. Is Wulfric doing here!?

While she was stepping in and out of reality, the two men continued with their argument.

"Nothing's over – just because you're losing? Fuck that. It stopped being a game a long time ago, anyway. It's not about that, and you're the fucked up one for keeping this going. Back the fuck off and remember who saw her first."

"Please, I was there before you even existed."

"I'm her fucking neighbor, her goddamn landlord – she's been living next door to me for years."

"And I was her neighbor ten years ago, so *I win*."

Winning? A game? I'm a game to them? How do they even know each other, let alone have a game about me?

"Get fucked."

"I'm done. It's over. It was all fucked to begin with. She was with me last night, and the night before – I don't care if you don't believe me, it's *fact*. Not a game, not a trick, nothing. I want her, she wants me. It's over between you two. *Over*."

"She was with you ..." Liam's voice trailed off. Normally, Katya would've felt bad about him finding out that way. But right then, Katya still wasn't thinking normally.

No, Katya was pretty sure she was having an out of body experience.

"Yes. We talked about a lot of things, agreed on some things. She can explain it to you herself. But trust me when I say you two are over, and if you so much as look at her sideways, I will fucking *end you*."

"If I so much as look at her? Sorry, pal, I hate to remind you, but I've fucked her. Lots of times. So I'll look at her any way I want."

Katya was going to be sick. She was actually going to be sick. She could feel saliva pooling at the back of her jaw, could tell her stomach was rolling back and forth. Hearing people talk that way about her, it was surreal.

"Watch what you fucking say about her."

"Screw you. You know what, you're right, *Ricky*. How's about I just give her a little call? Call her and tell her what a nice new boyfriend she has – a guy who told me to go out with her to see how good she was in bed, then sat around comparing stories with me. Let's see how she feels then."

"You'd be outing yourself, too."

"Ooohhh, little Ricky scared? Good, cause I'm not."

Katya took several deep breaths and concentrated. Ricky? Why was Liam calling Wulf by that name? Wasn't that … wasn't his business partner named Ricky? *Richard.* She could picture the business card in her mind's eye. Richard Mason owned half of Liam's business. Richard Mason hated to be called "Ricky", so that's what Liam always called him.

Katya's brain must've been a good lock pick in a former life, because some more of those tumblers squared up inside her head. A mason was a stone worker, or someone who worked with stone. Stone. Wulfric Stone. Wulf**RIC** Stone.

*They've known each other. This whole time, they've known each other. Known **about** each other. What did he say? '**A guy who asked me to go out with her …**' – Wulf asked Liam to go out with me. Asked him how I was in bed. Wulf didn't ask me out till after my night with Liam. Wow, must have been a hell of a conversation. Shit, I would've asked me out, too. Naive idiot who puts out on the first date. Hell of a catch, boys. **A hell of a catch**.*

She came out of her private reverie and realized everything had gone quiet in the office. The only noise was an odd jingling sound. It took her a moment to realize it was her phone. She looked down at her clutch, then pulled out her cell. Liam's office number was scrolling across the screen. He must have made good on his threat to call her. She put her free hand against the door and pushed, slowly opening it wide.

Liam was behind his desk, the phone to his ear, his jaw dropped. Wulf was to the left of the desk. He didn't looked shocked. He looked

… hurt. Like he was in pain. She took a couple deep breaths and held up her phone, showing the screen.

"I would've answered, but … seemed kinda pointless …" she let her voice trail off. Liam visibly struggled to swallow and set down his phone in its cradle.

"Katya, I don't -"

"I came here to talk to you. I didn't realize you were busy," she interrupted. He moved around the desk, taking tentative steps towards her.

Wulf stayed completely still, his eyes never leaving her face.

"I'm so sorry, Katya. I didn't want you to find out like this."

"No, sounded to me like you never wanted me to find out," she even managed a laugh. "But just to clear something up, Wulf is right – he saw me first. We became neighbors when I was five. He wins."

"Jesus, don't say it like that," Liam growled. She looked up at him. At his warm eyes and his lips that were made to smile. Smile and lie, oh so well. Everything, a complete lie. A photo book of memories closed in her brain, the pages flipping. Them on the roof, or laughing together in his kitchen, or exploring each other in his bed. All a competition.

*He brought you a kiddie pool for your roof – because Wulf had a real pool on **his** roof. He laughed when you almost walked in on his business meeting – because he'd known you were too stupid to realize the meeting was with Wulf. He'd talked about having a shitty investment with his partner – **you** were that investment. A shitty investment. Lovely.*

"Don't say it like what? Like it's the truth? It is. I hope you told him everything. Did he tell you about that first time?" she asked, turning to look at Wulf. "It was pretty goddamn amazing. Sex right there in the booth."

"I knew," Wulf said, his voice barely above a whisper.

He knew. So many private moments, building something special, and he was coming here and sharing them all with Liam. Talking about you. Comparing notes about you. **Laughing at you.**

"Did he tell you all the dirty details? What all we did?" she demanded, glancing between them. "Must be hard to know that he got to fuck me in ways you never did. Pity, if only you could've kept it a secret for a little longer."

"Stop it, Katya," Liam urged.

"And did I hear you say you '*traded stories*'? How fun! Was it here, in this office? Just some good ol' boys, talking about a bitch they'd both fucked. Man, I wish I was a dude, sometimes. *How fun.* Were you, like, telling Wulf about all the exciting new stuff you were getting me to do? Was Wulf telling you about how I would try out all those new tricks on him? I hope you two had popcorn. *How fucking fun.*"

No one said anything. Liam glanced at Wulf. Wulf stared at her. She shot fire at both of them with her glare. She knew she was right – their faces were giving away everything.

I was a game. A competition. My best friend, and quite possibly the only man I've ever loved, and I was nothing but a game to them.

Katya was halfway up the stairs before she even knew she was running. She braced her hands against the walls as she went, struggling to stay upright. When she got to the door, she burst through it so hard, she knocked over a waitress that was on the other side.

"Hey, watch it! What the hell is going on!?" Timmy yelled.

She ignored him. Ignored everything but the pounding of her feet. Of her heart. She pushed through the exit, startling Jan off his stool as she practically leapt down the stairs. He hollered after her, but he didn't stop her.

No, Wulf was the one to catch her first. She wasn't surprised. Liam was in great shape, but Wulf was an athlete. He could probably catch anything that tried to get away from him.

"Just talk to me," he insisted, holding her by her arms.

"I don't have to do shit for you!" she screamed, beating at his chest. Liam came running up next to them.

"Just come back inside. We need to talk!" he shouted. The rain was still coming down in sheets, soaking them all in an instant.

"Sounds like you two have talked enough. God, I'm so stupid. I'm so fucking stupid!"

She was crying. She couldn't help it. She wanted to be strong, but it just wasn't possible. These two men had stolen all her strength, in one awful moment. Violated her for weeks, and she hadn't even known it.

"Stop," Wulf's voice was low as he yanked her close. "You need to listen to me."

"I don't need -"

"*You said,*" he whispered, and she stopped struggling for a moment as she stared up at him. "You said you wouldn't leave me. That you trusted me. Your words, Katya."

"Are you kidding right now? Throwing my words in my face, after ... after ... *you lied to me!*" she shrieked, finally jerking free of his grasp. He held up his hand, like he was calming a rabid animal.

"I never actually lied," he corrected her.

"You cannot be serious. A lie by omission doesn't count, I guess. You knew I was sleeping with someone else, you said it was fine. You didn't care. You didn't think that maybe you should mention you knew the guy? Or that you were secretly meeting with him to talk about our sex life? Jesus, Wulf, I never shared those moments with *anybody.* Not with him, not with my roommate, not *anybody!* It was special to me. Special! *You* were special, you made *me* feel special, and it was all a goddamn filthy fucking lie!"

He was working hard to maintain his composure, she could tell, but he couldn't keep the hurt out of his eyes. She was glad to see it, hoped it would stay there for a long time.

"And you," she turned her wrath on Liam. His eyes were wide and he looked scared. *Good.* "You were something else. You invaded my life. Made yourself my best friend. You acted like you cared about me, like you were someone I could trust. *You lied to my face.* I said his name, and you didn't say a word. You acted like you'd never heard of him. Jesus, how did this all even happen!? How do you two even know each other?"

"I told you – I needed a backer for my business," Liam explained. "I didn't know shit about buying a place or anything like that. I had inherited the Twin Estates, and Wulf's company was managing it, so I went to talk to him, and -"

"Wait, wait, wait," she breathed, holding up her hands. "Wulfric's company *manages my apartment building?*"

Both men winced in unison.

"It's a subsidiary company," Wulf answered in a low voice. "Masonry Management solely handles property management. I spend most of my time at the realty company."

"You manage my building," she whispered. She'd been writing rent checks to Masonry Management and mailing them out on her way to dates with the company's CEO, and she hadn't even known it. Liam had confessed to owning the buildings, had even talked about the management company – but had conveniently never mentioned *who* was running said company.

What. The fuck.

"Yes. We have for about eight years now."

"I wish you would've told me."

"Me, too."

So many secrets. You'd think if they were going to lie and hide from me, the least they could do is get their jobs done right.

"Well since we're here now and discussing it, can you fix my *goddamn fucking oven!?*" she started screaming, hitting him in the chest again. "You're a fucking awful management company, you know that? *Goddamn fucking shitty! What the fuck is wrong with you people!?*"

Both men stepped forward and she practically leapt away. Touching them to hit them was fine – she *did not* want them touching her, however. Ever again.

"Calm down," Wulf growled.

"Please, you're gonna hurt yourself," Liam insisted.

"Fuck both of you," she hissed. "Is that how this all started? Liam sees me around the building, tells his little buddy Wulf, who also happens to manage the building? Did you guys go full on stalker mode?"

"No," Liam cleared his throat and glanced at Wulf once. "No, I told you the truth when we first met – I saw your profile on Eros, recognized you as my neighbor. Wulfric was in my office, he saw the profile, too. We were both surprised by your bio, he said he didn't remember you being like that. Told me I should go out with you and see if any of it was true. It was a joke, I never thought you'd go out with me."

"Oh, so this is all *my* fault."

"No! Not at all, no. But the next time I saw him, he'd heard about what we did in the club. One thing lead to another -"

"Oh, one thing lead to another, and suddenly we had a competition going for *who could be the biggest asshole!*" she was screaming again. Liam's hands went into his hair and he stepped towards her, but she took several back, keeping her distance.

"Jesus, this is all so fucking bad. It is, I know it is – *we* know it is," he gestured between him and Wulf. "We thought it was funny at first, sleeping with the same girl. But then it wasn't funny anymore. That's why we started fighting – it stopped being a joke. We both … we both sort of fell for you."

"You two are so fucked up," she was gasping for air as her gaze bounced between them. "That you can stand there and say this shit to me, and in the same breath say you fell for me. Who treats someone they 'fell for' like that!? That you can play with me like I was your toy, *like I was an object to be passed around*, and not even care, and then have the audacity to claim you felt something for me. Do you think you can just say that, and it negates everything else? *It just makes it worse.* That you could do something like that to someone you claim to care about … you need help. I'm not even kidding, you both need serious help."

"Katya, if you just let us -" Wulf tried to interject.

"*I thought I loved you!*" she screamed, whirling around to face him. Everything in the alley went silent. Wulf stared at her calmly, while the color drained from Liam's face. "I thought you were falling in love with me. But you don't know how to love."

"Don't say that."

"It's the truth! How could you do that to someone you care about? How could you look me in the face, and say the things you said, and then come back here and give those moments to someone else? Private moments, sacred moments, and you just blew them all away. You had so many chances last night! I shared *everything* with you. I was falling in love with you, how could you do that?" she sobbed, dropping her head into her hands. She could hear him groan.

"Please, don't. *Don't do this,*" he whispered, his hand running down the side of her arm. Again, she yanked away.

"Don't touch me," she growled, wrapping her arms around herself. "You're sick. Both of you. You objectified me. You turned me into a pawn, into a game. I stopped being a human being the moment you guys started trading stories, started keeping secrets – and you didn't even care. You robbed me of my right to know what was happening to me, my right to *choose* what was happening to me. Like I was … was a sex toy. Some inanimate object. You let it go on and on and on. I must have looked so stupid to you both. A strip-aerobics class with Liam, a strip show for Wulf. Did you set it up that way? Wulf suggests something he'd like, Liam sees if he can make me do it?"

She was trying to be flippant, but as soon as it fell from her lips, as soon as she saw their expressions, she knew it was the truth again.

Strip-aerobics. Blow jobs. Uninhibited sex. A pool on the roof. A trip to the old neighborhood. So many things, completely orchestrated.

"I swear, it was before either of us really knew you," Liam insisted. "It was just for fun."

"Do I look like I'm laughing?"

"Please, Katya. *Please*. Remember how we were the other night," Wulf begged. *Actually begged*. "Remember me. That was the *real* me."

"I wouldn't know, would I? I've never met the real you."

"You're the *only one* who's met the real me."

"I have to go," she blurted out, turning in a circle, trying to figure out the best path of escape. "I'm going to be sick, or pass out. I have to go."

"No, you can't leave like this," Liam said, stepping up to her side.

"Let me take you home," Wulf said, stepping up to her other side. She was boxed in.

"I don't need you!" she started screaming. "You ruined me! You broke me. I don't ever want to see either of you ever again, how's that for a fucking joke? A fucking game? Maybe this time I'll get a chance to play! Never again, never ever again."

She was sobbing and she was screaming and she was pushing at both of them, just trying to gain some space. They'd completely violated her trust and stripped her of her basic rights – couldn't they at least let her breathe!?

A hero finally swooped in to save her. She was glad – after the hour she'd just had, she'd almost thought there weren't any left. Jan the Bouncer came lumbering down the alley and grabbed both men by their collars, yanking them away from her.

"Alright, enough!" he roared, shoving them aside. Katya shivered in the rain and continued crying, one hand pressed over her mouth. "Both of you, get the fuck out of here, right now! Before I call the cops!"

"Who the fuck are you?" Wulf demanded.

"Are you kidding? *I'm your boss*," Liam reminded Jan.

"I don't give a fuck if you're the Second Coming – no one treats a woman like that, not on my watch. And especially one who's done nothing but be kind and sweet and generous. I should beat the shit outta both of you. You pay me to keep out the trash, right? Well, that's exactly what I'm doing, *boss*," Jan snarled, wrapping a protective arm around Katya. She leaned into his side and just sobbed, clutching at his leather vest. Wulf stood up straight, to his full height, and grabbed the edges of his jacket. Jerked it into place.

"Tocci," he said in a serious voice as he stared right at her. "*This isn't over.*"

He shoved past the bouncer and walked out of the alley.

"You bet your ass it's over, buddy!" Jan yelled. "I hear about you harassing this little lady in any way, I'm making a house call!"

"Please, Katya," Liam whispered, crouching down so he could look her in the face. "Believe me – it wasn't all a lie. It just got out of hand. I never lied about how I felt. You are the best friend I've ever had. You're more than that. I care about you. I didn't mean to hurt you. *Please.*"

She couldn't respond, she was crying too hard. Jan hugged her close and shot daggers at his boss.

"I hope you didn't think I was joking. Best get the fuck outta here, Eden."

Jan always called everyone by their last names. Despite being a beast and a former member of a motorcycle gang, he lived by a strict code of ethics. He was polite and he showed respect, and using peoples' proper names was part of that – so when "*Eden*" fell out of his mouth, it was like dropping a bomb.

Liam gave one last painful look at Katya, then stood upright. Glanced down the alley, back towards his club. Then he looked back at them.

"Make sure she gets home okay. Take care of her," he instructed his employee.

"I'll do a damn sight better job than you did, that's for sure."

Jan turned away then, gently forcing Katya with him. They were both already soaked, but she found it touching when he opened his umbrella over them. She wrapped her arms around his big belly as much as she could and hung on.

"Thank you," she whispered.

"No. No, don't you thank me. Anyone would've done that," he assured her.

"Don't be so sure. People are capable of lots of bad things."

"Don't you go thinking that just cause some spoiled pricks got their heads up their asses," he said. "People are good for the most part, Ms. Tocci. Look at you, and Ms. Bellows. You're great people. They're just pricks."

"Pricks," she echoed his sentiment. They stopped at a curb and he looked around for a taxi.

"I want you to know, I had no idea this was going on. Ricky Blue Eyes back there, I knew he was part owner. He would stop by once in a while, never paid attention to me, of course. I noticed he was hanging around more, but I figured it was shop talk with boss man. I had no clue," he said. She managed a chuckle.

"Ricky Blue Eyes."

"Yeah, the creep with Edenhoff. Ricky."

"His real name is Wulf," she whispered.

"Shit, his name is wolf? Shoulda been your first clue, right there."

She laughed with him and he patted her reassuringly on the arm. A taxi finally stopped, and Jan held the umbrella over the door till she was safely seated. She grabbed his hand before he could shut her in, though.

"Thank you. I mean it. I can't thank you enough," she breathed.

"You stop it, or we'll all be bawling."

"I don't want you to get in trouble with Liam."

"You kidding? Boss man loves me, I'm fine. You worry about you, little girl, alright? Take care of yourself. Tell Ms. Bellows she's staying home tonight, and to not worry about it – it's leave with pay. Tell her Jan says so."

Jan was not the type of person to be argued with, so Katya

nodded her head. Thanked him again and let him shut the door. Waved goodbye as she started rolling through traffic.

About halfway home, she started crying again, and didn't stop till she was in her apartment. Tori was nowhere to be seen, the place was empty, so Katya went back into her room. Collapsed on her bed and cried and cried and cried.

One fake profile. Two men. Liam had found her profile, Wulf had seen it. Liam had asked her out, Wulf had encouraged him to do so. Liam had told all her sexy secrets, Wulf had taken advantage of them. Liam had stripped away her inhibitions one by one, and Wulf had basked in her new found freedom. They'd shared moments and compared notes and come up with new ideas. She'd been their play thing. A pretty doll on a shelf – pull the strings just right, and little Katya Tocci will do a dance for you! Jump up and down for you! Bend over and do anything you want for you!

It was ridiculous. If in the very beginning, they'd both said the truth – that they both knew her, both wanted to pursue relationships with her, she probably would've been okay with it. Hell, she'd obviously been dating Wulf while she'd been sleeping with Liam, so they had proof she would've been okay with it. She'd always been open and honest, with both of them.

But they'd kept it a secret, on purpose. To have fun with her. Manipulate her. Liam, sitting with his feet in the kiddie pool and drinking beers with her. Wulfric, sitting at the bar and burning her up with his eyes. Each one of them knowing so much more about her than she knew about them.

Wulf never would've asked me out if I hadn't had sex with Liam. If Liam hadn't told him all about the sex. Jesus, this is my fault. Mother was right – save it for someone you care about.

She was hugging a pillow and sobbing so hard it hurt when Tori finally came home. The other girl dropped her groceries in the hallway and came sprinting into Katya's room.

"What's wrong? Honey, talk to me! Are you hurt? Did Wulf do

something? Did Wulf do this to you? What did he do!? I'm calling an ambulance!"

Katya clung to her friend's arm and wouldn't let her go. It was a couple minutes before she could calm down enough to talk, but eventually she was able to tell the whole story to Tori. And she meant *the whole story.* From beginning to end, every gory, kinky, sexy, awful detail. Every single thing between her and the two worst men she'd ever met in her life.

"So he would fuck you," Tori spoke in her blunt way as they laid in Katya's bed. "And then he'd sit down with Wulf and tell him everything you guys did together. And then basically Wulf would be like that's hot, see what else you can get her to do, see if she'll deep throat or use a sex swing or whatever. And then Liam would, and he'd tell Wulf, and then you and Wulf would do those things?"

"This is all my fault," Katya whispered.

"Don't you ever say that again."

"No, it's true. If I hadn't slept with Liam, none of this would've happened. Maybe it's karma – I was kind of using Liam to become more sexually open. This is my punishment."

"Katya, there's a big fucking difference between you having a casual, acknowledged, open relationship with a man, and a man lying to your fucking face while he shares all your most intimate details with another man, in the hopes that other man will have just as good a time with you. *Holy shit, that is so fucked up."*

"That's what I said. I told them they need help."

"They need to get their balls stepped on."

"Liam might like that."

"I'm quitting," Tori suddenly jerked upright.

"What? No! You can't do that, you need that job. Jan said you don't have to come in tomorrow, to take the day off with pay," Katya assured her, clinging tight to her arm.

"Are you kidding? I don't care if I have to suck dick to pay rent – at least then I'd know the money was coming from a better man than

Liam Edenhoff," Tori swore. Katya actually started laughing.

"Please," she panted. "Please, don't quit. Just wait. Let's settle down."

Tori stopped struggling with her and laid back down.

"You're right. I won't quit."

"Good."

"Because we need a mole on the inside."

"That's good, I – wait, what?"

"I don't want either of them trying to run this scam on anyone else. I'm gonna stay there, as a spy," Tori assured her.

"Oh. Uh … okay."

Katya didn't really need a *mole on the inside*, but she did need Tori to pay her rent on time.

"I'm really, really sorry," Tori whispered a couple hours later, smoothing Katya's hair out of her face. "I know you liked him."

"I think I might have loved him," Katya cried.

"I know you don't want to hear this, but I think … I believe Wulf cared about you, too. Maybe like how a sociopath would care about a cat, but comparatively speaking, that's a lot. You touched him, Katya. Through all the bullshit and game playing and crazy sex, I really believe you touched his heart," Tori insisted.

"Pity it didn't help him."

"No, it didn't."

"No. All it did was break me."

26

KATYA WOKE UP SOME TIME LATER IN THE MIDDLE OF THE NIGHT. IT WAS disgustingly humid in the room, made hotter by Tori sharing the bed with her. Katya slid to the end of the mattress and stood up, stretching onto her toes.

She grabbed her phone and headed into the bathroom. There were multiple missed calls and messages. All but one were from Liam.

Only one text from Wulf. Sent about an hour before she'd woken up, at two-thirty in the morning.

You promised me.

Boiling hot rage bubbled through her veins. He was reminding her of her promises? Promises to what, love him and stand up for him? Be there when he needed someone? Yeah right, more like he needed a toy to play with, an object to hold. Needed to control her and consume her. *Own her*. How could he possibly say that to her? She had needed him, and he'd let her down. Ripped the bottom out of her world. Lied, manipulated, made a mockery of – that's all he'd *ever* done to her. She felt so stupid.

I thought I could play in their world. That I could be a sex kitten. But I'll never be that girl from the profile. I'm just boring old beige Katya Tocci. I was out of my league.

No. **NO**. She would not fall into that trap. Liam may have helped, but Katya had made the decision to go out with him. Katya had walked into that club, and Katya had agreed to sleep with him. She had taken the leap, all on her own, without help from either of them. She was strong, and she was brave. She could be anything she goddamn wanted to be.

I'll show them that we're not even playing in the same league.

She started yanking open drawers in the bathroom and pulling out all their beauty products. She always wore her fresh-face make-up. *Cute and innocent.* Screw that – those men had fucked away cute and innocent a long time ago. She dragged some thick black eyeliner across her lids, then smudged up the line, giving herself a trashy, sexy, smokey eye. Next she found a deep red lipstick that looked great against her skin, so she put it on extra heavy, making her lips looker fuller. Pouty-er. *Perfect.* She raked her hair up into messy bun on top of her head, called it good, then left the bedroom.

She ran on tip toes into Tori's room and started rifling through the other girl's dresser. They were different sizes, but similar heights, and could occasionally swap clothes. Tori was a much sexier dresser, though, and that's what Katya was looking for right then.

She found a black fitted crop top. Or was it a bustier? It showed a lot of tit and all her stomach, that's all that mattered. A couple pins in the back and she had it fitting snug on her body. She wiggled into some tiny, almost microscopic, black shorts, then looked in a full length mirror.

It was probably more skin than she'd ever shown in an outfit. Awkward pins and all, the top still looked amazing on her, and even barefoot, her legs looked about a mile long. That brought back a memory from a lifetime ago. Wulf calling, asking her on their second date. She'd been so surprised – why on earth would Wulfric Stone want to see her again?

"Because you have amazing legs."

She'd thought it was just flirting. Now she knew it was only because Liam had asked to see her again.

She stormed back into the bathroom and only turned on the lights over the mirror. She leaned backwards and forwards, trying to find the best angle for her cleavage that would still show some of her body. She held her hand awkwardly above her head, made a duck face, then took a picture. Popped out her hip, took another picture. Winked, another pic. Licked her lips, another pic.

After about ten photos, she went into the living room and powered up her laptop. She transferred all the pictures to her computer, then looked through them. She didn't even recognize herself. All the makeup and the close up lighting had washed out her face a little, making her skin look flawless. Her chest was caught in the bright light, the rest of her body carved out of shadows, making her look curvy in all the right places. The red lips and smokey eyes completed the look. She looked like a walking, talking advert for sex. Raw, nasty, raunchy, filthy, sex.

The first picture she'd taken, that was the one. Her pursing her lips, blowing a kiss. Her lids at half mast, giving her bedroom eyes. Her breasts thrust high and center stage, demanding a second glance.

Fucking perfect.

She found her way to a website she hadn't visited in over a month. Dusted off a profile and reactivated it. Since she'd never changed anything and had only deactivated, all the original info was still there. Still the same party girl with some sexy personal hobbies – but now, that girl had the picture to match. She uploaded the duck face pic to the profile, then picked up her phone.

She had to redownload the Eros dating app, but once she did, she went straight to her own profile. There was the sexy party girl, blowing her a kiss from the top of the screen. Talking about being kinky at the bottom of the screen. Absolutely perfect.

She put down the phone. Shut off the laptop. Leaned back into the sofa and stared at the ceiling. It was so quiet in the apartment, she could hear her own heartbeat.

I don't need them. I don't need them. I don't need them.

"Kat?" Tori sounded sleepy from the hallway. "Why are you sitting in the dark?"

Katya took a deep breath.

"It's the only place I feel comfortable," she whispered.

"What?"

"Nothing, let's go back to bed."

She scrubbed off the make up and changed into pajamas. Crawled onto her bed and pressed her back against Tori's. As she closed her eyes, she took a couple more deep breaths, trying to keep the tears at bay.

Looks like little Katya Tocci finally grew up.

To Be Continued ...

ACKNOWLEDGEMENTS

I went through a super long dry spell. I wrote *The Bad Ones* in December of 2015. Of course there was lots of editing and rewriting that happened, but the rough draft and main content were done in December.

And then I didn't write anything else until August of 2016.

Oh, for sure, I started things. Started lots of things. Even got up to 40,000 words on one story (about half of an average length novel). But nothing stuck. Everything felt forced, I wasn't into it. Since publishing, that was the longest stretch of time I've gone without completing some kind of work. It wasn't even necessarily writer's block – I just didn't WANT to work.

I had gone through a move, I'm sure that had something to do with it. When things finally settled down, I went back home for a visit. One morning, I had a bizarre dream. I've been writing for basically my entire life, and I have never dreamed about my characters or written one of my dreams down.

I literally dreamed I was brainstorming a story. It was like watching a movie, while plotting it. I can remember coming up with their names so clearly, Liam's and Wulf's. Wulfric Stone was first, like he was introducing himself to me. Eden was second. Then Katya and Liam in the sex club, the crazy wild sex they had, everything, all the way up until she meets Wulf in her bakery. It was crazy! My brain did all the work while I was sleeping! Why can't it ALWAYS be like that!?

So yes, everything from the first word till Wulf meets Katya, is exactly how it was in my dream. I had no clue if it was going to take off or not, but the ideas kept pouring out.

As always, enough thanks cannot be said to Ratula. #CONGRATULATIONS, bitch, book number four in the bag! Through thick and thin, bitch fests, laugh fests, documentaries, scary movies, Tiny Dog – I look forward to our conversations each and every day, and I just want to say thank you for being an amazing friend.

For this book, I added a whole new slew of beta readers because it's fun to have strangers tell you when your stuff sucks, HAHA! No, but with every book, I usually add a new reader or two, to keep things fresh. This book, I added something like SEVEN. Some I'd never interacted with prior to them beta reading. And it was awesome, you all helped immensely, it was an amazing experience.

So thank you to my OGs, Angie, Sunny, Letty, Jo, Rebecca, Lheanne, Rebeka, Shannon, and Sue. Some of you have been there since the very first book – even the ones that haven't been published! Most have helped me since Separation. So thank you for sticking with me for so long.

To my new betas – Andrea, Jennifer, Berenice, Tink, Jennifer G., Deanna Pinklady, and Bex, you more than did a good job. You all proved to have great insights and wonderful advice, and taught me so many things. Sex clubs usually don't sell booze! I had no clue! Thank god you all filled out the form, this book wouldn't be half as good without you.

Thank you to Champagne Formats and Qamber Designs for giving me some of the best looking books out there! Each every one are stunning, in my humble opinion, and your work harmonizes so well with my vision. Thanks so much.

Special thanks to Christine at Shh Mom's Reading. You've done all my releases since Reparation, but you weren't able to do this book. I'm so sad that aspect of our relationship is over, but so excited and happy for your new adventures. Thank you for six amazing releases.

A NEW thanks to The Rock Stars of Romance, for stepping in at kind of the last minute and handling the release of *this* book. I'm a nervous person by nature, I don't deal well with "meeting" new people, online or otherwise, so it was important for me to deal with people I "knew", or who would get me. Milasy, you've always been amazing and supportive, thank you for helping out so quickly when I messaged you. Lisa, you're a rock star, and I wonder when/if you ever sleep – thank you for making this smooth and painless for someone like me, who expects everything to be difficult and uncomfortable.

Of course, thank you to every blog that has shared, posted, read, reviewed, done giveaways, made teasers, all of the above and everything beyond. What you do every day is amazing and when I feel like complaining, I try to picture what it's like to run a wordpress site, and then I shut up. Thank you so much.

All the readers. Each and every single one. Authors, bloggers, reviewers, stay at home moms, people reading at their desks at work. In bed at night, in their car in a parking lot, whenever there's spare time. Thank you for liking my words. This never gets easier and each time I'm sure it's going to be the worst book ever, but you all prove me wrong every time. I have a very magical profession – thank you for allowing me to pursue it.

To Mr. F. It's been an interesting year. Awful and wonderful and strange. I'm glad it happened, and I will be glad when it's over, but most of all, I'm glad you love me. Thank you for being such a big part of my life and for shaping me into the person I am today.

THE NEIGHBORHOOD

A TWIN ESTATES NOVEL

EXCERPT

Breathe. Breathe. Don't think. Breathe. Breathe. Did I sign that paperwork the office sent over? Breathe. Breathe. Have to check that escrow deal. Breathe. Breathe. God, what is she doing right now. How did this get so fucked up. I knew I should have fucking listened to myself and walked – **DON'T THINK**. *Breathe. Breathe.*

While Wulfric Stone's natural habitat was an Olympic sized swimming pool, it wasn't the only form of exercise he got – he had a stressful job, he had lots of different ways of burning off the tension. Running came a close second to swimming for clearing his head. It created a different sort of burn in his muscles, created a whole new plethora of aches and pains.

Sometimes, when he was particularly angry about something, he preferred it over swimming. After doing a couple miles worth of laps, he could just float away. Literally. Lay on his back and be weightless for a while. Not with running, though. How cruel – a sport that takes a person miles away from their starting point, and if they push themselves too hard, it just means they have to turn around and do the same distance back. Feel like collapsing? No weightless pond to float in. No, the best case scenario meant hopefully finding a cool patch of grass to collapse onto and pray his muscles didn't cramp up while gravity put pressure on every limb.

Yes, running was a very punishing sport, and Wulfric Stone was a bad man who definitely deserved punishment.

Breathe. Breathe.

His calves were burning and sweat was *pouring* down his body. He was pretty sure his lungs were getting ready to stage a coup and walk out on him. Still, he kept pushing, pounding his feet down harder against the ground.

How can I breathe when she's not here to help me?

Wulf let out a frustrated shout and ripped his earphones off. This wasn't working. He slowed to a stop. He knew it was a bad idea, he should jog for a while, reducing his pace slowly, but fuck it. Running away from his problems clearly wasn't helping. Maybe a massive charlie horse would successfully distract him.

Or maybe he could have a heart attack, that would be *perfect*.

He veered off the pathway, heading straight into the woods. San Francisco was entering fall and as a breeze hit his sweat slicked skin, he shivered. He grabbed the hem of his t-shirt and brought it to his forehead, mopping up sweat. When he lowered the material, he glanced around and realized he'd wandered so far, he couldn't see where the trail was anymore.

Good. Maybe I'll be lost in here forever. That would solve everything. Jesus, how did everything get so fucked up?

It was a rhetorical question – Wulf knew the answer. *He* had fucked it all up. Broken his own rules, gone against his own advice, and look what had happened. He was a mess, wandering around in the woods, cursing at trees.

Worse, was he'd known just how bad the ending between could be, he'd seen it all unraveling from early on, and he'd tried to avoid it by doing what he did best. Being an asshole. After all, if he told her about their little scam, she'd leave him. If he didn't tell her and she found out, she'd leave him. If Liam told her, she'd leave him. It seemed to Wulfric that the only possible outcome was Katya leaving him.

So, like a true gentleman, Wulf left her first.

Why did she come back? If she'd just stayed away, everything would be fine. Fucking fine.

Except it wouldn't be fine. He'd be a shell of man – or at least, a worse version than the one he'd already been – and she'd be convincing herself Liam was the perfect guy for her. Wulf couldn't stand that thought. Couldn't bear the idea of Liam touching her and kissing her and seeing her naked and making her sigh and gasp.

"*AH!*"

His fist slammed into the tree before he even knew his arm was moving. He hadn't pulled the punch at all, striking the trunk as hard as he could, but Wulf barely felt anything. He was numb.

So he hit it again. And again. And didn't stop till blood was running down his fist, and even then, he still didn't feel a thing. It was only the red staining his white t-shirt that gave him pause.

Of course I didn't feel anything. I'm Wulfric Stone, and stones don't have feelings.

The Kane Trilogy

degradation

Available Now

If you haven't met Jameson Kane yet, read below for a sneak peek …

Tatum plucked at her shirt in a nervous manner. She had tucked it into a tight pencil skirt and even put on a pair of sling back stilettos. If someone had personally requested her, she wanted to make an effort to look nice. She had blown out her hair and put curls in the ends, and toned down her make up. Even she had to admit it, she looked presentable.

For once.

Men in expensive business suits began to file into the conference room and she stood still, giving a polite smile to everyone who entered. A team of lawyers was meeting with their client. Six chairs were lined up on one side of a long table, with just a single chair on the other side.

Tate had been positioned at the back of the room, next to a sideboard filled with goodies and coffee and water. She fussed about, straightening napkins and setting up the glasses. When all six chairs were filled on the one side, she stared at their backs, wondering who the big shot was that got to stare them all down. The person who would be facing her. A door at the back of the room swung open and her breath caught in her threat.

Holy. Shit.

Jameson Kane strode into the room, only offering a curt smile to his lawyers. His eyes flashed to her for just a second, then he looked back. His smile became genuine and he tipped his head towards her, almost like a bow.

She gaped back at him, positive that her mouth was hanging open. What was he doing there!? Had he known she would be there? Had he been the one to request her? Impossible, he didn't know what temp agency she worked for – but what would be the chances? She hadn't seen him in seven years, and now twice in two days.

Tate felt like swallowing her tongue.

"Gentlemen," Jameson began, seating himself across from the lawyers. "Thanks for meeting with me today. Would anyone care for any coffee? Water? The lovely Ms. O'Shea will be helping us today." He gestured towards Tate, but no one turned around. Several people asked for coffee. Jameson asked for water, his smile still in place. It was almost a smirk. Like he knew something she didn't.

She began to grind her teeth.

She delivered everyone's drinks, then carried around a tray of snacks. No one took anything. She moved to the back of the room, refilled the water pitcher. Tidied up. Felt Jameson staring at her.

This is ridiculous. You're Tatum O'Shea. You eat boys for breakfast.

But thinking that made her remember when he had said something very similar to her, and she felt a blush creep up her cheeks.

She was pretty much ignored the whole time. They all argued back and forth about what business decisions Jameson should, or shouldn't, make. He was very keen on dismantling struggling companies and selling them off. They tried to curb his desires. His tax lawyer explained how his tax shelter in Hong Kong was doing. Another lawyer gave him a run down on property law in Switzerland. Tate tried to hide her yawns.

They took a five minute break after an hour had passed. Tate had her back to the room, rearranging some muffins on a tray, when she felt the hair on the back of her neck start to stand up. She turned around in slow motion, taking in Jameson as he walked up to her.

"Surprised?" he asked, smiling down at her.

"Very. Did you ask for me?" she questioned. He nodded.

"Yes. You ran away so quickly the other night. I wanted to get reacquainted," he explained. She laughed.

"Maybe I didn't," she responded. He shrugged.

"That doesn't really matter to me. What are you doing tonight?" he asked. She was a little caught off guard.

"Are you asking me out, Kane?" she blurted out. He threw back his head and laughed.

"Oh god, still a little girl. *No.* I don't ask people out. I was asking what you were doing tonight," Jameson replied.

She willed away the blush she felt coming on. He still had the ability to make her feel so stupid. She had been through so much since him, come so far with her esteem and her life. It wasn't fair that he could still make her feel so small. She wanted to return the favor. She cleared her throat.

"I'm working."

"Where?"

"At a bar."

"What bar?"

"A bar you don't know."

"And tomorrow night?"

"Busy."

"And the night after that?"

"*Every* night after that," Tate informed him, crossing her arms. He narrowed his eyes, but continued smiling.

"Surely you can find some time to meet up with an old friend," he said. She shook her head.

"We were never friends, Kane," she pointed out. He laughed.

"Then what is it? Are you scared of me? Scared I'll eat you alive?"

324

he asked. She stepped closer to him, refusing to be intimidated.

"I think *you're* the one who should be scared. You don't know me, Kane. You never did. *And you never will,*" she whispered. Jameson leaned down so his lips were almost against her ear.

"I know what you feel like from the inside. That's good enough for me," he whispered back. Tate stepped away. She felt like she couldn't breathe. He did something to her insides.

"You, and a lot of other people. You're not as big a deal as you think," she taunted. It was a complete lie, but she had to get the upper hand back. He smirked at her.

"That sounds like a challenge to me. I have to defend my honor," he warned her. She snorted.

"Whatever. Point to the challenger then, *me.* Defend away," she responded, rolling her eyes.

He didn't respond, just continued smirking down at her. The lawyers began filing back into the room and Jameson took his position on the other side of the table. She wasn't really sure what their little spar had been about, or what had come out of it. She was just going to try to get through the rest of the conference, and then she would scurry away before he could talk to her again. She didn't want anything to do with Jameson Kane, or his -,

"Ms. O'Shea," his sharp voice interrupted her thoughts. Tate lifted her head.

"Yes, sir?" she asked, making sure to keep her voice soft and polite.

"Could you bring me some water, and something to eat," he asked, not even bothering to look at her as he flipped through a contract.

She loaded up a tray with his requests and made her way around the table. No one even looked at her, they just threw legal jargon around at each other – a language she didn't know. She stood next to Jameson and leaned forward, setting his water down and then going about arranging cheese and crackers on a plate for him. She was about halfway done when she felt it.

Are those … his fingers!?

Tate froze for a second. His touch was light as he ran his fingers up and down between her legs. She glanced down at her knees and then glanced over at him. He was still looking down, but she could see him smirking. She tried to ignore him, tried to go back to setting up his food, but his hand went higher. Daring to brush up past her knees, well underneath her skirt. He couldn't get any farther, not unless he pushed up her skirt, or sunk down in his chair. She dumped the rest of the cheese on his plate and started to scoot away. She had just gotten back to her station when she heard a thunking noise, followed by groans.

"No worries. Ms. O'Shea! So sorry, could you get this?" Jameson's voice was bored sounding.

She turned around and saw that he had knocked over his water glass. He was blotting at the liquid as it spread across the table. The lawyers were all holding their papers aloft, grumbling back and forth.

Tate groaned and grabbed a towel before striding back to the table. She glared at him the whole way, but he still refused to look at her. She started as far away from him as she could get, mopping everything up, but eventually she had to almost lean across him to reach the mess. She stood on her toes, stretching across the table top.

As she had assumed it would, his hand found its way back to her legs. Only this time he wasn't shy, and her position allowed for a lot of access. His hand shot straight up the back of her skirt, his fingertips brushing against the lace of her panties.

She swallowed a squeak and glanced around. If any of the other gentlemen lifted their heads, they would have been able to see their client with half of his arm up his assistant's skirt, plain as day. He managed to run his finger under the hem of her underwear, down the left side of her butt cheek, before she pulled away. She stomped back to the food station, throwing the towel down with such violence, she knocked over a stack of sugar cubes.

When she turned around, Jameson was finally looking at her. She plunked her fists on her hips, staring straight back. His smirk was in place – as she had expected it would be – and he held up a finger, pointing it straight up. *One.* Then he pointed at himself. One point. *Tied.* He thought they were playing a game. She hadn't wanted to play games with him, but she hated to lose at *anything*, and she never wanted to lose to a man like Jameson Kane.

An idea flitted across her mind. Tate wanted to make him as uncomfortable as he had just made her feel. She coolly raised an eyebrow and then took her time looking around the room. The lawyers all still had their backs to her – not one of them had turned around the entire time she'd been there. Blinds had been drawn over every window, no one could see in the office, but she knew the door wasn't locked. Anyone could walk into the room. She took a deep breath. It didn't matter anyway, what was the worst that could happen? She would get fired? It was a temp job, that Jameson had requested her for – he didn't even work there. Did she really care what happened?

She dragged her stare back to meet his and then ran her hands down the sides of her skirt. He raised an eyebrow as well, his eyes following her hands. When she got to the hem of the skirt, she pressed her palms flat and began to slowly, *achingly*, slide the material up her legs. Now both his eyebrows were raised. He flicked his gaze to her face, then went right back to her skirt. Higher, up past her knees. To the middle of her thighs. Higher still. If anyone turned around, they would be very surprised at what they saw. One more inch, and her skirt would be moot. Jameson's stare was practically burning holes through her.

Taking short, quick, breaths through her nose, Tate slid her hands around to her butt. She wiggled the material up higher back there, careful to keep the front low enough to hide her whole business, and was able to hook her fingers into her underwear. She didn't even think about what she was doing, couldn't take her eyes off of

Jameson, as she slid her underwear over her butt and down her hips. As the lace slid to her ankles, she pushed her skirt back into place. Then she stepped out of the panties and bent over, picking them up. When she stood upright, she let the lace dangle from her hand while she held up one finger. Point.

Winning.

Jameson nodded his head at her, obviously conceding to her victory, then returned his attention to the papers in front of him. Tate let out a breath that she hadn't even realized she was holding, and turned around, bracing her hands against the table. She leaned forward and took deep breaths. She had just started to gain some ground on slowing her heart rate, when a throat cleared.

"What is that, Ms. O'Shea?" Jameson called out from behind her. She spun around, balling up her underwear in her fist.

"Excuse me, sir?" she asked.

"That," he continued, gesturing with his pen at her. "In your hands. You have something for me. Bring it here."

Now everyone turned towards her. Tate held herself as still as possible, her hands clasped together in front of her legs, hiding the underwear between her fingers. All eyes were on her. Jameson smirked at her and leaned back in his chair. She took a shaky breath.

"I don't know what -,"

"Bring it here, Ms. O'Shea, *now*," he ordered, tapping the table top with his pen. She glared at him.

Fuck this.

She turned around and pulled one of the silver trays in front of her. She laid her panties out neatly on top, making sure the material was smooth and flat. She was very thankful that she had gone all out and worn her good, expensive, *"I'm-successful-and-career-oriented!"*, underwear. She balanced the tray on top of her fingertips and spun around, striding towards their table, a big smile on her face.

"For you, Mr. Kane," she said in a breathy voice, then dropped the tray in front of him. It clattered loudly and spun around a little before coming to a rest, the panties sliding off to one side.

As she walked away, she could hear some gasps. A couple laughs. A very familiar chuckle. When she got to the door, she pulled it open before turning back to the room. A couple of the lawyers were gawking at her, and the rest were laughing, gesturing to the display she had just put on; Jameson was looking straight at her, his smirk in place. She blew him a kiss and then stomped out the door.

ABOUT THE AUTHOR

Crazy woman living in an undisclosed location in Alaska (where the need for a creative mind is a necessity!), I have been writing since ..., forever? Yeah, that sounds about right. I have been told that I remind people of Lucille Ball - I also see shades of Jennifer Saunders, and Denis Leary. So basically, I laugh a lot, I'm clumsy a lot, and I say the F-word A LOT.

I like dogs more than I like most people, and I don't trust anyone who doesn't drink. No, I do not live in an igloo, and no, the sun does not set for six months out of the year, there's your Alaska lesson for the day. I have mermaid hair - both a curse and a blessing - and most of the time I talk so fast, even I can't understand me.

Yeah. I think that about sums me up

Printed in Great Britain
by Amazon

74690062R00201